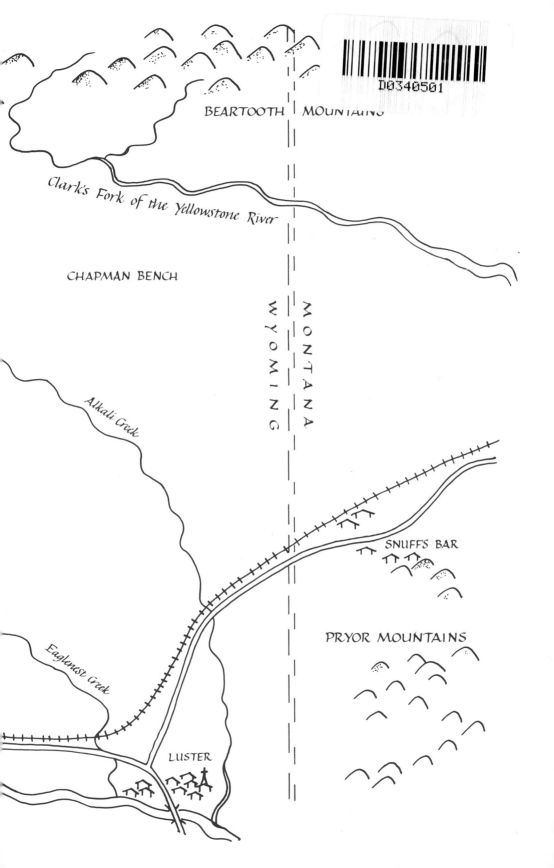

BEARTOOTH MOUNTAINS

Clark's Fork of the Yellowstone River

CHAPMAN BENCH

WYOMING

MONTANA

Alkali Creek

Eaglenest Creek

SNUFF'S BAR

PRYOR MOUNTAINS

LUSTER

D0340501

HEART MOUNTAIN

Happy Birthday to Dale
1-1- 89

ALSO BY GRETEL EHRLICH

The Solace of Open Spaces

ハート・マウンテン

グレトール・エーリック著

HEART
MOUNTAIN

Gretel Ehrlich

VIKING

VIKING
Published by the Penguin Group
Viking Penguin Inc., 40 West 23rd Street, New York, New York 10010, U.S.A.
Penguin Books Ltd, 27 Wrights Lane, London W8 5TZ, England
Penguin Books Australia Ltd, Ringwood, Victoria, Australia
Penguin Books Canada Ltd, 2801 John Street, Markham, Ontario, Canada, L3R 1B4
Penguin Books (N.Z.) Ltd, 182–190 Wairau Road, Auckland 10, New Zealand

Penguin Books Ltd, Registered Offices: Harmondsworth, Middlesex, England

First published in 1988 by Viking Penguin Inc.
Published simultaneously in Canada

1 3 5 7 9 10 8 6 4 2

Copyright © Gretel Ehrlich, 1988
All rights reserved

Grateful acknowledgment is made for permission to reprint excerpts from the following
copyrighted works:

The Unbearable Lightness of Being by Milan Kundera. Copyright © 1984 by Harper
& Row, Publishers, Inc. Reprinted by permission of Harper & Row, Publishers, Inc.
Two poems from *Ikkyu and the Crazy Cloud Anthology* translated by Sonja Arntzen.
© 1986 University of Tokyo Press. By permission of the publisher and the translator.
"Farewell Poem" by Tu Mu from *Poems of the Late T'ang* translated by A. C.
Graham (Penguin Classics 1965). Copyright © A. C. Graham, 1965.
Three poems from *Kokinshu: A Collection of Poems Ancient and Modern* translated
by Laurel Rasplica Rodd. Copyright © 1984 Princeton University Press. Reprinted
with permission of Princeton University Press.
The Plumed Serpent by D. H. Lawrence. Copyright 1926, 1951 by Alfred A. Knopf,
Inc. By permission of Alfred A. Knopf, Inc.

LIBRARY OF CONGRESS CATALOGING IN PUBLICATION DATA
Ehrlich, Gretel.
Heart Mountain.
I. Title.
PS3555.H72H4 1988 813'.54 87–40668
ISBN 0–670–82160–8

Printed in the United States of America by Arcata Graphics, Fairfield, Pennsylvania

Set in Electra
Designed by Fritz Metsch

Calligraphy on title page by Akiko Suzuki
Endpaper map by Press Stephens
Endpaper map calligraphy by Carol Fiorile

Without limiting the rights under
copyright reserved above, no part of this publication may be reproduced, stored in or introduced into a
retrieval system, or transmitted, in any form or by any means (electronic,
mechanical, photocopying, recording or otherwise), without the
prior written permission of both the copyright owner
and the above publisher of this book.

for those Japanese-Americans and their families
who were interned at relocation camps

and for
Press

History is as light as individual human life,
unbearably light, light as a feather, as dust swirling in the air,
as whatever will no longer exist tomorrow.
—Milan Kundera

ACKNOWLEDGMENTS

Heartfelt thanks to those who assisted me by generously sharing their wartime stories: especially, Carl Iwasaki, Frank Emi, and Estelle Ishigo, interned at Heart Mountain; Charles Kikuchi, whose diaries were begun at Gila; Miné Okubo, painter, who was interned at Topaz; Robert Broadwater, who survived the Bataan Death March and was a prisoner of war in Japan; Dr. John Merritt, who was both doctor and patient in the Pacific; Bea Iwasaki, whose brother was the first Nisei to join the Air Corps; the painter Masami Teraoka, who lived through the war a hundred miles from Hiroshima; and my parents, Grant and Gretchen Ehrlich, who participated in the war effort "stateside." Thanks also to those who provided research materials: the Bancroft Library, Berkeley, California; the UCLA Special Collections; the Smithsonian Institute; the National Archives; Pat Johnson of the Greybull Library; Wayne Johnson of the Wyoming State Library; John Roland, Northwest Community College Library; the Japanese-American Cultural and Community Center, Los

Angeles; Col. Pat C. Hoy II; Pat Crosby; Barbara Schenkel, bookseller; Brian Petersen; Elaine Moncur, rancher on Heart Mountain; Peggy Ann Lloyd, typist. For their interest, hospitality, and concern in Kyoto, Japan, deep thanks to the Noh mask carvers Aya and Noyetsu Iwai; and Professor Aseyeda, who gave us entry to Kyoto's Noh theaters. Thanks to those Japanese-Americans whose books, diaries, drawings, and paintings fleshed out an unfortunate event in history I was too young to witness.

CONTENTS

AUTHOR'S NOTE

On February 19, 1942, two months and twelve days after the attack on Pearl Harbor, President Franklin Delano Roosevelt signed Executive Order 9066, which gave the Secretary of War the authority to designate military areas and exclude all or any people from them. As a result, over 110,000 Japanese immigrants (Issei) and Japanese-Americans (Nisei) were removed from their homes, farms, and businesses and interned at ten camps: Manzanar and Tule Lake in California, Poston and Gila in Arizona, Minidoka in Idaho, Granada in Colorado, Topaz in Utah, Rohwer and Jerome in Arkansas, and Heart Mountain in Wyoming.

My novel, *Heart Mountain,* is a blend of fact and fiction. The Heart Mountain Relocation Camp did exist and the political realities are faithful to fact. For purposes of the narrative, I have compressed some of the geographical elements, conveniently eliminating miles between actual creeks, ranches, bars, towns, and highways, and have taken the further liberty of "relocating" a waterfall from Clark's Fork Canyon to Heart

Mountain. The town of Luster is fictional, as are all the characters in this story. Snuff's, the bar, served drinks until it burned down a few weeks ago.

—G.E.

Heart Mountain, Wyoming
February 29, 1988

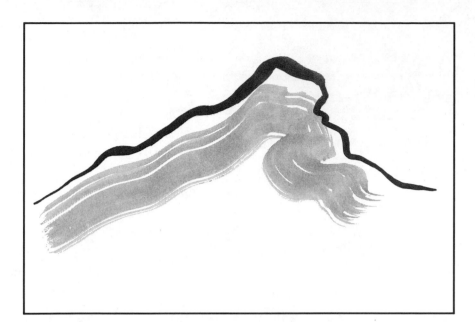

PART ONE
1942

1

Then it was the day McKay's brothers left for the front by bus to the county seat, train to San Francisco, troop transfer ship to the Hawaiian Islands, and from there, catapulted into what was known as the Pacific theater, as if war had a proscenium, McKay thought, as if its horrors could be contained.

After, he unfolded a cot on the screened porch of the house and took off his clothes. It was August and he was hot and he did not want to live inside the house anymore. The cot felt cool. He closed his eyes and listened to the wind for a long time. It brushed back and forth over the ranch like a massage gone on too long, everything under its touch getting sorer and sorer.

His parents had been dead for twelve years and his brothers had gone to war. The whole state had emptied out and now he ran the ranch with one Japanese cook who was afraid of horses and an aging, alcoholic cowboy who went on a binge every time there was a storm.

The ranch bordered the Heart Mountain Relocation Camp where ten thousand Japanese-Americans and their immigrant parents from the West Coast were to be confined. He had seen it come quickly into existence and heard the hammering and the dozing of the earth. He had stood with his strong hands flat against the screen, listening. The porch was his isolation booth, a cell in wide open space, and he heard the first guard tower at the Camp go up on stilts, forty feet in the air.

He lay down and rolled on his back and sucked the blood from his right hand where it had gone through glass. He had fought that morning with his brother Champ, who had a chip on his shoulder about McKay. "Prince fucking Charming," Champ called him, because McKay had more brains and common sense, good looks, and more natural ability than anyone in the valley; he rode broncs so gracefully, he made it look like ballet. Sitting in the backseat of the car that would take them to the train station, Champ had turned to McKay at the last moment.

"I don't know what's wrong here," Champ had said. "What makes you so goddamned special you can't go to war."

McKay grabbed the car door but Champ rolled the window closed. As the engine started, he recalled seeing his brother's stubborn profile, the bump where his nose had been broken riding saddle broncs and the deep-set, resentful eyes. McKay's arm had pulled back suddenly, bursting through glass until it collided with Champ's jaw. The driver quickly released the handbrake and the car rolled forward. Through the smashed window McKay saw the stunned look on Champ's face and his older brother, Ted, trying to get the driver to stop and the car moving ahead until it was taken by heat waves.

Now McKay felt with his tongue for slivers. The skin was torn back in long flaps from the middle knuckle and the breeze that carried the mountain air onto the porch made the cut sting.

He was young, only twenty-four, but his eyes looked tired. Sometimes he imagined one of the bombs dropped at Pearl Harbor had gone AWOL and was following him. "It's just us desperados left behind," Pinkey, the hired hand, said. "Just those ones of us too ornery to do any good over there." McKay hadn't passed the army physical because of the horse accident the year before. He was more legs than torso and his reedlike body was as pale and graceful as a sandhill crane's except for the limp. One leg was shorter now and something locked in the middle of his otherwise graceful stride. When he went to town, he found he could not share in the rounds of pride and hope and grief over the "boys" at the front because he did not know if going to war made you a hero.

Bobby tapped McKay on the shoulder. "It's time," he said.

McKay sat up. It was still dark outside.

"What time is it?"

"Four. But snow very bad."

McKay leaped out of bed and dressed. It was only September but two feet of snow had fallen during the night. He rode alone from pasture to pasture opening gates so the cattle, driven by wind, would not suffocate where snow drifted at fencelines. Heart Mountain towered above him. It was a geological freak. A limestone block, it broke away from the Rocky Mountain cordillera 40 million years ago and skidded east along a detachment fault shaking free and moving again just as the Shoshone River changed its course and Yellowstone Park was a nest of volcanoes that blew. McKay tried to imagine the mountain's choked, laggard polka into existence, when the earth around the fault quavered like jelly and blocks of lighter rock skittered and tumbled across the earth's unstable surface.

Now the wind blew out of the north, then came around from the opposite direction with a thumping, forward motion. McKay remembered that during the night one tree exploded, dropping branches into the lower limbs like bodies being carried home from war. Others broke from the weight of snow in sharp reports—reminders that there was a war on. He needed none. He'd had a bad dream. He was in a hospital looking for his brothers. Room after room was filled with bodies stacked up. Their heads and limbs had been cut off and the torsos were tied together in bundles like newspapers to be sent home. For the rest of the night he lay awake wondering if he was a coward.

At the upper end of the last pasture McKay rode the timber looking for bulls. When he emerged wet flakes of snow hit his face. He thought of these slopes as the neck of Heart Mountain. Its powerful torso was the ranch. The colt picked his way down the rocky slope. The saddle slipped forward on his withers and McKay watched the shoulder muscles bulge and lengthen and let his own body sway from side to side with the colt's gait. McKay had not been happy at college or on the trips to Mexico with his father but only here under the clipped top of Heart Mountain where he imagined there was an eye that saw him, sometimes the only eye, and a beacon light which led his grasping, solitary thoughts home.

McKay heard rock tumbling. It was getting dark and he strained to see. Far below the lights of the ranch house came into view and to the south, the lights of the relocation camp. He heard the noise again, then made out a bull elk trotting down a steep sidehill. It was a massive animal with a hump over its shoulders and a swept-back rack of antlers attached precariously to its head.

When the bull stopped, McKay stopped. The animal lifted its head and a long, looping whistle came up through its neck, followed by heaving grunts. Then the bull started down the slope. At the bottom, he cut through a field of grain to the reservoir. The sky had cleared in the west. McKay saw the sun shine for a moment, then sink below the horizon. When the bull pawed at the water, it looked as if he were pulling his leg through shattered glass. The pink in the sky stained the water and the bull lowered his neck and drank.

McKay heard hooves clatter on rock. He turned in the saddle and saw a herd of fifty or sixty cow elk with calves and young bulls flooding down the slope. They waded in. Their backs were dusted with snow and they kneeled down in the lake until water covered their bodies and rose up suddenly with a whooshing sound. One calf walked to the back of the bull and sniffed his rump, then immersed himself and came up dripping and mewing for his mother.

When McKay's colt stretched his neck forward and coughed, the elk turned nervously, shaking off water. The lake was all silver now and the banks of the lake and the alfalfa field surrounding it were almost black. McKay looked up at Heart Mountain. The band of light in the west had been extinguished. Snow began again. Some of the older cow elk climbed the dam bank. Others followed. Now the lake itself was dark and the silver showed around the legs of the animals only when they moved. The young calves went last. They dipped and splashed while their mothers looked on and called to them in seal-like barks and the bull stood on the bank and bugled. His long, sinuous whistle sounded like a whale's song.

McKay rode home. He couldn't see the trail but the horse knew the way. He wondered what Bobby was making for dinner. Not that the ranch needed a cook when there was only him and sometimes Pinkey to cook for, but Bobby Korematsu had become a fixture. In his sixties now, he

had come to the ranch when McKay was seven. Hired to cook for the
haying crew for one month, he stayed seventeen years, and now, he
would live out the rest of his life at the ranch. He had already chosen
the place where he wanted his ashes buried.

"Bobby?"

The kitchen was dark. McKay shook the snow from his jacket and lit
a kerosene lamp. He had feuded with the Rural Electric Association and
they had cut off his electricity. The lamp smoked at first, then the light
came up beautifully in the chimney. Wind made the doors rattle and he
heard the tin roof on one of the sheds heave and flatten, and when he
pressed his face to the window, snow came at him in swirling waves. He
opened the door to the pantry. In the near dark of the room Bobby held
a dead snake's head under one foot and the tail under the other. He
lopped the rattles off with a pocket knife, made a circular cut, then peeled
the skin like a sock.

"Funny snake. Think he come in here for winter. Smelled him first,
then heard him rattle."

"What did he smell like?"

"Cucumber. Strong ones."

With a swift stroke Bobby slit the skin so it lay flat. Then he hung it
in between McKay's undershirts on the clothesline.

McKay set the lamp on the table and took down the bottle of whiskey.

"Nice weather, huh?" he said cynically.

"Too early. Garden ruin now."

"Pinkey showed up yet?"

Bobby shook his head and shrugged his shoulders. "You look like
drowned rat."

"A hungry one," McKay said.

McKay peeled potatoes and Bobby stoked the wood stove hot enough
to sear the steaks cut from a side of beef that had been a bull. The sound
of split pine shifting into embers made McKay think about bodies falling
from a burning plane and also, bodies burning from sexual heat. . . .

"Does that powder really work, Bobby?"

Bobby wiped the sweat from his forehead, then pierced the steaks with
a sharp, two-pronged fork and dropped them into the black skillet. When
the steaks were arranged perfectly in the pan, he turned to McKay.

"Don't know . . ."

"What do you mean you don't know?"

"Don't know any women now."

"But you have—"

Bobby smiled and turned back to the steaks. The grease they threw onto the top of the stove skittered and shone. "You young man, don't worry about these things. . . ."

Bobby filled two plates with steak, potatoes, and marinated green beans he had put up that summer. They sat facing each other with a lantern and a bottle of whiskey between them. Except for the booze, everything they ate came off the ranch. Bobby's summer garden was an acre of squash, beans, carrots, beets, lettuce, tomatoes, corn, peas, and broccoli, beside a plot of herbs whose English names he did not know, as well as a Japanese garden of daikon, cabbage, eggplant, scallions, and winter melon.

McKay cut into his meat. "Poor old Heber, the Mormon bull. . . ," he said as he chewed. "Where the hell's Pinkey?"

"No see him. Probably drunk now since it snowed."

"I ought to move that sonofabitch to the Gobi Desert, where it never storms. . . . Want a shot?" McKay asked, uncorking the whiskey. Bobby shook his head. "The elk are down," McKay added.

"Where?"

"By the lake. About fifty head and a big bull."

Bobby stood up, went to the kitchen door, and stepped outside. A few snowflakes blew past him and frizzled on the stove. McKay looked at the old man. He was wearing his padded winter kimono and it swayed in the breeze. Beyond was blackness; then, as the wind shifted and blew up from the south, the sound of a bull elk bugling carried through the air.

Bobby returned to the chair whose legs had been cut down so his feet would touch the floor. He stabbed a piece of cut meat with his fork and held it to his mouth, then put it down again. "Everything sad now," he said solemnly.

When they finished, McKay cleared the plates and Bobby brought the sheet cake down from the cupboard. The cakes he made every week were too large for just the two of them, and he ended up giving them to the dogs and chickens, but refused to use any other pan.

"They're not dead, you know," McKay said, meaning his brothers.

"No." Bobby stared at him. "They fighting Japanese."

McKay's face flushed as he filled Bobby's shot glass. He remembered the first night after his brothers had gone to the front—how he had found Bobby in the dark kitchen crying.

"Bad war. Not good for heart," Bobby had said. "See, make me cry," he had continued, pounding his chest with his small hand.

"What if Korematsus kill your brothers?"

McKay looked fondly at the old cook. "I don't think that will happen. Ted's not even a soldier, he's a medic, he's saving lives, not taking them . . . and Champ is . . ." McKay stopped. He pulled a letter from his pocket. "It's from Ted. Shall I read it?"

Bobby nodded.

"Dear McKay,

"A war is a hell of a place for an idealist, that's all I can say. I requested a hospital ship. Is it illogical to suppose that in a war doctors are needed? Instead, they put me on a light cruiser, Brooklyn class, with a single bunk, clean sheets, and a Negro boy who wakes me at 7:00 A.M. every morning. My medical duties consist of ministering to heat rash, jock itch, athlete's foot, and colds. It's about as stimulating as giving the dogs worm pills. There are a thousand men on board. Once a week we eat with the enlisted men. The food is awful—mostly ram from New Zealand, canned spinach, and boiled potatoes. It's 110 degrees down there and stinks to high heaven. There's a movie every night. I've never felt so useless.

"I guess I can't tell you where we are, but the natives here are infested with parasites and malaria. The women go bare-topped. One of the guys said their breasts look like hounds' ears. I read *Time* magazine and everything else I can get my hands on from the library. It's the way I get lost and stay lost.

"Sorry I sound so depressed. What a shock to feel stirred up by patriotic duty, then get this . . . when I could be helping, even saving lives.

"Champ's in the middle of things as usual. Last week, before we left, he squeezed a girl so hard he broke her ribs. She showed up at sick call on the base and I had to bandage her. He was down in the dumps about the quarrel he had with you that last morning and says he wishes you'd hit him harder. Funny kid. I guess Henry's the big shot now and really seeing some action in the Coral Sea.

"Sometimes I think it's worse being on this end of things because we have too much time to think. By now Bobby knows where we are. Must be tough on him. It's made being here kind of confusing for me and Champ. Henry too. We talked about it the last night we were all together. A week ago I dreamed we were at cow camp and a breeze was blowing off a snowdrift and something smelled dead and our hair had turned white and we were laughing. Love to Bobby. Madeleine too.

Your brother,
Ted"

Bobby looked up. "He's not lying? He's really doctor?"

"You know Ted. He never did like a fight."

"Not like you, huh? You big fighter. Ask Champ," Bobby said, making fists.

After dinner McKay went to his sleeping porch and sat on the edge of his cot. He knew the elk were bedded down in the alfalfa field, snow deepening around them, the ridges of white resting in the bull's tines.

He lay down, his arm across his eyes. He wondered what it was like to be an elk. What did they think? What did they dream? An image of the lake came into his mind. The water was green and choppy. Then it became the ocean. Big swells lumbered past, the spray flying backward and stinging his eyes. He was swimming. Bobby came out and stood on the beach to look for McKay. What he saw were hundreds of elk heads bobbing up and down just behind where the waves begin to crest, and the big bulls' branching antlers and the one human face in the midst of them. McKay's . . .

2

Pinkey had been up since four but sat by the cook stove and moved a spoon around in his cup until six-thirty or so. The calendar above his head read December 1942 even though it was actually September because the first gust of wind that brought the front in had blown the pages of three autumn months to the floor. Pinkey decided December sounded good enough to him, so he left November, October, and September underfoot and later, used them to start a fire.

When the wind calmed he put on his coat and overshoes. The storm clouds slid to the East. He cut the wires on the bale of hay he had used as a couch all summer and fed a third of it to his mare. He looked up. He heard the drone of a plane but could see nothing. The sky, like the ground, was white. Yesterday it had been purely blue. One cloud had passed overhead. It was shaped like a human penis and rode the airwaves erect, pointing heavenward, Pinkey had thought, so that now, his usual nuisance morning erections, ordinarily reminding him of his solitary state, became something blessed.

Before leaving he added another layer of clothes: three pairs of socks, four shirts, a coat, a muffler, gloves, and a Scotch cap with the earflaps pulled down. Then he rode toward the highway. As he looked at the sky it occurred to him that yesterday's phallic cloud had softened and drained and come apart like cooked meat into the white smithereens falling on him as snow.

Across the road from Snuff's Bar a calcium mill spewed pink dust across the state line into Wyoming. Two front end loaders, a long wooden shed, and three cars on a railway siding were dusted pink and for a mile thickets of greasewood and sagebrush leaning south away from shouldering winds caught the mined chalk, as did the cattle who grazed there.

Pinkey left his sorrel mare tied between two pickups at the bar. With her back leg cocked, her whole body looked crooked. One rein dangled straight down into the mud. Someone had written "Ride me" in the snow that covered the saddle. Later, Pinkey thumbed a ride to town. The white-haired woman who owned four city lots and half-interest in the bank picked him up in her Cadillac. People are nicer now there's a war going on, Pinkey thought, and was glad he wasn't drunk so he wouldn't dirty the seat and felt proud of himself for suppressing the desire to put the touch on her for five dollars. She let him off in front of the clothing store. He tipped his sweat-stained hat and said, "Thank you, ma'am."

His paycheck, saved from a spring and summer at line camp, went toward new wool pants and a winter jacket because the one he was wearing, though still warm, had bloodstains all over the front from calving the winter before. He looked at himself in the mirror for the first time in four months. Next to the salesman, a hulking Mormon man who wore a reddish toupee and a diamond ring on his little finger, Pinkey looked small. His short legs were bowed, his windburned cheeks looked like polished apples and from his cracked lips a line of blood drove down his chin and dripped on the floor.

He went to the bars. They had tin ceilings and coal stoves set in the center and sunlight came off the mirrors behind the back bars like comets. "Drinks for the house," he yelled in each one, though "the house" rarely consisted of more than two or three old men and women—sheepherders or barflies or cowboys too bunged up to work—plus the bartenders, who never drank at ten in the morning so early in what Pinkey called "the drinking year," which began when the first storm of the season blew through.

At the Cactus, Pinkey downed a shot of Cobb's Creek whiskey from a bottle marked with his name. He dabbed at his lip with a handkerchief and read the new sign behind the bottles: NO JAPS.

He ordered another drink and read the sign again. He didn't like it.

"Even Bobby Korematsu?" he yelled down the counter to the bartender.

"What say?" The barman looked up from wiping glasses.

Pinkey went around behind the bar and pulled the sign down.

"Hey . . ." The barman rushed forward as Pinkey tore the sign in half so the word *Japs* fell to the floor beside his scuffed boot and the word *No* drifted sideways, teetering on the edge of the counter.

Pinkey stood braced.

"Get the hell out of my bar," the bartender yelled, picking up the torn sign.

"What about Bobby Korematsu?" Pinkey repeated.

"Yea, what about him? He's a Jap just like all the others. . . ."

The barman's teeth showed like a dog's.

Pinkey squatted in the alley between the Cactus and the Medicine Wheel bars and wiped blood with the sleeve of his shirt. His lip was cut and blood flowed from one nostril where the bartender had hit him squarely, just once, then dragged him out the front door onto the street. Pinkey had hidden in the alley, "just like an ol' dog licking his wounds," he mumbled to himself and wished the Mormon bishop's dogs would come find him and take him home.

He sat with his head tipped back against the brick wall. Now all he could think of was his wife, Janine . . . the night in Hardin when both of them had ended up cut and kicked and had hidden out in an alley just like this one while their noses bled and after a while she had leaned over and wiped Pinkey's face with a dirty red kerchief he kept in his back pocket to wipe the long blade of his pocketknife after castrating or earmarking a calf. How sometime later that night they had ended up lying under a stock truck in the parking lot and made love hurriedly and drunkenly with their pants twisted down their legs, and how afterward she had felt something wet on her shirt, right over her breast and said, "I think it's milk," but later, in the daylight, found that a bad U-joint had leaked grease, but knew she was pregnant anyway and nine months later to the day gave birth to their one son, Vincent.

Pinkey did not drink all the time then as he did now, because he had her, and they rode together on some of the big Montana outfits and it was a long way to town. When he did drink it was with her, when they went on a party after shipping or branding or calving, and it was just for one or two nights, nothing more; then they went back to cow camp or headquarters and ate a big breakfast to soak up the alcohol in their bodies and rode for another two or three months before they saw a town again.

But it was always there. The bottle. Sometimes, riding in the high country, he thought he saw it shimmering behind a screen of pines, or lying at the bottom of a river, some kind of call, like the way a priest is called, he thought, but it was a beckoning to a physical place he wanted to hide his eyes from, some brightness into which he could not help but fall.

Janine had tethered him in a way no one else in his life had. The night she cut that line, not a night like in Hardin, but a night when the baby had colic so bad he cried for four nights and days and Pinkey had left because he couldn't stand the sound of such human agony. He had not even gone to the bar—that was the thing that always got him—but had only slept in the barn as in Depression days when people took beds and food where they could and were at the mercy of strangers.

And when he had gone back home the baby was well but Janine was so tired she had aged and Pinkey's things were packed and she would not let him enter the house. That night, he heeded the other calling. He knew he should have fought to stay, implored, demanded, slept at the front door until she let him in, but he gave up without any fight whatever. That was the September night a cloud rolled in and, backing into it, he felt the moisture on his neck, and in the next second, it swallowed him.

Pinkey dabbed at his face, though the blood had dried, then went into the Medicine Wheel Bar.

Inside the rear door Pinkey tripped on a junkpile: a 410 shotgun with a broken stock, three rolls of pitted barbed wire, and a box of rusted D-rings and buckles.

"Is that your dowry?" he asked a man wearing a red neck scarf.

"That's Jimmy Luster's stuff. Backed his wagon to the door last night and just started auctioneering things off. Said his old lady quit him and he was going to travel light for a while."

Pinkey stared at the goods on the floor. "Did Jimmy say where he was headed?"

"Didn't know," the old cowboy said. "See, the thing is, he just found out his kid was killed in the Pacific. Them Japs sank his ship and he was in some kind of lifeboat deal for a week and he went plumb nuts. Jumped overboard. Couldn't swim."

Pinkey looked out the front windows of the bar. The bright morning light hurt his eyes. Fat flakes of snow were falling fast. "He'll just winter-kill out there," he muttered as if talking about himself. He drank for the rest of the day.

McKay reached Pinkey's cow camp at noon. The snow was knee-deep. For a while, the sky cleared and what was left of the moisture in the blue air sprinkled down like glitter. Pinkey's mare was gone. That meant he had ridden to the bar. McKay hobbled his horse and let him eat the mare's hay. Then he went inside the cabin and lit a fire. The cabin was damp. There was food on the shelves but it had been chewed by mice. McKay reset the three sprung traps and warmed himself by the stove.

He had been a little boy when Pinkey first came to work at the ranch. He taught McKay how to rope, how to handle a calf on the ground during branding, how to split wood, how to tell if it was going to rain by the look of the entrance to an anthill, how to kill a sage hen with a rock and barbecue it for dinner . . . and how to drink enough Cobb's Creek—a special brand of whiskey no one else had ever heard of—to keep aches of all kinds, saddle sores, and stiffness at bay.

When he was fourteen and he and his father and Pinkey were moving cattle to spring range, and he had accidentally let the calves get separated from their mothers and run back, RJ was so mad at McKay he took his rope down and chased the boy through the sage. McKay ran as fast as he could, but his father was swinging the lariat at his back, hitting him sometimes, and when McKay tripped, his father's horse had to jump over the top of him. McKay lay on the ground with his hands over the top of his head. He was too scared to cry. Then RJ stepped off his horse and, standing over McKay, said, "It's all over now," by which he meant the incident should be forgotten.

After, McKay had gone with Pinkey to cow camp. They picketed their horses and grained them. Inside, Pinkey looked at the boy. "You did good, kid. My daddy whupped me a few times and I wasn't near so brave." Then he cooked a dinner of elk steaks, potatoes, and gravy. Even now, when they bunked up together, Pinkey always asked McKay if he was hungry and he always was and Pinkey cooked for him.

Now he sometimes wondered if Pinkey was worth the bother. He was always "elsewhere" when there was work to be done—"elsewhere" being the bar—and McKay was tired of working alone.

"There's no fun in it," he told himself and thought glumly that there wasn't even anyone to tell that to. After his parents died, he had kept thinking he could at least write to them, tell them what he was doing on the ranch, what decisions he and his brothers had made for the coming year: how he had decided to cull the cows for lower birth weights and higher conception rates, how they had bought twenty bulls at a sale up in Montana, and about the colts he was breaking. He resolved to write his brother Ted a letter.

The cabin was warm now. McKay swept the floor and wiped the table. After the coffee boiled and he drank some, he closed down the stove and rode home. On the way he picked up straggling cows and calves—the ones the storm had not brought down. They plowed through fresh snow and by the time McKay rode through the last gate, he counted 150 pairs.

Pinkey found his dentures on the sidewalk between the Cactus and the Silver Spur bars and lost them a third time. A tremor had begun in his neck and passed all the way down to his fingertips and legs so even his knees shook when he walked. A pickup full of young cowboys passed.

"Come on up to the Outlaw and we'll buy you a drink," one of them yelled.

Pinkey looked up. A face in the cab gave him a start. It was his son, Vincent. Pinkey dove into an alley. His empty stomach convulsed.

"Dad?"

Pinkey supported himself between the brick walls of two buildings and looked up. "I thought you was up to the Outlaw," he said, trying to straighten up. He had wanted to see his son. He always wanted to see him. It was a hunger like the tug of a good woman in town, but stronger. He remembered he had promised he would take the cure.

"I came back to say hello. You in town for a couple of days?"

"You could say that," Pinkey replied dryly. "Oh Christ, I'm gonna be sick. You better go."

The dry heaves scratched up through Pinkey's body and ended in his open mouth. He gasped and spit. Vincent held his father's head until the nausea passed.

Pinkey looked at his son. "When did you get so growed up?"

The young man shrugged shyly but the wounded look in his eyes was there. Pinkey knew the look and concluded he needed one last drink before he quit for good. They walked to the Cactus. Pinkey had already forgotten he had been kicked out of there once that day. A row of icicles fell from the eaves of the building and speared a hump of drifted snow behind their backs. They went in. Tall, lithe, and slender, Vincent had a broad face that bore the scars of acne and from under his tall-crowned black hat, two braids hung down.

"Who's your friend?" the bartender asked.

"This is my kid, Vincent," Pinkey replied proudly.

"The hell . . ."

"His mother's Crow; that's why he's so tall and good-looking."

"Yea, but who's the father?" one of the drunks yelled from the back of the bar. The chirp in his voice sounded more like choking.

"Well I've never seen a half-breed looks like that," the bartender said.

"That's because you've never been two steps out of this sonofabitchin' Mormon town." Then Pinkey stood on his toes and leaned toward the barkeep. "The whole goddamned country is breeds. We're all half this and half that and half something else, and any one of you show me some thoroughbred blood and I'll show you a phony sonofabitch."

Pinkey stepped back from the bar. He was still mad about the NO JAP sign. He turned, kicked the jukebox until it lit up and played a tune, then followed Vincent to the street.

"Hey, Pinkey, you owe me for the drinks," the barman yelled.

When Pinkey reached the sidewalk he slipped on the ice. Vincent helped him to his feet.

"I'd better catch that ride back to the ranch," Vincent mumbled. "You got wheels?"

"Yea, sure," Pinkey said. The color had drained from his face. He watched Vincent walk east along Main Street. He moved like a wildcat, Pinkey thought. Smooth and swift and careful. Maybe I'm not the kid's daddy, he thought, then brushed the snow from his new coat, adjusted the gray Stetson, and walked the opposite direction, toward Snuff's and home.

Stores gave way to small frame and brick houses where lawns burned under the snow. Pinkey's hat was cocked sideways on his head and his legs were so bowed. A few dogs barked as he passed. He smiled as though acknowledging applause. Past the last house the sky closed down like a dark awning unreeled from the mountains, lowering what Pinkey thought of as infinity, all the way down to the pint bottle in his back pocket from which he stopped to drink. A skunk ran out from behind a rosebush. Pinkey howled with laughter, brushing against the red blossoms already skewed by heavy snow. He wiped his mouth as the liquor slid down. The skunk zigzagged down the road, the stripe on its back crossing the road's white line, like crossing his *t*'s and Pinkey thought the highway would spell out messages for him if he walked far enough along its edge.

The dogs came out from behind the Mormon church and trotted at Pinkey's heels. "Hello, Bishops," he said and clucked to them. For twelve years he had trained the stock dogs at McKay's ranch. He didn't have any theories or methods. "It's just a meeting of minds," he liked to say. He was happy now. He had wanted company and now he had these dogs. They were the Mormon bishop's Border collies, raised to work sheep. Pinkey laughed when he thought how mad the old bishop would be when he found they were gone.

He looked at the sky. The clouds had curdled and thickened. Sure enough, the penis cloud he had seen the day before had knocked up some old gal and now there was this.

Pinkey stood on the side of the highway and looked west. A red and white grain truck approached. The dogs sprinted ahead, leaping up and changing directions midair to chase the truck. "Atta boys, get 'em out, way around," Pinkey yelled, then he took another swallow from the pint bottle. The dogs came back to him and jumped up on his leg and he patted their heads.

Another loaded truck barreled toward them and the dogs repeated their act. Pinkey crouched down and followed the action with his head like a first base coach. They nipped at the hubcaps. Pinkey whistled and they came back to him and licked his face. Then he stood. The road was empty. No trucks, no cars. The snow had started again so he and the dogs clambered down into the borrow pit. Like swimmers, they waded through tall grass, their feet rolling over discarded beer bottles as they walked.

Finally the headlights of a car appeared. Pinkey crawled to the road, clutching at bunchgrass. The headlights bore down on him. "You jacklightin' sonofabitch." Then the lights were on him like crossed eyes. He crouched down, barking in unison with the dogs, a magnificent high-pitched crooning cut off suddenly by a whomp.

The car shuddered, fishtailed, and slid to a stop. A cyclone fence on the far side of the borrow pit vibrated. Pinkey, half sprawled against the fence and half on the ground, moaned.

The driver of the car ran to the collapsed figure. "God almighty, mister, are you . . . ?"

Pinkey looked up. The man crouching over him had dark eyes. Like Vincent's. Was this Vincent? No. Then Pinkey remembered why he had come to town that day. It was Vincent's birthday and until now, he had forgotten.

"You killed me, you sonofabitch," Pinkey said.

The driver dropped to his knees.

"Well hell, I ain't really dead," Pinkey said, grinning.

The driver just looked at him.

"I know I'm good-lookin', but don't stare. Take me to the hospital. I think my leg's busted."

The man pulled his jacket off and spread it across Pinkey's chest. "I'm sorry, man, I'm really sorry."

"Oh shut up," Pinkey said. He slid his hand across the overcoat. Camel hair, he thought, or maybe cashmere.

Two women rolled Pinkey into the X-ray room on a gurney. The hospital was understaffed because of the war and there were no orderlies. Pinkey lay back, his hands folded behind his head.

"Do you want to take my pants off now or later?" he asked the two nurses and winked. They smiled and said nothing.

The transfer to the examining table proceeded with difficulty. Pinkey refused to help. On the contrary, he was a deadweight for the two women. McKay burst in. The hospital had called him when Pinkey arrived, and with one motion he lifted his hired hand to the table.

"For God's sake, Pinkey . . ."

Pinkey gave McKay a grin. "Where's the cards, the flowers, the candy?"

"Oh, they're just floodin' in."

Pinkey turned to the nurses. "Are you going to strip me now?"

"Sorry, old man, maybe another time," the heavier of the two replied. Then she split the seam of his trousers with a razor.

"Stop it! My new pants . . . ," Pinkey howled.

"Just slap the sonofabitch," McKay said, smiling and motioning to the nurse to continue cutting.

The hospital let Pinkey sleep it off in the vacant labor room for no extra charge. He slept until the pain in his leg woke him. When he opened his eyes the walls of the room folded around him and spun. He closed them again. The beads of darkness under the lids spun too, zooming backward then bursting against some inward wall the color of garnets. He felt a terrible weight in his body. Maybe they put a body cast on with my arms inside so I can't hold a bottle, he thought. He tried to move his arms and there was a sickening crash. The room filled with light.

"Did we fall out of bed?" a big woman in white asked. She helped Pinkey up.

"I guess my wings broke," he said.

"Up we go. Now we'll put these sides up so we don't try to fly again."

Pinkey felt the hard bed under him again. When the nurse's face came close he thought he heard a terrible roar like snow falling from a roof. Then the room went black. He tried to lie still but his shoulders twitched and his body splintered like rotten wood. He saw a bottle somewhere in front of him and when he reached for it, it broke, but the whiskey didn't spill. It had turned solid, like something frozen, then all at once, it shattered. His arms lengthened, reaching for it. He tried to think of why the need came on him. Then his arms were fifty yards long, his hands like tiny knobs, and still he could touch nothing and the need grew, a malevolent bloom.

"You havin' a baby or do you want to go home?" McKay asked, throwing light into the room.

Pinkey sat up and looked around. "Am I dead?"

"How the hell do I know. I ain't the doctor."

"What time is it?" Pinkey asked.

"Time to get out of here before we're snowed in for the winter."

Pinkey suddenly felt clearheaded and slid off the bed. He hopped a few times, hanging on for balance. McKay handed him his hat, then the crutches. "God, if you don't look like a jackrabbit . . ."

A fog swallowed the road ahead of McKay's pickup and mixed with steam off the river. They drove north in the dark. Ahead the sky began to clear.

"What'd you have to go and get drunk for?" McKay asked. He was tired.

"That's why."

"What's why?"

"Because I'm tired of having reasons. Why can't a man just go and do stuff?"

"Well you ain't going to be doing much with that thing on your leg."

From out of the dark a road sign loomed: WELCOME TO BIG MONTANA. A horse ran in front of the truck. McKay swerved hard.

"Hey, that's my mare," Pinkey shouted and motioned to the sorrel horse eating grass on the side of the highway, which McKay referred to as "government feed."

The truck skidded to a halt. Pinkey looked. He could see the blurred outline of the calcium plant. A half-moon shot up from an empty railroad car and shone like a pinhole in ice. Pinkey's saddle had been dumped on end under the bar sign, which pulsed, throwing a bloody pool onto the snow every second or so.

McKay backed his pickup to a sidehill and loaded the mare. Pinkey rolled down the window. "I named her Eleanor. For Eleanor Roosevelt."

When McKay slapped the mare on the rump, she jumped in and the top of her back steamed where snow had melted and the ice hanging in her mane clanged like crystals.

McKay turned his truck around. Now the sign read: WELCOME TO WONDERFUL WYOMING. Pinkey inspected his cast as if seeing it for the first time. He drummed on it here and there and discovered some of the plaster was still wet.

"Don't you worry about them cows. I left them on autopilot. And don't worry about this cast neither. We'll cut her off in a coupla weeks and I'll be good as new."

McKay smiled. Pinkey pulled his coat tightly around him and cradled his head with a gloved hand. A wheezing snore came from his half-opened mouth as soon as he closed his eyes.

McKay drove slowly on the ungraded ranch road so as not to jar Pinkey's leg. Once he stopped to check the depth of a mud hole, and when he climbed back in, he glanced at his passenger. Pinkey's beard was growing out gray and his pink cheeks were a mass of capillaries broken into a fine mesh.

The truck lurched. Fins of slush sprayed up on either side. In his sleep, Pinkey felt McKay's eyes on him. It was like heat penetrating his heavy lids. He wanted to laugh but his body made no sound.

3

Kai Nakamura lay across the bed with only a shirt on. It was late and it was raining again. After Li made love to him she rested her head on his stomach.

"You nervous. Everything noisy in there."

Kai shifted, laughing, and pulled one knee up. He reached over her hip and lit a cigarette. The room smelled of green vegetables and cooking oil. Li climbed off the bed.

"Here," she said, pinning a badge to his shirt. She kissed his chest where the shirt was open. His shoulders were big because he was on the Cal Berkeley swim team. He read the badge. It said, I AM CHINESE.

The noise of the city wallowed in the room, a mechanical gargling of horns, rain, music, and engines. On the fire escape the potted chrysanthemum he had given Li for her birthday tossed about in the wind. He ground out the cigarette until it looked like a pig's flared snout and clasped Li's head tightly in the crook of his arm. He thought her hair shone like the stalks of black bamboo. He rolled her from side to side. Locking his arms across the small of her back, he entwined his legs with hers until she wriggled from him. He grabbed her again and pinned her on her back with a wrestler's hold.

"Hello," he said.

Li smiled. She knocked at his shins with the tops of her feet, then went limp. Kai dropped heavily to her side. He was thinking ahead, about the next day and the next, and a coolness had gone through him. Li examined his face.

"Who are you?" she said.

There was a knock on the door. Kai scrambled under the covers as Jimmy Wong, Li's older brother by twelve years, burst into their room. "No more Chinese women for you!" he announced, laughing. He handed Kai the *San Francisco Chronicle*. The headlines read, ALL JAPS MUST GO. Kai sat up propping himself against the wall. He leafed through the newspaper: ". . . it makes no difference whether the Japanese is theoretically a citizen. He is still a Japanese. Giving him a scrap of paper won't change him. I don't care what they do with them as long as they don't send them back here. A Jap is a Jap. . . ."

Jimmy sat on the edge of the bed and stared out the window. The building that housed the dumpling shop and mah-jongg room across the street was dark. A fire escape clung tentatively to its side and the green dragon—a symbol of vitality and long life—used in the New Year's parade where he had met Li lay unfurled against three upstairs windows.

Jimmy turned to Kai and whispered: "You stay here. Wear badge. Marry Li. Keep go to college. Change from great Japanese scholar to great Chinese scholar."

Kai laughed. "I'm not either. I'm just American boy with slant eyes. Chinese wouldn't have me," he said.

Li reentered the room with two bottles of Coke. She uncapped them with the bottle opener by the bed and handed one to Kai and the other to her brother. The rain intensified. It slapped hard at the one window. Against city lights the drops looked black and fog enclosed the streets of Chinatown like sea-lanes leading to places no one in that room knew.

Kai unpinned the badge and twirled it between his fingers. It pricked his thumb. A drop of blood appeared and Li licked it away. After, Kai flung his hand over his head in a mocking backstroke. He thought about swimming from this dank room so redolent with intimacy. He would swim backward from the trancelike, forward motion of time, starting in San Francisco Bay, doing the backstroke under the bridge, the crawl out into the channel, then float past the Farallon Islands into rough seas.

Li opened the window. A surge of wind rushed past the bed. She pulled the chrysanthemum, whose heavy blossoms were bent completely over, into the room.

"Look what's happened," she said.

Kai didn't look at the plant but at her. Perhaps this was the last time he would see her. In two days he would be evacuated. Whatever else happened he would remember her diminutiveness and the tart taste of her skin.

After he left Li on that last night of freedom, Kai waited for sunrise at an all-night upstairs teahouse where he was known by the waiters. It would have been dangerous for him to walk the streets because a curfew and a five-mile travel limit had been placed on "all persons of Japanese ancestry." Even the binoculars he used for baseball games had been confiscated. Evacuation notices were posted on power poles all over the city. He and his friends had read them and had taunted the man pasting them up. Now, he sipped black tea and waited for sunrise alone.

At eight he boarded the ferry for Richmond. He hadn't seen his parents for two years, though they lived less than ten miles apart. When he was twelve, Kai had been sent to an orphanage and later, to live with a Caucasian professor and his wife to learn "the American Way." The American Way had brought him, at twenty-four, a Ph.D. candidacy in history.

The man at the ticket office, a Filipino, hesitated before giving Kai passage on the ferry, adding insult to injury because the Filipinos hated the Japanese as well.

Kai walked the streets of Richmond. Turning a corner, he saw his parents' tiny frame house. In the front yard, a cypress had been pruned into an odd, windblown shape, and a single vine crawled a trellis up one wall.

He knocked on the door. When Mr. Nakamura opened it, he did not recognize his son. "Who are you looking for?" he asked briskly.

Kai shoved his hands into his pockets and stepped back, chuckling.

"Pop, it's me," he said, but his father only stared uncomprehending.

He heard his mother. She pushed past her husband and let out a gasp. "Oh . . . it's you—come in."

"Don't mind him," she whispered, "it's just that you've changed," she said, smiling. She turned to Mr. Nakamura. "He has grown so big, *desu-ne?*"

Kai's father stood to one side and nodded yes.

The house was bare. All the furniture had been sold or stored for safekeeping. In the living room Mr. Nakamura sat on a packing crate and bent toward the big radio. It lit his face like a jack-o'-lantern.

Kai's mother called from the kitchen. She was stirring scallions into broth, shoyu, and sake, then eggs and eel.

"I don't eat this food very much anymore," Kai said.

"Oh, this is special for you. *Unagi donburi.* You always liked it," she said, though Kai could remember liking no such thing.

He looked at his mother. He resembled her in build and the shape of his face but he still wondered if these were his parents. When they spoke during the meal he could not understand what they said.

After lunch Kai and his father drove to Japantown. Mr. Nakamura wanted to show his son the store. On the way, he saw a sign in the morgue: I'D RATHER DO BUSINESS WITH A JAP, and a crudely handwritten one in the barber shop: FREE SHAVES FOR JAPS. NOT RESPONSIBLE FOR ACCIDENTS.

"How's business been going, Pop?"

Mr. Nakamura grunted. "No good now."

It was a Wednesday but Japantown was deserted. The noodle shop, the mochi shop, the restaurants were all closed. Mr. Nakamura pulled up in front of his hardware store and unlocked the door. It was housed in a triangular building at the end of a block flanked on two sides by narrow streets.

Inside Kai walked up and down the aisles. There were shelves of tools: planers and chisels and saws, garden tools and seed packets, and a ceiling-high stack of black twine rolled into balls. In another aisle were kitchen goods: bamboo steamers and water ladles, cast iron pots with wooden lids, chopsticks and scrub brushes, and a penny jar full of bubble gum.

Mr. Nakamura took his place behind the counter. When he came to America he worked as a laborer on a celery farm, a chicken-sexer, a flower grower, and now the owner of Japantown's only hardware store. Above his head was the business license he had framed austerely in black and next to it, a photograph of the Great Buddha at Nara.

"For God's sake, Pop, take that down," Kai said, pointing to the photo.

Mr. Nakamura stood motionless. Kai slid a penny into the gum machine and popped a jawbreaker into his mouth. His father turned away in disgust and struggled with a locked door. Kai helped him. Finally the door swung open. Instead of the street, there was a garden, no bigger than a closet, with stepping-stones, mossy banks, a stone water basin, three flowering shrubs, and, against a tall fence, a thicket of black bamboo.

"I sell business yesterday," Kai's father said solemnly. "Seven hundred dollar. The car too. But didn't show them this."

Kai spit the gum into his hand and stared at the massive block of stone under his feet. Already the moss had begun to grow beyond its borders. Across the street a gong in the Buddhist temple rang. Kai heard glass breaking. He turned around. His father had broken the picture frame and held a match to the photograph of the Buddha. The glossy paper lifted and curled toward him and became ash.

They locked the store and drove home in the Studebaker. Sometimes the horn stuck and Mr. Nakamura had to lift the hood and pinch a certain wire, but not today. They glided through empty streets. Their first night of evacuation would be spent at a racetrack in converted horsestalls. The idea amused Kai at first, and he thought of getting a rake from the store for the manure, but changed his mind.

"Seabiscuit, here we come," he said, though quietly, so his father would not hear.

The next morning Mrs. Nakamura swept the floors a last time though the house appeared to be spotless. Three large suitcases and a bulging duffle bag were set out at the front door. At the last moment Mr. Nakamura parted with his beloved possession: a potted bonsai he had grown from seed. The neighbors, who were Danish, were to care for it. Mr. Nakamura explained the strict watering and pruning schedule, then handed the tree to the sea captain.

"It is very beautiful, this little tree," Jan Carlson exclaimed. He was tall and in his big red hands the tree looked even smaller. "Don't worry;

it will live longer than this damned war," he shouted. "It will be very healthy tree when you return. I will have it for you, sure."

Mr. Nakamura looked at the man, his eyes glazed with shame, then bowed deeply.

Two days later Kai and his parents were on a train. All through the cars he could see only black hair, dark eyes, the sound of a language his parents had forbidden him to learn. The journal he began keeping that day was a way of steadying himself against drastic change. Already, the lullaby rocking of the train felt deathly to him. He dreamed the tracks were his arms. He was holding Li. The heavy cars rolled over them.

When Kai woke his arms were asleep. He had been sitting on his hands to keep warm. Out the train window he could see the desert under a moon. He thought it looked like the palm of a hand on which no lines had been drawn.

Like a great elastic band the train stretched Kai away from the places and people he knew well. He opened his journal:

As I look out the train window I can see green hills dotted with houses. Strange but I hadn't noticed the soft greenness before. I remembered in the hurried retreat I had left my room in turmoil. An Issei would have been ashamed to leave the place in less than perfect order so as not to betray any confusion in his mind. But as for confusion, I'm feeling plenty. Everyone on the train is asking what will happen to them when we get to the Camp, but I'm asking what will become of us when we return—if we ever do.

The train clicked and swayed. Kai continued writing:

A child is crying. I think it is very young, only four or five days old. The mother described her experience of hearing news of Pearl Harbor. She said, "I felt as if I had lost all the color in my body." Then came February 19 and the signing of Executive Order 9066:

Whereas the successful prosecution of the war requires every possible protection against espionage and against sabotage to national-defense material, national-defense premises, and national-defense utilities as defined in section 4, Act of April 20, 1918, 40 Stat. 533, as amended by the act of November 30, 1940, 54 Stat. 1220, and the Act of August 21, 1941, 55 Stat. 655 (U. S. C., Title 50, Sec. 104):

Now, therefore, by virtue of the authority vested in me as President of the United States, and Commander in Chief of the Army and Navy, I hereby authorize and direct the Secretary of War, and the Military Commanders whom he may from time to time designate, whenever he or any designated Commander deems such action necessary or desirable, to prescribe military areas in such places and of such extent as he or the appropriate Military Commander may determine, from which any or all persons may be excluded, and with respect to which, the right of any persons to enter, remain in, or leave shall be subject to whatever restrictions the Secretary of War or the appropriate Military Commander may impose in his discretion. The Secretary of War is hereby authorized to provide for residents of any such area who are excluded therefrom, such transportation, food, shelter, and other accommodations as may be necessary, in the judgment of the Secretary of War or the said Military Commander, and until other arrangements are made, to accomplish the purpose of this order. The designation of military areas in any region or locality shall supersede designations of prohibited and restricted areas by the Attorney General under the Proclamations of December 7 and 8, 1941, and shall supersede the responsibility and authority of the Attorney General under the said Proclamations in respect of such pro- hibited and restricted areas.

I hereby further authorize and direct the Secretary of War and the said Military Commanders to take such other steps as he or the appro- priate Military Commander may deem advisable to enforce compliance with the restrictions applicable to each Military area hereinabove au- thorized to be designated, including the use of Federal troops and other Federal Agencies, with authority to accept assistance of state and local agencies.

I hereby further authorize and direct all Executive Departments, independent establishments and other Federal Agencies, to assist the

Secretary of War or the said Military Commanders in carrying out this Executive Order, including the furnishing of medical aid, hospitalization, food, clothing, transportation, use of land, shelter, and other supplies, equipment, utilities, facilities, and services.

This order shall not be construed as modifying or limiting in any way the authority heretofore granted under Executive Order No. 8972, dated December 12, 1941, nor shall it be construed as limiting or modifying the duty and responsibility of the Federal Bureau of Investigation, with respect to the investigation of alleged acts of sabotage or the duty and responsibility of the Attorney General and the Department of Justice under the Proclamations of December 7, and 8, 1941, prescribing regulations for the conduct and control of alien enemies, except as such duty and responsibility is superseded by the designation of military areas hereunder.

> *Franklin D. Roosevelt.*
> *February 19, 1942.*

A man such as Roosevelt could not have thought of such a thing, could he? Surely he was coerced by bigoted, anti-Asian businessmen in California. What did he know of coolie labor and exclusion acts? And now, it's the Camps.

We pulled out of the station this morning with the blinds drawn. So we could not see out or so no one could see in? The seats on the train are wooden benches. Hard on the old Issei bones. A week after Pearl Harbor the U.S. Treasury Department froze our bank accounts and we are allowed to withdraw no more than $100 per month. Now, looking around, I see many people who have already lost their farms and homes and equipment— anything they were making payments on—so we are not only exiled, but destitute. No money, no home.

The train lurched to a stop. There was no town, only a water tank and a switch box. Kai closed his journal and ran to the door. He jumped down, tilted his head back and inhaled dry air. Two army soldiers eyed him. They had guns. Steam from the train's engine hissed and the great trunklike water hose swung against the black cab. Ahead, Kai could see the Rocky Mountains. Snow covered the higher peaks. "Bring clothes suited to pioneer life," they had been advised. The thought made Kai chuckle.

Kai climbed on the train and returned to his parents' seat. They had slept through the stop. His mother's mouth was open and his father's head was tucked against his shoulder the way a bird sleeps and his glasses hung crookedly from his nose. Kai began a letter.

Dear Li,

Can you imagine how I feel? I don't even know myself. A little while ago a wave of loneliness came over me like nothing I've felt before. It's a kind of wrenching ache. Tell Jimmy we crossed a river called the Virgin. It runs red, can you beat that? When we left the Assembly Center I saw a man with his arms stuck through the fence, holding his girlfriend, and it made me think of you.

For the time being I'm a family man. Isn't that funny after all these years of being an orphan. Mom and Pop are awfully scared and sad. I've been trying to make the trip as comfortable as possible but it's not easy. Some of this American food doesn't agree with them. They probably never had a hamburger before—after all those years in Richmond. By the way, I told them about you.

Pop has hardly said a word since he closed up the store. I don't know how to get him to talk. I can't believe I won't be going to classes in the morning and in the evenings, coming to you.

We heard that at another camp someone sent a box of oranges with a sword inside. A Nisei ran with it and the MPs shot him dead.

I guess I'll try to get some sleep now. It feels strange being apart—like a big hole that grows bigger and bigger where my heart has flown back to you.

love, Kai

Kai folded the letter, tucked it in his journal, and tried to sleep, but couldn't. He looked at his parents again. They would not have approved of Li because she was Chinese and they would have thought her vulgar. Now their heads bobbed with the swaying and jerking of the train and the stale air in the car rose like something solid.

The stories he had heard on the train about the early arrests of Issei shocked him. Men his father's age who taught in Japanese language schools, or were Buddhist priests, or owned a fleet of fishing boats, or big farms along the coast, were taken off the streets by FBI agents, given twenty-four hours to pack, loaded in the back of produce trucks covered with canvas, and shipped to county jails.

One fisherman from Terminal Island had gone out as usual at two A.M., but noticed no boats followed him. When he looked back a last time, he saw the lighthouse go dark. They made their haul and on returning at sunrise, found the harbor had been closed off with a piece of wire. A launch approached and three FBI men boarded. They arrested the captain and confiscated radios and binoculars, and a logbook the captain had been keeping.

The train's whistle blew long and hard and Kai heard the crossing bells where a county road intersected the tracks. There was nothing to see but grainfields, unfenced grazing land, and a tiny town in the distance shrouded by cottonwood trees. He opened his journal again:

Shikata ga nai. *There's nothing to be done. That's what some Issei say. But is history so irremediable, so foreordained that we can't move it this way or that, we can't choose?*

I heard some of these "evacuee cars" have been hooked up to the back of freight trains. Ours isn't. There are too many of us. To outsiders we must look like a ghostly procession—blinds partly drawn, guns silhouetted against lamplights. History is an illogical record. It hinges on nothing. It is a story that changes and has accidents and recovers with scars. We are history tonight.

In the dark, the train with its five hundred passengers reached Heart Mountain Relocation Camp. The Camp was on the western edge of a wide basin. The land was dry and rough and broken, covered with bunch-grass, Great Basin rye, cactus, and sage. A series of benches tilted up toward the mountains and the Camp looked down on farmland below. As the train slowed, jackrabbits zigzagged out of its path. One or two were crushed under the wheels of the engine. Kai thought the sagebrush looked like people huddled low to the ground.

There was no station house. Only a platform. Kai helped his parents down and worked his way through the crowd. Then a bus took them to the top of the hill, through the sentry gates. The Camp was a ghastly, monochrome city of tar paper barracks lined up along avenues, surrounded by guard towers. They said it took up a square mile.

A handsome couple joined Kai. They introduced themselves as Will Okubo and Mariko Abe. He was Kibei—a Japanese-American educated in Japan. They had been living in Paris. She was a painter, but Kai didn't catch what Will said about himself. He spoke with a strong French accent and seemed to have difficulties with certain English words. He was tall and pale and used a cigarette holder. His khaki pants were held up by suspenders and he sported a white beret. Some pioneer, Kai thought. Mariko was tall for a Nisei and had a haughty look and wore trousers. She pursed her lips when she listened to someone speak and her eyes fastened on one thing, then another. She stood apart from the men with her hands on her hips. "Look at all this. I've never seen a jail with so much air."

Kai took a match from behind his ear and struck it with his thumbnail. The noise startled one of the guards. He turned his gun on Kai. Mariko quickly put her body in front of the gun and looked the soldier in the eyes.

"Why must you do that? We are innocent, you know. We're not criminals."

The soldier stared at her unblinkingly. Will Okubo pulled the cigarette from his ivory holder and threw it on the ground.

"Fascists," he said and spit at the soldier's feet.

Outside the mess hall Kai found his father sitting on his suitcase in a crowd of people. His glasses were still askew because the frames had become bent during the long train ride. He was looking down an avenue toward Heart Mountain. It rose up from sparsely timbered slopes like a pediment cut crookedly across the top, and he wondered aloud if there was a small shrine up there. Then he fainted.

When Mr. Nakamura came to, Kai and Will helped him to his feet and carried his suitcase to their assigned barrack.

The rooms were sixteen by twenty feet. There were three iron cots with no mattresses and a big coal stove and an inch of red dust on the floor. Otherwise their living quarters were unfurnished. Kai helped his parents settle in. When the beds had been arranged and some of the clothing hung on what would later become a partition, Kai went out and stood in the dusty lane between barracks. He felt unsteady, as if he were still on the train, still moving, and it made him nauseous. He wondered whether, as an exile in his own country, he would always have this motion in him, this sickness.

"Hello . . ."

Kai turned. It was Will Okubo.

"Are you in this block?" Kai asked.

Will tipped his head in the direction of a door. His face looked ashen and his eyes were squeezed together in a squint. He twirled the ivory cigarette holder in his hand.

"You're next door to us," Kai said and Will shrugged indifferently.

When Kai looked up again he saw the woman—Mariko—standing in the doorway. A cyclone of dust spun toward them as she watched. Kai covered his eyes when it hit but Will stood unflinching.

The two men walked to the northern edge of the Camp. Light rode the sidehills and the sage-covered bench above them. In the distance Kai saw a band of antelope and closer, a family of deer. The grass had turned fawn-colored and the does and fawns had begun to turn their winter color—gray. Will lit a cigarette and gave one to Kai. Above, a single nighthawk plunged and climbed above them. It made a stuttering, high-pitched cry as if its vocal cords had shattered, and its shadow looked like a cross, shrinking and swelling on the ground.

"Do you believe in God?" Kai asked.

"*Mais* no, certainly not. And you?"

"No," he said and shrugged. "Did you meet up with Sartre when you were in Paris?"

"I saw him once. At the Café Flôre. That's all."

Kai nodded. He was looking at the hills above the Camp. A line of cattle filed by. A blackbird rode the back of a bull and a lone rider with long legs and a dark hat brought up the rear.

"A real cowboy. Do you think he sees us?"

Kai laughed at Will's Parisian accent. That'll throw them, he thought, a "Jap" who speaks French.

Will's cigarette burned to the edge of his ivory holder. He was shivering so Kai gave him his jacket. When the sun reached the Camp it threw a grillwork of shadows across the two young men and the shadows of the guard towers leaned sideways, penetrating the barracks and moving across the beds inside.

"*Très formidable*, huh?"

Kai threw his cigarette on the dry ground and stepped on it. "God, there's nothing here," he said and smiled incredulously.

4

The handrail over the footbridge to Bobby Korematsu's cabin was made of barbed wire. Each evening, on the way home from the main house, he steadied himself on it the way he had held the ship's railing forty-seven years before when he made the crossing from Japan to America. He had come by ship on the sixty yen he had saved from a job as an apprentice to a pickle-maker in Osaka. From working in cold salt solution every winter, his hands became sore and cracked though he was only thirteen at the time, and the other boys in the factory beat him and stole his food.

The night Bobby's ship, *Saibei Maru*, docked in San Francisco, he was taken to Angel Island to go through immigration, and on the third night released into the city, where he became lost in Chinatown. He couldn't believe he was in America because all the men wore long pigtails and tunics over pantaloons and no one spoke English. That disappointed him because on the passage across the Pacific he had learned enough English to get by. The next day he wandered into a narrow room with no chairs and writing on a blackboard he couldn't read and was asked by a white man smoking a cigar if he was looking for work. The man thought he was Chinese and Bobby didn't correct him and took the job as cook for the Chinese crew on the Union Pacific Railroad in a place where there were mountains and snow called Wyoming.

The Chinese men who laid track across the southern part of the state until it met the track of the Union Pacific, thus joining the continent in one continuous ribbon of iron, were not allowed to eat or sleep in the section cars with the white workers. They hung hammocks between the trees to one side of the tracks and Bobby cooked over an open fire. He made thirty-five dollars a month, twenty dollars less than the white cook for the same work, but still thought it was a better job than working in a pickle factory.

When train service commenced, Bobby stayed on, graduating into the dining car of passenger trains, making his home base in a working man's hotel over a Chinese laundry on a Laramie, Wyoming, street that faced the very tracks his crew had laid.

He had come north in the summer of 1926 because he had never seen Yellowstone Park or Custer's battlefield. The day he stopped in a store to buy a Coke was the day he overheard a handsome, vivacious woman with sparkling eyes tell the grocer about her son McKay's illness—he had whooping cough—and how the other two boys had come down with the measles, and she had a haying crew to feed and couldn't find anyone to help her because the county had slapped a quarantine sign on the ranch gate. Bobby had stepped forward and offered his services. He had never taken a vacation before and after only three days, he was tired of it, and he wasn't frightened of contagious diseases. "One week, that's all," he told the gray-eyed woman. She smiled, drew a map of how to get to the ranch, and left the store.

"And I'm still here," Bobby thought.

Besides cooking, he took care of all three boys, Champ, Ted, and McKay, but ministered most often to McKay, who was sicker. Secretly, he credited himself with saving the boy. He brewed special teas from medicinal herbs he had learned about from an uncle in Osaka, added to the ones he came across living with the Chinese, and in the evenings, made a "chest cloth" and "a sleep cloth"—steaming hot compresses which he applied to McKay's chest and head.

He had loved the boy the minute he saw him. He was pale blond, almost white-headed. Bobby noticed a look in the boy's eyes—soft, deep, and comprehending. "You no little boy," Bobby had mumbled to him as he thrashed with fever. "You no grown-up either," by which he meant that McKay was neither distracted by the whims of most seven-year-olds nor jaded by adult burdens.

At the end of the week he wired his Union Pacific boss and said he would not be returning. "Sixteen years ago . . . ," he thought. Now he looked to the south. The lights of Heart Mountain Camp kept intruding on his thoughts. He was not used to lights and noise out at the ranch. Now there was a steady hum and the sound of trains coming and going, bringing more evacuees. He could not help wondering if some of his own people—Korematsus—were there. He had heard once that he had an uncle living in San Jose, and a sister, born long after he had left home, was rumored to have married a lettuce farmer in Guadalupe, California. He found it difficult to think of them as his family. This ranch and these boys were his home, and before that, it had been the Chinamen. Yet, how could he help but wonder? He looked up. The sky had cleared since the first heavy storm. Now a cloud rolled in and for a moment, the Camp's blazing light hung inside it like a swinging lantern.

For the first time he felt his loyalties shift—not away from McKay and his brothers, but crowded now, by the possibility that members of his own distant family were near.

A wasp, still comatose from the previous night's hard frost, fell from the ceiling and burned to a crisp on the back lid of the cook stove. Bobby watched it writhe and twist but did not try to save it as he usually did. That's how he felt about the war now. It was out of his hands. When he thought about wasps, he knew they were part of a long progression, linked and curved through the seasons like the deer spine he found draped across a rock outside his cabin door. Rain, flies, and mud swallows were followed by heat, mosquitoes, and deerflies; followed by rainlessness, rattlesnakes, and grasshoppers; then, as a last gasp before the glittering apocalypse of winter—wasps and the first snows.

But the war was different. It had no progression, no seasons. He thought about the two uniformed men who had come to the ranch the week before. McKay had talked to them from horseback. They said they were looking for Bobby Korematsu to warn him that if any suspicious activity was observed, he would be detained, or worse, sent to prison. Bobby remembered the one man had a crew cut, a cactus stand of hair, and the other one had fingers that bent up at the ends like those of wealthy men who had never worked the land. McKay had sat his horse stiffly, then ordered the two men to get off his ranch. He kicked the horse toward them as if pushing cattle down an alleyway and they retreated to their army car, backing quickly out of the yard.

But when Bobby thought about actual fighting, everything jumbled in his mind. He knew he could no longer keep things separate—his "boys": Champ, Ted, and the neighbor, Henry, from his own blood relatives; strangers from friends; enemies from allies. Which was which? When he looked out the window again he thought he could see them falling. As he crossed the rickety bridge to his cabin that night, the lights of the Heart Mountain Camp blazed and, clasping the handrail suddenly for balance, he punctured his hand on a barb.

Dripping eaves woke him. But when he went to the house to fix breakfast, he heard another noise.

"Who's that?" he called out, thinking a pack rat might have gotten in. The noise stopped, then he heard laughing. "McKay?" he called out again but there was no answer. The long hall from the kitchen smelled musty. He threw open the door to the living room. It was a two-story-high room with huge mullioned windows that looked out on Heart Mountain and the floors were covered with Navajo rugs. Bobby stood at the windows. He saw elk a great distance away, moving single file into the timber.

"Owwwww . . ."

Bobby spun around. Behind the couch Pinkey sat on the bare floor propped against the liquor cabinet, whose lock he had opened with a hacksaw. His face was smeared with blood and he laughed when he saw Bobby—a sound like a cry. His broken leg, newly casted but already filthy, stuck straight out.

"Why you do this?" Bobby implored, leaning toward him. There was a note of pity in his voice.

Pinkey's eyes hardened. He picked up the hacksaw and began shaking it. The sharp teeth almost cut Bobby's face.

When Bobby took it from him, Pinkey blinked. His empty hand still shook in the air.

Bobby sat cross-legged before him. "Stop it now," he said.

"I'm dying," Pinkey mewed, rubbing his dirty face.

Bobby helped the old man to his feet and led him down the long hall to the kitchen. He heated water and made a thin broth as Pinkey looked on.

"I need some medicine now . . .," Pinkey stammered.

Bobby poured two tablespoons of whiskey into a glass and held it to Pinkey's mouth, then wiped his face with a hot towel.

Pinkey smacked his lips. "Thank you, Bob . . .," he said gratefully and leaned back in the chair. The room was warm from the cook stove and after sipping some broth, he dozed off quickly.

Four buckets of water came to a boil on the cook stove. Bobby poured them into a big galvanized tub on the floor. Naked, except for the cast which went from his knee to his ankle, Pinkey insisted on bathing with his hat on. Bobby tested the water with his elbow.

"Hey, this ain't baby formula we're cookin' up, is it?"

Bobby shook his head.

"How the hell do I get in?"

Bobby offered his shoulder for support. Pinkey leaned on him, hopping on his good leg to the rim of the tub. Then, holding his casted leg in the air, eased himself in with a splash. He rubbed his face with the warm water.

Bobby looked in the direction of the Camp. He felt his resolve not to go there weaken, then busied himself at the stove, stirring the broth which Pinkey refused to drink now. When he thought of Ted's disgruntled letter, he felt relief and disappointment at once. He could not bear to think of Champ and the neighbor boy, Henry, at all.

Pinkey hummed as he washed behind his ears. He let his hands float on top of the water and gathered bubbles toward his chest until he had amassed two prodigious breasts. When they dissolved, he asked Bobby to help him out of the tub. He hopped to a chair and Bobby handed him a towel.

"You think I bad now, should go to Camp with other Japanese?" Bobby asked the old cowboy.

Pinkey stopped drying himself. He looked up, then dabbed his mouth dry as if he had just finished an elegant meal. "What the hell are you saying, Bobby?"

Bobby just stared at him. Pinkey cleared his throat.

"Well the way I see it, Bob, you and I've been on this outfit a long time and I figure we're just about the same man. We both come away from home when we was kids and we know how to survive without having nothing of our own. And we know what makes people tick because we've had to put up with so goddamned many of them, like 'em or not, just to get a damned paycheck. And we're both gettin' old." Then he slapped his belly and pulled at the extra flesh around his middle. "And under this is just an ol' boneyard, ain't it? Just a bunch of bones. And once they're scattered on the ground, who will know which is Japanese and which is American, which is a cook's and which is a cowboy's, which is the coyote's and which is mine or yours?" he said in a slow, deliberate voice, then finished toweling himself dry.

Bobby let himself down on a chair in front of Pinkey. He was wearing a padded silk jacket one of the Chinamen from the railroad had willed to him. He dug into the pocket and pulled out a news clipping, unfolded it, and ironed it out smooth with his hand on Pinkey's leg. Pinkey looked.

"You read it. I ain't got my readin' glasses on," Pinkey said, though Bobby knew he was illiterate.

Bobby read the headlines: PARK COUNTY SAYS NO TO JAPS HERE.

Pinkey listened, his head tilted to one side, his eyes closed dreamily, then he looked at Bobby for a long time before speaking.

"Well hell, Bobby . . . that's just a newspaper. . . ."

Bobby finished the ranch chores early that day. Pinkey had fallen asleep by the fire and Bobby was careful not to wake him. In the hallway he bundled up in a wool coat, boots, and a muffler and left the house by the kitchen door. He walked south toward the Camp. Two of the ranch dogs followed him, whining dolefully. At the place where the road became the creek and the creek the road, Bobby thought about how easily one thing can become another. By midafternoon he reached the gates of the Heart Mountain Relocation Camp.

Three young Nisei boys goose-stepped by the guardhouse and saluted. *"Heil Hitler!"* they boomed out, then ran as the guards stepped toward them. Bobby slipped through the gate unnoticed.

There were so many people, and rows and rows of buildings stretching almost to Heart Mountain itself, Bobby thought, and a commotion he had not experienced for many years. He walked, down one "avenue"— a muddy track—between barracks, crossing by a bathhouse, then a mess hall, and down another avenue to the end, and up the next one among so many people with Japanese faces.

Bobby watched new evacuees pick through piles of scrap lumber at the end of each barrack for building material. Teenage girls passed him and said hello in perfect, unaccented English. Old women wearing kimonos and getas shuffled between the shower houses and the apartments, holding soap and towels. He looked at faces. Were there any Korematsus here? he wondered.

At the end of one barrack building, on the Heart Mountain end of camp, two old men hunched over a Gō board. One player made his move, then the other one grunted something in Japanese. Bobby listened. He gargled the words in his mouth. He could say them—the sounds hit his throat in a familiar way but no longer carried any meaning. He felt dizzy. How could he have forgotten so much? His throat stiffened and there was a hammering inside his head as he tried to repeat the words in a way that meaning came with them.

The other player took his turn. The sound of the black stone snapping against the wooden board was like a switch going on inside Bobby. He made a slight bow. Speaking Japanese, the men asked if he would like to sit in on a game.

Bobby watched as the black and white stones moved across the board. He thought they looked like sheep, wandering over the countryside, for Gō is a geographical game in which the player who takes the middle way— accumulating not too much territory, but enough to hold sway—wins.

"Korematsu?" Bobby asked suddenly, interrupting the game.

The two men gazed at him.

"Anyone here named Korematsu . . . from Osaka . . . old man like me, farmer in San Jose . . . girl . . . no . . . woman now, fifty years old . . . Guadalupe, California . . . marry lettuce farmer?"

Again the two men looked at each other and shook their heads at Bobby, then continued the game.

When the Camp's dinner bell rang, it was getting dark. Bobby stood up from the table, alarmed at how quickly the time had passed.

"*Kon ba wa,*" the two old men said and bowed.

Bobby bowed and they parted. At first, he could not remember the way back to the gate. He walked the length of the mess hall the wrong way. Inside, he saw all kinds of people sitting down on long picnic benches, eating. The food did not smell good. He rounded the building, realized his mistake, then went back the other way, crossing "avenues" until he came to the gate. A sentry guard came out.

"Where are you going? Do you have a pass?"

"No live here. Cook for twenty year, Heart Mountain Ranch," Bobby said and pointed up-country.

The MP turned to his partner. "We have another joker out here."

The other guard appeared. "What's your name, boy?"

"Not boy. Old enough to be your grandfather."

The two guards laughed uproariously. On the hill behind them a family of coyotes began yipping and howling. Bobby's dogs, waiting patiently, growled and took off. Bobby tried to call them back but they wouldn't come.

"What's your name?" the MP asked.

Bobby gave his name. He looked in the direction of the ranch but could see no lights. He patch of clear sky the Big Dipper bent its elbow down where the ranch should have been. To the northwest, a haze of white snow clouds was taking the sky. Bobby thought of the trains that had brought the evacuees here. They had traveled over track he had helped to build: they were bringing everything he had forgotten he was back to him.

The soldier motioned Bobby into the guardhouse. They had been reading comic books and drinking Coke. Bobby sat down and folded his hands. He stared at the floor and a feeling of shame passed through him. The dogs had run the coyotes off and now there was a terrible, raw silence. Then a voice outside the guardhouse said his name, and a short ruddy man wearing a gray Stetson cocked sideways on his head and propelling himself forward on crutches appeared, talked to the guards, and took Bobby home.

5

Saturday, October, 1942. The first edition of the Heart Mountain Sentinel came out today and I think it's going to be a fine weekly paper. I say this, because I'm a copy editor along with Ben Iwasaka, also from Berkeley. He's a law student there. "Now we're both members of that suspect species, the journalist," he said when I walked through the door this morning. No one else thought it was funny but that's because they haven't grown up reading Hearst newspapers. But what harm can there be in a little local paper? We try to put forward national news having to do with relocation. There's a social page, a column that gathers news from the other nine relocation camps, and the usual editorial page, camp sports, activities, letters, and classifieds. Issei-owned businesses from Utah, California, Oregon, and Washington are buying ads. Anyway, it's a job, which I need— both for the money and to keep my mind off other things . . . this deep wrenching away from things and people I love . . . like yesterday when I woke and thought I was in Chinatown . . .

A journalist . . . a historian . . . I wonder what the difference is, because I fear my tendency as a scholar is to put thing in neat blocks, to control what has been the uncontrolled destinies of other peoples . . . I've resolved not to fritter all my time, and to give some thought to definitions.

Ben asks, Why history, why not politics, something that exists in the present. . . . In response, I came up with this: History, in our case, is not the event of evacuation, transfixed in time, but an accumulation of the movement of human wills over time and continuing now. . . . There was not one cause for our internment, but many—a deep-seated racial prejudice working on top of fear, distrust, and greed. So how is one to say exactly where history begins or ends? It is all slow oscillations, curves, and waves which take so long to reveal themselves . . . like watching a tree grow.

Journalists, beware! History is not truths versus falsehoods, but a mixture of both, a mélange of tendencies, reactions, dreams, errors, and power plays. What's important is what we make of it; its moral use. By writing history, we can widen readers' thinking and deepen their sympathies in every direction. Perhaps history should show us not how to control the world, but how to enlarge, deepen, and discipline ourselves.

Sunday, our day off after the Saturday edition is out. I feel light-headed and oddly happy, like a criminal with a new identity. When you've lost everything, what's there to worry about? I went to Block 7-22-3, where Ben lives, and we walked together to the mess hall. He said he hated school and someday wanted to run for a political office. Now that would be something, a Nisei governor! Just then, I stuck my hand in my pocket and pulled something out: it was the badge Li had made. I gave it to Ben and he laughed, because it said: I AM CHINESE.

Monday. It was so cold this morning my mother's hair turned white with frost as she walked from the bathroom to the barracks. It snowed, and after, there was a ground blizzard. It's nature's way of getting at you twice—first on your head, then up between your legs, and both ways, it blinds you. Mom is disgusted at how late I sleep in when we're not on deadline at the paper. She doesn't know I'm part owl and get my work done at night. Whenever I can, I skip breakfast, get up about ten, have coffee, then help Pop build furniture for our "home away from home" . . . Already, the many domestic and aesthetic touches are showing . . .

there are curtains, tables and chairs, bookshelves, paintings and drawings hung on the walls, and outside, rock gardens are taking shape here and there.

One of the many differences between the two generations here is that while we Nisei feel like caged lions, the old folks are taking a vacation for the first time in their lives, and dedicating their time to their beloved arts and crafts. Already, Mom has signed up for a class in ikebana, and Pop has joined a group that sings old Japanese ballads—unusual for him. It's ironic that Uncle Sam, by putting us all together, is only encouraging the very thing Caucasians hate and fear—our Japaneseness. Every day, this camp looks more and more like a Japanese village. This nostalgia for the old ways bothers me, though, because in the end, I'm afraid it will be damning.

Pop told me how ashamed the Issei women are about using the toilet with no privacy. That's when being a simpleminded jock comes in handy. I suffer no shame! At dinner, another old Issei said, "When you don't have something, you fight for it. When you aren't allowed to fight, you get numb." I wonder if that will happen to me? I went back to the office, my resolve strengthened. I'm trying to get a grip on what's happened to us and what it implies. The terrible failing of the democratic process nearly blinds me when I try to sort it out. Why, for instance, aren't the German and Italian immigrants behind barbed wire? I guess we all know the answer to that, but it's damned hard to swallow.

Most everyone in this "city" is sleeping now. Here and there I see a curl of smoke going up or hear a baby cry or see an old Issei stumbling toward the bathroom with his kimono on. I like to look at the stars. That's something I didn't have time for in Berkeley. The little window by my desk faces north and the Big Dipper is so big I can't quite see it all.

I really came to the office to think about Li. Living in the same room with Mom and Pop, I find I censor my thoughts. But here, I can imagine lying with her in the little room we had in Chinatown. It was much noisier there because so many restaurants stayed open late, but it was a sweet noise, our secret love music. She'd lie under me and I'd tell her we were swimming and I'd make her lie on my back the way baby whales do, then I'd tell her we were on our way to Mexico and I'd spread her legs. She didn't have much hair down there and it was beautiful to see how she was built. When it rained hard we seemed to be able to make love longer—sometimes four or five times in a night.

I have a hard-on now. Well, what did I expect? It thumps against this desk and makes a sound like a bird flying against the window. Even though I say these things, Li is beginning to seem remote to me. How long has it been? I don't want to start counting days like a damned prisoner. It seems like years. But that's the purpose of exile, isn't it? To fortify our feelings of separateness (not to speak of helplessness). Love is an attempt to bridge the distances between us, to conquer separateness. Now I'm standing at a road-cut where the bridge has washed away. Do I really love Li? Or was our affair only an entertainment? Perhaps what I've thought of as love has been only self-interest, a vanity.

6

McKay woke with a start. He had slept hard without moving and the blond curls on one side of his head were punched in flat. His leg hurt where it had been broken and he rubbed it as he swung his feet to the floor. He was supposed to remember something, but what was it? The tequila had been passed around at the roping arena the night before.

When he stood the room went black. There was no heat and he trembled as he pulled on his long underwear. One side of his face looked old; the eye twitched and the soft flesh under the eye was gray, as if ash had been smeared there. The other side, the bright side, looked childlike, and his mouth was pulled down, then up, in a wry, effortless smile.

It was the third day of a savage unseasonable storm. He had to ship cattle and hoped the storm would blow over. He limped into the hallway of the big house and called for Bobby. No answer. The house had never seemed so quiet. He could feel the cold coming up through the pine floor and the toes on his left foot that had once been frostbitten ached. He stood at the entrance to the living room. It was still dark but the room glowed. A thin layer of snow covered everything—couches, chairs, the inside of the fireplace, the Navajo rugs on the floor. Where wind had driven under the doors, there were mounds of snow, like tiny dunce caps toppled over. He knew what day it was now: the anniversary of his parents' death.

He lit a kerosene lamp and stood at the fireplace. On the mantle was a silver-framed photograph of his parents, taken the day they drowned. His mother was bundled in a fur coat. Her gray eyes sparkled. Her head was turned to one side and she was smiling at McKay's father, whose black hair stood on end. It had been windy and he had the hurt, far-off look of someone who only finds happiness elsewhere.

McKay remembered the bull sale in Red Lodge, Montana, when his father disappeared with a woman who came out of the stands and stood by the door. McKay did not see him again until late that night when he came back alone to the bar. He looked shaken. McKay ordered him a shot. After emptying the glass RJ started talking. "I love your mother," he began. "That woman was someone I've known many years, someone I could have married. But things happen. I met her after I married your mother. Life's a lot of compromises. But that's good, that's human, that's how the coyote survives."

McKay had looked at his father and asked, "What happened tonight?"

RJ had stared straight ahead. "I still love her. We just fit together. . . ."

"Here," McKay had said and shoved another full shot glass between his father's crumpled hands.

Afterward, McKay had understood his mother's fierce resolve and her loneliness better. Once, she might have become hardened or else crushed, but she succumbed to neither. Each time RJ had a distant look in his eye, she softened with accommodation. She might have done the same if she had had the chance to roam as he did. And she loved her boys.

His parents' death felt as if a black wave had sprouted legs and walked out of the sea and rolled over them, taken them in the night. The freedom he had thought he might feel did not come. Quite the opposite: he sensed his parents' watchful eyes more strongly now than when they were alive, and he could not shake them.

The kitchen door swung open and Pinkey roared, "McKay, you lazy sonofabitch, ain't you up yet?"

McKay heard Bobby's soft footsteps and Pinkey's hobbling, then the sound of the cook stove fire being laid. He went to the kitchen.

"Me and Bob went on a tear last night—did you miss us?"

McKay looked at the two old men. "Well I'll be-go-to-hell."

"Bobby only had one, but he got drunker than a waltzing billy goat," Pinkey said and plunked himself down on the kitchen stool. "I thought we was shipping today."

"You're not with that thing on your leg."

"Well let's saw her off then."

"No. Because I ain't taking you back to that hospital . . .," McKay said, then looked at Bobby. "You're not saying much this morning."

Bobby shoved another piece of pine into the firebox. "Did bad thing yesterday," he said.

"Like what?" McKay said, laughing softly.

"Don't bullshit him," Pinkey said.

McKay winked at Pinkey as he pulled the kitchen table out from the wall and added two middle leaves to make it big enough for the roundup crew. Then he sat back against the wall with his coffee. His spurs jangled as he hung his feet on the rungs of the chair. Bobby looked at the table. The surface was badly scarred from years of use. Some of the hired hands had carved their brands into the wood.

"They're not there," Bobby said to McKay.

"Who isn't where?"

"Yep . . .," Pinkey crooned apropos of nothing.

"Sister . . . uncle . . . not living in that Camp."

"You went to the Camp?" McKay said in amazement.

Bobby nodded, then continued. "Asked. No one heard of them."

"Well that's that, then," McKay said finally.

"Then those army pricks wouldn't let Bobby out. . . ."

"Ah hell . . .," McKay growled.

"So I went and straightened the bastards out," Pinkey said proudly.

McKay tipped the chair forward and set his coffee down. "I bet you did. . . ."

"Ohh . . . many many faces . . . all kinds . . . young and old . . . some rich ones, wear cashmere coat and hat . . . some like me . . .

they've got everything in there, all penned up like pigs . . . not good . . .," Bobby said.

"What else?" McKay asked.

"Worst thing happen."

"What's that?"

"Couldn't talk . . . can't remember Japanese."

"The hell . . . you're always running off at me in Japanese. . . ."

"I mean really talk. . . ."

"But those are Americans in the Camp . . . they speak English," McKay said.

"Not the old ones like me, not very good English."

McKay looked Bobby in the eye and, smiling, nodded his head.

McKay stepped out the kitchen door to spit out his snoose. It had begun snowing lightly and the sky was pale gray. He saw someone hunched over, sitting on the stairs to the main part of the house. He walked toward the figure.

"Madeleine?" he called out, alarmed. She was his closest neighbor and friend.

She did not raise her head. Since the war began she and McKay had run their cattle together because her husband, Henry, went off to war with McKay's brothers and there was too much work for both of them to do alone.

"Madeleine," McKay repeated and knelt by her. She was shivering. Snow filled the brim of her hat. She held out a telegram, which McKay read.

WE ARE SORRY TO INFORM YOU THAT HENRY HEANEY HAS BEEN REPORTED MISSING IN ACTION SINCE JULY 1942.

McKay led Madeleine inside.

McKay told Bobby and Pinkey: "Henry's missing in action."

Pinkey pulled a chair out from the table for her. "You sit down now and we'll fix you up . . . sonofabitch," he grumbled and hobbled to the stove for coffee.

Bobby pulled down a pint of brandy he kept to resuscitate birds who flew into the windows and added some to Madeleine's coffee. She wiped tears from her cheeks as she drank while McKay leaned toward her and held her other hand.

"It could mean all kinds of things . . . not that he's dead. . . ."

"I know," she squeaked out.

She had long blond hair pulled back in a braid and ruddy, freckled skin. She was sturdily built though not big.

"Did you put your horse up?" McKay asked.

She nodded yes.

"Hell, you must have been riding in the dark to get here this early."

"That damned horse of hers has headlights," Pinkey said.

Madeleine smiled then.

"You better stay here for few days," Bobby offered. "I fix room upstairs."

She glanced at McKay, who looked shyly down.

The snow worsened. When the kitchen door opened again, Jesse, Orval, Frank, and his daughter filed in. They stomped their feet to get the snow off and piled their overcoats and hats on the floor.

Pinkey surveyed the crew. "Well ain't this a ragtag-lookin' outfit. . . ."

Madeleine did not look up.

"She had news about Henry," McKay said, interpreting her silence.

Jesse stepped forward.

"Tell me what it was," he said.

"He's missing in action," Madeleine said.

"I'm real sorry, Madeleine. You just let me know what I can do, day or night. . . ."

"Thanks, Jesse, I will."

"Sorry to hear it, ma'am," Orval mumbled, then sat at the table, as did the others.

There was a silence, then Bobby served a fine breakfast of calf's liver, bacon, biscuits, gravy, and fried eggs. They ate quietly.

"Can I see it?" the other girl said. "I've never seen a telegram before."

Everyone looked up at Madeleine. "Sure you can," she said and handed the girl the telegram.

Pinkey hobbled over to the table with the coffee pot and filled the cups.

"How's that leg, Pinkey?" Madeleine asked.

"Short, just like the other one."

Bobby pulled a gooseberry cobbler from the oven.

"Oh boy . . . doesn't that smell good," Frank said.

"I can't believe it," McKay mumbled, meaning Henry.

Madeleine did not eat, but went to the living room.

McKay went to find her. "What are you doing?"

"Watching it snow."

He sat beside her on the window seat that faced Heart Mountain. The snow came down in tiny grains.

They were silent. McKay thought about how his life had opened up when Henry came on the scene. The years working alongside Champ had been years of dogged competition and Henry's good-naturedness diluted Champ's hostility. McKay thought of the day Henry's horse had fallen on him when they were doctoring calves for pinkeye. The fall had broken Henry's pelvis and while others went for help, McKay lay on the ground beside him, holding him, telling him jokes to keep him from going into shock. When the ambulance came, the driver had found the two young men on the ground, laughing.

"That was real good, Bobby," Jesse said as he pushed his plate away and filled his lower lip with snoose.

"I'll go jingle those horses," McKay announced. Jesse nodded appreciatively. His hair was slicked down flat and dented where a hatband had ridden his head for forty years. Of all those present, except for Pinkey, he was the only one to have ridden roundup with McKay's father.

McKay used a flashlight to get to the corrals. It was so cold his nostrils froze and he could smell the moisture in the air as it sailed down the escarpments onto the plain. Wind whistled through woven wire. It pushed against McKay and he pushed back, tilting his body into it until his hat brim bent down to his nose. Snow flew sideways in a cross fire and the wind, roaring now, swept the old snow up, held it whirling in the air, until the ground beneath was bare. McKay stopped to get his bearings. A piece of roofing flew by. He thought he could make out the stackyard fence where the hay was kept but he couldn't be sure. The wind heaved and broke him at the waist and took his hat and pushed him forward. He yelled, not because he thought anyone could hear, just to throw his voice at the storm, but the wind took the sound from his mouth and carried it away.

McKay walked. It didn't matter whether his eyes were opened or closed. He couldn't tell if time was passing, or was passing him so fast—at the speed of the wind—that he would be dead when the storm stopped. He heard a terrible noise, then he saw that part of the stackyard fence had snapped and blown into the hay and stuck there like cracked ribs. He circled around the stack to the shed where he fed his saddle horses. The horses were bunched together in the far corner. Snow had drifted through unchinked logs and buried them to the shoulder. They could not move. McKay talked quietly. The snow rose up their necks like a tide. He cupped his hands and dug quickly, like a dog eager to unearth a bone. Steam rose from the horses' backs and their flanks quivered, and the hair around their muzzles and eyes and under their chins was frosted white. McKay exposed the shoulder of the horse closest to him, then the belly. He was breathing hard and the mucus froze and hung down from his nose in an icicle. The first horse stepped out of the collapsed drift. He dug more and the second horse came free, then the third and fourth. He waved them through the corral gate and closed it, tying it shut with a piece of barbed wire.

He turned toward the house. Now the wind was in his face and he had to loosen his scarf and wear it around his nose and mouth in order to breathe. He had heard the stories of men's lungs freezing, but that was when the air was much colder, thirty-five and forty below. He tried to sense his bearings and remember the dips and rises of the ground. He began counting his steps. How many steps would it take to get from the corrals to the house, he wondered, then laughed at himself. He counted to six hundred.

A tiny light shone in his face. It was Madeleine.

"Here, hold on."

They linked arms.

"It's a little breezy . . . ," McKay said.

Madeleine led him to the kitchen door.

The roundup crew waited out the storm in the house. It lasted twenty-two hours. Bobby busied himself sweeping up snow as it sifted beneath the north-facing doors. When night came, the men bunked up, two to a bed; Frank's daughter slept in the living room; and Madeleine slept upstairs in the room Bobby had made up for her.

Before dawn the wind stopped and the clouds broke apart. Above where the light came, the sky was indigo, almost black, like the mind at the point of unconsciousness. McKay padded through the house waking his guests. Their tall boots, lined up by the fire to dry, had tipped to one side and the other, anchored by spurs, and their hats were crown-down beside them.

He walked to the horse pasture. Drifts of snow skidded back and forth. It looked as if everything were floating, everything except himself. He was pinned by the movement of his feet sinking through new snow to the ground.

He roped out seven horses: four bays, a light sorrel, a red roan, and a blue roan. The blue roan was his "long circle" horse. He had a big roman nose, feet round as pancakes, and a deep heart girth. When McKay looked over the withers of his horse he saw Madeleine walk into the corral.

"Morning," she said.

"Good morning, sunshine."

The others followed.

"Don't you have no lights out here, for God's sake?" one of the men asked.

McKay grinned. "I like saddling my horse by moonlight."

"Well ain't you a romantic sonofabitch . . . I wish'd I was a girl."

"I don't," McKay retorted.

The blue roan flinched as McKay swung the saddle on.

"Watch out for that bronc."

"Yea, I'm awful scared."

Madeleine pulled her cinch up, then recoiled her rope and fastened it to her saddle. McKay watched her affectionately. They had been childhood friends, then lovers. By the time she surrendered her virginity to him and he to her, wrapped in a canvas dam that smelled of mildew in a dry irrigation ditch, they had already punched cattle, roped, and ridden colts together and continued to do so. They had been born on the same day in the same hospital, McKay in the delivery room and Madeleine in the labor room—there being only one of each in the small country hospital—and years later when she came home with Henry on her arm, McKay felt as welcoming as he did betrayed.

When the horses were saddled, the riders trotted out into the white pasture eight abreast, like cavalry. Madeleine edged in between McKay and Jesse. It was cold enough to make their eyes tear. The horses snorted rhythmically, blowing air on every second step, and McKay felt the front legs of his horse pounding up through him like pistons.

After two hours of trotting, the riders puffed hard, too, their breath spraying in white bursts, and the smell of sage, bruised by horses' feet, lifted to them. When they came to water they let the horses drink. They startled two coyote pups at the spring. The pups backed up a few feet, then sat and watched curiously. Light crept down the tops of the hills and as the riders started off again, they could see the cattle.

It was a mixed bunch—calves, yearlings, two-year-old steers, and bulls. McKay sent pairs of riders to the top of the draw. From there they sent cattle running downhill for half a mile on either side of the creek. McKay and Madeleine stayed low and caught the gather. They moved steers out in a long line. The riders took positions on either side of the herd—two on flank, three on drag. Madeleine and McKay rode point, steering the lead cows down the draw, then across the high bench toward town.

They stopped for lunch at a pond and took turns holding the herd. McKay unrolled his slicker on a rock. The sandwiches, cookies, and fruit tumbled out from it. From their perch they could see a corner of the Heart Mountain Camp. Madeleine gazed down on it silently. There was a guard tower and some men were marking out a baseball diamond in the snow. McKay pulled the cork from his flask and offered her a drink. She took a big swallow, inhaled sharply, and wiped her mouth with the back of her hand.

"Maybe Henry is playing baseball in Japan," she said caustically.

"I was just thinking of him, too."

"Maybe he's dead, or worse. . . ."

"Don't, Madeleine."

"I can't help it."

"It doesn't do any good."

"Yea. Nothing does."

"I know," McKay said.

"I just feel so damned useless. Going through the motions . . . of what, I don't know. Hoping, I guess. But what's hope anyway? It's just a joke that doesn't really mean anything. But if I don't hope, then what am I?"

McKay drank from the flask again.

"We're just used to being able to do things, Madeleine. That's how we were raised."

"Then how do I learn to do nothing?"

McKay rolled the uneaten sandwiches in his slicker and tied it to the back of his horse. Now he and Madeleine could make out the whole baseball diamond at the Camp and the three men on hands and knees mounding up snow where the pitcher would stand.

"I can't wait to see them start hitting snowballs," McKay said and climbed onto his horse.

Madeleine led her horse behind a clump of sage and squatted down to pee. After, she gathered the reins and put a foot in the stirrup. A sage hen flew up. The horse crow-hopped sideways away from the bird, into Madeleine, then jumped again with Madeleine's foot hanging from the stirrup, and started trotting downhill. Madeleine's head banged against the ground and one shoulder dug a trench in the snow. Then her foot came free. She sat on the ground and rubbed her ankle. McKay quickly retrieved her horse, loped back to where she had fallen, stepping off before his horse drew to a stop beside her.

"Babe, are you okay?" He held her.

She started laughing, then struggled free. "Yes."

She walked slowly to the horse, touched his shoulder, rubbed her hand up his neck, then pulled his head all the way around with the one rein and kneed him hard in the belly.

"Goddamn you. Stand still now," she said and with the horse's head still checked, stepped on.

After they held herd while the others ate, McKay and Madeleine moved the cattle out. When she rode ahead once to keep a young steer from turning back, McKay noticed her jacket was torn at the shoulder and a line of blood stretched across her back where she had lost some skin. When she turned back, he saw her tears.

"Are you hurt, Madeleine?"

"No. I'm okay."

"You don't look too damned okay."

"I'm scared."

"From the fall?"

"No . . ."

"Do I have to work your jaw to make you talk?"

She looked wide-eyed at McKay. "I'm scared about Henry."

She kicked her horse into a lope and McKay caught up with her.

"I love you."

"What?" She hadn't heard.

"Christ," he mumbled. "I love you," he roared.

"Shut up, McKay."

She slowed her horse to a walk and McKay rode so close their legs touched. He leaned toward her mischievously.

"I think you were the first person I saw when I was born."

The shipping corrals loomed black against the sky. Dust hung in the air as they approached the yards. McKay, Jesse, and Madeleine moved back and forth behind the herd, whooping and yelling, and the dogs, normally silent, broke into excited barks.

The yardmen opened the gates. Bunched tightly and surrounded by riders, the cattle finally went in. The sorting corrals and smaller pens had gates that swung into wide alleyways. These ended in loading chutes where cattle cars were shunted to a stop and the wooden doors rolled open. Madeleine and McKay rode through the cattle quietly and began sorting the steers from the bulls and taking out any strays and cripples. The dust was pulverized into a fine powder and the riders wore neck scarves over their noses and mouths. They took small bunches of steers down one alley while Jesse and Frank took another bunch to a waiting railroad car. Their horses nipped the rumps and necks of the animals, pushing them with their chests until, at the end of the day, their fronts were smeared with green manure and dust ran from their soft eyes and muzzles in streams. The parts of the riders' faces left uncovered were black with dirt—raccoonlike—through which only the whites of their eyes showed.

"Unto you I give these animals," McKay mumbled to himself as he passed back and forth through the alleys. "Whom I have loved and nurtured, bosomless," he continued. He felt sad and relieved and didn't think of their impending death, only their safety.

Madeleine unsaddled her horse and let him drink and roll in an empty pen. The windows of the café across the road had steamed up and the lights looked like an ornament against so much desolate land. She walked toward McKay and took hold of his arm. "Come here," she said in a wooden voice. She pulled him closer. He thought about the night before when she had found out about Henry and had slept in the bedroom above his. He had felt rage at first because he could not hold her and comfort her. He had blown out his lamp and lain on his narrow cot and watched snow cover his sleeping bag.

Madeleine's horse rolled in the far corner of the pen. His black hooves glistened under the yard lights. They flailed like pieces of hard coal in the air. Madeleine unbuttoned McKay's shirt, then his long underwear, and pressed her hand into the blond hair on his chest.

McKay made a sound and his head tipped back. It seemed they were naked. He was moving in and out of her like a furred animal, long and warm and sweet, standing on his hind legs like an elk. To be inside her he had to hitch his whole body up. There were elk around him—cows barking at calves, bulls whistling and grunting. They were both on their knees now and when he came or imagined he came, water whooshed over the tops of their backs.

Madeleine held him obstinately. He did not know what she wanted of him. First she had opened to him, her body undulating against his. Now she was still.

"I'm so tired of waiting," she said and sighed.

He felt the rim of his penis rise and push against her through his jeans. She looked at him.

"Oh, McKay . . ."

"I can't help it."

"Damn you," she said.

"Damn me?"

"I love you too," she said.

"Quit it."

"I know."

McKay turned from her.

He carried his dog into the café. It was hot inside and the floor was greasy with melted snow and mud. He swung over a stool at the long counter. The dog curled up at his feet and began snoring. The room was full with men. Those who weren't eating stood behind those who were and each time the door opened the noise inside the café redoubled with the sound of bawling calves.

"McKay?" Carol Lyman stood in front of the young rancher, a coffeepot suspended in air. He nodded. She poured, then turned, catching a glimpse of herself in the mirror, and primped her brittle hair.

"And I'll have a piece of that pie," McKay said.

She slid a plate toward him.

"And the little shit probably wants a hamburger," he said, indicating the dog on the floor.

"With everything?"

"No onions," he said and winked at her.

"You heard about Henry, I guess . . . ," McKay said when she came with coffee.

"No."

"Missing in action . . . that's all we know."

"Oh no," she gasped. She had known Henry when she was a girl and began coming west to a ranch in the Pryor Mountains—not a dude ranch, just an outfit that took in guests during hard times.

The noise in the café increased. More bodies crowded in behind McKay, men he had known all his life, men his father's age, bundled in long overcoats.

"I'll have a whiskey and a piece of that pie," one of them shouted.

"Which kind?" Carol snapped.

"I don't care. Just one of them round ones," the man said and broke into laughter.

Two old cowboys shouldered in behind McKay and set their cups on the counter to be refilled.

"Hell no, I was tied hard and fast and when that ol' bull hit the end of the rope he whipped around . . ."

Carol Lyman returned with the pie.

"Where's my whiskey?" the man asked.

"It's too damned early for you to be starting on that stuff," she said curtly and poured the coffee for the cowboys.

". . . and my horse backed up so fast the saddle rode up on his neck. Hell I was sittin' plumb between his ears. . . ."

"Well it's been a crazy goddamned storm. Those guys over in Sheridan really got it bad. Lost forty-five percent of their lamb crop, I heard. . . ."

". . . and she went out in the morning and they was just dead, cows and horses everywhere. Then her hired man come up froze to death. Christ, things is bad enough with this war going on without a mess like that. Poor woman."

Carol Lyman brought the dog's hamburger and refilled McKay's cup. "No onions."

"No onions," he replied.

One of the yardmen talked to someone behind him. "Hey did you hear about Fred's boy? He was taken prisoner of war by them dirty Japs. And Henry's missing in action over there."

"I think I could stand anything but that," a voice behind McKay said.

"Carol, where's my whiskey at?"

"You eat that pie first."

"Well when was you hired on to be my mother?"

Carol snorted and turned on her heel. Steam from the coffeepot flew over her shoulder like a feather boa.

The seat next to McKay emptied and filled up again.

"How'd you fare, McKay? Get those ornery old cows of yours loaded up?"

"Yep, I guess we did."

Carol Lyman removed the empty pie plate from in front of McKay. Her quick movements reminded him of his mother. Carol had come back to Luster in 1930 and had helped Margaret Allison cook during haying and branding.

McKay looked out the window. Someone had cleaned the panes. The sorting pens were full again with another man's cattle, and through the slats of the cars he could see the bulge of a rump and protruding horns.

"There goes more Japs," someone yelled excitedly.

A passenger train slid behind the cattle cars on another track. The shades were all drawn.

"I don't see how they could get any more into that Camp."

"They say there's going to be ten thousand of them."

"Hell, I ain't even seen that many cattle in one bunch before."

Instead of the news, music came on the radio. An old cowboy with a hat shaped like a volcano and no front teeth grabbed Carol Lyman's hand

and tugged at her until she came out from behind the counter. "I don't feel like dancing," she protested. The crowd made a space for the old man and he waltzed.

Carol glided by again.

McKay thought about the day his parents' car had been pulled from the canal. He remembered Carol Lyman standing in the doorway of the beauty parlor, watching the rescue crew. A curler had dropped from her head—like an antler, McKay thought—and bounced on the ground.

"I heard Madeleine's gonna ride with them cows," the man next to McKay said.

"Yep. She sure is."

"I wonder what poor old Henry would think of that."

McKay warmed his hands around his coffee cup and said nothing.

The blacksmith went behind the counter and started pouring coffee. He stopped in front of McKay.

"I've been thinking about your ma and pa this morning," he said quietly.

"Well thank you," McKay said.

"I guess you must be having a time out there . . . kinda lonely on that ranch, isn't it? Kinda lonely for a young man . . ."

McKay looked down, then out the window. His face reddened. When Madeleine entered, every man in the café turned to look at her.

It was dark when the "all-aboard" sounded. Snow blew across the tall yard lights like black gravel. Madeleine boarded the train. She wore a long yellow slicker over her trousers and her hat was pulled down low against the wind.

"Call when you get to Omaha," McKay yelled up to her. "And watch for that shipping fever. I had Bobby pack the medicine kit. And if you need help that kid from the Two Dot Ranch is on board somewhere."

"Yes, McKay," she said and winked.

"And be careful. . . ."

The train lurched once and stopped. They could hear cattle scramble for footing, then the train lurched again.

"McKay, I'm sorry."

"For what?"

The train moved and she slid from him.

*   *   *

McKay took the shortcut home in the dark. Even so, the ride would take three hours. His horse climbed through the breaks. Snow from juniper branches spilled down his neck as he brushed by. His companion, the errant bomb, made a little wind just above his head. When the horse climbed to the top of the bench McKay could see the train shooting south, out of the basin.

He didn't know how long he rode with his eyes closed. He had been drinking from the flask in his saddlebag. Blasts of snow scratched his face and the electric needle of hard cold punctured each toe. When he opened his eyes he knew he had reached the lower end of the ranch.

He passed the gate and climbed the knob toward the family graveyard. When he reached what seemed to be the top, he stepped off his horse. Snow from the ground blew up in his face, then plummeted down, mixing with the new snow. For the second time in two days, he found himself in a whiteout. He leaned out and pawed the air. Then the reins dropped from his numb hands.

"Roany, you sonofabitch . . . come back. . . ." The horse was gone. His foot hit something hard. He crouched down and brushed away the snow but it was a rock, not his parents' headstone. Something—either the booze or the blowing snow—made him close his eyes again.

McKay woke with a start and whistled. His dog came to him and licked his eyes and the top of his nose and behind his ears. He stood up and called for his horse, circling one way, then the other. He tripped against something taller and thinner than a rock. That's how he knew it was his father's grave.

"Hello, Pa." He threw one arm around the headstone and cupped his ear to it.

"Talk to me. I need a little help." He paused. "I've lost my roan horse. Tell me where he is . . . please?"

He pressed his ear against the polished rock. His nose was running and his blond hair stuck out from under his hat. A dark form appeared in front of him. He stood up quickly.

"Well, you dumb sonofabitch." He grabbed the horse's head and planted a kiss on his big jaw.

As he brushed the snow off the seat of the saddle, he thought about how his parents had been extracted from the car and pulled dead from the ditch, up through a thin layer of ice that broke over his mother's head in long, translucent staves; how her gray hair had come unbraided and floated like sea grass. He remembered his father's wounded, wistful eyes—how they had still been open and when he tried to close them with his own hand, he couldn't. How the lariat, always kept on the front seat of the car coiled neatly, had opened across his father's chest as if to spell out one last cry of dismay: ooooooo.

When McKay reached the ranch no lights were on. He lit an oil lamp and wandered through the house. The living room had been straightened up and swept clean of snow, and the photograph of his parents had been set on the mantle with incense burning on either side. That's what the brothers had called "Bobby's witchcraft."

McKay went upstairs. The old pine staircase creaked. He opened the door of the bedroom where Madeleine had slept and set the lamp on a small table. For a long time he stared at the bed. His hands were blue from the cold and he had trouble taking off his clothes. Then he pulled the blankets back and rubbed his lonely, aching body on the sheets where she had been.

7

When Carol Lyman's shift at the shipping yard café ended that afternoon, she drove to Snuff's Bar. It was located on a bend in the road that came from nothing and led to nothing for a hundred miles and the mill's pink dust blew back over the gaunt building as if to conceal its ramshackle edifice and clothe it decently.

Out back an archipelago of small cabins made a line up the hill. In the twenties they housed the only madam in that part of the state and her three employees, though after a few years they moved back to Butte, Montana, where they had come from, because business was brisker there. When the Depression hit, Snuff opened the cabins again, fitted the beds with worn sheets, and let jobless men and women coming through on freights sleep in them. Carol had left Luster in 1932, moved on with those seeking work in California, vanished, without saying good-bye. Now she was back.

She lived in a house on the edge of town. The neighbors had a yard full of roosters who awakened her and her retarded son each morning. They strutted and crowed and brawled until Mañuel fed them. Carol looked like a bird herself. She had long legs and gnarled toes and the skin on her neck showed gooseflesh in the winter. She had a handsome, haughty presence, a regal posture, and carefully kept red fingernails. Sometimes she walked in the badlands looking for arrowheads or, when she had enough gas, she'd drive to another town and drink a milkshake at a drive-in restaurant there. She thought of her ability to step out of routine as a discipline—the way some women her age do volunteer work or take up ballet.

She began going to Snuff's the day the Mormon women invited her to their Relief Society meeting. They felt sorry for her and because wartime heightens people's sense of community (in direct proportion to their bereavement), the women issued an invitation to the solitary Carol Lyman. She attended once. To show her gratitude, she made a banana cake and a gallon of nonalcoholic punch, but sat back as the women made Christmas presents for the soldiers and never joined in. During a break she went outside to have a smoke. From behind the currant bush, she watched the kindly women reconvene. They kept looking toward the door, expecting her to return. Instead, she stubbed out her cigarette against the wall of the church and drove north, wearing her dark glasses. That was a Thursday. She decided she would be obligated to no one from that Thursday on.

Normally, she was a guarded person. Her life was as narrow as a pine needle. But Snuff's was the loneliest place she had ever seen and on a whim, she began stopping there.

Stepping out of the car, she straightened her dress, took a deep breath, and walked in. She had never gone to a bar alone. A chandelier in the center of the room swung in the draft of the opened door. Its bottom tier was bent and only four crystal prisms remained. A long cord descended through the middle of the fixture and a bare bulb hung down in the room like a punching bag. She walked to the middle of the floor and turned slowly. It was a big, drafty place with a cream-colored tin ceiling blackened by soot. A sour smell moved stiffly through the air and mixed with something antiseptic. Flannel curtains with scenes of duck hunters aiming their shotguns hung limply over unwashed windows and the ten-by-ten linoleum dance floor was badly nicked and stained. Tables and chairs and spittoons were arranged at the far end and in one corner, there was a card table sparsely padded with green felt. Snuff stood behind the bar and looked at the woman who walked in.

"You want to buy the outfit, or do you just want a drink?" he asked jovially.

Carol Lyman turned to him. He was tall and dapper and nearing fifty. He wore a trimmed mustache and his hair rose in a tuft at the top of his skull. His face was windburned and when he smiled, his thin lips turned white.

"A Manhattan," Carol said. "Do you make them here?"

Snuff looked askance at her and went to work. He poured and shook and strained and in a moment, held out the drink she requested. She ate the cherry first, then drained the glass of its reddish orange liquid.

"Very good. Thank you," she said, handed Snuff the correct change, and left the bar. That was the first time. After, Snuff looked for her through the greasy porthole window at the end of the bar and a week later to the day, saw her coupe glide in—like a black swan—snapped on his red bow tie, and made another pitcher of Manhattans.

Inside the door, Carol pulled a compact from her purse. She did not like the way she looked. She touched her cheek. The skin was dry. "Oh well," she thought. When she saw the drink waiting for her, she gave the bartender a hesitant smile. She was not used to being waited on; it made her uneasy.

"How very sweet," she said and swung one hip onto the barstool.

The tall man extended his hand. "Hello, I'm Snuff."

"Carol Lyman."

"Which side of the line are you from?"

"Wyoming. Luster. I work at the shipping yards. In the café."

She drained her glass and dabbed at the corner of her mouth with one finger. "I'd like a card game. Is that possible?"

"Yes, ma'am. Poker or blackjack?"

"Five-card draw."

A pool of light lay on the green felt like a full moon. Snuff opened a new deck. His bony fingers were so long they almost wrapped twice around the cards. He shuffled, she cut, he dealt, she asked for a card and won.

Snuff dealt another hand, stealing a look at Carol while she contemplated her new cards. He was good at sizing up people, but this woman was not easy to know and he savored the challenge.

"You looking for work?" Snuff asked.

Carol glanced up from her cards. "Who, me?"

Snuff laughed, then straightened his bow tie.

"Oh, heavens no. I like my job at the café. This is just my day off," she said, discarding a seven. "It's not much of a job. I used to help Margaret Allison. . . ."

"McKay's mother?"

"Yes," Carol said, laying her cards down. "That Margaret had a lot of snap. Got things done. Her eyes were so bright. . . . There's no one like her around here now. No one that reads books like she did. There wasn't anything she didn't know. She liked everything." Carol looked at her cards again and picked up a ten of hearts. "I was there when they dug her and RJ up out of the canal. I watched them come up through that ice. I'll never forget it. I was at Arlene's. Remember her? She's gone now too. She was giving me a permanent. Ever since, I've hated that smell. . . ."

Snuff looked at her questioningly.

"That smell of permanent. It reminds me of Margaret dying."

Snuff noticed her eyes were yellow and silver like a wolf's. It was the time of year when the sun had begun falling southward and the light it cast was like her eyes—yellow and silver mixed, with the richer color dominating—and the only thing that broke the awful silence were wasps hitting against window glass and, where there were trees, the sound of frost-blackened leaves scattering.

"Here, let me get you another one, on the house," Snuff said, jumping up and carrying her glass to the bar. He poured himself a drink.

Carol swiveled around in her chair. "You ought to have dances here," she said. "It's big enough. . . ."

"We've had a lot of things go on here—"

"But not during a war, I suppose."

"I guess not. Not yet, at least," he said coming back to the table with the drinks.

Carol studied her cards, then laid them face down on the green felt.

"Henry Heaney . . . missing in action," she said as if repeating something to herself.

Snuff looked up. "Yes. I heard. What a shame . . ."

"Did you know Carter too?"

"Henry's brother?"

"Yes."

"I remember him. He was the strange one. Made things very difficult for the family . . . always disappearing, then making up things about his life."

"I knew him too," Carol said stiffly.

Snuff looked at her, then back at the cards.

"You've won again," he said.

"Oh, so I have."

They smiled at each other. The card game didn't matter and they both knew it.

"Another game?" Snuff asked.

"Why not?"

This time Carol dealt and Snuff cut the deck twice. Carol's hand was promising. She had three queens of hearts, a four of spades, and a nine of hearts.

"We were engaged to be married," she blurted out.

"Who do you mean?"

"Carter Heaney."

"But when? He's been . . ."

"He asked me the night he died."

"I'm sorry. And I apologize for what I said about him."

Carol waved her hand in the air as if to say it didn't matter. "What about you, did you ever marry?"

"I was supposed to be a priest, but I got derailed."

Carol sized him up. "You could have been one." She leaned forward over her cards. "I knew someone who met the pope once. Took Communion from him. Right out of his hand."

"I never had that," Snuff said.

"Right out of his hand," she repeated.

When Snuff discarded, Carol leaned back in her chair.

"Well it's churchlike enough in here. You see, there's the altar," she said, pointing to the mirrored back bar. "And those are the pews. But it needs that incense. . . . I like the smell," she said, surprised at how voluble she had become.

"*You* should have been the priest . . . ," Snuff said.

"Oh goodness no. I don't believe in anything."

Snuff smiled. What was impersonal about her had given way to something else—a nervous bantering he liked.

"I help out old Father McGuvey once in a while. Even served Communion a few weeks ago. Some of the old guard in town think it's wrong for a bar owner to be an altar boy," he said, smiling.

"It makes perfect sense to me," Carol said. "You're in the business of serving spirits. . . ."

Snuff laughed and resorted his cards. "It's hard to make something of nothing," he said, meaning his cards.

"You're lucky to believe in something," Carol said solemnly.

Snuff snorted. "My life's been dictated by chance. . . . Do you believe in chance?" he asked.

"You mean like this?" Carol said, laying down a royal flush.

Snuff peered over his cards. "Yes," he said, then caught her eyes with his.

"Ooooooooweeee. Look at all that money!" A short man on crutches wearing a dirty Stetson appeared in the middle of the dance floor.

"What can I do for you, Pinkey?" Snuff asked.

"Cut me in."

"That's hers," he said flatly.

Pinkey doffed his hat to Carol. One of the crutches fell from under his arm.

"I need a saw," Pinkey said.

"What kind of drink is that?"

Pinkey squinted hard at the man. "You're dumber than I thought you was. What's wrong, don't you savvy English?"

Snuff laughed.

"You've got to get me outta this sonofabitch," Pinkey said and swung his broken leg in the air.

When Snuff refilled Carol's glass Pinkey peered over the rim.

"What's that hummin'bird food you're drinkin'?" he asked.

"Here, try it," she said.

"Hell no, that'd clog up my pipes."

Carol inspected the mutilated cast. It was blotched with mud and the bottom edge was badly frayed.

"How long have you had that on?" she asked.

"Too long . . . a couple of weeks, I guess."

Snuff disappeared, then returned, carrying a meat saw.

"What are you going to do with that?" Carol asked.

"Pinkey, sit up on that table there, will you?" Snuff said. "Carol, grab his heel and kinda steady the thing."

Pinkey lay back on the long oak table, a relic from the neighboring town's one lawyer, who died and whose office sat idle for twelve years. Pinkey watched as the saw sank into white plaster. Soon the cast was halved and Snuff pried it apart. They peered down at the leg.

"God it looks wormy, don't it?" Pinkey said. "Can't you put that thing back on?"

Snuff held up a piece of the cast and laughed.

"Then get me a shot of whiskey," Pinkey said.

Snuff brought the drink and Pinkey gulped it down. He slid off the table slowly until both feet, the one with the boot on and the pale one covered by a sock, touched the floor. He put weight on the broken leg, then lifted it gingerly. His face turned white. He tried again. Then he looked at Snuff, and at his foot, and at Snuff again.

"I'm healed. I'm healed," he cried out and waved his crutches in the air like wings. He stood up. The leg held.

"Just send me a bill, Snuff," he said and hooked the crutches on the chandelier's bent frame. They watched as he hobbled out the door.

Carol Lyman turned on her heel and gasped. A man stood directly behind her. Clean-shaven, he had matted black hair, olive skin, and a dappling of black moles—beauty spots—on his jaw.

"What are you afraid of?" he asked. He had a soft voice.

"Carol, that's the Wild Man," Snuff said. "He lives out back."

Out back meant one of the cabins, Carol thought. She had never been inside any of them.

The Wild Man's face collapsed. "My dog is sick," he said.

Snuff put down the bar towel he had been wiping his hands with and followed the Wild Man to his cabin.

"May I come too?" Carol asked and Snuff nodded.

Inside, the cabin was cramped but tidy—not anything like the Wild Man's appearance. A narrow bed had been shoved up against one wall, a steamer trunk against another and, leaning sideways, a tall bookcase crammed with miscellaneous titles: *The Virginian*, a set of encyclopedias, *Don Quixote*, everything Tolstoy had written, and a 1942 *Saturday Evening Post* folded back to a story called "The Bear."

Snuff and Carol looked at the dog who lay curled on the bed. He was a Heeler-Kelpie cross, smaller than a coyote but with a coyote's head and ears.

"What's wrong?" Snuff asked, bending close to the dog. His eyes were clouded and he made a hoarse noise.

"He's dying," the Wild Man said leaning helplessly against the door.

Carol looked at the man. If he were cleaned up he'd have movie star looks, she thought, but . . .

"Let's take him in where he'll be warm," Snuff said, and the Wild Man gathered the dog in his arms like a child.

Outside, Carol noticed that the afternoon was nearly gone. In the northwest dark clouds humped up and moved toward the desolation around Snuff's. Despite heavy snows the week before, the air felt tropical and Carol thought she could smell the sea.

"Ten years ago I found this dog in an irrigation ditch . . . he was just a few days old . . . about as big as a rat. Someone tried to drown him, but they forgot to turn the water into the ditch, I guess," the Wild Man said as he walked down the narrow hall that opened out onto the dance floor.

They made a soft bed for the dog under the oak table where he always liked to sleep. He gave them a grateful look. Snuff went to the porthole window and looked outside. In the distance heat lightning domed the dark sky with its ghostly hood of light and thunder exploded overhead. Then the lights in the bar went out.

"Snuff. What's happening?"

Snuff pressed his face against the grimy porthole. Outside it was dark too: the neon light off, the mill dark, no moon. The door swung open. A small figure stood in the entry and did not move.

"Come on in," Snuff said.

Still the visitor remained motionless.

"Who's there?" Snuff asked again.

When there was no answer Snuff came out from behind the bar falling against the bottles.

"Snuff, can't you light a match or something?" Carol yelled. She heard a match being struck behind her, then another. The Wild Man held up a silver candelabrum.

"Where did you get a thing like that?" Carol whispered as they approached the silent figure at the door. A wizened Japanese man appeared before them. When the light shone on his face he hid his head in his hands. Then he regained his composure.

"They leave me. Cannot find way back. So confused," he began.

"Who are you?" Snuff asked.

The old man looked at Snuff timidly but gave no answer. Snuff took the candelabrum from the Wild Man and went to the phone. The line was dead. He put back the receiver slowly.

"Christ," he mumbled, then rejoined the others.

A plane flew over. It made a high, uneven whine that deepened into a drone as it veered away. Snuff and Carol looked up at the tin ceiling. Then they heard a car and two gunshots.

"What's going on around here?" Snuff asked. "Maybe we better find some cover for a while."

"Oh Snuff . . . ," Carol protested, but when Snuff led the old man away from the door, Carol and the Wild Man followed. They all joined the sick dog under the table.

"Here, give me that light," Carol said and held the candelabrum up to the old man. Under coal-black eyebrows he had an elfish face and a delicate nose. Gray hair was swept back from a long, grooved forehead.

"Are you from the Camp?" she asked.

"*Hai*. Heart Mountain. *Hai*," he replied cheerfully and broke into a timid smile.

"Mr. Abe," he said and made a slight bow.

"You better blow those out now," Snuff said quietly.

The Wild Man held the dog close. In the dark they could hear the animal's labored breathing. Another plane droned overhead. This one was farther away.

"War and peace," the Wild Man whispered and chuckled at his private joke.

In the confusion Carol's hand touched Snuff's under the folds of a coat he had thrown down for them and she did not move it away. They braced themselves, though for what they weren't sure: for a Japanese army to burst in, for sudden death. Snuff positioned himself so he could see out the porthole at the end of the bar. Beyond the bent geranium the sky was a blank.

Carol leaned back against the table's thick pedestal. It was like a tree, she thought, the trunk curved and smooth, and branching into a sheltering canopy. For a moment the window went white with lightning. A clap of thunder jangled the chandelier's crystal prisms. Carol imagined she was on a boat. Wind whistled and the air slipping under the door into the stale room smelled of a failing sun and seaweed.

They waited. Each tried to comfort the dog, passing him from lap to lap. When the dog was passed to the old man Carol whispered, "He's just old. There's nothing to be afraid of." Then she looked at the man again. "Where did you relocate from, Mr. Abe?" she asked.

"Los Angeles. I was flower grower. Then had to come here. Plant garden. No good, no grow," he said forlornly.

The Wild Man looked at him. "Nothing grows here," he said dryly.

Mr. Abe gave back the dog.

The night was divided by long silences and short interludes of whispered talk. Snuff spoke first. He told of an upbringing in the mining town of Butte.

"I worked for Marcus Daley. He owned just about everything in Anaconda and Butte. Besides the mines he had a big hotel. It was quite a place. Everything in it was made of copper—even the toilet seats. All kinds of people came through: boxers, opera singers, movie stars, gangsters. They said Butte was an island of easy money entirely surrounded by whiskey. I was an orphan. My dad died in the mines. Oh, death was common. One man died every day in those mines; the cemetery held forty thousand. Money was easy; death was easy. I guess it was living that got to be hard.

"I grew up on Venus Alley. Do you know what that was? A whole street of whorehouses. When Mr. Daley put me to work I didn't have a dime. He taught me something about making money. I even had a little string of racehorses all my own. Then I lost them in a poker game. And in exchange I got this place."

Snuff paused and looked at his surroundings, then laughed.

"I told Carol earlier that I was supposed to be a priest." He looked around. "But things happen; things get lost along the way. This is my hardship post."

When Snuff finished talking, no one spoke. The rumbling of the Wild Man's stomach broke the spell. Carol smothered a laugh, then crawled on hands and knees behind the bar. She returned with a handful of elk jerky and four pickled eggs, shared by all. The Wild Man broke his egg in half and gave the yolk to his dog.

"What about you?" Carol asked, looking at the Wild Man.

His eyes bounced like dark berries when he smiled, but he didn't speak.

"He fell out of a boxcar from a moving train one night," Snuff interjected, looking at the young man. "When I found him his ears were frostbit. Had to have old Doc Hoffman up here to cut them off."

Carol found herself staring at the Wild Man's head as Snuff talked, but the long matted hair hid the ears.

"Snuff took me in," the Wild Man said. A silence followed.

Carol looked at him intently. "Is that all?"

"After I healed up and spring came I worked as an irrigator. Up on the Heaney place, then down here on that Mormon farm. That's back when they ran their livestock together . . . back when they were true socialists. . . ."

"Tell her about the Depression," Snuff urged.

The Wild Man stared at him. "We wore rags. Like everyone else," he said flatly.

"We'd drive around in the middle of the night and deliver boxes of food he put together on people's doorsteps. Clothes too and books . . . lots of books," Snuff said.

"I was just the chauffeur; that's all."

"Like hell you were . . . ," Snuff said.

"I liked irrigating. It's child's play. There was a coyote who used to follow my pup around . . . walk right behind him about fifteen feet. . . ."

"But what about before? Where did you come from?" Carol asked.

The Wild Man stroked his dog adoringly. "Before?" he asked. "Before that I went to college . . . in Cambridge . . . Harvard. One day I came home from classes and my house had been robbed. Then I looked out on the streets and I knew why. It was the thirties. I had lots of things and other people had nothing. I left my door open and walked back to school and told them I was leaving. That night I hopped a freight. It was full of hoboes—guys my age too. When I returned, my parents, who had been wealthy, had lost everything. I wanted to spare them the embarrassment of having an extra mouth to feed, so I took off again and landed here."

The small dog groaned, stretched his back legs, and collapsed again in the Wild Man's lap. Snuff looked through the window. Two stars shone, then one was overtaken by clouds.

"I wonder what's happening out there," Snuff said.

The Wild Man looked at him. "Nothing. Same as usual."

A long silence followed. Then Carol Lyman said, "What about you, Mr. Abe?"

The old man's eyebrows rose and he looked timidly at her. "Oh no, is no very good story."

"All stories are good," she said.

He looked from one to the other. "I come on ship. I'm opposite him," he said and pointed to the Wild Man. "Start out with nothing. Come here to make money. Before—mask-carver in Noh theater. Kyoto. Master died. Then I come here." He paused and pursed his lips.

"Ship take long time. Very rough. People sick all over. Only one other man on board. All others—girls. Picture brides. You know? Mail order. Have photograph of man they marry. That's all. Never meet before. Just picture. Two days before reaching San Francisco, one girl so scared she jump overboard. That girl's friend . . . she very beautiful . . . she come over to me. Write poems to each other every day. Like in Heian times. The day we are coming to port, don't know what to do. She stand in bow of ship and look at picture of man she supposed to marry. When she see land, she tear picture up and throw over railing. We get off boat, and he's there. Right in front. Oh, so ashamed. She grab my arm like married woman and we walk by. Very bad thing we do, but in those days, love matches not common. Not common at all. After, I work for farmer. Then lease own land. Couldn't buy; no Japanese can. Land on coast. Very beautiful, like Japan. Grow daisies. Many, many acres of them. So thick—like snow."

The Wild Man rearranged the dog and covered him with a torn blanket, then he looked up and smiled at Mr. Abe.

Carol Lyman thought of the places these people had lived; how the places she had come to looked as if a river had run through them and swept all the small comforts away. Because it was dark in the bar, her eyes were closed sometimes, sometimes open. Maybe she would die tonight, she thought, flanked by three strange men. Yet her body felt light. She had not touched any part of a man for many years and now Snuff's arm pressed firmly against her back. A fly trapped under the dog's blanket buzzed. The dog's eyes opened, an ear twitched, then sleep overtook him again.

"Carol?" Snuff said.

"I can't."

"Why not?"

"Because I've never told anyone."

Mr. Abe looked at her. "Nothing to lose, huh?"

Carol smiled. The Wild Man relit the candelabrum and their faces glowed. Carol cleared her throat.

"I spent a summer near here twenty years ago. I was young and had come to stay at a ranch. In August there was a party at the Heaney ranch on the other side of the mountain. We started out horseback and rode all day. We arrived just as the fiddle players were tuning up. It was a lovely party. Paper lanterns had been strung across the veranda and through the trees. There were tables and tables of food. Everyone came. Even the sheepherders. I remember how they stood at the door and wouldn't come in at first. They had their dogs with them.

"During the evening I wandered down a long hall into another part of the house. I heard someone coughing, so I peeked in. Henry's brother, Carter, was lying in bed. He was the handsomest man I had ever seen. He had thick wavy hair the color of chocolate and a straight nose and big glowing eyes. Every feature was perfect. He looked like a young god. He told me he had pneumonia. His cheeks were very flushed and he kept clutching my hand and asking me to stay and talk to him. So I did.

We talked about everything. I had never spoken that way to a man before. Once someone came in and checked on him. We were alone for the rest of the night."

Carol paused, then continued.

"He was the father of my son, Willard," she said quietly.

A long silence followed. Not disapproval as Carol suspected, but rather, they were waiting for more. She looked at her audience. Mr. Abe was sitting cross-legged straight as an arrow. He didn't look old now. His face was bright. The Wild Man stroked his dog.

"The terrible thing was . . . ," Carol began, looking around. "I didn't even know his name until I read it in the *Billings Gazette* . . . it was his obituary. He died a few days later—the day I left on the train."

Snuff gave her a surprised look.

"I lied before," she said to him. "He never asked me to marry him. It was only that one night. Half a night. That's not very much time for two people to have when they love each other."

Snuff put his hand on her arm. She continued.

"The doctors didn't know what made Willard not right. He's retarded. Maybe it was Carter's illness, transferred something . . . or maybe it was something in me. He was so handsome, though; that's the strange thing. . . ."

Carol looked at the others. All at once the arbitrariness of their lives seemed absurd. This bend in the road and the little towns on either side, linked by great acreages of desolation, had neither accepted nor refused them. There was room here, that was all—a geographical accident. What they had done, how far they had drifted was of no concern. The convulsions of weather and seasons would always be greater than they were. That was a comfort, too, Carol thought.

She felt tired and cold suddenly and laid her head against Snuff's knee. A warm wind rattled the doors and windows of the bar. After a while she slipped into a light sleep. She dreamed she was on a boat, though the sea swells she thought cradled her were Snuff's arms and the back legs of the dying dog, and the Wild Man's knees, and Mr. Abe's folded hands. The boat passed over a school of fish. Then she could see herself from up in the air as though she were flying. It was not water that held the boat, but fish. A clap of thunder woke her.

"What time is it?" she asked, startled.

Snuff looked toward the grimy window and shrugged. Rain undulated across the darkened mill, slapped at the road and the windowpanes, then ceased. A car drove by. There were three gunshots this time. The Wild Man stood excitedly and ran out the door, shaking the candelabrum at the sky. "Here I am! Can you see me? Go ahead, shoot me. You can have me. Come on!" As he yelled, wind extinguished the candles one by one. When he went back inside, he found that the dog had died.

At daylight, they stood, stiff from the long vigil. A red belt of light had widened in the east. It looked like a shield held up to do battle with night. Outside, the Wild Man walked away from the others. They watched as he clambered up the pink dune of mineral tailings—over the crest of one, down the backside, up another. Mr. Abe's eyebrows lifted. His long forehead was like something you could land a plane on. He pointed to the pink mounds.

"Like cherry blossoms," he said. "Same color."

Carol smiled at the wizened old man. She thought she had never seen a morning like this, a more exquisite bend in the road. She wrapped her long arms around herself and felt ribs under her sweater. Trembling from the cold that comes just before sunrise, she rocked back and forth on her feet. Snuff touched her shoulder.

"You look like a bride," he said.

When the pink came out of the sky, the pink mounds turned to the color of snow and the air took on a transparency—like the hottest part of a flame.

A car barreled down the highway toward them. It was Pinkey and two other cowboys. They waved wildly as they passed, then the one in the backseat drew a pistol and shot three times in the air.

The Wild Man sat perched on a pink mound. The candles had fallen out of the holder and he held the empty candelabrum above his head as though proposing a toast. He started laughing. Then he stretched his legs straight out and let himself slide. He kicked over to his side and rolled. Pink dust coated his body. He rolled and rolled, laughing, and when he hit the bottom of the mound, he stood up and shook like a dog.

Abe-san held his hand over his mouth.

"You look like geisha," he said and patted the Wild Man's white cheeks. The Wild Man's black eyes gleamed. He lifted his head to the sky and howled. After, he walked back toward the bar followed by the others. A buzzing noise stopped them and they looked: the neon sign over the bar door lit up suddenly and began its habitual blinking once again.

8

McKay watched the elk move out of the alfalfa field at dawn. He had been walking the pasture beyond the lake with a .22 rifle slung on his back. The lake was green and still and the elk ran, single file, up Eagle Nest Creek toward the falls.

The chatter of a prairie dog stopped him. They were a nuisance to ranchers, turning an acre of grain into a desert. McKay scanned the hill. Three prairie dogs stood upright on mounds of excavated dirt—like pitchers in a baseball game. He shot once and missed and shot again. A scream came from behind a windbreak of cottonwoods at the top of the hill.

McKay dropped his gun and ran toward the trees. Jumping the ditch, he saw an old Japanese man, blood-covered, holding his arm. Working quickly, he unknotted his neck scarf and tied it above the wound.

"I didn't see you," he said, trying to sound calm. "I didn't see you. . . ."

The man had a delicate nose, upswinging eyebrows, and a long shining

forehead. His face was covered with sweat. He watched the young man
tie another piece of cloth around the wound and thought his eyes were
as blue as delphinium.

"What's your name?" McKay asked.

"Abe."

"You'll be all right, Mr. Abe," McKay said.

McKay was surprised at how light the man was—light as a banty rooster,
he thought—as he turned onto the dirt road that would eventually lead
to town.

The old man watched the sky as he was being carried. "Yellow singing
bird," he said. His arm felt as if sharpened rocks had been screwed into
the bone. He wanted to hear the song of the bird he had been looking
for when the bullet took him down, the bird with the yellow chest, but
he didn't see any now.

It began raining softly. McKay hadn't noticed the clouds. They rolled
in so low, they seemed to skim his head. Even though the old man was
light in his arms, McKay's bad leg started to hurt. He realized he was
limping. He would pace himself, and tried breathing in a deliberate
rhythm, but the air came up through his chest in quick bursts.

McKay thought of his brothers in the war. They had been wounded
and someone was carrying them. Their blood dripped on the ground and
looked black where it mixed with sand. They were on a beach and there
were planes crashing into the water near the horizon. The two brothers
hung limp because they were dead.

McKay stopped for a moment to get his breath. He looked at the old
man. Where had he come from, McKay wondered. Did I shoot him out
of the sky? "You're going to be all right. I didn't mean to hurt you. You'll
be okay."

"Came out with harvest crew. Went for walk to see birds. Ones with
yellow chest, big song . . .," Mr. Abe said.

"Meadowlarks."

"*Hai.*"

McKay looked at the old man. "Are you all right?"

"*Hai.*"

They were rain-soaked now. When McKay stumbled once, Mr. Abe
let out a cry. Otherwise he was silent. At a spring on the top of a hill
McKay put the man down. It was dry inside the grove of junipers. McKay

cut off the tail of his shirt with a pocket knife and dipped it into the water and wiped the man's face with it. Then he cupped his hands and brought water to his lips. When they had rested, McKay cut the shirt away from the wound and squeezed water over it so he could see how deep it was. Then he cut another piece of shirt, covering the wound again and the two men continued on.

Not long after they reached the fork in the road that led to the town of Luster, an army car came into sight and stopped by the two men. They had been looking for Mr. Abe, they said. A woman in the backseat pushed forward frantically and stepped out of the car.

"*Grandpère* . . . what have they done to you?"

She stroked his forehead and touched his wounded arm and looked at McKay.

"I shot him by mistake. I didn't see him. He was behind some trees."

They slid the old man onto the backseat of the car. Mariko cradled his head as they sped toward the hospital. In the rearview mirror McKay watched the woman. She looked up once.

"Why did you do this to him?" she asked.

McKay, in the front seat, turned around to face her. "I'm sorry."

"So you had a little farm accident, huh?" one of the army men said to McKay smugly.

"I said it was an accident."

"I thought you was a Jap-lover," the other man said.

McKay glowered at him. "I looked at the wound. It's not too bad. He lost some blood, that's all." Then he stretched out his bad leg, rubbing it where one of the breaks had been, and closed his eyes.

On the highway, they passed the hermit's green shack on a hill where three dogs were chained to a post and gunny sacks spilled over with tin cans near the door. They passed the Mormon church's grainfields, and the victory gardens with signs commemorating a son's or brother's or husband's batallion. They crossed the Heart Mountain canal where McKay's parents had drowned, passed the beauty shop, and started down the main and only paved street of Luster, where almost every other building housed a bar.

When McKay opened his eyes he turned to Mariko again. Mr. Abe had a smile on his face and seemed to be resting comfortably. Mariko stared straight ahead. The cords in her neck stuck out and McKay could see the quick intelligence in her eyes. She had a fine nose and a downward curve to her upper lip and cheekbones that spread sideways like gull wings. Her hair had tumbled out of the tortoiseshell barrette and each time she pulled it back, the gloss of it shone in her white hand. Her hair was so black it looked blue.

"Our ranch borders the Camp."

She stared at him.

"I'll take full responsibility. Anything I can do."

Mariko nodded yes. . . .

The hospital's only two nurses greeted the army car at the front door and helped Mr. Abe to the examining room. After a wait, Doc Hoffman arrived with his black bag. He had come out of retirement as part of the war effort to replace the town's younger doctor, who had gone to the front. He had a double chin and heavy-lidded eyes and always looked as if he had been awakened from a long sleep and everyone knew he was incompetent.

After the nurse cleaned the wound the doctor inspected it. McKay had been right. It was a shallow wound and the bullet hadn't hit bone, but he needed blood. McKay rolled up his sleeve and offered his arm. Mr. Abe shook his head.

"Not O type. O negative."

The doctor looked embarrassed. He had forgotten even to ask the old man's blood type. McKay and the fat nurse looked at each other and the nurse rolled her eyes.

"Pinkey," McKay said.

The nurse groaned. "Oh no, not him again."

The army men were dispatched to McKay's ranch. McKay wrote a note for them to give to Bobby. It explained that the men were not there to take him away, only to take Pinkey into the hospital.

The nurse gave Mr. Abe something for pain. He sat cross-legged on the examining table and refused to lie down. He was thirsty and Mariko brought ice water. The sheriff arrived and questioned McKay and Mr. Abe about the incident. When he asked the old man if he wanted to bring charges, Mariko looked sharply at McKay and the old man said no.

The sheriff left. Now McKay was alone in the room with Mr. Abe and Mariko. She frightened him. Sometimes their glances met, and they would both look away.

When Bobby Korematsu saw the army car pull into the yard, he ducked behind the kitchen sink. The man with the crew cut knocked on the door. Bobby stayed down.

"We're not here to arrest anyone. There's been an accident. Open up," the man yelled.

Finally Bobby let them in. They showed him McKay's note, which he read carefully.

"It's his blood type. This hired hand of yours . . . he's the only one around whose blood matches."

Bobby looked at the army man, then at the note again. "Okay. I get him."

When Pinkey finally arrived, accompanied by the army men, he stood at the entrance to the emergency room, then walked to Mr. Abe. "I sure am sorry about this and I hope you don't mind taking in an old cowboy's blood. It ain't nothing to brag on and it's a little whiskey soaked, but I don't mean no offense by it," he said and stepped back.

"Have at it, Betsy," he told the nurse and rolled up both sleeves.

McKay looked at his hired hand. "You're too drunk to give blood."

"I'm as sober as a pig in high heels," he announced and tiptoed around in a tiny circle.

Mr. Abe tipped his head back, laughing, and his face—most of it forehead—shone.

"Sit down, Pinkey," the nurse commanded.

"I forgot to tell you; I faint when I see needles."

"Don't look."

"I already seen it."

"I'll just throw a bucket of water on you, if you do."

She jabbed the needle into Pinkey's arm and Pinkey whimpered. The nurse who took the blood doubled as the lab technician.

"Doc, do you think you can handle things while I'm gone?" she asked and winked at McKay.

Now Mr. Abe lay on his good side and rested. Mariko brought more water, then paced the floor. The four men simply watched her. After another long wait the nurse returned with Pinkey's blood. It filled a whole bottle. Mr. Abe sat up, resuming his cross-legged posture. The nurse had been called from home and her hair was still in pin curls. She had fat arms. Pinkey watched as the flesh swayed under the part of the arm where the muscle should have been. He flinched as the needle slid in then pushed his white stool closer and watched, almost mesmerized, as his blood began sinking from the bottle, traversing the tube, and disappearing into another man's body.

McKay felt weak in the knees and sat down. His cheeks were flushed and he wondered whether he might not be coming down with something. He looked at Mariko holding her grandfather's hand. It wasn't her Asian features that made her seem exotic, but the expression on her face—unguarded, and comprehending; wild, indignant, and hurt. Like an elk, he thought. Her dark eyes blazed.

"Does it hurt much?" she asked her grandfather.

"Much better now. Getting new blood," he said and pointed to Pinkey brightly.

"It ain't exactly new," Pinkey said out of the corner of his mouth.

McKay excused himself and went downstairs for coffee. He was having trouble keeping warm. The cafeteria was empty except for the other nurse, whose ribs showed through her sweater when she bent over. She had long teeth like a jackrabbit's and had made clucking sounds when Pinkey had come in weeks before with a broken leg. McKay poured a cup of coffee, then set it down because he felt dizzy.

"Excuse me," he said to no one in particular and left the room hurriedly.

He met Mariko in the hallway, nodded, then ran to the door at the end of the hall. It opened out to the parking lot. He heard a train whistle and wondered when Madeleine was coming home and whether the steers had sold well. When his head cleared, he went back inside. Mariko was leaning against the wall with one hip stuck out. He approached.

"They say you're a painter," he said at last.

"Yes. Do you like painting?"

"I saw some van Goghs once. And Gauguins and Picassos. . . ."

"Yes," she said, smiling.

It was the first time McKay had seen her smile. He felt the flush in his face creep up. Mariko offered him a Gauloise. He thanked her but refused. They walked to the picture window at the end of the hall. Beyond was a cornfield. The dry stalks moved stiffly in the breeze and streaks of crimson climbed the bleached husks. The hall smelled like the inside of Snuff's bar, McKay thought—heady and antiseptic. His head throbbed and he felt cold and hot at the same time like a piece of marble propped next to a fire.

"They said your grandfather can go home tonight."

"Home?" Mariko repeated the word cynically.

"I'm sorry. Look, I'm awfully sorry."

Mariko walked away, then stopped to dig a cigarette from the crumpled blue package. She turned to him.

"Are we much hated here?" she asked, pulling on the cigarette. It hadn't been lit right and the fire burned to one side, then went out. She smoothed the wadded package and stuffed the cigarette back in.

"I don't hate you at all," McKay said.

A quizzical smile came over Mariko's face.

She paced the hall. Once she stopped and peeked through the emergency room window; Pinkey was leaning on one elbow. His eyes were closed, and her grandfather rocked back and forth as Pinkey's blood dripped into his arm.

Mariko moved back toward McKay. He watched her soft, deliberate stride. Her feet seemed to reach too far forward as if trying to get away from ground that might break through. He thought he was going to cry. Then it passed. Mariko was standing in front of him. Her eyes were stern and sullen and swelled under the lids like dark waves coming in. She leaned forward and looked right into him. He knew she saw how his blood vibrated, how he was faltering, always faltering, like a wall pulling away from a beautiful half-built house.

She smiled. McKay's chest was so congested, he found it difficult to breathe. He had to turn away from her while he coughed. Then he saw his hand extend toward her. He didn't know where he wanted to make it go, he only wanted to make peace with her for the terrible thing he had done. She clasped his wandering hand with both of hers. Her fingers were warm and a little rough on the ends. She looked at him as though to say something, but didn't.

*   *   *

When Pinkey's head slipped off his hand, he jerked awake. At this, Mr. Abe's elfish face lit up and he let out a peal of laughter. The nurse slipped the needle from his arm, then looked at Pinkey in disgust.

"You might as well be renting a room here, the amount of time you spend in this hospital."

"Times are tough; that's all, Betsy."

"Yeah, who needs a war when we've got you around."

Doc Hoffman came from a room at the end of the hall and joined McKay and Mariko. In the emergency room he took Mr. Abe's pulse, checked the wound, and declared him "good as new," speaking in the loud voice reserved for "foreigners," as though volume compensated for words they didn't understand.

Mr. Abe dangled his feet over the edge of the table, then stood up. He was the same height as Pinkey, but birdlike. He bowed to the old cowboy.

"*Domo arrigato gozaimashita.*"

"You bet. Hell, we're blood brothers now. You can't get much closer than that," Pinkey said proudly.

The nurse with the fat arms pushed a wheelchair under Abe-san and made him sit down, then wheeled him from the room. Mariko turned to follow. She shook the doctor's hand.

"*Ciao,*" she said.

Pinkey looked up. "Yea. That's a good idea. Let's eat."

9

Am I like the optimist who, while falling ten stories from a building, says at each story, "I'm all right so far"?

No, I'm not. Because the news that Abe-san was shot by a hakujin—a white person—whose ranch borders this camp shocked me out of the lethargy I'd been feeling. Are we going to be picked off like geese, one by one? Will Okubo jumped to the conclusion that it wasn't an accident and insisted I do some "investigative reporting." Now how in the hell am I supposed to do that from behind barbed wire? Went to the director's office and asked for a special pass to interview the sheriff and the doctor who treated Abe-san. The pass was denied. So much for muckraking. "I'm sitting on it for now," I told Will when he asked. "Like a hen," he said, glowering.

The weather is godawful—blustery winds and spitting snow. I don't feel warm anywhere. The tip of Heart Mountain is white. It comes and goes inside clouds and looks "like a man being carried on a palanquin," *my father said; the mountain moves, the sky is still. Tried refilling my fountain pen this morning and the ink was half-frozen. I went back to bed. Mom and Pop were off early—she goes to her class in ikebana, and Pop to his in English-language. Optimism is for the fainthearted, I decided, lying there. How much more absurd can things get? There's a war on and my mother spends her days learning to arrange flowers.*

Sunday. Spent the day shoveling dirt against the foundations of the barracks to keep the cold from coming in. Pop joined in and we worked in a line with Mariko and Will. Just before sundown, the smell of cooked liver permeated the Camp. Will tied a scarf around his nose and mouth. When we cleaned up and went to dinner, he sat alone in his room. For such a tough thinker, his senses are easily offended. Later, I shared one of those foul-smelling French cigarettes with him and listened to the Issei fire patrol clacking wooden blocks as they strolled through the Camp. "It's the old way," Mom explained. "Back home." (By which she meant Hikari.) "They still do it this way. Japanese buildings are nothing but wood and paper. Very old; very dry. Many fires . . . very bad. I remember one house that went up in flames down the street from us. Old man there had gone crazy. Poured gasoline all over the house and himself, then lit a match. Fire destroy three houses, kill five people, and took half of Shinto shrine at the end of the street. He kill himself and many others."

This morning, helped Ben pass a petition around to keep the War Relocation Authority from stringing barbed wire completely around the Camp. Some kids joined us, singing, "Don't Fence Me In." Strolling through this square mile of humanity is an education in itself. Such variety! We met and talked to farmers and fishermen, tough guys from downtown Los Angeles, Buddhist priests, and rich housewives, schoolteachers and koto-players. . . . One Issei told me that when he came to America by ship, they fed him bread and butter. He had never seen butter and the taste of it made him sick. The first hakujin *he saw had red hair and green eyes. He thought the person was sick. "I didn't know there were different colors of hair and eyes then," he told me and laughed.*

Halfway around the Camp, Emi joined us. Ben had introduced us a few days before. She's fresh-faced and smart and already I've grown quite fond of her. As we walked between barracks, she told me that her mother

was a picture bride and their first house was a shack on the edge of a field
of onions, with no water and a dirt floor. "My father loved gambling more
than rice," she said. "He'd work all day, then disappear in the basement
of someone's house and gamble his day's wages away. Sometimes he won,
but mostly he lost. We never knew what the next week would bring." She
said he died one night in his sleep and the next day they were informed
that he had lost everything they owned in his last bet—even the samurai
sword that had been in the family for centuries. . . . "So this camp doesn't
seem all that bad to me," she said. Almost cheerfully.

Tuesday. Abe-san came home today. In lieu of investigative reporting, I
merely recorded his arrival. An amateur photographer from the town of
Lovell donated a press camera, so I was there when the staff car pulled
up. Mariko was with him and helped him from the car. As he stood,
bandaged arm in view, I pressed the button and there was a minor explosive
flash.

Abe-san hid his face. "Why you do that to me?" he asked angrily.

I told him I had never used this camera before and didn't know it would
go off like that. Will laughed. I followed them from the car, down the
lane, to their unit, and asked at the door if I could come in. Abe-san
nodded.

"Put that thing away," he said, pointing to the camera, and I laid it
on the floor, then took my pad and pencil out to get the story.

Abe-san looked right through me and said nothing. Finally I asked him
if he thought it was an accident and if he had thought of bringing charges
against the guy.

Abe-san looked amused. "Why he waste bullet on old man like me?
Better for him to come and shoot you young people . . .," he said, laughing.

"Well, did he act like he wanted to hurt you?" I asked. I was already
feeling frustrated.

"No. He's good boy."

"Who's a good boy?" I asked.

Abe-san turned to Mariko. "What's his name?"

"McKay Allison," she said.

"Sooo . . . good memory," he said.

I looked from one to the other in disbelief.

"You might have been killed . . .," I said.

Abe-san scowled. "Oh . . . yes . . .," he said, then smiled.

"Frankly, I don't see what's so funny about it."

"It's not," he said matter-of-factly. "It was accident. Like stubbing toe."

"Death is like stubbing your toe?" I asked.

"Hai."

What could I do but shrug it off? Another crazy conversation with this madman.

"But if you changed your mind and did decide to bring charges, would you—or any of us—have any legal rights here? I mean, if they can abrogate some of our democratic rights, can't they do away with others?"

A twinge of pain crossed Abe-san's face. He held his wounded arm. "Why meet bullet with anger? That makes you just like bullet."

"No it doesn't," Will whispered.

Abe-san ignored him and stared at me. "Understand, desu-ne?"

Understand? Not really. I understand the theory, all right, but how to put it into practice without closing my eyes to reality, without being naive? I don't trust myself, and I don't know what to think of Abe-san.

Friday. Went to press. I was one of the lucky ones who got to go to Cody with the paper. It's printed at night on the big flatbed presses of the Cody weekly. While it gets printed, we go for a steak at the Mayflower and sometimes catch part of a movie in town. We get some stares, all right, but so far, no one's shot at us! Then we go back, fold the paper, and take the whole load to Camp for delivery.

Sunday. Another black day. For twenty-three years I've looked in the mirror and never seen my face as "Japanese." How naive could I have been? Now I hate what I've come from. I try to appear calm and good-natured, but inside I'm seething. How can a nation that purports to fight fascism use fascist techniques to solve problems at home—and expect not to get caught in its lie. And that would be the worst thing—the hypocrisy is one thing, but getting away with it would be the real tragedy.

Monday. Snowed like hell, then warmed a little, then froze again last night. Went skating between the barracks with some young kids. They ordered their skates out of the Monkey Ward catalogue. They laughed every time I fell down. Said my ankles looked like udon.

Thursday. Yesterday, the last of the evacuees from the assembly camps in California arrived here. Good-bye horse stalls, see you later Seabiscuit, I say. It's reported that 107,000 Nisei and Issei are in ten camps now and here at Heart Mountain, we've reached our quota of 10,767. I found one little kid in a sandbox crying and when I asked what was wrong he said, "I don't like Japan. I want to go home to America."

The guards say it will snow within the week and this time, we should expect it to stay on the ground until spring. How can we expect something we've never experienced? The children are ecstatic. They can't wait to build snowmen. All I know is that with no more trains coming in, it feels settled in an odd sort of way.

10

The day after Thanksgiving Carol Lyman drove her retarded, pear-shaped son, Willard, to the grocery store where he worked. In the mornings he scattered fresh sawdust behind the butcher counter and swept the aisles. His mother let him off on the street corner, threw him a kiss, and drove away. The pale pink willow branch he took everywhere with him waved in the wake of the car. The horse trader's truck appeared at the edge of town. It was green with a red stock rack and rolled passed Willard like a Christmas tree. Two sorrel horses in back swung their heads from side to side, nostrils flared. When the horse trader nodded hello, Willard raised his willow high in the air, as high and sailing as the horses' heads, he thought, and pumped it up and down like a baton.

"Morning, Willard."

Rose bent over the shelf which held peaches and fruit cocktail and stamped "12 cents" on top of each can. Her platinum bun, encased in a hairnet, teetered as she leaned.

"You put the willow down and get to sweeping. We're quitting at noon. Don't you remember?" she said. Then she grabbed Willard's wrist and wrote "12 cents" on the back of his hand with her grease pencil. Willard laughed out loud like a horse squealing.

"You're getting pretty high-priced, aren't you?" Larry, the butcher, wrapped a pound of hamburger in white paper. "You can take this home to your Mom tonight, okay, Will?"

Willard stared hard at the meat case. It was white with a big window in front and inside, on shaved ice, a few steaks and chops and sausages. He thought it looked like the insides of someone's body.

At noon, Rose, Willard, and Larry ate egg salad sandwiches in the back office, then went out on the street. Some of the men had cut a big fir and placed it where the one paved street in town ended at the railroad tracks. They made a stand for the tree in the highway maintenance shop— once the livery stable—and Willard watched as they nailed the tree trunk to it, saw the sap dropping like opals smeared over the bark by the men's big hands; bent down and put his face into the soft needles and drew in his breath; saw the tree tipped up, brushing past his cheek and ear until it stood straight again.

The smaller trees, the pines, were wired to the streetlights as Willard sorted bulbs into foot-high piles by color. Rose and Larry carried a large box of tinsel between them down the alley. Later, when the lights had been strung and the dark had come down on the town, Rose gave Willard his own tinsel. The thin package, damaged in shipping, was torn open and the long skein of silver wrapped on shirt cardboard pushed through the cellophane window at front, disheveled like hair. Willard pulled out a handful and held it to his willow branch as if the tinsel were hay and the branch could eat. Then he dabbed the bright stuff onto nearly leafless twigs and began to walk. He held the decorated branch like a torch and marched down the nearly empty street. The little pines, the ones held captive to the lampposts, flickered with light, and loudspeakers, attached that same afternoon to the eaves of the Mormon church, blared Christmas carols, and a river of cold wind came down hard and all at once and blew every strand of tinsel away.

Pinkey stood at the window and looked down at the street. The door behind him slammed shut because of the wind. He had moved to town from the ranch during the week, taken a room at Rose's boardinghouse because McKay had kicked him out after he hacksawed the lock off the liquor cabinet again and began mixing drinks. He had pulled the bottles McKay's father had brought home with him after cowboying in Mexico—tequila, mescal, Kahlúa—as well as the ancient bottle of Benedictine he had given to his wife on Valentine's Day the first year they were married. Pinkey arranged three glasses in front of him and poured crème de menthe, scotch, and schnapps into one; vermouth, blackberry brandy, and mescal into another; Kahlúa, gin, and bourbon in a third; and drained the glasses one by one, licking his lips clean.

McKay had awakened Pinkey by poking him in the ribs with his boot. He had passed out on the Navajo rug in the living room. McKay told the cowboy to get out and not come home until he was ready to work.

Nor was Rose happy to see Pinkey. She led him into the dining room, where a hot lunch was being served family style, and dangled a room key in front of his face.

"If you can hold your dinner down, you can have a room."

Pinkey hadn't shaved for five days. His whiskers had grown in silver and his red cheeks sprouted above the stubble like hothouse bulbs. The wind howled. It was already dark and strings of Christmas tree lights had fallen from the small pines in long loops and whipped like tails against the sidewalks. For days a blizzard of tinsel filled the air and fell in bright shoals against the buildings. When the five o'clock train pulled into the station at the edge of town, Pinkey leaned out over the windowsill to see. Canvas sacks of letters and packages were unloaded, then a black coffin was pushed to the edge of the boxcar. The coffin was long and dark like a tree trunk felled in the rain. A hearse backed up to the train and three men slid the coffin into its dark hold.

Pinkey reeled backward and sat on the bed. His hands felt clammy. A gust of wind tore another string of lights from a pine across the street. Who the hell's in that box, he wondered. The pavement shone under the Christmas tree. Pinkey stood again, steadying himself at the window. When he looked down everything was in twos—like a dowser's stick, he thought. Then there were two of him—one in the room and the other one, the proud one, trying to make the two one again.

When he sat the bedsprings squeaked. He heard the train's steam engine pant in the dark, heard the whistle pierce the roaring wind with another kind of roaring and the train moving away. He would go back to the ranch now, he decided. He was ready. He would go downstairs and call McKay. His broken leg ached all the way into his groin. He reached under the mattress for the bottle.

The door swung open.

"Look who's here." Dutch stood in the hall with his arm around a woman. "It's Loretta."

Pinkey hobbled toward Dutch, who had ridden the rails with him to find jobs cowboying in Montana, and the woman, Loretta, who had taken up with them on a St. Patrick's Day in Butte, ten years before; even ridden the rails to Seattle, where they ate salmon out of trash barrels behind the good restaurants; and ridden back with them as far as Miles City and disappeared. She had black hair in a pageboy and a hard face. She was a head taller than Pinkey and when he lurched into her, he nuzzled his head on the swell of her opulent breasts. Dutch pulled an open bottle of beer from his coat pocket and offered it to Pinkey.

"Come on down, you're missin' a good party," Dutch said.

Pinkey noticed Dutch's ears and nose had grown grotesquely large. Dutch tipped the bottle up and held it to his mouth until it was drained, then dropped it to the floor and stepped toward the woman again.

"I can't, I'm on my way up to the ranch."

Now the woman edged away from Dutch's grasp, toward Pinkey.

"Just one more little kiss?" she asked, then pressed herself against him and put her lips to his bald head.

"Oooowee! Do that again," Pinkey said.

After, arms entwined, the trio descended the stairs to the bar.

When the hearse approached, Willard stood to one side of the street. The willow branch, stripped of ornament, looked narrow and closed up like an arrow. Some of the fallen tinsel had caught on Willard's shoes and as he dragged his feet onto the sidewalk, silver strands let go of his ankles and blew away. He waved at the hearse driver, then looked at the small pines whose strings of light looped to the ground like jump ropes and the big tree at the end of the street, blinking and shuddering. The grocery store was locked. Willard pressed his face to the window. His breath made a balloon of frost which he scratched away, then saw how the one bare bulb in the back of the store cast a light over the hard butcher's case, saw his package of meat abandoned there.

The cactus on the sill of the south window cast a green light in the bar. Pinkey cut off the top of one paddle, peeled it with his pocketknife, diced the green flesh, and dropped the pieces into his whiskey.

"Listen to this." The bartender read from the newspaper: " 'Help Uncle Sam Nip the Nipponese! Come to the Big Horn Hotel, Saturday, 4:00, where a representative from California's aircraft industry will interview you for a job. Contribute to the war effort!' By God, that sounds better than the Red Cross sewing and knitting clubs. . . ."

Loretta took her hand from Dutch's thigh and dug into her purse for her sunglasses. She looked at the bar clock: three forty-five.

"I think I'll just go over to that hotel," she said.

Dutch yanked her arm. "I thought your dance card was already filled up for the night. Now don't go shippin' out on me. . . ."

"Oh Christ, Dutch, shut up," she said, pulling away.

" 'Draft Board calls Men for Examination. All able-bodied men under the age of forty-five years, with or without dependents, will now be called for a physical examination on Monday, November 29, 1942. However, because of the shortage of farmhands, some men will be deferred from service if they are found to be regularly engaged in an agricultural operation. All men must come to the courthouse. . . .' " The bartender stopped reading.

"Hell, they couldn't run the outfit without me," Pinkey drawled.

". . . and Bud here and his old bar is just as important as . . ."

"That means me," the bartender said.

"What means you?"

"I'm forty-four. I won't be forty-five until spring."

"Christ, Bud, I thought you was way older than that."

"You are when you have eight kids."

"All out of the same mare?"

The bartender scowled.

"Well here's to you, Bud. No, I mean it. Goddamn, we need a little patriotism around here," Pinkey said.

"Let me buy you a drink."

"Thanks, Dutch, I think I'll take you up on that."

They drank. The rectangle of green light moved from the floor in the middle of the room to the bartender's face and broke up on the cluttered wall behind him. Two men Pinkey had seen before but couldn't remember where came into the bar. One had a crew cut and a square face. His head looked like a box. He ordered a shot with a water back and his friend ordered the same. They sat at the end of the bar close to the door and the shaft of shamrock light caught the tops of their heads. Pinkey drained his glass and poured the pieces of cactus into his hand.

"Hors d'oeuvres, anyone?"

The man with the crew cut turned to him. He wasn't sitting on the stool but standing with his short legs spread wide apart and he didn't smile. Then Pinkey knew it was the army man in civvies, the one who had taken him to the hospital to give blood. He dumped the cactus back into his glass, and ordered a round for the house.

"There better be some of that cactus left when I get back from wherever the army sends me . . . if I do . . . hell, even if I don't!"

Pinkey grinned. "You bet, Bud. Harvest's over."

When the taller of the two men reached for the drink Pinkey had bought he saw the tattoos just above the man's wrist and a tangle of brown hair raked over it. He thought it might be a sailfish or a seahorse but he couldn't be sure.

"Hey boys!" Loretta sashayed past the army men to the far end of the bar. "I got me a job."

"As what?" Dutch asked and howled with laughter.

"In one of them airplane factories," she said indignantly. "In Los Angeles."

"Ooowee. . . . Ain't that near Hollywood?" Pinkey asked.

She turned a sour face to him. Pinkey reached up and took her dark glasses off. He whispered. "What'd ya have to do to get this job?"

Loretta grabbed her glasses back. "I just signed my name is all."

"Well I'm proud of you," the bartender chimed in.

Dutch and Pinkey turned to him.

"Well ain't you getting to be a patriotic sonofabitch all of a sudden," Pinkey said.

Bud stopped drying the beer glass and the army man, the one with the crew cut, shifted his feet to look down the bar. Pinkey hiccuped, grabbed a stirrer, and plunged it into his new drink until chunks of cactus swirled upward in the brown liquid.

There was a scratching sound.

"Look," Loretta whispered.

A boy with a Japanese face stared in. His eyes had the same hooded look as Willard's and he uttered a sound—something between a rooster's crow and a human whine—then scratched at the broken screen door. Before Pinkey could think about that face and sound, a bar stool skidded sideways across the floor and knocked into him, spilling his drink. He felt the sudden wetness on his broken leg and thought he had pissed in his pants. Then he heard a scream like a gut-shot fawn's.

The army men had the Japanese boy on the ground. He was half in and half out of the bar and the screen banged against the men's elbows and backs as they dropped the boy. Pinkey and Dutch reached the two men at the same time, but Loretta was already there. She jabbed one high heel into the back of the tall man's knee and when he lurched, she grabbed his shirt collar, yanked him off the boy, and let the man fall. The one with the crew cut staggered toward her.

"You can't do that," he stammered.

She waited until they were face to face, his hands on her, then she kicked him in the groin.

"Eeehaa," Pinkey yelled. He leaned down toward the face with the hooded eyes. The boy screamed.

"Hell, I ain't going to hurt you. That hurtin's all over now." He fell, sitting, beside the boy and groaned with the pain in his leg. Another terrible sound erupted. This one didn't come from the bar but from somewhere in town. It was the harsh whistle of an air raid horn.

Pinkey listened for the drone of Zero fighters. There's no hiding now, he thought. I might as well just sit here and order me a last drink.

"Bud . . ." He had to yell to be heard. "Drinks for the house . . ."

Something bumped into him.

"Oh my God," Loretta squealed.

When Pinkey looked up he saw the two army men fighting with each other. The boy whimpered and Pinkey shielded the boy's head and every once in a while hammered a fist spastically in the air as the two men reeled above him. The air raid whistle roared on.

"Where's that drink?" Pinkey hollered into the bar long since vacated by Bud, who hated fights. Pinkey looked at the young boy. His jaw had swollen and blood oozed from a cut by his mouth. People flooded the streets, scanning the sky for bombers. They formed a circle around Pinkey and the boy because the army men had fled down the alley. When Pinkey looked up he saw Willard, his body oval and oversize, his eyes, like the young boy's, holding the same bottomless stare.

Willard dropped his willow branch to the ground and it lay like another downed body. He had seen the two army men burst out of the bar and descend on the boy. He felt as if the blows were aimed at him instead and, when the air raid siren started, thought the noise was issuing from someplace inside himself. He saw Pinkey on the ground next to the boy and had seen the things Loretta had done to the men, saw the men flee, and remembered how, just before the Nisei boy's head had seemed to gyrate all the way around on his neck, his jaw made a snapping sound and he had screamed, how he—Willard—had thought it was the kind of sound the bird of paradise would make if it were backhanded, its long jawbone flower breaking into flame.

By the time Bud came back Pinkey had made drinks for Dutch, Loretta, and himself, and anyone else who came in. Pinkey had picked up the paper and wondered aloud whether his name would be in next week's issue for heroism. When Dutch asked him what was at the movies, he said he couldn't read and handed the paper back to Bud, who said *Woman of the Year* with Katharine Hepburn.

"Anyone wanna go?" Dutch asked.

Bud shook his head.

"Sure, Dutch, since you're treating," Loretta said.

Pinkey stirred the cactus in his glass to the top again and watched it drown.

Pinkey lay flat on his back on the bed. A big crack had cut across the ceiling since the last time he had rented the room. It ran its course like a creek, its headwaters in the middle of the ceiling, widening where it met the wall. He rolled on his side and pulled the pint bottle from under the mattress. I'm going to thumb a ride to the ranch, he said aloud to himself and took a swig. He heard cars on the street below and went to the window. The black hearse filed by, then a line of pickups and cars. Across the way, Rose and Larry and Willard stood on the boardwalk. After the procession passed, someone at the end of the street turned the Christmas tree lights back on.

He sat on the bed with a thud and thought about the war. The United States had lost in Bataan, won in the Coral Sea, lost again in Corregidor. He thought about the trains that brought the war prisoners from the West Coast and the ones that brought the dead bodies home. He sank back wide awake. The ceiling only spun if he closed his eyes. He heard the door to Dutch's room squeak open, then close, and a woman giggling.

Pinkey listened. "I thought you was up to the picture show," he yelled into the other room without moving his head from the pillow.

The sounds stopped. Pinkey's eyes moved like hard globes. He took another swig. Now the sounds were muffled. He heard a bed creak and laughter and a low groan. He lay motionless. Now the muffled laughter exploded into a hissing sigh.

"You bitch," he whispered. His face stiffened the way it had before he was sick in the alley with his son watching; then it went soft and tears stood in his reddened eyes.

In the morning a fog covered the town. It was so thick Pinkey could not see the grocery store across the street. He heard the 10:10 pull in and depart and wondered how many more coffins had been unloaded.

"Look," he said, meaning his hands. They were shaking. Dutch had come in the room and Pinkey asked for a shave.

Dutch held the straight razor at an angle to Pinkey's jaw and pulled against the graying whiskers with uneven strokes. The fog was not a solid thing but, like self-hate, sank and once in a while, pulled apart as if to let in fresh air. One of those times Pinkey saw Willard traipse across the street toward the boardinghouse. Then he saw Carol Lyman's black coupe pull up and Carol, eyeless behind dark glasses, stand by the car, put two fingers in her mouth and whistle, and after, Willard run out and climb in.

It was more frozen air than a true coastal fog. And so heavy, it wrapped tree limbs and lampposts in frost. Pinkey had seen that Willard's willow branch had turned white. It glistened like sequins threaded together and tied in a knot at one end.

Dutch shaved the other side of Pinkey's face, then the upper lip and chin.

"Do you think we'll make green grass?" he asked.

"Hell, my crystal ball's broke," Pinkey said.

"You know, I get tired of town sooner than I used to," Dutch said.

"Ouch." Pinkey wiped a spot of blood from his chin. "I'm ugly enough without you adding to it."

". . . to where I don't even know if it's worth coming into town at all anymore," Dutch continued.

"Not even for last night?" Pinkey asked, grinning.

Dutch left his hand, the one holding the straight razor, suspended in air.

"Well you . . ." He stopped, embarrassed, then finished up the shave. "I guess two old men like us only deserve one girl."

Pinkey remembered Loretta's breasts. Then the fog was not of a piece but rolled into muscular forms that flattened out quickly. Her breasts were like clouds wound tightly by strong winds above the mountains, Pinkey thought, and smooth. Smooth.

Dutch stood back to examine his shaving job while Pinkey touched the left side of his face, then the right. He wanted to look in the mirror but was too weak to stand. He had made love to Loretta sometime during the night; that much he remembered. She had come into his room from Dutch's and when she climbed into his bed he asked her if she wasn't Dutch's girl and she said, "I'm no one's girl," which was the same as saying "I'm everyone's girl," as if it made any difference, as if we could own anything—a piece of land, a dog, the weather, even bodies which form so slowly in someone else's body and come apart so fast in front of a gun.

Now he remembered how she had leaned in toward him. He could have lit a match with her breath. The moles on her chest looked like hailstones coming fast and her too-black hair bent sharply under as if recoiling from the strength in her shoulders. He had drawn her closer until he could not tell where his body stopped and hers began and thought how all opposites come to nearly the same thing: how a hailstone like a hardball can knock you out with its coming; how her pendulous breasts, clanging together like buoy bells, could make him deaf; how her banking into him—an undulation of fog—was like not being able to see. When he woke she was gone.

11

The first funeral for a boy killed in the Pacific had to be moved up a day because the ground had started to freeze and the gravediggers didn't want to open the grave with pickaxes unless they had to. It was December and an arctic front had pushed down from British Columbia. There had been snows and thaws all fall but cold that came to stay smelled different, McKay thought as he filed by the boy's gold coffin, like a rubbed flint and the sparks were snow.

He had looked in the mirror that morning when he was naked and shivering and saw how skinny he was, as if life were a subtractive process, not an additive one.

"I know life is supposed to be a great thing but I can't shape it to my liking," he had written to his brother Ted. "Any advice?" He could feel the letter in his breast pocket as he shook hands with the boy's family after the last graveside prayer. He had added, "Nothing new here. You know how November and December are. I'm like a fish on ice. I'm already tired of winter and of national pride that feeds on world ruin and winter hasn't even happened yet. Girlwise, I'm no better off than you probably are. I continue what Mother called 'my questionable practice' of sleeping with the dog. I suppose that for someone like Champ, going to war maps out one's life for a while, or forever, but why follow a map that leads to hell. Hell's right here at home, and Pinkey would say, 'Ain't it lovely?' "

On the way home McKay stopped off at Snuff's. He always stopped there before weddings and after funerals. The desolate look of the place cleansed him, the way certain foods clean the palate.

"I'll have a shot of that Cobb's Creek," McKay said.

"You mean out of Pinkey's bottle. . . . He'll be mad," Snuff said and winked. His untied bow tie hung around his neck and the front of his white shirt was wet from washing glasses.

"Yea, Pinkey just bought me a drink only he isn't here to pay." Snuff smiled as he filled the shot glass. Restless, drink in hand, McKay swung off the bar stool. He was wearing one of his father's tweed jackets and it was too big for him through the shoulders. The bar smelled of ammonia and for a moment McKay couldn't get his breath.

"A funeral's a hell of a thing to go to first thing in the morning," Snuff remarked. His boney hands were covered with soapsuds.

McKay walked to the back door and yanked it open. On the other side Carol Lyman's eyes met his. She was bent over the Wild Man, scissors in hand. A mass of thick hair lay strewn on the ground and in the sagebrush and the snow that had begun to fall an hour before when the pallbearers lowered the coffin into the hardening ground, covered it.

"Hello, stranger, need a trim?"

"Hello, Carol. You taken up barbering now?"

"He needed it bad."

"I'll say," McKay said. He couldn't look at Carol without thinking of the day his parents drowned and he didn't want to think about that now. Something else pulled at him. He turned back to the bar.

"Hey, Snuffy, would you drop this in the mail for me; I've got to get home," McKay said. He wanted to get out of there and he had forgotten to mail the letter to Ted in town.

"Will do."

"And put that Cobb's Creek on Pinkey's tab, goddamn it, not the ranch's."

Snuff laughed because he knew it came out to the same thing.

A week before Christmas, Abe-san invited McKay to the Camp's Christmas party. When he arrived, an Issei Santa Claus gave out gifts to the children. The Santa was an old man with a narrow face, so skinny, the costume fell in folds from his neck, but his eyes shone and he squeaked in delight with the children.

After refreshments there was an art show: flower arrangements by the ikebana club; charcoal drawings of Camp life by Estelle Ishigo, a Caucasian who had relocated with her Nisei husband; and Mariko's "Fifty-two Views of Heart Mountain," in the style of Hiroshige, a card said.

McKay was not prepared for what he saw when he came to Mariko's work. The paintings were ink washes on smooth, double-folded paper that accordioned out into a scroll. The images themselves were a kind of blank composed of only a few brushstrokes. Yet, something strong appeared in the emptiness. She had used yellow, blue, and black ink and a tenacious softness washed over the desolate landscape rendered there.

Some of the views were imagined—parts of the mountain she had never seen, like the alluvial fans above his ranch. In one, the mountain soared beyond the picture frame. Only its midsection could be seen. Yet no other image had given a sense of the mountain's wholeness in quite this way, McKay thought. Another view showed the top of a waterfall. How had she known there was one behind his ranch? A wide swatch of water cascaded over the rock. Almost the whole painting was a vertical tongue of water.

The last five were not landscapes but Camp scenes. Heart Mountain was included, the view straight down the long rows of barracks, its blunt peak barely inked in. In the foreground of another painting three women, dressed as courtesans, appeared to be playing samisens, but when McKay looked more closely, he saw they were holding machine guns.

After, the Buddhist and Christian children gave a joint pageant. Joseph, Mary, and the Buddha all slept at the same inn, a *ryokan*. In the crush of people McKay had not been able to find Mariko. He sat on a hard folding chair next to Mr. Abe and when the play was over, he rode home.

An antelope heart is not big. No bigger than a man's fist and in some light it shines. McKay had saddled his "long circle" horse before dawn and ridden the old mail trail south along the creek lined with house-sized boulders. He thought of the day the finches and pine siskins had passed through the ranch, down from the high mountains. How slender their necks looked as they balanced on thick stalks and reached across the emptiness—the same emptiness Mariko's paintings were about—for seed. Now he heard only the three-note whistle of the red-tailed hawk and the wind, less fitful but more labored, bringing winter in.

The wind, having shifted away from the north, was in his favor and with binoculars, he glassed the small band as he rode the edge of the juniper. Finally, he picked out a dry doe and got off his horse. He pulled his rifle from the scabbard—slowly, as if there were no such thing as motion or gravity—then stepped out in front of the trees and fired, a 250-yard shot.

The antelope that fell had been drinking. She lurched forward on her knees, then tilted her head to one side as if trying to see down into the earth where the dead go. When McKay reached her, he could see where her black horn had carved a crescent shape in the dirt. Heart Mountain rose amid spears of gold light and the mountains behind, the Beartooths, were the color of wild plums. After he gutted out the antelope he held the heart in one hand and traced the route of the main artery with his finger. The thought of the steady, racing pump as the antelope ran, mouth opened to the wind, made him want Mariko.

McKay covered the carcass with cedar boughs, then tipped his horse into a trot, not north toward the ranch, but south again, out onto a long terrace of land that overlooked the relocation camp. He rode hard and when it started getting dark he closed his eyes. The thought of winter, of whiteness unobstructed, made him feel sick. What the hell was he doing way out here at dinnertime, he wondered. He opened his eyes. There was a white flash. Then he saw: the lights in the guard towers had been switched on.

Loneliness does not originate in one particular thing, an old Japanese poem his mother had taught him began. He could not remember the rest. Evening came over the pines on the mountain, inking them black. There were no leaves on the trees so the wind modulated a sky suspended between sunset and moonrise and McKay knew he had come to see, no, to behold Mariko.

He did not ride directly to the front gate but instead turned north and west away from it. He circled the entire camp once. It was dark and he could see into some of the barracks: framed lives like cartoon strips of people who shouldn't be there, but on their farms and fishing boats and stores. Where the fence drew near the living quarters, the mass of lights stunned McKay. His pulse raced. He felt as if the path made by the fence builders around the Camp were a drug, a black vein. This is the way a hyena circles, or a bachelor coyote kicked out of the den. Was it that or a pilgrimage? He thought of the Mexican *penitentes* he had seen as a child walking on their knees and the bits of flesh left behind on the steps of the cathedral, and of the first time he had made love, wrapped in a canvas dam in a dry irrigation ditch, how his face had rubbed into the red dirt on the side of the ditch. A clod had fallen into his open mouth and he had laughed as the taste of it mingled with the taste of Madeleine.

She had called him from Omaha. The calves had sold fine and she said she wanted to stay on and visit her parents if she wasn't needed at the ranch. When she asked McKay how he was, he had replied, "I'm fine. I'm great. I'm like a fish on ice"—the same thing he had told his brother.

In her absence, in everyone's absence, McKay and Bobby had taken to eating *oyaku donburi* for breakfast every morning. The *donburi* was made of chicken, scallions, and eggs sautéed in shoyu and sake, put over rice in a bowl. "A meal in a bowl" it was called. They washed it down with more sake than they needed so early in the morning, but they didn't care because it was the only way to bridge the gap between Ted's letters, the long wait for word about Henry, and Madeleine's return.

McKay thought about the day Madeleine came home with Henry on her arm. "My husband," she announced. McKay thought it was a joke being played on him. But the look of elation and discomfort in Henry's eyes told him something different.

"How could you?" McKay asked. "Without me?"

In the months to come he and Henry grew close. They rode colts together and in the summer, when the rodeos began, Henry heeled while McKay headed steers in team roping. "I love you, you sonofabitch, but only because you love Madeleine," McKay told him.

The three of them went to dances together. McKay and Henry took turns cutting in on each other. The time they drove home in a blizzard and went off the road, the three of them had to bundle up in two sleeping bags zipped together until morning.

"Don't you think there can be too much of a good thing?" Henry quipped. Madeleine laughed but McKay poked his head out into the frosty air and in a solemn voice whispered, "No."

McKay slowed the colt to a walk as he neared the buildings. A heavy carapace had come down on him, front and back like a hard chitinous shell and under it he felt his heart beating and the cold trickle of antelope blood on his chest. He kicked his horse into a trot.

A smell rose from the path. No. It came from a vent in the mess hall— a smell of beef hearts stewing. He thought of Mariko's feet. Now he couldn't even think of what her face looked like, but her feet were cloven hooves and she could run, open-mouthed, like an antelope, to or from him—either way.

He rode south toward the gate. Pools of light lay on the rough ground. As McKay approached, a man's voice boomed out in the darkness.

"Stop where you are."

Now the light reeled in McKay's direction and he kicked his colt into a lope.

"Harry, you bastard, it's me," he yelled.

There was a burst of rifle fire over his head.

"Stop where you are."

McKay's horse made a sliding stop and he dismounted hurriedly.

"Harry, you bastard, is that you up there?"

"Who's there?" a voice shouted sternly.

"Stop shooting and look."

"Name, please." The man shone a flashlight in McKay's face.

"Who the hell do you think it is?"

The guard leaned over the railing of the tower. "Well, you SOB . . . why didn't you tell me it was . . ."

"Shit, you must need a hearing aid. And you always did need glasses."

"I didn't hear anything but that horse."

"That's because you were too busy shooting."

"Well you could have let me know you were coming."

"The walkie-talkie on my pony's broke."

"McKay, what are you doing out here at this time of night?"

"Need to see someone."

"Jesus, you're goofier than ever."

"You're still a lousy shot."

Harry, the guard, descended the stairs from the tower. At the bottom he squatted on the ground beside McKay and whispered conspiratorially.

"What can I do for you, McKay?"

McKay looked his old high school friend in the eye. "Harry, I need to get into this sonofabitch," he said, motioning beyond the wire.

"I can't do that for you. Visiting hours are over."

"You can damn well look the other way."

Harry stared at the cold ground and drove a stick through the dust. "Jesus."

McKay stood impatiently.

Harry stood too and rubbed his forehead wearily. "Okay, I'll write you out a pass."

"Thanks, Harry," McKay said and handed him the colt's reins. He turned his back, unbuttoned his pants and relieved himself. Then he stepped through the wire.

"Hey, wait. I've got to give you your pass."

"Keep the paperwork for me. I'll just lose it," McKay said, grinning in the dark.

The colt nudged Harry's arm. "Hey, is this the colt bucked me off last spring?"

"Yea, but he's copacetic now. You can ride him."

"You lyin' bastard."

McKay walked in the direction of Mariko's barrack. It was dark now and the ground was rough and he didn't have a flashlight. He wished he had taken the flask off the saddle. Hell, Harry's probably drinking out of it or maybe he's gotten too damned righteous for that, he thought, and walked on unsteadily.

On a little rise above the barracks, he came on two lovers silhouetted by the lights. Their heads moved together, then apart. He called out. They stood abruptly and straightened their clothes. When McKay limped toward them, they ran. He sat where they had been necking and thought he could still feel the warmth of their bodies in the dirt. That morning he had read in the papers about Guadalcanal and the fight to keep Henderson Field and wondered what it was like to be there, at close range, under fire. The lights below looked like an airbase. McKay imagined walking down to the landing strip, climbing in a plane, radioing the tower for takeoff. He would fly over dark water dotted with ships, yes, Japanese ships, and for once the errant bomb that for some time had been flying beside him would be stashed underneath, neat and tidy in the belly of the plane until he let it drop, and once he had sent it plunging, the air would suddenly feel light—light as a summer night in Wyoming— and he would be dead.

As McKay walked between the barracks his chest pounded and he wondered if he was having a heart attack. He didn't care. A door slammed and opened again and he saw Will Okubo storming out of the last apartment and Mariko standing there. She didn't see McKay at first, then her eyebrows lifted straight up into the middle of her forehead with an elegance and innocence he had not expected. She grabbed McKay's hand and pulled him into the doorway.

"Why are they shooting? Who are they shooting at?"

"Me. But I know the guy. He's a lousy shot anyway," McKay said nonchalantly and smiled.

"They shot an old man in another Camp last week. He was looking for arrowheads."

McKay looked at her. She was still holding his hand. He could smell her French perfume. He felt as if the errant bomb which had been following him all these days was *her* body—the slim hard torso moving close, then keening away like the hull of a boat, a hull of desire.

The evening breeze that had inked the pines black lifted her hair. Then his head was under it, his lips against her neck, and they were turning in a circle away from the door and he heard the whistle of a distant train coming closer, the train bringing Madeleine home—a Christmas Eve surprise—and forgot about it when Mariko's strong painter's fingers pressed into his back like dowels and he felt the length of her body against him. And once, when he opened his eyes, he saw the Northern Star.

"Why are you here?" she gasped.

McKay reached into his pocket, badly stained with blood now. He felt the firm, slippery muscle—not his own, but the antelope heart—and, holding it in the palm of his hand, presented it to her.

12

The night before Madeleine boarded the train for Wyoming after a month away she bit her tongue so hard in her sleep, there was blood on the pillow in the morning. Henry had come to her in a dream. He was sitting on a stool with one leg crossed over the other, talking to her. He said he had tried to make arrangements to see her but there wasn't time; he had to go somewhere. Outside, planes were flying up a narrow canyon and crashing into a rock wall. When she saw him next he was naked, standing by a window with his back to her. Then he turned around and said he couldn't watch those planes; he couldn't look anymore. She always called Henry her little monkey because he wasn't tall and whenever she woke from nightmares, he made faces until she smiled.

In the morning she pulled all the shades in her parents' big house and sat on the floor of the closet where her prom dress still hung. She counted—the number of letters in Henry's name, the number of days, weeks, months since she had taken the train to Omaha, then gone to

Kansas City, where her parents lived. Their house was built high on a hill overlooking the river. At seven, her mother came into the darkened room. "I'll make you some hot milk," she said upon seeing her daughter curled up on the closet floor.

"I feel like a bum calf when you do this to me," Madeleine said and when her mother said, "What?" Madeleine said, "Never mind."

The house was decorated for Christmas with a spruce that touched the living room ceiling and a gingerbread house and silver bowls in the shape of shells filled with ribbon candy.

"Everyone's waiting for someone," Madeleine's mother continued. "And everyone's waiting for this dreadful war to end. Remember, you're not the only one."

When the Rocky Mountains came into view, Madeleine was sitting in the dining car of the train. A waiter served her a sliced chicken sandwich and a single rose shook in its silver vase. The triangular shape of Long's Peak looked like geometry: she was on the south end, Henry was west, McKay north.

She thought of Henry, his green eyes, the one deep line that traversed his forehead and funneled sweat to his temples. It had been a year. Her parents thought she had married down. They asked for what she called "his pedigree." She told them he didn't have one but he made her laugh and had a feel for livestock and was gentle with her and could raise animals from the dead. That hadn't been enough to satisfy them but she was married to Henry anyway on a weekend by a justice of the peace who had given them a speeding ticket on the way into town.

When her father asked what had happened to McKay, she had answered, "Nothing, he just didn't ask me to marry him, that's all." As the train moved toward Long's Peak, she thought of the way Henry's chest felt against hers, the back of his neck, his knees, but every time—as if an electric wire had jogged her memory the wrong way—she saw McKay.

In the tiled bathroom of the Denver train station, where she had to change trains, Madeleine took stock of herself. Everywhere around her were men and women in uniform: WACs and WAVEs, army nurses and medics, men in the infantry, air corps, sailors and navy flyers. . . . She wore brown gabardine riding pants, a white shirt, cowboy boots, and the belt buckle she won roping with McKay in high school. When she leaned forward to put on lipstick, the tube dropped to the floor. The tip, shaped to the contour of her lips, chipped off. A woman in a WAC uniform stepped on it by accident and a woman holding a crying baby who had probably never seen its father bumped into her from the behind. Madeleine walked out the door.

Outside she gazed north. One side of Long's Peak was flattened and bright with sun on snow. The air was crisp. She took a deep breath. She might have been going to see Henry but where do you go to see a man missing in action, she wondered, then walked out to the platform where the train to Wyoming awaited her.

"How do I look, honey?" Loretta twirled around in front of Dutch and Pinkey at the train station. She was wearing wool trousers and a white shirt with the scarf Pinkey had bought for her at the dime store.

"You don't look like a honky-tonk cowgirl no more," Dutch said a little wistfully.

She pressed against him. "Keep it buttoned up, okay?" she said, placing her hand flat against his fly.

"What about me?" Pinkey asked just as the steam engine came down on them with a deafening roar.

"You, too," she yelled to Pinkey, fumbling nervously in her purse for the ticket.

They walked her to her car. A Negro porter descended the steps, looked at her ticket, and directed her inside. Pinkey stared at the man: his eyes glittered and the inside of his mouth looked like bleeding flesh. Pinkey couldn't remember the last time he had seen a black man. It made him smile to think he had seen so much of life, even here, in Luster. "I'm getting plumb cultivated," he thought.

Loretta hung out the window and let her arm down to the two men. She looked uncertain about her decision to leave. Pinkey noticed the way her breasts filled her white blouse as she leaned. He wanted to touch them one last time.

"Will you miss me?" Loretta asked.

"You bet we will," Pinkey volunteered. "We'll be true. Hell, I can feel myself turning back into a virgin already."

Dutch laughed nervously as the train clunked forward. The sky had a smothered look and steam from the engine added to it. Loretta threw a kiss and the train that brought Madeleine home for Christmas took Loretta away.

Madeleine stood on the end of the platform with her slicker over her arm, clutching her vet bag. Some of the men nodded as they walked by, assuming that McKay would be there to pick her up. But no one came.

"Hello, you little heifer."

Madeleine wheeled around, then gave Pinkey a hug.

Pinkey looked over his shoulder at Dutch. "See how easy it is: out of the arms of one, into the arms of another."

"Oh shut up, Pinkey," Madeleine said. "Are you giving me a ride to the ranch? Where's McKay?"

Pinkey studied her for a moment, then pushed his hat back on his head. "Don't know where McKay is. Hard to say these days."

"We'll give you a ride if you find us an outfit to drive," Dutch volunteered.

"Yea, let's steal us a nice Caddy," Pinkey mumbled.

A black coupe swerved in alongside the platform and Carol Lyman put on her dark glasses, then came around to the front of her car.

"Need a ride, Madeleine?"

She picked up Madeleine's suitcase and hoisted it into the trunk and the two women drove off. "Merry Christmas," Madeleine heard Pinkey yell, and looked out the window. It had been fall when she left and now the country was covered with snow.

"Where's McKay?" she asked.

"Busy I guess," Carol said flatly as the car pulled away from the station, north through town.

"What's new around here since I've been gone?"

Carol thought for a moment. "There's been a funeral, for that Dickens boy; McKay said he'd gotten two letters from Ted, nothing from Champ, of course. Anything from Henry?"

"No," Madeleine replied and looked at her driver. Carol sat very straight when she drove. Her dark glasses were on the dashboard and from time to time, she touched them, folding the bows back, or held them in her hand on the seat.

"How's McKay?" Madeleine asked.

"Don't you know?"

"What do you mean?"

"Oh, I just thought you would know more than I do. . . . Well . . . he's been awfully damned nervous. Just looks kind of upset all the time; of course, that's been since the shooting."

"What shooting?"

Carol looked at her again, then back at the road. "Oh . . . thought you knew . . . shot a Jap. Really tore him up pretty bad."

"Tore who up?"

"Oh, not the Jap . . . he's an old man . . . just wandered off and McKay's bullet grazed him."

"God," Madeleine said.

"Just a scrape really. Lost some blood. Carried that old man on his back for miles. . . ."

Madeleine rolled the window down. The closed car made her feel sick. She looked out at the familiar landscape—the one paved street of brick and frame houses giving way to grain and hay fields, and those to rangeland studded with sage.

"Sometimes when you've been away and come back, everything looks so big . . . so much bigger than I remembered . . . kind of empty almost. . . ."

"Things always look that way," Carol said.

13

Before everyone came back that night—everyone being Pinkey and McKay—Bobby lit the candles on the Christmas tree. It was a tall cedar McKay had cut in the draw above the heifer pasture and dragged in behind his rope horse. Bobby lay down on the rug under it. It would be a long night, and, expecting no one, he let his mind wander. The room was dark and he thought looking up into the lighted tree was like looking into a city—each light was a room with a stranger inside.

The last year Bobby cooked for the railroad crews, when he was thirty-nine, he spent a Christmas Eve like this one alone in a section car. It had been put off on a siding near Laramie and when the other men went into town, Bobby stayed behind. He remembered lying on his bunk looking out at the foot of snow that had fallen and blown into hard drifts against the car. Once a train passed on the other track and a long time after the whistle sound dissipated, a man knocked on the door and stepped inside.

Bobby knew the man. He delivered groceries to the railroaders every week, mailed their letters, bought their cigarettes, advised them on where to go to get girls when they went to town. He was young but his face had weathered and he had pale red hair. The diamond ring on his finger shone in the window light. Bobby had known him only to say hello, though the man had brought Bobby special treats—a cake from the bakery and a bottle of whiskey on occasion. Bobby was pleased by the visit. The man set a small gift on the table between them.

"It's Christmas Eve," he said quietly. That was all.

Bobby made coffee and they sat for a long time while the red-haired man smoked nervously. He informed Bobby of some of the local news— a restaurant that had burned down, an illegitimate baby, and so on. Bobby liked the way the smoke curled up one side of the man's face and tangled in his hair. In the dark, the red tip of the cigarette moved like a wand, carving designs that vanished between them.

He asked Bobby about Japan, what the rooms looked like, and Bobby told him of the kimonos and the baths and the Osaka wharves. Then the visitor told how he had been born in a sheep wagon on the edge of town during a blizzard that killed a hundred ewes and lambs as well as the camptender. After, his father had gone on a two-year binge and later, his mother was committed to the state institution.

"I was really raised by the herders," he said. "And I was born on Christmas Eve. So you see . . ."

The gas lamp flickered as the man spoke, as if taking breaths between words. It made the narrow car seem to move again, clicking over tracks, and Bobby wished his friend a happy birthday.

At midnight the man asked Bobby to open the package. It wasn't much, he warned. Inside was a silk scarf. Not the kind the cowboys wore, but patterned, with bars of silver and blue, like the sky, Bobby thought, and he tied it around his neck. When he stood to adjust the lamp, the red-haired man jumped abruptly to his feet, grabbing Bobby by the waist. Bobby didn't move, and when he looked up, the man closed his eyes and turned his head away.

"What's wrong?" Bobby asked in a small voice.

The man didn't reply. They just stood that way for some time.

The man's hands finally dropped. Quickly he unfastened Bobby's trousers and let them fall. He clasped his hands at the small of Bobby's back where it felt so warm and pressed his cheek to him.

They lay together on the floor of the section car with the gas lamp faltering, naked except for Bobby's long scarf. Another train passed. Its whistle sounded like something green, Bobby thought, and the trembling he had felt in his own body seemed to spread everywhere now. The silverware in the drawer above their heads rattled.

He couldn't remember whether they slept then but he remembered remembering: the time his parents had taken him on a boat down the Inland Sea of Japan. The first night, the son of a samurai practiced swordplay up and down the decks and on either side, the lanterns of tiny villages glowed, and the next day, when they reached the southern island of Kyushu, he saw the single spray of steam from a hot spring jetting into the frigid air.

On the way home from the Camp, McKay put his colt into a steady, even trot. The horse wove a path through the sagebrush until he came to the creek that divided the Camp from the ranch. He stopped when he saw the water. It had frozen and thawed and a middle strip of blue water showed under the thinnest pane of ice. The colt lowered his head and snorted, then balked. McKay worked him up and down, backing and turning and bringing him forward to the crossing again, letting him smell the frozen water. Finally the colt stuck his neck out, almost pulling the rein from McKay's gloved hand, and leapt over the creek like a jaguar, McKay thought, because he had seen one do that in Mexico when he was a boy, and when the colt came down on the other side he kept running. McKay squeezed him hard with his left knee and turned the colt uphill and let him run until he wasn't scared anymore. Near the top of the hill the colt stopped. McKay backed him a few steps, gave him a loose rein, then turned him toward home.

It was night. In the breaks, the pine tree tops creaked. The day before Christmas Eve merged in his mind with Christmas Eve, because he had been going back and forth to the Camp so often. A train whistle shrilled across the open space. He would be too late to pick up Madeleine, he thought, a little ashamed.

When he reached the corral, his horse was wet with sweat and the long hairs of his winter coat were frosted. McKay lit the Coleman lantern and hung it from the saddle shed. Then he pulled the saddle and rubbed the horse down with a clean towel and began walking him.

The three bright stars of Orion's belt rose and the long tail of Eridanus hung down over the Camp—over Mariko's head. The lantern swung and McKay and the horse moved in and out of its stirring light.

When he stopped to feel the horse's chest, he saw the lights on the tree inside the house. Bobby must have lit them. It was Christmas Eve after all, he decided. He wondered whether Madeleine had gone straight home. The lantern's constant whirring sound sputtered as it ran out of fuel, and when he put the horse away, the lantern faded slowly like the fade at one of Harry Vermeer's movies. McKay looked up. A single falling star seemed to come right at him, then opened out into a reddish gold glow and vanished. "Well this sure as hell ain't Bethlehem," he said aloud to the sky. His spurs rang as he walked to the house.

14

As if it mattered. His screened porch felt more like a cell than the Camp did to him. He could not see the Camp from there, only the flare of lights like the sun's corona. When the screens were wet they smelled like rotting mineral. Extreme cold had taken all the other fragrances away.

He had received another letter from his brother Ted, who said he had been transferred to a converted hospital ship and had seen so much dying going on, he had forgotten that the human body is capable of giving birth. The lagoon reeked of decomposed flesh. He wanted McKay to know that he was all right and that no new news had been learned about Henry. Then he added a postscript. One of his friends from the Stanford Army Medical Unit heard from his wife that she was leaving him. He jumped down the stairs at the hospital in Palermo. "He would have been the best doctor of all of us," Ted said. "He had the biggest heart. But then again, that quality might have made him unsuitable for the job."

McKay lay on his cot. His head felt as if it were unraveling. He had circled the Camp like the bituminous raven, gliding for days on a single wing beat. The people in the Camp slept on cots too, though they'd had to make their own mattresses by stuffing straw into ticking cases. He knew, because he had provided the straw.

Just after Christmas word got around that he was visiting the granddaughter of the man he had shot. Someone wrote him a hate letter which expressed shock at the idea that he had "allowed an intimacy to develop with a dirty Jap." After he read it, he held the paper with a gloved hand and stuffed it into the cook stove to burn.

Now McKay stood with his hip pressed against the cold screen and thought of how Mariko had hated him at first, then turned inexplicably toward him. Sometimes the fierceness of their attraction made everything go black, as if burnt, or else it was a black thing tunneling through ordinary air. He thought passion was like war. It was weightless and heavy at the same time. It became a catch in the breath every breath and left a long wake and widening rings of concentric circles as if to mark the place where a rock had sunk in a lake or a trout had surfaced.

He thought of the day tears broke from Mariko's eyes and fell down the side of her face into her ears and how he had caught them with both his fingers and tasted the tears. At that moment the carapace broke. He saw it float from him. It had not been anything like a tortoise shell, but metallic, the outer skin of the errant bomb that had come too close and held him rigid all those days.

Now Christmas was over. Later that week Pinkey went to work again cleaning the calving barn and Bobby pointed out the ridge where he wanted his ashes buried when he died—above the ranch on the flank of Heart Mountain, the very ridge where McKay watched the elk walk single file almost dutifully, down the frozen creek bed that divided the ranch from the Camp into the year nineteen hundred and forty-three.

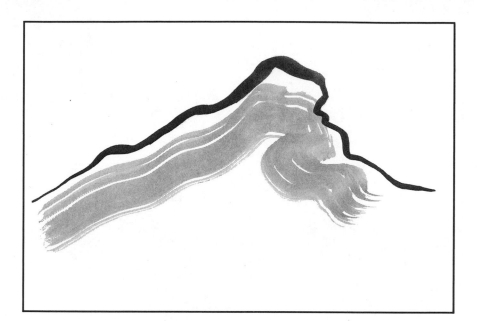

PART TWO
1943

What is this flooding me, childhood or manhood . . .
and the hunger that crosses the bridge in between?
—Walt Whitman

15

To hell with everything, that's my New Year's resolution. I'm a different person than I was, with an altered destiny, but who cares? My interest in history has taken a political bent, and swimming, which was my discipline, my art so to speak, has been beached for a while. I've gotten a good, strong dose of my Japanese heritage, but really, what's there to celebrate? A year of war in the Pacific, a year of legalized racism, a year in a concentration camp.

After too much sake, I sacked out at Ben's. In the morning went "home." Mom and Pop were sitting together on the edge of the bed. I knew something funny was going on when they asked me to sit down. Boy, oh boy, did they drop a bomb on me. "Your father has something to tell you," Mom began. Pop cleared his throat and began speaking without looking at me. "You have older brother we never tell you about," he said. "He's in Army Air Corps. He fly twenty-six mission so far in Europe and North Africa. We just find that out too. He ask us to tell you, so we tell you, now."

I sat down on a stool in front of them. Mom was wringing her hands. I couldn't talk for a long time. Everything around me shut down and all I could hear were the words "You have a brother." Finally, I tried out his name: "Kenny."

I have a brother. Stephen Kai Nakamura has a brother. I'm not an orphan; I'm not an only child.

It's useless asking Issei questions, even my own parents. They just grunt or look away. I flew off the handle, picked up a stool and smashed it against a bed. Mom screamed something in Japanese. I stopped thrashing about and looked at her. "Why have you done this to me?" I asked.

This afternoon they showed me a picture. Kenny sure doesn't look like me. He's smaller and leaner. He's the only Nisei flier in the whole country and here I am, an "enemy alien" locked away. When I asked Mom how I was different from Kenny she said, "You're both smart, but he's not cocky."

Went to the latrine in the middle of the night, sat on the can and cried.

The next day I tried to stay calm but it's just too much to take in at one time.

Fixed the stool I broke. Pop even helped me and finally we were able to talk. I asked them why they had sent their two sons away to be raised by strangers. What was wrong with what they had to offer? Mom cried and cried, then Pop spoke. He told me how poor they were when we came along, and afraid for us. They weren't treated well in California—"Things were done to us, or behind our backs, and we want you to be real Americans," he said. "To own land and become citizen and to speak without accent. How could you have that living in a shack with them, in a household where only Japanese was spoken?"

"I wouldn't have cared," I said.

Kenny is a turret gunner on a "Liberator"—that's a plane. According to the casualty lists, turret gunners don't last very long. They sit in the tail with a gun, very exposed. Will I ever meet him? Maybe it would have been better never to have known of his existence. But Mom keeps saying he has a lucky charm—an Issei wives' tale—something about tiny holes behind his ears that indicate a charmed life. "He'll live," Mom says. But I'm not counting on that or anything.

We have a small library here and I've been reading Defoe on the plague,

The Narrow Journey to the Deep North *by Basho, Samuel Pepys, some World War I journals, and Ernie Pyle. All my ideas of history have broken apart. Aren't diarists really historians and aren't historians really failed novelists?*

These thoughts—while stuffing myself on Li's New Year's box full of my favorite foods: cookies, dried ginger, panettone, jasmine tea. The accompanying letter was less bountiful. It went something like this: "How are you? I am fine. Jimmy Wong says to come home; he has a job for you." But what the hell. War is war and absence does not make the heart grow fonder. Shared the food with the usual gang—Ben Iwasaka, Emi, Mariko, Will, Abe-san, and Mom and Pop. We sat in a circle on the floor by the stove and ate and drank tea until there was no more. I told everyone about Kenny. Odd feelings overtake me when I talk about him. I'm not "me" anymore; I'm someone's brother.

The next day, the talk at work was about the Nisei girl found screwing an MP in the linen closet. We had a good laugh imagining the look of the Issei who opened the door on them. The MP jumped up and pulled his gun. The old woman ran, and the girl buried her head in the towels and screamed. If this is consorting with the "enemy," who cares? C'est la guerre. . . . He was probably a nice guy. Harry something . . . No, I'm lying. He's probably a cad and she's a lost little girl, and he's ruined her.

Afterward, a committee approached the administration with a proposal for a red light district. The idea was met with scorn. Yet it's true—things have gotten out of hand around here: illegitimate births, etc. Like all prisoners, we find that our hungers intensify and we do almost anything to satisfy them.

Later. I've retreated to the latrine again because the lights are on all night and I can't sleep. Mom told me stories about when Kenny was a baby and I feel I'm getting to know him. But I've had this crazy thought too: maybe everything they say is a lie; maybe there is no Kenny; maybe I'm not their son.

Took off all my clothes and got in the shower. As soon as that warm water hit me, I began to cry—not out of sadness, but rage. I banged my fists against the shower wall. Who am I angry at? I wondered. At my parents, at society for not accepting us, at myself for all the bitterness that's in me?

Something caught my eye and I turned. It was Abe-san. "Why are you wasting water when you have so much in here?" he yelled, pointing to my eyes.

I turned the water off and stood naked before him. He just smiled and walked away.

January 23. The weather seems to be mimicking the calendar. It's the twenty-third of January and it's twenty-three below zero tonight. Went to bed early because it was the only way to get warm. Mariko woke me. In whispers, she ordered me to get dressed so I put on all the clothes I could find and followed her outside. Then I saw for myself what the excitement was all about. The Northern Lights filled half the sky. It was mesmerizing. Thick rays shot up like church spires, and an intersecting cloud pulsed with color so that the ceiling of the sky slanted low over us— but it was all a mass of gases, nothing solid. Will and Abe-san came out and the four of us huddled together, our necks craning. . . . Isn't it odd that such extravagant, otherworldly beauty goes hand in hand with desolation.

January 28. Today, Secretary of War Henry Stimson announced that a special combat unit would be open to Japanese-Americans. How can this be when, after Pearl Harbor, we were all reclassified 4-C, citizens ineligible for military service because of ancestry, then, for those of us in coastal areas, put behind barbed wire? In the next week it's said we will first be required to fill out a questionnaire "to determine our loyalty"—this apparently rigged up from a Navy Intelligence form. Many here were already in the service before Pearl Harbor, then jerked out, and I'm sure others would have gladly volunteered when they came of age, had we not been summarily incarcerated. Perhaps it is us who should be questioning them.

The "leave clearance form" was given out today. A staggering confusion has beset the camp. It's four pages long and poses thirty questions. The purported purpose is to determine who among us is suitable and eligible to leave the Camps on a permanent basis to return to college or work in any one of the inland states. In other words, Uncle Sam wants us off his back, though we're still not "allowed" to return to our coastal homes. Furthermore, I don't think it is a coincidence that the army recruiters are showing up to enlist volunteers into an all-Nisei combat unit.

Two ways of looking at these events has become painfully clear in the last twelve hours. The Sentinel *editorial, called "Vindication," states that the Nisei unit is "an epic milestone in the long uphill battle to reestablish ourselves as Americans."*

Will Okubo and the like are calling it the "Jap-Crow Unit" and the loyalty questionnaire "an insidious trick."

The two crucial questions are as follows:

27—"Are you willing to serve in the Armed Forces of the United States on combat duty whenever ordered?"

28—"Will you swear unqualified allegience to the United States of America and faithfully defend the United States from any or all attack by foreign or domestic forces, and foreswear any form of allegiance or obedience to the Japanese emperor, or to any other foreign government, power, or organization?"

To ask us to answer these questions is adding insult to injury. How can we be prisoners and answer question 27 in the affirmative? And if we answer yes to question 28, it implies we did in fact have an allegiance to Japan which we are now relinquishing.

On top of it all, recruiting officers appeared this afternoon to enlist volunteers into a segregated, all-Nisei combat unit. The message is implicitly clear: in order to get a leave clearance pass and get out of this Camp—even if it means we can't go back to our California homes, which are still off limits—we have to offer ourselves up to be slain.

Got together with Ben and came up with a way to answer the Leave Clearance Form: "Under the present circumstances, I'm unable to answer either question." This, we wrote out as an example for others to use and we pasted them on the mess hall and latrine doors. I think it will help those who are undecided on the issue and feel as Ben and I do, that the government has done us an injustice. How could anyone feel otherwise?

When people saw what we had written out, they began coming to us for advice. It's an outrage to ask young Nisei men to sign up for a war which purports to protect democracy when our own democratic rights have been unconstitutionally withdrawn from us. I told one of them: "If we were let out of these camps and allowed to return home, then I'd be the first one to sign up. I believe in defending my country and I feel it's my duty to do it. But first, we must take a good look at our own government policies before we start throwing stones."

February 1. The Army recruiters have taken over my office and one other at the Sentinel. *Let them have it and we'll show them how little good it will do. I noticed they closed the blinds for fear that the guys who sign up for combat duty will encounter problems with those of us who don't.*

The two questions have split the camp. While standing in line to use the latrine, Joe Fukubata said he'd answered no-no, even though he'd tried to enlist before evacuation. But he's seen how the camps have broken the backs of a lot of guys and now all he wants to do is fight for the rights of those in the Camps. "When I have to give up my life for democracy, I want to see the goddamned thing first," he said.

Many families have one son in Camp, and another son in the army. Others have one son here and another son caught in Japan when war broke out. Pondering all this, I've come to understand the conscientious objector's view as well (though we resistors are only saying no on constitutional grounds, not religious ones). Many people here have close relatives in Japan. For them it comes down to shedding blood. And if shedding the blood of a relative is unthinkable, then shedding the blood of someone else's relative is just as bad. It's simply a matter of the Golden Rule.

February 8. The Sentinel's *editor described the registration-volunteer program as "a forward step to what the great majority of Heart Mountain residents have been striving for since evacuation" and as "an indication of the possibilities now opened following officialdom's change of heart."*

Will and Ben countered the editorial with the formation of something called the "Heart Mountain Congress." Their first act was to send a letter to all other relocation camps telling people that the Japanese American Citizen's League—JACL—whose voice our editor was parroting, did not represent the feelings of the majority. Furthermore, they offered as an option what we've now begun calling "conditional registration," i.e., full restoration of citizenship rights as a precondition to registering and volunteering for the army.

Already, some people are calling our actions "dissident" and "disloyal." "Disloyalty" implies treason, but under the Constitution, the crime of treason is defined very narrowly as "offenses of espionage, sabotage, and seditious conspiracy." Yet, thinking something without acting on it in any way is not a crime. Not a single person of Japanese ancestry has been indicted for a crime of treason since the war began. Even so, the two thousand Issei rounded up immediately after Pearl Harbor and sent to special prison camps—with no evidence on which to make a charge—have since been "paroled" to war relocation camps. Furthermore, we Nisei are constantly referred to as "enemy aliens," "Japanese," and "Japanese aliens," and in the same breath we're now being tricked into giving our lives for "our country."

Saturday. All activities in the Camp have been suspended in order to facilitate registration. The Camp has polarized into little knots of "Yes-Yes" JACLers and "No-No" militants. Bull sessions run all night long every night. In the midst of it all, found myself with Emi. On Iwasaka's advice, went to an empty room in the hospital—since he works in the X-ray room and lets us in, nobody's the wiser. We clung to each other out of mutual desperation—and it was fine.

February 10. Will and some of the other activists have drawn up a petition. Will delivered it as a speech on the eve of registration:

The minds of many of us are still shrouded in doubt and confusion as to the true motives of our government when they invite our voluntary enlistment at the present time. It has not been explained why some American citizens who patriotically volunteered at the beginning of the war were rejected by the army.

Furthermore, our government has permitted damaging propaganda to continue against us. Also she has failed to reinstate us in the eyes of the American public. We are placed on the spot, and our course of action is in the balance scale of justice; for our government's honest interpretation of our stand will mean absolute vindication and admission of the wrong committed. On the other hand, if interpreted otherwise by misrepresentation and misunderstandings, it will amount to renewed condemnation of this group.

Although we have yellow skins, we too are Americans. We have an American upbringing. Therefore, we believe in fair play. Our firm conviction is that we would be useless Americans if we did not assert our constitutional rights now; for unless our status as citizens is cleared and we are really fighting for the high ideas upon which our nation is based, how can we say to the white American buddies in the armed forces that we are fighting for the perpetuation of democracy, especially when our fathers, mothers, and families are in concentration camps, even though they are not charged with any crime?

We believe that our nation's good faith is to be founded on whether it moves to restore full privileges at the earliest opportunity.

Mid-February. Life is always a lot of problems. Mom said she thinks that any Nisei who volunteers will be put on the frontlines and killed off. Now the Kibei, Japanese-Americans educated in Japan, have become a solid anti-WRA group. They go around in little gangs at night and threaten JACLers. Last night someone in another block was beaten up. Pop was so scared he hid under the bed.

We're not the only Camp having trouble. The army and the WRA are pressuring everyone to complete the questionnaire, making threats of twenty years' imprisonment if we don't comply. I abhor this. But I also abhor the news that when an army man showed up at one of the other camps to give a conciliatory talk, the Kibei stood up and sang the Japanese national anthem!

At Tule Lake we heard that many Kibei, Nisei, and Issei lined up at the Internal Security Office to apply for repatriation to Japan. That same week, a whole block refused to register and when the army sent the trucks around to pick them up, they wouldn't board. The agitators were arrested and thrown into a stockade. A minister, reportedly pro-registration, was set upon and severely beaten. Same thing at Gila and Manzanar.

Mom and Pop sat me down tonight to have another talk. I started laughing before they said anything. These "talks" of theirs suddenly struck me as funny. Were they going to tell me I had a sister now? Or were they announcing their intention to repatriate to Japan?

Mom had to get me a glass of water to settle me down. Felt like a kid again. They said I should answer "Yes-Yes" and finish my doctorate, get on with my life and not worry about them anymore. At first I felt pleasant surprise, then distrust. What did they have up their sleeves now? I didn't tell them I had applied to the University of Chicago. I don't feel constrained to tell them my plans—they didn't ask me if I wanted to be raised by strangers.

Woke up in the middle of the night. Went to the latrine. Felt like I was entering some kind of black wave just cresting. Couldn't move my eyes off the ground as I walked. Sitting on the john, realized my feet were numb—stupid me. I had on sandals and there's a foot of snow on the ground.

This Camp has come to symbolize everything I've hated: exile, deviousness, injustice. I've never known bitterness like this. I want to live!

Went back to the apartment and lit a match over Mom's and Pop's heads and just stared at them. They looked like strangers—an old Japanese couple asleep. Nothing they are has anything to do with me. My looks betray who I really am.

16

The day an arctic blast sent the thermometer to thirty degrees below zero,
McKay grained the saddle horses, doctored a sick bull, and soaked an
old gelding's foot in a bucket of warm water and epsom salts for a wire
cut below the pastern. The lake that had thrown up its diamond surface
to him every day, summer and fall, was now a solid block of ice, six
inches thick. He, Bobby, and Pinkey had loaded hay the day before; now
they harnessed the team and fed from the back of the wagon as they
bumped over frozen ground. McKay's breath whitened on his wool scarf
and patches of frostbite appeared on his cheeks like medallions. The
cough that had begun the week before deepened. That afternoon, when
he started back to the ranch after putting the team away, it hurt to breathe.
He held the scarf over his mouth as he walked. Once, he stopped to lean
on a fence post and wondered whether he could make it to the house.
He tried to take shallow breaths. The pain in his lungs felt like heat, a
tissue searing. Inside, he didn't take off his coat or his scarf, rigid with

frost, but lay down on the floor by the cook stove, all the heat escaping above him, and when the scarf finally thawed, drops of water fell from it and froze again on the pine floor.

When McKay woke, he thought Mariko was in the room. Something warm pressed on the small of his back. Was it her hand? Lying on his side, facing a window, he could see the ranch enveloped by snow clouds. Once in a while they broke, like a fever, and pulled apart, and the land sloped up and became Heart Mountain.

The cough intensified. It made everything in his chest break like the rubble of European cities that had been bombed. The rubble rose to his throat and he choked, his mouth open for breath. The clot passed and he lay back and wiped his eyes.

"Madeleine . . ."

"Oh, McKay . . . you're so sick. . . ." She leaned down to him.

"I just can't get warm; that's all." His voice was faint and he suppressed another cough. "When did you get here?"

"Two days ago. I've been sleeping on your floor."

McKay saw his mother's quilt beside the bed. He looked at Madeleine again. "Where have I been?"

She laughed softly. "Right here, in bed. You just don't remember."

McKay closed his eyes. He thought back through the days since he had unharnessed the team, but they did not separate out and come into his head clearly. Mariko had pressed against his back once. Or had that been Madeleine? The rest was time in a lump, with shadows and chills and light drifting across bedcovers and black skies with points of light and something that made him wonder if he was dead.

Madeleine unbuttoned his pajama top and rubbed a salve on his chest. Was it eucalyptus? The smell of it reminded him of Mexico, and his father's ranch there.

"Who's been feeding?" he asked.

"All of us. Don't worry. The work's getting done."

McKay smiled weakly. He tried to summon up the details of what had to be done each winter day, but couldn't. He slept again. When he woke, the room was dark and Madeleine was under the quilt on the floor. She was lying on her side, and he could see the curve of her waist and hip —he had been coughing and his pillow was wet from sweat.

He had dreamed he was at the hospital waiting for Abe-san's arm to be treated. Mariko's hair was blue. Her hand, reaching out to him, was the head of a worm. Then McKay was holding a sword. Legs and arms and clothes and faces kept falling as he sliced. Then he tried to cut away the false engagements of fever; his desire for her dropped until nothing was left but her head, rolling. He laughed hard, but was it a laugh anyone could hear? He tried to stop, but the head rolled and rolled. . . . Sitting up suddenly, he yelled. "Mariko."

Bobby shoved two pillows behind McKay's back and helped him sit. He held a cup to McKay's lips.

"What old bush did you cut down to make this stuff?" McKay asked. He had been drinking Bobby's potions since he was seven and claimed he had never been cured.

"Just drink," Bobby commanded. "It's good for you."

And he did. Later, McKay realized he had been moved from his screened porch to his parents' bedroom. He had never slept there before, but it was close to the kitchen and the heat from the wood stove warmed it, as did the sun. He smiled. He had been conceived in this bed, and now perhaps he would die there.

"Bobby?" McKay spoke with his eyes closed as if he were blind. When he opened them, Bobby was sitting on a chair by the bed. "I'm going to get married."

"Oh . . ." Bobby looked surprised. "Who you marry?"

McKay's face dropped. Then he fell back, laughing, but it was a sad laugh, and his head turned from side to side. "I don't know," he squeaked. He slept again.

When the sun slipped from the window, he didn't know if he was awake or asleep, until he saw himself in a white room or else a dark room, covered with sun. He was swimming. There was a tunnel and water and blue bubbles breaking against his unshaven face. Sometimes he lifted far above the water, and it was a blue string suddenly blackened by the shadow of wings. Then he dropped, and the impact of his body on the sea made it burn.

Madeleine lay curled on top of the blankets beside him. His hand was under her and his arm had gone to sleep. When he pulled it free, she sat up with a start.

"I was dreaming about Henry," she said sleepily. "His eyes looked so green. . . ."

McKay's gaze shifted to the window. He watched the moon rise. The last night he had ridden to Camp to see Mariko something broke as if a vase had been thrown and the water had washed warmly over his feet. Ablution. That was the word he had been waiting for. The holiness of water touching the body of a loved one. . . .

Madeleine wrung out a wet towel. She wiped his forehead, then held the warm cloth against his chest and let the steam rise. When the compress grew cold, she dipped it in steaming water and laid it on him again.

The room was quiet. Sometimes McKay heard the wood stove tick and a log fall into itself. Winter fastened things together. He stretched his arm out and it fell against Madeleine's leg. She put the towel down and knelt. Her long braid had come undone and the hair lay in three cords down her back. She held his rough hand to her lips and rubbed her cheek against the hard knuckles. In a voice so soft he could barely hear, she said his name over and over. He thought it sounded like a bird calling to another bird.

She kissed his fingers. When she began telling him what she had not known she would say—that she loved him, and Henry too, and wasn't it possible to love two men at once—she saw that he was sleeping.

The next day McKay's breathing worsened and Pinkey called Dr. Hoffman at the hospital. Betsy, the nurse, answered the phone.

"Betsy, I think McKay Allison over here has taken a real bad turn for the worse. Where's Doc Hoffman, sleepin'?"

"Who is this?" she asked.

"Pinkey, over at the Allison ranch."

There was a silence. "You're sober, aren't you?"

"Yea, I'm sober and we've got a problem with this kid. Could you tell the damned sawbones to get over here soon as possible. I think he needs something . . . he can hardly breathe."

"Right away, Pinkey," she said seriously.

"That's better . . . ," Pinkey said, his voice trailing off.

He hung up the phone and dialed another number.

"Who's in charge over that outfit? I need to speak to him."

"The Camp director?"

"You bet . . ."

"I'll ring Mr. Roberts."

"Thank you, ma'am."

When Mr. Roberts came on the line, Pinkey tried to make his voice sound gruff and official.

"This is the cow foreman over at the Allison Ranch. I'd like . . . well, you've got a gal over there who's being called for by my boss, McKay Allison. He's awful sick and they don't know if he's going to make it through the night. He's been callin' and callin' for her. . . . It's Mr. Abe's daughter. How about letting her come on over for a very short visit to a kid who might die. He's kind of all alone out here, parents are dead, see, and it's just me and one other hired man is looking after him. I'd be obliged."

When the details of the visit were agreed upon, Pinkey gassed up McKay's truck and drove out of the yard.

Bobby watched Pinkey from the bedroom window, wondering where he was going. He applied another hot compress to McKay's chest. The room smelled like eucalyptus and the steam made his hair damp and his breathing came hard. He'd been up all night with McKay. Sometimes McKay talked—and sometimes he called out for people, once for his mother, a few times for his dog, and for Mariko. . . .

Who is this woman? Bobby wondered. To think of McKay with a Nisei . . . what a strange thought.

"Bob . . . ?" Pinkey called out.

Bobby heard footsteps in the hall.

"Bob, I've brought Mariko Abe."

Bobby looked at the woman. She was taller than any Japanese woman he had ever seen, but then, she was American, he reminded himself. Her stern face frightened him. No, this was not a woman like his mother, and she did not bow to him as he approached.

"Come this way," Bobby said.

Mariko looked at Bobby, equally astonished. "Who are you?" she asked, squeezing past Pinkey.

"Hell, that's Bobby," Pinkey interjected. "Everyone knows Bobby. . . ."

"Not from the Camp?" Mariko asked.

Bobby looked at her. "No. Not from Camp."

"God, he's been here since the Punic Wars," Pinkey said.

Bobby looked Mariko up and down. "McKay never say you so tall."

Mariko leaned close to Bobby. "Is he going to die?" she whispered.

Bobby stared at her wide-eyed.

She went to McKay.

Kneeling beside his bed, she stroked his forehead. "I'm here; I'm here now."

McKay opened his eyes and searched her face.

"I met Bobby," she said.

Finally he smiled. She put her hand on his chest. "Breathe," she said. "You must breathe."

The fever went down. After, McKay had the sensation of having passed through a cavernous body, like the body of a horse. The day he saw Pinkey sitting in a chair by his bed, whittling on a piece of wood, he knew he would live. Pinkey looked up.

"Hell, you've been in that bed so long, I thought you was homesteading," he drawled. "Them heifers are starting to calve. . . ."

"Turn on the lights," McKay whispered. He sat up. "Who's calving nights?" he asked. His chest rattled when he talked.

"Madeleine."

"Then what are you doing up?" he said, clearing his throat.

Pinkey laughed. "God, you are growly . . . you must be healing up."

McKay looked out the window. It was night and he could see no moon, no stars. "I feel like I've been out somewhere and came back in."

Pinkey leaned back and rocked. The piece of pine he was trying to whittle split and he put the two pieces in his pocket.

"Bobby's all fired up about something," he said, wiping the blade of his pocket knife on his pants.

"About what?"

"Some girl you was calling for."

"What girl?" McKay asked indignantly.

Pinkey grinned. "You tell me."

McKay fell silent. Pinkey fumbled with the pieces of wood in his pocket. Then he looked up. McKay's face was contorted.

"Yea, that's the one."

"I didn't, did I?" McKay asked, embarrassed.

"You bet your ass you did. I had a hell of a time jerking her loose from that sonofabitchin' camp to come see you."

"Come on, Pinkey . . ."

"Hell kid, we were giving you your last rites."

"She came here?" he asked incredulously.

"Sure did."

McKay slumped back and pulled the covers up on his chest.

"What did you go do that for?"

Pinkey threw the pieces of wood into the wastebasket.

"Well, I'll be go-to-hell . . . you could show a little gratitude. If I'm ever about to die, you better bring me some girls . . . lots of them. . . ."

"Hell, Pinkey, I'd have to blindfold them to get them near you. . . ."

Pinkey grinned. "Why do you think them lights was out in here?"

Winter nights in Wyoming come early like a form of blindness, Madeleine thought, even though she knew there was nothing to see when you had a husband missing in action for one year, then two, because there was no landscape in which to imagine him, no future to contemplate, and, like an iceberg, very little of the present showed. She was happy working nights because she couldn't sleep. She thought night fed off her, clung to her, tarnished her.

Every two hours she and Pinkey checked the heifer pen, their flashlights riding over the bodies of pregnant cows, and the little circle of light worked as a sounding line with which to fathom her future and the darkness. At least, that's what she told Pinkey, to which he retorted, "Hell, you don't look calvy at all."

She saw no sky or mountains, and hardly any faces other than Pinkey's that winter. Jesse and Bobby worked days. Watching the young heifers struggle in labor—switching their tails and rubbing their rumps against trees—Madeleine came to think waiting was one of the things that go with being a woman, and she hated it. But during a war, everyone is waiting, everyone is powerless, everyone is offering himself up to become dead in some way—all because someone who had power felt impotent and struck out against the feeling. But by the end of calving she came to think of waiting as a slow gathering, a prodigiousness. She had exhausted all her thoughts about Henry. She tried to visualize "missing in action" and ended up with a string of unkempt images: Henry tossed into the air by a blast; Henry doing a nose dive out of an airplane; Henry's swept-back hair. . . .

"Pinkey," Madeleine yelled. "We've got one here."

The heifer had fallen to her knees and rolled onto her side. She lifted her head and bellowed loudly and her sides heaved. When the feet showed they were upside down, the hooves pointing skyward, not down toward the ground as they should have been.

"There's a backward calf here," she yelled out again, rolling her sleeve up above her elbow.

She looked up. Pinkey rode through the heifer pen. Two bottles with black nipples for suckling calves stuck out of his saddlebags: one milk, one whiskey. He stepped off his horse with a groan.

"I'm feeling kinda gant myself," he mumbled and reached for one of the bottles. He opened his mouth and stuck the long black nipple between his lips and drank.

"Jesus, Pinkey . . . help me push this calf back."

Pinkey stood at the back of the cow and peered under her tail. "Does he feel real big?"

"No."

"Last time I tried to turn one of them calves around I got him all tangled up. Let's just go with it now," he said, wiping his mouth on his sleeve.

Madeleine pulled her arm out and held the two back hooves in place while Pinkey attached the rope, which was tied hard and fast to his saddle. He looked at his mare. "Eleanor . . . you ready?"

Madeleine rolled her eyes in exasperation. "Let's get this calf out before he drowns in there."

Pinkey shook the rope which stretched between the horse and the calf's feet. "Hey, you old bitch, wake up," he growled.

The mare backed slowly and the rope stretched taut. Pinkey and Madeleine supported their feet on the cow's rump. The calf's back legs came, then the body, and the neck. . . .

"Eleanor . . . back up . . . ," Pinkey commanded, and the mare buckled her haunches, dug in, and pulled.

When the calf's head popped out, the cow bellowed again and looked around. Madeleine slipped the rope off the calf's hind feet and cleaned his mouth with her finger, then stuck a straw up one nostril to get the breathing reflex going.

"Christ, he sounds worse than McKay. Let's swing him."

They stood and held the calf by the back legs, then swung him in a half circle and laid him down again. The calf coughed and shook his head, and after the cow stood and began licking him off they swung him again and cleared his mouth, until finally his breathing came more easily.

When the snow started again, the flakes were small and hard because of the cold. While they were pulling the backward calf, another one was born in the corner of the corral and froze to the ground before the cow could lick him off. Pinkey took the gunny sack out of the other saddlebag and rubbed the calf dry, then threw him onto Eleanor, who carried him to the barn.

They had been working thirty-two nights in a row, and there were fourteen or so more to go, Madeleine thought as she sat on the bench by the stove and rubbed the calf with a towel. It was a little black bull calf—black because the neighbor's Angus bull had bred a few of their Hereford cows—and as she rubbed him she thought he looked like Henry—stocky, shiny, dark, hard-muscled—but the way he breathed reminded her of McKay.

Between births they suckled weak calves, milked out cows with tight bags, doctored calves for scours and pneumonia, and logged in pertinent information about each calf: birth weight, mother's number, sex, color, and remarks about calving problems when they occurred. There had been a calf with a crooked neck, a strangled calf, one with no tail, one with crooked legs; calves whose presentations at birth were breech, backward, one leg back, upside down; or else calves too big to be pulled, requiring a cesarean.

It wasn't just the problems Madeleine noted in the notebook, but temperament and behavior of cows and calves—how long it took to stand and suck, how aggressive or sluggish they were, how quickly the cow accepted them, how much milk she had, how difficult she was to handle in the corral—so that in the fall, when they shipped the calves, McKay could also cull the cows whose traits he did not care to perpetuate: extreme belligerence, big teats, bad mother, calves with birth weights too high or with deformities.

From the bench by the stove, Madeleine could see Pinkey riding through the corrals, stopping every once in a while to pull the nippled bottle of Cobb's Creek from his saddlebag and satisfy his thirst. She had laughed the day he tried to suckle a calf with the wrong bottle. He jammed the nipple into the calf's mouth, and when the calf refused again and again he let out a string of expletives longer than the calf was tall. She tapped him on the shoulder and gave him the bottle containing milk.

The week the weather turned to twenty below, she and Pinkey built a small pen around the stove and filled it with weak calves. They opened all the gates in and out of the sheds and spread straw anywhere the cows found shelter—under trees, in ditches. Jesse and Bobby fed oat straw along with grass hay and cake—a protein supplement—and for two nights no calves were born at all.

"I believe they've closed up shop for a while," Pinkey said about the cows. Madeleine wondered if it was cold where Henry was—if he was— then she wondered what it felt like to be dead.

Pinkey brought in a heifer. She had been in labor for a few hours and was straining hard. He leaned toward his mare's ear. "Eleanor, you got your pulling hat on?" The horse flicked one ear back and one ear forward toward the cow. He made a loop and roped the cow around the neck and one front foot, and she rolled onto her side. When the calf's front feet appeared, Madeleine grabbed them and put the loop of a second rope around them. When the calf's head came, they saw how big it was. The cow strained and moaned. She was opened up as far as she could go without tearing, and when the shoulders hit against her pelvic bone, Madeleine poured mineral oil over her hands and tried to loosen the opening.

"Come on, baby . . . push a little harder," she said.

When the shoulders were out they let the cow rest a few minutes, because they knew the hips would be bigger. Madeleine reapplied the oil, then Pinkey told Eleanor to back up and the rope went tight. When the hips came, the cow bellowed. Madeleine could see where the skin was tearing.

"Pull real steady now, Eleanor," Pinkey said to his horse. Then he turned to the half-emerged calf. "Come on, you little hip-locked son-ofabitch . . . squeeze on out of there," and the calf came.

Madeleine tore the delicate placental sac. It was blue, and from its confines the calf lifted his white face and shook his ears.

"Hello, you little rat," a voice said.

Madeleine and Pinkey looked up. McKay pulled the cashmere scarf from his mouth and smiled.

When McKay gained back some of his strength, he worked the night shift with Madeleine, and Pinkey worked days. The cold had lifted, then a chinook blew in and the tops of all the drifts loosened, and the snow underfoot melted to mud. Sometimes he was so weak he lay down on the straw with a cow and calf, and Madeleine would find him there, bundled up and sleeping.

The rest of the calves came more easily despite swings of weather—from short blizzards to snow-melting days. McKay kept his cashmere scarf wrapped around his neck and mouth and wore four sweaters under a long wool coat. He made sure the coffeepot was full and the potbellied stove hot and hung a piece of baling wire where they dried their gloves in the rising heat. The cold and wind chapped their faces and hands, and the tips of their fingers cracked painfully. They dipped their fingers into a can of axle grease McKay found in the shop.

"Ain't this ranching life glamorous?" Madeleine quipped.

McKay dabbed grease on her cheeks and nose.

She looked at him. "Are you warm enough?"

"Yes," he snapped. He was tired of being mothered. He looked at Madeleine sheepishly. "I've always loved your nose."

She butted her forehead against his shoulder, over and over, and McKay put his arm around her.

"I'm so tired . . . ," she said. "God, I'm tired. . . ."

17

Abe-san beckoned me in as I was on my way to dinner. When I stepped inside, I saw three bowls and three pairs of chopsticks set neatly on a straw mat.

"You eat here tonight," he said gruffly, and I sat where he told me to sit.

He and Mariko had cooked a pot of rice on the wood stove. On top of rice, we had Chinese greens which he had grown under a cold frame made from old windows. He stirred the rice, greens and three eggs into a frying pan, then served it. Mariko made Mormon tea from the twigs of a plant that grows here, much milder than the usual green tea.

"You know these?" Abe-san asked, picking up his chopsticks, and when I nodded, laughing, he looked relieved—one less thing to teach me.

We ate in silence and I found it pleasant after the din of the mess hall. But I felt a little guilty, thinking how much Mom and Pop would have liked that meal.

When I put my bowl down, Abe-san started laughing at me. He put his hands on his thighs and lifted his chin. What strange, delicate noises he makes! Then he looked at me.

"Your mind—so loud!" he said. "Must learn to be quiet."

His remark bewildered me. Here, I'd been quiet as a mouse all during the meal.

"No . . . I mean all the time, it's noisy. You come back—sit with me."

With my eyes, I appealed to Mariko for help, but she gave me none.

"What do you mean?" I asked.

"You'll see."

"When should I come?"

"Three."

"Tomorrow?"

Abe-san laughed.

"This morning."

Had to hide the alarm under my pillow. What was I doing, getting up in the middle of the night for this crazy old man? Dressed and went next door at three. Tried to open the door, but couldn't. It must have been barricaded. "What the hell?" I said aloud. Tried again. Wasn't he in there? No luck, so I stood in the middle of the frozen lane. Then I saw Abe-san's face at the window. His hair was loose and he gestured angrily for me to go away.

"What's wrong with you?" I yelled. "Are you crazy or something?"

Just then, Mom came out. She shook her head when she saw me because she thought I was drunk, then shuffled to the latrine, stooped over.

The next day I didn't see Abe-san at all. He wasn't in when I finally woke up and he wasn't at meals. Dropped by Iwasaka's. Emi was there, showing off a new dress she had made to one of Ben's sisters, but really, she was flirting with me. Had to work on the paper for a few hours, ate dinner, then went to bed. In the middle of the night I felt someone shaking me. "Get up. Get dressed." I thought it was Mom or Pop, but it was Abe-san. So I dressed and followed him. When I asked what had happened the night before, he looked at me as if he hadn't heard.

"I'm not sure I want to do this," I said.

He ignored me again and showed me where to sit. I slumped, bracing myself with two hands, and he walked around behind me and kneed me in the back, then lifted one ankle so it rested on the opposite knee.

"There."

"Now what do I do?"

His eyebrows lifted. "Nothing," he said.

It's easy to lose track of time in the dark. I don't even remember whether I had my eyes opened or closed. All I knew is that my ankle hurt like hell and I was bored enough to fall straight over sideways, asleep.

Abe-san righted me. He was sitting too, but facing the wall. I kept thinking about thinking, and about how much my feet and legs and butt hurt and about getting laid. But what did all that have to do with Abe-san's Zen?

Finally, he got up and said I could go home. Was it still night or was it morning? I could barely put any weight on my feet at first, but I felt good. Not sleepy, but relaxed . . . but good God, that's hardly worth the effort.

Effortless effort. I'd heard him say that a few times. Another riddle that makes little sense to me. Saw Mariko on her way to class and she asked how I'd liked Zazen. I gave her an unenthusiastic shrug and said it was all right. "But what's the point?" I asked.

"Oh, there isn't one," she said and went on her way.

Monday. Mariko and Will had a fight today. He calls her "Mariké." Sometimes they speak in French, then English with a little Japanese as asides. It was all because Mariko isn't militant enough. "I want to paint." That's what she finally screamed. Will accused her of all kinds of things— he called her inu *("dog" or "informer" in Japanese) and said she was a bourgeois and nothing else. His heroes are Gandhi and Baudelaire—he quoted from them, and she said, "I can paint. That's all I can do." Then I heard him hit her.*

Oh God, that hurt me when she cried out. I started to run to their room, but froze at my own door. There was a long silence. I heard Will apologize, then he said in a little boy's voice, "What about me?"

Later. Mom said Will is hinekureta, *which means "warped" and "twisted," a person who pretends he doesn't need love and doesn't know how to love others. He came to see me after the fight and I pretended to be asleep.*

Something about when Will hit her made me go crazy. When I went to her studio she acted as if nothing had happened. But the walls between us are paper thin . . . she must have realized I heard them. Anyway, her eye was beginning to swell and turn black. "Hello Mar . . ." That's all I could say. She must think I'm a dolt. What a beautiful woman she is. She wears Will's clothes and piles her hair on top of her head samurai-style, but tussled with long strands hanging down. "Are you okay?" I asked. She bit her lip and nodded yes. I wanted to hold her safely in my arms but instead, I asked her if she would do a series of sketches for the newspaper—of Camp life. She agreed to the idea and then showed me some of her work.

Her "Views," à la Hiroshige and Hokusai, are stunning. One set is a series of "pillar prints"—hashira-e—five inches by twenty-eight inches laterally, to hang on a pillar. They're portraits of people in the Camp doing what they do—sitting around a potbellied stove, working in their rock gardens, playing baseball, sleeping, using the latrines, washing clothes, lining up for the mess hall, holding hands at the movies.

The other series is painted on long horizontal sheets. They're done in the style of the Genjii scrolls with a "roof blown off" perspective. One is allowed to look down into many rooms at once, at many lives. The perspective is flattened and skewed on a diagonal. There's a feeling of movement in time, not because we're fooled into thinking we're seeing frozen bits of action, but because the design is so overpowering. It picks you up and takes you where it wants you to go and you surrender to its flat, imperious momentum. I might add that in these she has laid our block wide open.

She told me about Hokusai's life. He was poor and lived haphazardly. He moved ninety-six times in his life. Dipped a rooster's feet in paint and let him run over big sheets of paper; made a sixty-foot-high painting of the Daruma, and was also a master of the shunga, erotic prints. Every time he started a new series of paintings, it seems he changed his name.

After, Mariko gave me something strong from a little bottle on the table where she mixes her paints. She told me about drinking absinthe in Paris. "What it does to your mind . . . oh! là là . . . ," she said in a lilting French accent. She laughed and when I blushed, she pressed her knuckles against my cheek. I felt like a fool.

Saturday night. Talked with Will. Didn't mention the fight. He looks paler than usual; his skin is like marble and there are black circles around his eyes. Some of his "comrades" came by. He surrounds himself with *punks and troublemakers. Like me in Chinatown. I can't forgive him for hitting Mariko, but it's not my business. Instead, things are subdued between us. I know he senses the change and the thought of it makes him even angrier.*

Looking around the room where he and Mariko live, I see she's messy and he's neat. There's a flat river rock on the floor beside his bed, which is pushed next to hers, and on it, a red leather-bound volume of Baudelaire and a Japanese fan. He's the kind who doesn't need much. I wonder whether he'll ever feel at home.

Turned into a regular all-night bull session. Finally moved to the mess hall so we didn't keep everyone awake. Yuri and Eddie are fishermen with tattoos all over their arms. Yuri smokes a pipe and when he laughs he sounds like a seal. Tom runs the liquor combine here. I guess that's where Iwasaka gets his sake. He's big as a sumo wrestler and mean, but he has a soft voice. Carl's the smart one, the clever city boy and the worst troublemaker. I believe he would kill anyone who obstructed his beliefs. Will lets them yak and argue, then clears his throat and lays down the law. It's amazing, but they listen. He orchestrates their temperaments, the extravagant differences between them, and at the end of the night, they are of one mind. We've decided to take turns reading and interpreting the American Constitution, to come to a better understanding of our loyalty questionnaire case.

Monday. Two days of gloom. The ground is bare and the sky is gray and the trees are leafless. I've never seen a place that looks so dead. The Issei are in a state of shock over it. They had such high hopes for spring, thinking it would be like Japan, with cherry trees blossoming. I asked the guard just when spring did come to the Big Horn Basin. He gave me a funny look and said, "How do I know? I've only been in this state eighteen months." When I told Pop the joke, he didn't understand.

18

"Willard, you drop that blind."

Willard did as he was told and when the blinds clapped shut, dust blew onto his arm. He had been watching Mañuel's roosters.

"Get ready. You'll be late for work," Carol Lyman snapped at her son. It was Thursday again and she was eager to get on the road and enjoy her "day of freedom." She watched Willard walk across the living room as she put the final touches of red polish on her nails.

"And get a coat. It's winter, you know. . . ."

On the way back through the room, Willard peeked at Mañuel's yard a last time. He wanted to touch the roosters' red combs. Then he wondered what it felt like to have feathers.

"That's enough for one morning. They'll be here when you get home," Carol said. After she helped him into his coat, they went to their jobs in town.

The next week the Stockyard Café closed down because of the rationed meat, coffee, sugar, and fuel oil to heat the place. Carol took the news calmly, bought two magazines at the drugstore, and drove to Snuff's.

That same week Rose had found Willard slumped between the aisles of the canned goods and dry cereals. She thought he was sick. When she looked into his vacant eyes, he lifted his head. His face was round and sweet and had not hardened. His mouth opened as if he were going to speak, but the sound that came out was like a horse's groaning when the cinch is pulled up too tight.

"Willard, are you going to get to sweeping or do you want to go home?" Rose inquired.

No one knew if Willard could talk. He lifted his heavy body and shook his head.

"Willard, what's got into you?" Larry asked, coming around from behind the meat counter.

Willard gazed at the street as if he hadn't heard and his hooded eyes didn't blink.

"Willard . . . ," Larry said.

Willard picked up his willow from the floor. Three strands of tinsel hung from a broken branch. He regarded the small tree with affection and reverence, then tipped it away from his body like a flagpole and marched out the door.

The lunchroom of Rose's boardinghouse across the street was dark. She served meals family style, then shooed everyone out, because once she had come back in the evening and found Pinkey and Dutch cooking steaks for everyone in the bar next door. It was a big room with shiny floors and long tables with bench seats. Willard leaned his willow against the picture window that framed a piece of the town and gathered in the failing light of a January day. An odor of food still hung in the room. Willard liked the smell. He saw his mother's black coupe parked out front.

"Willard? Are you in there?"

When she entered the lunchroom she saw the willow silhouetted against the picture window first. It made her think of the dead tree she had seen by a lake once, filled with herons—one to a branch. From a distance their oval bodies had looked like severed heads.

"Willard? Where are you? Rose said you're sick or something. . . ."

Willard hiccuped, stood, and grinned in the dark.

The next day Carol took Willard back to work because he wasn't sick. He did not stay long. He helped Larry spread fresh sawdust behind the butcher counter and refilled the spindles with string, then ambled out the front door of the store and walked east, toward home. His branch pendulated. He took a firmer grasp and leaned into the northwesterly blast.

When a truck rumbled to a stop, Willard saw it was Mañuel.

"Weelard . . . *venga* . . . get in. . . ."

Willard pulled himself into the narrow cab. In the back, on the pickup bed, empty bird cages were stacked crookedly and rattled when the truck jerked into motion. Mañuel's favorite rooster rode in the front seat. The bird had picked all the stuffing out of the upholstery, and Willard sat on the bare springs. Mañuel liked to sing when he drove. The rooster stood on the seat between the two men and tipped his head to one side when Mañuel's quavering voice broke and slid into an even higher note. Once, Willard eased his hand to the chicken's head and let his finger run over the ruffled, rubbery comb.

When they reached Mañuel's house, Willard helped carry the cages into a south-facing shed and watched attentively as the birds were watered and fed.

The next morning Willard refused to go to town. Instead, he climbed over the fence that divided his mother's yard from Mañuel's and stood among the caged birds all day. When Mañuel came home from his job at the sugar beet factory at four, he did not seem surprised to see Willard there. Wordlessly, he handed the boy the watering can. From that day on, Willard didn't work in town again for a long time.

It was a seven-day-a-week job for which Willard received twenty-five cents a week, plus the fine meals which Mañuel and Porfiria allowed him to eat with his hands: *chile verde* or *carne asada* wrapped in a flour tortilla, strong coffee, and posole. One Sunday, after Mass, a tequila bottle was passed around. The first time Willard took a swig, he thought fire had erupted around his Adam's apple and burned upward, fanned by the oxygen he knew must be trapped in the globe of his head. With the second swallow, he thought of kerosene and hoped he would burn like a lamp.

That night, when he climbed the fence and went into his own house,

Carol met him at the door and gave him a kiss on the cheek. She pulled back in disgust.

"You smell like something. I hope you haven't set anything on fire."

Willard wanted to say that he was made of fire, that he was the color of a rooster's comb, because then she would be proud of him.

"Oh, I get it," she said and sniffed again. "You've had a little nip. Well, that's all right, Willard. . . ."

Willard looked at her, disappointed. Then, exhausted from the excitement of the day, he went to bed.

That evening in the living room, Carol could feel the cold coming up through the floor. It was February 20, 1943, and she read in the paper that so far, 61,126 men and women had been killed or wounded or were missing since the beginning of the war. The movies were listed on the next page. *Springtime in the Rockies* was playing. She noticed that the worse the war got, the more cheerful the movies became, and did not know whether this was American perversity or Yankee ingenuity. When she mentioned this thought to Velma Vermeer the day they had tea together—a ritual they started when they first met and continued once a year—Velma said, "Oh, that's Harry's domain. I have no ideas on the subject," then ran in to answer the switchboard. Velma was the first person Carol had met on returning to Luster after a long absence. Some people thought they looked like sisters, though Velma was twenty years older. "And she was married to such a strange little man," Carol thought. "No one I would have married."

Carol poured herself more tea. She thought about Harry Vermeer, Velma's husband. He had owned the one movie theater in town. Every Saturday night he threaded up the film and, at six-thirty, opened the doors, took tickets, sold popcorn. At exactly three minutes to seven, he ran up the narrow stairs, dimmed the house lights, and switched on the projector. He had wanted a real movie palace with velvet curtains and padded seats, and little lights in the ceiling to look like stars. Instead, he had only what Luster could offer—a stucco building with hard seats and a projector whose light was growing dim.

Velma swept through the door carrying a plate of madeleines—sweet, shell-shaped cakes sprinkled with powdered sugar.

"Oh goodness, I've never had these before," Carol said. The one she took crumbled in her hand.

"These were Harry's favorites. . . . Proust made them famous . . . the writer, you know."

Carol gave Velma a blank look and ate the crumbs.

"Do you remember when Harry tried to bring opera to Luster?" Velma continued. "That terrible woman who came by train from San Francisco. I'll never forget how thin she was . . . just like I'm getting . . . ," Velma said. "Harry was so disappointed . . . no, worse. . . . I don't think he ever recovered from the shock of his failure. He had advanced her a hundred dollars and all she did was cough in his face and collapse on the platform. She died right there, before a single note of music escaped from her throat."

"Then there was the circus," Carol said.

The memory made Velma clasp her hand to her mouth. "Land's sake, I'd forgotten about that," she said, her mouth full of cake.

"That giant . . ."

"All folded up in the back of that station wagon."

"Was that all there was to it—just one man?"

"The poor thing . . . I don't know how he managed . . . he was like a big dumb animal, standing there for people to stare at . . . but he was a human after all . . . ," Velma said.

"But how does someone get that big?" Carol wondered.

Velma looked out the window at the street. "Harry and I had a terrible row after the circus ordeal. I told him he looked like a badger." Velma looked down. "Have another, please."

"What are they called?" Carol asked.

"Madeleines . . ."

"Like Madeleine Heaney?" Carol asked.

Velma looked disconcerted. "No, Proust."

The switchboard buzzed and Velma ran into the next room to answer the call. Gazing at the tiny switchboard lights going on and off, Carol felt envious. She took another cake and held it in the palm of her hand and wondered why it was shaped like a shell and whether Madeleine Heaney had been named after them and who this Proust was.

She remembered the night Harry killed himself. She had been at the movies with Snuff, but it must have happened after they left the theater:

he slit his wrists inside the projection booth and lay in a pool of blood all night with the white leader turning round and round on the reel. That was the night the projector bulb burned out.

When Velma returned Carol noticed how thin she was. Her skin was becoming transparent. "You must know everyone," Carol said appreciatively.

Velma looked surprised. "Oh, I wouldn't say that—it's just voices." She poured more tea. "I don't think I would want to know everyone— like a doctor does—would you?"

"I wouldn't mind. Here, have a cake. You haven't eaten. . . ."

"And there's less and less of it, now that Harry has died."

"Less of what?" Carol asked.

"Oh, you know, rubbing elbows."

"But isn't it lonely?"

Velma gazed out at the street. "Not at all. I'm quite content . . . as long as I have that," she said, meaning the switchboard.

"What a comforting thing for people to know you're here . . . on the other end. . . ."

"At the middle," Velma said. "Isn't that what they call me? The Middle?"

"Yes," Carol said smiling. "The Middle."

Velma wrapped her hands around her waist. "Some people think I do this just so I can listen in. . . ."

Carol looked up from her tea. "Oh? But you don't, do you?" she asked, and both women burst out laughing.

Now Carol thought about Velma. "We really are nothing alike," and for the first time she was glad to be who she was and not someone else, at least not Velma. "But I wish . . ." She stopped the thought before it grew out of control. "Why am I always hungry for more?"

Much later she tiptoed down the hall and stood in the doorway to Willard's room. His breathing was labored and she thought it odd that he was alive at all. To have a living being come out of your body—whole and separate, a complete stranger. Her eyes moved over the salmon walls of the room. At night, when Mañuel's yard light was on, they looked like flesh, and the shadows of roosters paraded across the ceiling, grotesquely oversized. She thought of the room where she had conceived

Willard. Its walls were not fleshlike at all, but log with the bark still on. Willard's father had smelled bitter. It was a sick person's smell, and his hands were hot from fever. Sometimes she felt his presence so strongly she spoke to him. It had happened in the black coupe, in the hallway, at Snuff's. He seemed to fill the whole room but he wasn't big, and she could feel his warmth against her shoulder. "Dear one," she began. "How are you? Do you see him?" she asked and pointed to the lump under the covers that was Willard. "Don't laugh at me. They say you were always laughing, but when we met you hardly laughed at all. You were so sick. I love you. . . ."

Willard turned in his sleep and groaned.

When Carol lay down on the carpet in front of the furnace that evening, her black shoes looked like rocks tied to her ankles and part of her plain white slip slowed. Sometimes when she dreamed about Willard's father, his skin was gray like ash and when he smiled his dimples showed. In one dream he was lying on a coffin and winked at her when she filed by. In another she tried to hold him, but he shook out of her grasp like some object moving very fast, and she couldn't make out his eyes or lips, which are what a lover needs to see. Then he came back in full color and before her eyes, disappeared.

Carol stood. The side turned toward the furnace felt hot. She buttoned her sweater down to her waist and walked into the kitchen. One of the pears a railroader brought from California toppled onto the counter into her hand, and she lifted it to her mouth and took a bite and let the juices run down her chin.

She bent her head under the faucet and washed her hair. She wanted to sing, but she thought it might wake Willard so she hummed softly to make it seem as if there were more than one person in the room. Ghosts don't do things like that—they don't sing, she thought, but they laugh, except it's always with a funny look in their eyes.

She rubbed her wet hair with a clean dish towel, then, fishing bobbypins out of an ashtray, made curls so tight they pulled the skin away from her skull up into tiny points.

She sat down in the armchair in the living room and turned out the light. She leaned her wet head back. The word *suicide* came into her mind. It was a word she had carried around with her for a long time. She was a fastidious woman, and the idea of cutting her wrists or making any kind of mess did not appeal to her. Yet the word lay calmly under the skin of her forehead. Sometimes she opened the word like a suitcase and brought out various instruments of death, held them close, then put them away.

In the kitchen she shone a flashlight on the thermometer. Twenty below zero. "I feel so unfinished," she said aloud, but only to herself this time. No blood or melodrama for her. She only wanted extinguishment, something quick, an end to restlessness. She put on a coat and boots and went to the car. The air was so cold her feet and hands became numb immediately. The door of the coupe had frozen shut and she had to yank it violently to make it open. She wondered how long it took to die in such cold. Inside, she opened the glove compartment. Then, by the overhead globe light she counted her ration cards—"A" for gasoline—and computed how far from herself she could travel in one day.

19

The song of the western meadowlark, the very bird Mr. Abe had been looking for when McKay had shot him, awakened McKay. When the sun came up the sky looked like a flame blown sideways. Between the ranch and the Camp the country was still dark and Heart Mountain's one east-facing slope took on the color of fire.

"Could it really be spring?" McKay wondered. He turned on his back, then rolled forward and stood on the shaky cot, touching his hands to the ceiling of the screened porch. He felt as if he had slept all winter and was getting up for the first time.

"Bonsai," McKay said when Bobby burst into the room with a cup of green tea.

"*Bonzai* or *bonsai?*" Bobby asked, looking up at McKay.

"Bonsai. Want to get some with me this morning?" he asked.

"Get down from there," Bobby said, trying to hand McKay the tea.

McKay jumped off the cot lightly and took the cup between his hands.

When he was a child, McKay, with his mother and Bobby, had taken the team and wagon to a rocky slope of Heart Mountain where the pines grew stunted and bent by constant prevailing winds. They'd dig up one tree and take it home and plant it somewhere around the house or in front of Bobby's cabin, and each year they looked forward to finding a new one.

"Bonsai cultivate your mind," Bobby always said. "It improve you, relax eye if look at it long time. Don't need to sleep after. . . ."

McKay had liked the part about not needing sleep when he was young. It meant he could stay up and watch the constellations shift. His father had learned celestial navigation in Mexico and had taught McKay to read the sky. For this reason, McKay gladly helped dig up each new tree, then, replanting it, he'd sit before it, staring hard. . . . "I'll never have to sleep again," he reported enthusiastically to his mother. He remembered she let him stay up as late as he wanted that night, playing checkers and looking at the stars, until finally, he fell asleep.

"Did you carry me to bed that night when I was about seven and Mother said I could stay up all night?"

"Yes. You very heavy too!"

McKay dressed.

"Who these trees for? Here?"

"No. They wanted some at the Camp."

"For that woman?"

McKay looked up. "No . . . for her father and some of the other men who want to make gardens over there."

Bobby folded his arms.

"Now what?" McKay said.

Bobby looked into McKay's eyes. "That woman . . . ," he said tentatively.

"Who? Mariko?"

Bobby nodded.

"Well, what?" McKay asked impatiently.

Bobby shook his head.

"Because she's Nisei?" McKay asked, grinning.

Bobby clucked his teeth. "She won't be happy here. Like caged lion. I know. I watched her. . . . It's not good."

"It's good for me, Bobby," McKay said and walked to the kitchen.

Bobby and McKay ate a breakfast of deer steaks and eggs. The extra leaf had been taken out of the table after roundup and now they sat wedged against the kitchen wall again. When McKay poured coffee, the lid fell into his cup.

"Shit," McKay snapped.

Bobby looked at him. McKay had lost weight during his illness and now he was irritable. As soon as they finished eating he pushed his plate away.

"I'm going to harness that team now. See ya, Bobby."

Bands of clouds hung around the mountain. McKay drove the team into them, then rose out of the mist, and was obscured again—like a moon rising—Bobby thought. He watched until the wagon was no bigger than a toy.

When McKay reached what they called "the bonsai field," he stopped the team, tied the lines, and jumped down with the shovel. There was no wind and the tortured shapes of the trees seemed oddly unnecessary. Junipers and pines grew out of cracks in rocks, the trunks twisted and bowed away from the prevailing wind and the green needles reached up like opened hands. The thaw was coming out of the ground and when McKay dug down the soil was wet and flecked with frost.

Choosing the trees carefully for their unique shapes, he dug wide and deep, sliding a hand under the roots still clotted with dirt, as if under the head of a baby. He lined them up on the back of the wagon. They had grown singly on the mountain. Now, in close company, the needles of the wildly twisted trees touched.

When McKay pulled up to the sentry gate he saw Harry, the guard, who shook his head and groaned. "Now what?" he said, peering at the back of the wagon. "Wait here. I'll call. Jesus, McKay . . ."

In the guardhouse, Harry picked up the black receiver and dialed while McKay looked on. McKay didn't know whether Harry could be trusted. He hoped Harry didn't like his job.

"The Camp boss'll be right over. Sorry, but he's got to inspect this sonofabitch before I can let you drive to the living quarters."

McKay filled his jaw with snoose, then offered Harry some.

"Can't . . . not on duty."

"What'd you take a shitty job like this for, Harry?"

Harry's face froze for a second.

"You could have at least got a defense job," McKay continued.

"In one of those sonofabitching cities?"

McKay shrugged.

"My ma and pa needed me around . . . but not full-time, see, so I got me one of these stay-at-home-army jobs. . . . It's not so bad, really. . . ."

McKay squinted at him.

"What have we got here?" the Camp manager asked and walked all the way around the wagon.

"Just some trees . . . for some of the old-timers. . . ."

The manager looked over the rims of his glasses at McKay.

"Um huh . . ." He reached his arm in and touched the dirt around the roots of the tiny pines.

"That's all that's in there . . . just dirt and trees."

"And where do you mean to take them?"

"I'd like to drive it down to Block 4 E. Mr. Abe's block, down at the end there."

The manager looked McKay up and down. "I knew your father. . . ."

"Yes . . . ," McKay said quietly.

"Just this once . . . Harry, let him through."

"Thank you, sir." McKay tipped his hat and climbed on the wagon.

It was an old gentle team, and the commotion of children playing, radios blaring, teenage girls strolling arm in arm did not bother them. McKay turned down the lane that faced Heart Mountain, which Mariko referred to as the Champs-Elysées. In the distance, the edge of a front moved toward the Camp. Clouds flew in three directions at once, and the belly clouds, the ones that hung low and black under the limestone tusk, broke into soft screens of snow. A trance held McKay. The snow stopped and the wind turned a funnel of dust and debris toward the horses, then veered away. McKay slowed the team. A single thought fastened to the bottom and top of his mind, and the noise of the Camp peeled away as he drove straight west, toward Mariko, toward Heart Mountain.

When the clouds shifted north, they looked like long tattered sandbars. "I wish I could be more moderate in my desires, but I can't," he said half-aloud though he did not think there was anyone to whom he could address such a prayer. He pulled to a stop at the westernmost block facing the mountain. The wind eddied around his head a last time, then the front pushed northeast. The notes of "September Song" came from an apartment whose one door had been thrown open by the wind. The mare pawed the hard ground.

"Quit," McKay barked, and she did. He tied up the lines.

A young man with round glasses and broad shoulders greeted him. "Hello," he said and extended his hand. "Kai Nakamura . . . I talked to you for the *Sentinel* after that accident."

McKay half stood, looking down from the wagon, and nodded his head. "You bet. How you doing?"

Kai made his way around to the back of the wagon. "What have you got in here?"

"Just some trees . . . for Mr. Abe . . . hell, anyone that wants one." McKay jumped down.

Kai looked at McKay squarely in the eyes.

"Would there be an extra one for my father?" Kai asked.

"Hell, yes." McKay looked up again and smiled. "Any one he wants." He hopped up on the wagon box and began moving the little trees to the back, where they could be inspected. The left side of his chest hurt.

"This is my father, Mr. Nakamura," Kai said.

McKay looked around, then held out his hand. The old man bowed. His glasses were still bent and the pained expression on his face seemed to have frozen there. McKay straightened up and tipped his hat politely.

"Why don't you come around to the back . . . no, this way—you don't want to step in front of those old horses; they're kind of skittish—and you can take a look at these trees."

Kai steered his father to the back of the wagon. He stood some distance from it—a formal distance, McKay thought—even though the old man's eyes darted from tree to tree. Kai nudged his father forward.

"He wants you to pick one out," Kai whispered.

"My family always went once a year to get one of these . . . kind of a family tradition . . . ," McKay explained, picking up one of the trees and holding it out to Mr. Nakamura. The old man shielded his eyes from the sun and gazed flatly at the specimen. McKay looked at the tree, a juniper whose trunk looked like a twisted lock of hair, then at the old man. Kai sighed audibly.

"Do you like that one, Pop?"

Mr. Nakamura did not appear to have heard his son.

McKay put the little tree down and brought another one forward. Mr. Nakamura stood rigidly and made no response.

"Pop?" Kai asked impatiently.

"That's okay . . . there's plenty here," McKay said.

Standing on the wagon box, McKay looked for a tree he thought would please the man. He picked up the pine whose trunk bowed twice before shooting up and back the other way. "Two waves," he said, meaning the shape of the trunk of the tree.

Mr. Nakamura gave the young rancher a quizzical look, then smiled.

McKay held the tree out to him. Mr. Nakamura inspected it closely. He did not touch the wind-tortured trunk or the green, fanlike needles with his hands, but twisted his head this way and that so as to see each part of the tree from a different angle. Then he stepped back and bowed.

Kai helped his father carry the tree to the front of their apartment and, when the old man decided where he wanted it, dug the hole.

"Good morning," McKay said.

"Ohaiyo," Abe-san said, his eyes squeezed against the bright sun. He looked at the trees admiringly. "These trees are trying to decide who wants to come home with me," he exclaimed.

A song blared from a radio somewhere in the block.

"Ahsooo . . .," Abe-san hissed, and light as a deer on his feet, sprung forward until his chest pressed against the wagon box.

"They're all for you . . . ," McKay began.

Abe-san shook his head, smiling.

"This one?" Then McKay lifted a shaggy juniper whose double trunk twisted together straight up in a rigorous embrace.

Abe-san squealed with laughter, nodding his head yes. "Big lover, like you," he said, beaming.

McKay regarded the tree. Then he looked at Abe-san and a crooked smile broke across his face. "Where is she?" he whispered.

Abe-san's face dropped. "She's very bad now."

"Where?" McKay insisted.

"Not want to see anybody."

McKay jumped off the wagon and stood face to face with Mariko's grandfather. "Please . . ."

"Yes," Abe-san said, but there was something sad in his smile.

"As long as I'm digging . . . ," Kai broke in, holding up the shovel. "Where do you want this?" he asked.

Abe-san pulled away from McKay and looked at the shaggy juniper. He was wearing a kimono and getas, and when he walked, his body didn't move up and down, but glided. "Here . . . ," he said to the young reporter, indicating the spot where he wanted the hole dug.

McKay saw Mariko in the doorway. Her hair was disheveled. She had a cut on the right side of her mouth and a black eye. He walked slowly from the back of the wagon. His hands were black with dirt, and some of it had rubbed across his face, and his hat was pulled down low on his forehead because of the wind.

He wanted to hold her but couldn't. "That's a hell of a shiner," he said, trying to sound jaunty, but his voice cracked. He remembered the first time he had stumbled across the flats to her block, and how she had stood in the doorway, pulled him against her suddenly, and turned with him to the middle of the room where they could not be seen, and when the spinning stopped, how the room kept moving and made him think of the spiral shapes of seashells with tiny animals crouched inside.

"Are you okay, kid?" he asked gently.

Over his shoulder he heard Kai whistling loudly, as if to draw the attention away from the apparition in the door. Mariko stepped back into the shadow and McKay followed. He saw how the bruise had begun to yellow on the top of the lid and cheekbone, and the clotted blood by the side of her mouth was peeling away. He didn't know what had happened and he wasn't sure if he wanted to know. Mariko turned her back to him.

"I'm not in the mood to talk now . . . ," she began.

There was a long silence, but McKay didn't leave.

"I'm sorry I haven't been to see you for so long. . . . I've been stuck in a maternity ward," McKay said.

Mariko turned around, surprised.

"Heifers. Two hundred first-calf heifers. They need a lot of attention." Mariko chuckled. "Oh . . ."

McKay looked nervously out the door. "Look, I can't stay very long, the MPs are on my ass. . . ."

Mariko lay down on the straw mattress and held her arm over her bruised eye to keep the sun out. "I'm not sure that I know why you come at all," she said weakly.

"What do you mean?"

"I don't know what you want with me."

McKay's face fell. He tried not to let it show. He wanted everything he had done and said to be a lie so her words wouldn't matter, but he couldn't stop the sudden sliding, the blackness that came. . . .

"I mean, what do you want with someone with a Japanese face? You love me because I'm strange, isn't that it? Why me, when there must be so many others . . . I don't understand. You barge in here, into our lives, but I don't get it . . . sometimes I wonder if you find all this merely amusing. An entertainment until the war ends . . ."

"Jesus Christ . . ." McKay turned. His shoulders lifted up and down as if he were sobbing, but when he turned back his blue eyes were dry. "What have I done to make you think these things?" he asked.

Mariko sat up and touched the top of McKay's head as he knelt by her bed and looked out the door where her grandfather was hunched over his bonsai. "Oh, McKay . . . I want to be wrong. . . ."

He looked at her, deadly earnest. "Or can't you understand? Was it expecting too much?"

"Don't insult me," she snapped.

He moved closer to the bed.

"Please don't."

"I'm sorry about your eye," he said, because that's all he could think of to say.

"We had a fight."

"Who? You and Will?"

"Yes. It's been very bad around here. He thinks I'm *inu* . . . a dog, a stool pigeon for the JACL."

"Why?"

"I'm not, of course. I just want to paint. That's all I'm capable of doing. I'm not political."

McKay rubbed his forehead.

"He sees that as betrayal," she said. She pulled a Gauloise from a blue package and did not light it, but held it in her hand and walked around the tiny room.

"What does it mean to sign one of these papers the army passes around? What does it matter whether I say yes or no on their lousy questionnaire?" She thumped her heart. "They don't know what's in here and they never will." She stopped pacing in front of McKay and he lit her cigarette. She took a long draw. "I will not be segregated from the others and go to Tule Lake. Did you know? That's where they are sending the trouble-makers. Yes. Will is on the list." She strode around the room again. "I will not go." She sat on the edge of the bed and her knee touched his shoulder. "He likes causes. My causes are inside. I paint from them, not about them," she said bitterly.

McKay nodded.

"I count the days until he leaves. That's sad, isn't it?"

McKay turned on his knees to her and she lay back on the bed. Her eyes were closed and he could see how the bruised eyelid had swelled to twice the size of the other one. She looked out the window. The bright sun had gone.

"Do you think it's going to snow?" she asked after a while. Her face grew softer when she looked at him.

Someone knocked. "Hey, McKay . . ." It was Kai. "Those MPs are on the prowl."

"Thanks . . . I'm coming," McKay said.

When Kai left, Mariko grabbed McKay around the knees where the cloth of his pants went loose, and slid up until she was standing in his arms.

He brushed his lips against her hair.

"I don't really hate you at all," she said softly.

He rested his chin on top of her head. "Please, you must try to get a pass to come to the ranch. I'll come for you," he said, looking down at her face.

She gave him a strong questioning look. "Yes?"

"Yes." She put her nose against his collarbone and nodded.

"It's like being dead," McKay said to himself, as he went home, think-ing about Mariko. "Everything else is seared away." Where the road cut through an enormous rock cliff, he looked up and saw a hawk snatch a swallow right out of the air.

*   *   *

A week later McKay read in the papers about the restriction of passes to and from the Camp, because the town councils of Cody and Powell had made it clear that there were "too many Japs floating around town." The article incensed him and he burned it before Bobby read the mail. He decided to drive to the Camp. When he pulled up to the sentry gate, Harry stepped out.

"Hello, Romeo, want a Coke?" Harry leaned on the car door and thrust an open bottle through the window.

"What the hell is going on around here with this pass deal?"

Harry drew back and grinned. "You just can't stay away, can you?" he said.

"I put in for a pass for . . ."

"No deal. They've shut her down."

"Christ, the goddamned bigots in town again."

"I heard that," Harry said, jeering. "I heard that."

McKay got out of his truck and leaned against a fender. He scratched at the dirt with the toe of his boot and looked in the direction of Mariko's block. "No special deals today, huh?" he said and looked Harry in the eye.

"Sorry, asshole . . . I'm fresh out of deals today. Orders."

McKay rubbed the scarred knuckles of his right hand. "You've got yourself one hell of a job, Harry. . . ."

"I guess I don't carry a torch around in me for these Japs like you do, that's all," he said, lifting the bottle cap with a jerk. Then he picked the cap off the ground and rotated it between his thumb and forefinger.

"You're ignorant, Harry," McKay said, glaring.

"That's what my ma always said."

"Yea," McKay said and climbed into his truck. Harry appeared at the passenger window and leaned in. "Hey, I was just fooling around. . . . Stop fightin' your head, McKay . . . I mean it."

Pinkey sat on the front step of Snuff's bar and listened to the roar the wind made somewhere far above him. Dust from the mill covered the road. A car sped by, leaving black tracks in the white mineral, and after a while the dust healed over again. The bar door opened. It had been painted black and the paint was peeling, and every time someone opened it another flake fell off.

"Here." Snuff handed Pinkey a shot glass. "Anything else while I'm out on the veranda? Hors d'oeuvres?"

Pinkey tipped his head back and swallowed the whiskey in three gulps. "Just right," he said, handing the glass back. Snuff snorted and disappeared inside.

Pinkey took a deep breath. He loved the smell of the earth when it first came in spring—part sage, part clay, part skunk, part stinkbug. He vowed not to go inside again until winter. He had one spur stuffed into his shirt pocket and no horse. "I was going to ride over here, but then I just got to walkin' and everything smelled so good, I forgot to stop," he had told Snuff. Now he wished he had his horse.

He decided to flag down the next car that went by, but that might be quite a wait because it was getting on past dinnertime. He'd been waiting for McKay to show up at the headgate north of the ranch, then at the calving barn, then for the noontime meal.

"Snuff . . . hey in there . . . ," he yelled in the direction of the battered door, but there was no response. "Well shit, I suppose I have to wait on myself now," he mumbled, getting to his feet. He heard a horse and turned. His face brightened. "Hello, you lovesick sonofabitch . . . where the hell have you been?"

McKay rode up to Pinkey and peered into his eyes. "You sober?" he asked.

"Hell, yes. I've been doing your damned work all day. Anyway, I'm on the wagon. One shot a week, that's all."

"Yea, I know what your weeks are like—about an hour long," McKay said, stepping off his horse.

"I was just settin' out for home. . . ."

A car pulled up and a tall man unfolded himself from behind the steering wheel. McKay strode toward him with his hand outstretched.

"Jesus, I thought I was seeing a ghost . . . ," he began.

"How are you?" Rocky asked. "I seen your brother about two months ago. We shared a can of C rations under a palm tree. It was Christmas," he said with a laugh.

He was dark and lanky and when he talked, his head wobbled as if he had rested his chin on a marble, and when there was a silence in the conversation, he always looked up at the sky and squinted.

McKay offered his chew around and each man took a pinch. Rocky spit on the ground before he spoke, pulled one foot up under him against the running board. He and McKay had ridden colts together and rodeoed some, taking turns helping each other in the chutes, and once McKay saved his life when a bucking horse flipped over on him.

"It's pretty good to be home," Rocky began, spitting again. "I'll tell you, fighting those Japs—no offense to Bobby—isn't like fighting normal human beings. They just don't want to live very bad, is how I see it. They move around the country like a damned band of sheep. God almighty, I saw one officer line his men up and cut their heads off . . . didn't want to surrender. Hell, we're surrenderin' sonsofbitches compared to them. They take it serious in a little different way. . . ."

"Let me buy you a drink," McKay offered.

"Yea, get three go-cups," Pinkey chimed in. "I ain't going in there. I'm celebrating spring right out here."

McKay ducked in and Carol Lyman came out with three shot glasses of whiskey, which the men emptied quickly. When McKay passed the chew around again, Rocky's hand began shaking violently, then his shoulders lifted up and his head wagged from side to side.

"You need another shot, Rock?" McKay asked.

"It's not what you think . . . I've got me a tich of malaria is all. Seems like everyone got it if they ran out of them goddamned quinine pills. That stuff makes you ringy."

McKay looked at the ground and smirked. "I guess I'll have to find Champ a hard-mouthed colt so he won't go jerking on him, then . . . ," he said.

Rocky laughed.

"So, it's pretty tough over there, huh?" McKay said.

Rocky looked at him. "Real tough . . . I don't know, it's got so everyone's fighting to the death. I mean both sides. Where we was, we weren't taking any prisoners. Hell, we shot 'em out of the sky like a bunch of damned ducks if they parachuted into one of the forward areas. . . . Some of the guys, you know, took themselves some souvenirs. I couldn't believe it: one guy—and I'm not shittin' you—sent a Jap's ear back home to his girlfriend. . . . I'm sure as hell glad to have it over with. Got a couple of colts has growed up since I left—one's coming two; the other's a long yearling. God, they're nice."

McKay smiled at his friend. "Let's put some miles on these colts when this thing is over," he said. "I'm tired of getting bucked with by these waspy sonsofbitches all by myself. . . ."

"You've got yourself a deal," Rocky said, holding out his hand. "I best be going now. They're waiting on me up home," he said and pushed away from the car. When he smiled the gold caps on his front teeth glinted, and McKay noticed that his eyes had that wide expression of astonishment people get just before they die.

McKay turned to Pinkey. "How are you travelin'?"

"I'm afoot," he said.

"I suppose we have to ride double." McKay handed Pinkey the reins. Pinkey put his foot in the stirrup.

"Heave ho," McKay yelled and pushed Pinkey so hard he almost went over the other side. Once he was on top, his feet did not reach the stirrups. "I'll take the backseat," McKay said, swinging on gracefully.

"Watch how you hold on to me . . . I don't want no one to start talkin'. . . ."

McKay jabbed the horse in the flank. He humped up and kicked out.

"Hey," Pinkey yelled. He turned the horse toward home, after which McKay felt the pockets of Pinkey's coat.

"Don't you have something hid out on you?" he asked.

"What the hell do you take me for, some kind of wino?" Pinkey said indignantly.

"Jesus, I could use a drink."

"Why didn't you think of that at the bar?"

McKay shoved his hand into the pocket of Pinkey's coat. "Are you sure?"

Pinkey reached into the breast pocket of his vest and pulled a slender flask out and handed it over his shoulder to McKay. McKay pulled the cork with his teeth, then took a long draw.

"Let's go on a tear," he said, wiping his mouth and handing the bottle forward.

"Hell no, never touch the stuff," Pinkey said.

"You bugger," McKay said and took another swallow. "Come on," he coaxed.

Pinkey fended off the bottle with his free hand.

"You're hard to please," McKay said.

"Hey, first you kick me off the outfit for being inebriated, then you get the red ass because I won't go on a tear with you. Didn't they teach you anything at that college?" Pinkey asked, swiping the flask from McKay and taking a gulp. "Anchors away . . . ," he sang, drinking.

"I suppose you're going to tell me you were in the navy," McKay said.

"Merchant Marines," Pinkey quipped. "Goddamn, all those ports, all those women . . ."

"The hell . . . you've never even seen the water."

Pinkey laughed.

"And you can't swim."

"Who needs to swim? That's what a boat is for, isn't it?"

"Give me that bottle again," McKay said.

"What's eatin' at you?" Pinkey asked.

"Everything."

"Girl problems?"

McKay put the bottle to his mouth and let the whiskey flood out on his lips before swallowing.

Pinkey sat against the edge of McKay's bed on the screened porch. The moon rose behind a veil of clouds. Pinkey called it "a virgin moon" or "a moon that took vows."

"Or a Hindu moon, a moon in purdah," McKay added, staring with glazed eyes. For the first time in a week the wind had stopped. The silence was overbearing.

Bobby had left dinner out for them, but they went on through the kitchen to the liquor cabinet, and when they couldn't find the key to the lock, McKay broke it open and took three bottles to what he called his cell, his screened room. The cell felt crowded with Pinkey in it, but McKay welcomed the company because thoughts of Mariko were too easily conjured up and worked their way around the room until McKay deadened them with another drink.

"Isn't there anything to laugh about?" he asked.

Pinkey scratched his head, then told the story about the time he opened the barn door and four buck deer ran out over the top of him. "Them hooves was so sharp, they liked to scalp me," Pinkey said. McKay knew the story by heart. "They liked to cut me to ribbons," Pinkey continued. "Had to get my hair sewed back on." He paused and waited for laughter. McKay grimaced.

"You kids used to think that was funny," Pinkey said.

"It is funny. It just doesn't make me laugh anymore."

McKay uncorked a new bottle of whiskey. It wasn't Pinkey's brand and it went down more smoothly. He sat on the floor beside the old cowboy and filled two glasses.

"Here's to the Merchant Marines," McKay said, laughing.

Pinkey touched the glass with his and drank. "Here's to the goddamned war," he said.

"To the end of the goddamned war," McKay added.

"Yea, you bet. To the end of the stinkin' thing."

"Here's to you, Pink. . . . You're a hell of a drunk," McKay said, lifting his glass.

"To the boys," Pinkey said, swallowing. "Champ and Ted . . . and Henry."

"Here, here."

The dog shoved the door open and stood on McKay's lap, and McKay let him lick his face. "Buster, you old fart, here's to you."

"Shall we get him drunk?" Pinkey asked, with a gleam in his eye.

"Hell no, someone's got to do the work tomorrow."

"You're right," Pinkey agreed. "You're a hell of a manager."

"Yea, I'm sharp as hell," McKay said, sneering.

Pinkey looked at the young rancher. His eyes were bleary. "So they closed up the Camp, huh?" he said tentatively.

"Idiots."

"Who?"

"The assholes in town. They want them to sign something saying they won't stay here after the war is over. Well, who would want to live in this godforsaken place anyway?"

"Can't you write her or something?" Pinkey asked.

"Well, ain't you getting practical. You sound like my mother."

"Excuse me all to hell," Pinkey said and uncorked the bottle again. "Round two," he announced, tipping his head back.

McKay took the bottle from him when he had finished.

"You'll survive, kid," Pinkey said.

McKay wiped his mouth. "Thanks, that's swell news."

"Hell, I've been waitin' for one damn thing or another all my life, but it don't do no good. It's just something to make time pass. Now I can't remember long enough to know what I was waitin' for."

McKay smiled at the old cowboy. "You're right . . . to hell with it," he said.

Pinkey slept a while, sitting up against the edge of the bed, and when he woke, McKay was standing by the screen watching the sky get light.

"What are you all hot and bothered about?" Pinkey asked groggily.

McKay turned. "Will you come with me?"

"Where to?"

"Town. I'm going in to sign up."

"For what? Bowling?"

"The army, you asshole," he said and hiccuped.

"I thought you'd already been culled out."

"I was, but they're more desperate now."

"You said it, desperado. . . ."

"I said desperate."

"What the hell's the difference?" Pinkey asked.

McKay's hiccups came more quickly. "Shit," he said and began to laugh.

Pinkey struggled to his feet. His head only came to McKay's shoulder. "I'm ready, sport."

McKay filled his car with gas at the tanks and the two men drove into town. Even a town as small as Luster looked big and bright to him because he hadn't been off the ranch for so long. He pulled up in front of the hotel, and when he stepped from the car, the empty flask dropped out of his coat pocket. He hiccuped.

"Shhh," Pinkey said.

The two men strode inside and the recruiter looked up warily.

"Good morning, young men. What can I do for you?"

The poster tacked to the wall behind him showed Uncle Sam reaching down from a cloud.

"I want to join up," McKay announced. He showed the man his classification card.

The recruiter put the card squarely on the desk in front of him, then thumbed through his files until he reached McKay's.

"I see you've been here before. How's that leg?"

"Good as new," McKay said, then clapped his hand over his mouth as the next hiccup came.

"Why don't you walk over to that post and then walk back to me," the recruiter said.

McKay rolled his eyes at Pinkey, then walked to the post and back.

"That's a pretty bad limp you've got, sonny."

"It's on the mend. Look, I've got to get out of here. I've got to go over there with my brothers . . . ," McKay pleaded.

The recruiter scrutinized the pair once again. "I appreciate your interest, and I'm going to put a note right here on your file about your willingness to do service for your country, but at the moment I think you'll be doing more good raising food. It's the fight we can wage here at home, the fight against food shortages."

The recruiter folded his hands over McKay's file.

"Come on, we've got chores to do," Pinkey said, pulling at McKay's arm.

When they were out on the street, McKay saw the director of the Heart Mountain Camp pass in a car.

"Hey, I've got to talk to you," he yelled at the man, who turned, bewildered, and kept driving.

McKay laid his head back against the seat. He let Pinkey take the wheel, even though Pinkey's license had been suspended for drunk driving years before. "Is there anyone here with me?" McKay wondered, as Pinkey ground down through the gears. McKay swallowed. Something hard stuck at the back of his throat. Though it was midday, the moon was still visible, and he thought the sun and the moon were only stones—fatuous in their illusion of mass and brilliance. A raven winged over the hood, and he could not help but think of Mariko lifting over him.

Pinkey grinned. He was going only thirty miles an hour, but he straightened his arms against the steering wheel as if taking turns on a racetrack. McKay tried to count how many times he had bailed Pinkey out of jail. Twenty times? "Let's cut the sonofabitching wire," he said, breaking the silence.

"What wire?" Pinkey asked.

"At the Camp . . ."

"They'll just shoot you down. . . . Is that what you want?"

McKay closed his eyes. He saw the fire a bullet makes in the dark and the zinging sound of its passage. His lips were chapped and he licked them with his tongue, then pressed his head against the frosty window. He knew the truck was moving—when he opened his eyes the landscape strobed by. The sun shot hard through the glass, rolling geometric shapes over the dashboard. He held his head. His mouth opened, and from it came a silent, then barely audible cry.

20

March. Out of 2,300 men in Heart Mountain eligible for the draft, only 38 have volunteered for the all-Nisei combat unit. Approximately 400 Issei and Nisei here have applied for repatriation to Japan. I think they've signed their lives away. They won't be welcome there or here. Sad.

Much to everyone's surprise, the resistance has become quite solid. Even the block leaders—the "blockheads"—who have been conservative in all things refused to capitulate and made a declaration of nonpartisanship, refused to take on the responsibility of forcing their residents to comply with the army. Good for them.

Jack, Taki, and Emi came over with some rumba records tonight. It was fun watching them dance. Emi insisted on teaching me the tango. It was something to laugh about. Had to turn the volume up high because the wind's roar had become deafening. It felt good to drown everything out. There's so much bad blood here, coming from within and without. I don't know which is worse. We're split in so many directions at once, even our self-hate, at which we're becoming expert, is fractured. Which self should we hate—the self that hates the Issei and is a patriot, the self that sides with the Issei and is a disloyal, the self that feels betrayed by his slant eyes and American stomach?

What the press refers to as "the Japanese problem" has seen a revival. One of our congressmen who has never deigned to visit the camp reported that we're being "pampered" and "coddled"; that we're idle, fat-waisted; that we have wine with meals; that we hoard food which was intended for the citizens of Wyoming; that while we're luxuriating here, the boys in Guadalcanal are starving. I invite him personally to come live among us, to eat stewed beef hearts and sour milk; to rot—not idle—the best years of our lives away; to be jailed, having committed no crime; to be peered and poked at by outsiders as if we were in a zoo; to be hated, spat upon, turned away at restaurants and barbershops; to be the brunt of vicious cartoons.

Saturday. Got only one letter from Li. How can I blame her? It must seem as hopeless from her point of view as it does from mine. Can we even be sure that if the war were over tomorrow we would be allowed to return home?

Monday. Had tea with Abe-san, Mariko, and Will. The Heart Mountain Congress has reached a stalemate since the end of registration. Will is skinnier than ever, downright gaunt. He talks emphatically, cynically, brilliantly. But I fear for him. From reading the newspapers, the mood of the country seems more racist than ever, and surely there will be repercussions for those who protested, if not for all of us.

Asked Abe-san where he thought racism came from. He smiled and touched his head with his long fingers and said, "No imagination." Then Mariko asked what I thought, and I said hating others must come from hating ourselves. Abe-san threw his head back and, sucking in air, said, "Same thing!"

Friday nite. Tonight is the "anniversary" of my coming together with Li. Funny, I should be thinking about it so hard now, when I feel her attentions waning. It makes me wonder if human beings' drive to "pursue happiness" is fuelled solely by discontent. We seem to be at odds with the world and spend our lives struggling trying to make it fit us, and not the other way around. So it is with my feelings for Li, for anyone. How I ache for what I cannot have tonight.

Looked up a map of China. We're getting quite a good library together now, considering where we are. The River Li runs north and south. She was named for it; her family fished and farmed on its banks a century before.

Went home after a short bull session with Iwasaka and a cup of sake. Thought I'd talk to Will. Instead, found Mariko asleep on her bed. She had thrown off all the covers and lay sleeping, curled and smooth and perfect as a seashell, naked.

It shocked me. Not the nakedness, but her beauty. What a fool I've been all evening, drowning myself in sorrows over things past, when what is before me, what is in the present can move me so.

Later. Looked in the mirror for a long time. It's not narcissism—I'm trying to see "the mask," the Japanese in me, the American. But the more I look the less I see. The racial mask is inside the head, a projection, as if the flesh were a blank screen on which we inflict stereotypes. If I look Japanese and think American, does that change my facial characteristics? Am I more than who I think I am; am I double?

Sunday evening I put my journal away and went to Abe-san's. I can't remember when I started taking off my shoes at his door—just like an old Issei.

Found him in a pile of wood shavings, carving a new mask. He looked up at me, then continued working. Light from the window cut his face in half, as if he, like the mask, were only half-finished. "Every cut I make is a cut toward Nirvana," he likes to say. I sat down on the floor in front of him. Ever since the night I came to sit Zazen and he refused me, I've gotten a little nervous, never knowing when I'll get the boot again, or why.

Finally he put down his chisel and swept the floor. He gathered the shavings in a dust pan and poured them into the wood stove. Flames shot up under the lid, then died down.

"Do you know Ikkyu?" he asked.

"Who?" I thought he meant someone at the Camp.

He put his hands on his thighs and tilted his head back. I could hear the wind rattle the windows and doors. He began reciting:

Ten years spent in brothels, elation difficult to exhaust.
Now, forced to live amid empty mountains and gloomy valleys,
Thirty thousand miles of cloud spread between here and those delightful
    places;
The wind in the tall pines around the house grates upon my ears.

"What's that?" I asked.
"Ikkyu talking."
Abe-san sat with his hands on his thighs:
"Ikkyu was Rinzai Zen master. Later, was abbot of Daitoko-ji in Kyoto.
They say he was crazy—call him Unsui—'Crazy Cloud'—because he
didn't follow rules. He live in Kyoto in 1400s—very bad time. There were
wars, droughts, corruption in Buddhist temples. Kyoto burn down and
when people go hungry, monasteries have food. Ikkyu hate all this. When
he was young—younger than you—and he go find teacher, but teacher
would not let him through gate, so Ikkyu sat outside with nothing to eat
or drink, nothing to sleep on. He wait. Finally, teacher send someone out
with bucket of water—throw on Ikkyu's head, but still, Ikkyu would not
go away. Finally teacher let him in and he attained enlightenment."
Abe-san grasped his knees and rocked backward.
"Why does he talk about brothels, then?" I asked.
Abe-san scowled. Then replied with this:

Crazy Cloud, who knows to what wild wind he belongs?
Morning in the mountains, evening in the city . . .

"Ikkyu would say to you, 'Good and evil are not two; false and true are
same.' "
I shifted restlessly, and Abe-san continued.
"If you are enlightened, does not mean there is no pain, no confusion
in your life. To Ikkyu, desire and—letting go of desire—same thing."
I made a sound—embarrassed laughter, because I knew he saw I didn't
really understand. But who could unless they already knew these things,
then there would be no need to understand.
"Ikkyu wander all the time and write poems. He live like hermit in
mountain. Other times, he live in very poor section of cities, Kyoto and
down by Osaka, in Sakai. He fight with abbot of temple; that abbot was

corrupt man. Ikkyu have lover, blind woman—Mori—and when he become abbot of Daitoko-ji, she live next to temple ground. Ikkyu spend
whole life fighting. He live like old Tang master. They were eccentric.
They practice wild and free. He was only monk to talk about sex. Others
did what he did too, but they try to hide it. This is what he thought of
them:

In the midst of pleasure there is pain in Ikkyu's school.
Each frog fighting for respect at the bottom of the well;
Day and night busy thinking about the words of the scriptures;
Right and wrong, self and other, fussing away a whole life."

Abe-san tipped his head to one side and looked into my eyes. "When Ikkyu
abbot, he move far from temple to mountain. Many artists come there.
He was fourteenth-century bohemian. Artist, poet, and painter, gather
there; tea ceremony and Noh theater begin then. He was first monk to
live Zen outside monastery . . . he follow no rules. But what are rules
for? In Zen, they are only reminder. Ikkyu don't need them. He was
furyu—full of passion. He see everything, he mix with everyone, afraid of
nothing. . . . Whole world was his monastery—his discipline."
    Abe-san grasped his knees again and tilted so far back I thought he
would fall over, but he didn't. He righted himself. "That's how I wish I
lived my life," he said.

Went for a walk that evening. It was cold but I continued on. I did not
like what I had become. That's all I knew, but maybe that's all I needed
to know. . . . I remember stopping in front of one of the barracks to listen
to a jazz band play over the radio. The music sounded flat—it had the
kind of depth that comes from bitterness, not wonder. That's how I was
too. I walked on. I kept feeling a pocket of something inside me, a ruined
well. "But I'm too young to feel like that," I said aloud. At the end of
rows of barracks, I looked back at the Camp. For a minute I hated Abe-
san and all those old Issei with their ideas. . . . Then I remembered how
he had gazed at me while talking about Ikkyu. . . .
    The Camp looked as if something had collapsed even though all the
shabby buildings were standing; the people walking around were steel

bearings rolling aimlessly, and the dust—always the dust—rose senselessly like exhaled smoke.

I walked to the waterhole, the one used by children in the summer. The water was shallow and cold. What was I doing here? I took off my clothes hurriedly and sat down on the "beach." Some beach. I could see snow on top of Heart Mountain.

The water numbed my feet but I went all the way in, crouching to let it wash over my back. For a moment, I floated. When I saw how white I was and how my belly had grown, I felt disgust. Once I asked Abe-san where in the human body the soul resided. Barefoot, sitting cross-legged, he laughed. Then he picked up his foot by his little toe and said, "Here!"

A half-moon sailed through clouds. "Deliver me," I said out loud. "From myself." I rolled over and dogpaddled in a circle. When I stood up, my feet sank in the muck. The water tickled my waist. I tried to see the whole moon, not just the half that was reflecting sunlight, because I knew my inclination was to reduce everything to controllable parts . . . just like those monks Ikkyu hated . . . right and wrong, self and other. . . . That's what "historical detachment" will do for you. Bullshit. I'd been fending everything off, protecting myself . . . but from what?

When I pounded the cold water with my fists it splashed into my face and came down like tears.

21

The morning the last of the river ice went out, fifty elk came down to the river. They drank, then waded to the island. Their tracks flattened the sand where it had mounded up in tiny dunes and in among the river stones their black scats lay polished as pebbles. Heart Mountain rose above them. It was misted rock, the top vermillion half floating above the base and the base floating above the ground. "It looks torn," McKay thought, as he finished morning chores and reconnected a water line that had frozen during the winter. He felt as if he had stones in his throat; the exacerbating fact of Mariko's absence stood up in his mind like a tree.

McKay rode out through the west pasture, roping, doctoring, and eartagging calves. He and his brothers had always loved these early spring days "when a man could get his rope down and let his horse run awhile." When he finished, he rode to the river. Overhead the clouds looked more like waves, the kind of waves that come toward shore but never break, whose cresting swells suddenly flatten and return to deeper water. He thought he had reached the bottom of his loneliness, but now another depth revealed itself—one that he could not push beyond and as he approached the river, orange and scarlet clouds traveled over him without breaking.

He stepped down, slid the hobbles from the D-ring at the back of his saddle, and hobbled his horse. Since the day he had been turned away from the Camp, unable to see Mariko, his mouth and head had felt thick and spongy, as if his craving for her had become waterlogged. He walked to the tip of the gravel bar and lay down on the rocky edge. Where the current had scooped out a deep hole, the water was turquoise. Two or three small trout headed into the stream and held themselves, fluttering, near the bottom. When he put his hand into the water, it turned numb.

McKay walked. Halfheartedly, he twirled once, because he was thinking of the way he had circled the room with Mariko in his arms. Then he sat with his back against a piece of driftwood. He pulled his heavy coat on and closed his eyes. When he was a child, Bobby had told him that if he listened—really listened—he could hear everything in the world. He could even hear the future coming.

He tried to make his mind quiet. Every few seconds a chunk of ice floated by because upstream, at ten thousand feet, it was still winter. The wind came out of the northwest and all along the tops of mountains snow sprayed straight up and came down finely sifted, like flour. He listened. At ten thousand feet, wind blew through pines, but above, where there were no trees, who knew how long those spring winds had been blowing, since sound is only a function of resistance to what no longer flows freely.

He heard the ache in his body fasten itself to his throat and groin and over that, gusts skating down the river and the river sounds rising in the interludes. The gravel bar was a bridge whose connecting ends had washed out. What was on the banks that he so hungered for? The ache set up in him like cement. He unfastened his pants. He did not want to think of her now because he did not want to use her this way, but her face streamed in, shunting against him like a train. A chunk of ice knocked the shore, then bumped out into the current. He held himself. It was not pleasure he wanted but knowledge: full knowledge that surpasses consciousness. Then he did not need to think. Her presence moved his hips skyward, toward turbulent winds no one could see, and the river flooded through his body soundlessly.

By the time the last five hundred cows had calved, the first five hundred were old enough to brand and turn out into spring pasture. Bobby cooked wild turkey and a side of beef, and the women brought potato salads, bread, cakes and pies, and the neighbors who came worked. Madeleine, Jesse, and Pinkey roped while Bobby vaccinated and McKay branded, and some of the children from town held the calves when the ropers dragged them to the fire. When Pinkey tired, he changed jobs with McKay and held the red-hot branding iron to the ribs of each calf while the hair and flesh smell curled over his face. After their ordeal the branded calves bucked out across the pasture, and four days later McKay, Pinkey, Madeleine, Jesse, and his children moved a thousand pairs to spring pasture. At the first water crossing, the calves tried to turn back. McKay dismounted and carried one or two across—and after much whooping and hollering, the others high-stepped through. It is wind and water that bring spring in, McKay thought, water that takes the ice away, and he was happy to ride with his chaps dripping. The cows moved slowly because of the calves. The crew drove them up the great alluvial fans of Heart Mountain, crossing three ridges at its base—buttresses for the limestone tower above them.

McKay and Madeleine rode point at the head of the herd and turned the lead. When the cattle broke into a run, they rode hard and fast, down through willows, spooking the herd up and out of a creek bottom, loping across a wide bench through the last gate to a ten-thousand-acre pasture.

As they rode back in the dark, a bottle of schnapps was passed. Bobby drove the chuckwagon and fed the roundup crew as they moved up and across the mountain. He kept the fresh horses watered and grained, because the riders could use the same horse only every third day. So there were forty or fifty horses in the remuda. Because of the war they never knew whom they could get to ride with them, so they had to have plenty of gentle horses, and during the rest of the year McKay worked hard with up-and-coming colts as well as the older ones in the herd. He tried to use them enough so they weren't bored but rest them enough so they didn't turn sour.

Pinkey had always trained the stock dogs, though the word *train* didn't describe what he did. There were no shouted commands such as "Heel" or "Come." He merely let a young dog follow him everywhere while he talked softly, cautioning him about this and that, letting the dog feel his way around a horse or a herd, calling him back from retrieving a cow, feeding the dog whatever he, Pinkey, ate, and letting him sleep on the bed.

Because Pinkey was in his sixties, McKay gave him only gentle horses to ride. "Dog gentle," Pinkey liked to quip as Eleanor, his favorite mare, ate cookies and drank beer out of his hand.

On roundup, their nights were spent talking about the personalities of animals, what a horse's mind was like, and no one there ever tired of such talk. And every year, after the dug-in routine of winter, McKay was glad for the long stint on horseback, of living with the herds. Sometimes when he looked out over them he failed to see how anyone could think an animal was stupid or uninteresting. The more years he rode, the more minds he was exposed to, the more it seemed as if there were no fundamental differences between a human and an animal, except that maybe animals were smarter. They rarely staged wars.

By the end of April all the pairs had been moved to spring pasture. The last day McKay wanted to ride the northernmost fence and check the youngest calves. He and Madeleine stopped at the spring where an old tin cup hung from a nail in the tree.

"I'm so stiff I don't know if I can get off," Madeleine said, so McKay brought her all the water she wanted. Then he drank too. From there he could see Bobby and Pinkey driving the chuckwagon home and hoped they would stay sober.

They rode up through the breaks where the soil turned sandy and pine trees grew. Their horses moved in unison. The air smelled moist and fresh and the sage smell was sharp under the horses' feet. McKay stopped a few times to mend the top wire of the fence where deer had broken it down.

They reached Pinkey's cow camp just before dark. McKay lit the kerosene lamp on the table. After, he helped Madeleine picket the horses. He lit a fire in the stove and Madeleine went through the cupboards for food but found only whiskey. The cabin was always neat but better stocked with booze than food. She took down the bottle of Cobb's Creek and sat at the table where Pinkey had left a game of solitaire the fall before, and finished his game. McKay dipped a bucket of fresh water from the spring and put a pot of coffee on. He and Madeleine had spent so many summers of their life at this cow camp, they did these small chores without having to say anything.

When the water boiled, McKay dumped in three large spoonfuls of coffee, then poured cold water over the grounds. Madeleine found two old cups in the back of the cupboards and wiped them on her shirt.

"Do you want to play?" Madeleine said.

"No . . . do you?"

"No . . ."

Madeleine turned her chair so it faced McKay. She put her elbows on her knees and looked down.

"What?" McKay asked.

"I don't know . . . I've missed you."

"But we've been working together day and night."

"I know."

"You've seemed so distracted, though . . ."

"I guess I have been."

Madeleine held his hand tightly, then gathered up the other one and held them both and he put his face down so the backs of her hands touched his cheeks. "He's been gone almost two years. . . ."

McKay looked away.

"What's the point?" he asked in a flat voice, and she knew he was bitter.

"There isn't a point. There's just right now, that's all."

McKay lay facedown on the bed. Madeleine filled the coffee cups and took them over. With one hand she rubbed his back. She was trembling and she had to keep looking outside because she felt herself filling and emptying over and over until the sensations became blurred. The whiskey touched the back of her throat and the warmth of the room softened her. She pulled McKay's shirt up and touched the skin on his back and realized how rough her hand had become during months of feeding and calving.

"I still love you, you know," she blurted out.

McKay turned slowly until he was on his back facing her. "Madeleine . . . I'm seeing someone else."

Madeleine's hand stopped moving.

"You know who it is, don't you?" he asked.

"Yes." For a long time neither of them spoke or moved.

"It's just like us to have our timing all off," Madeleine said at last.

McKay laughed. "It's all right. . . ."

"No it isn't—nothing's all right," she said.

McKay put his hand on her leg. "Give me some of that coffee."

Madeleine passed the cup to him and he sat up to drink. When he was finished she leaned forward and pushed her head into his shoulder.

"I want you," she said.

McKay stood suddenly and went to the door. He threw his coffee out on the ground and set the empty cup on the table next to the cards. He took off his boots. Madeleine's eyes moved from McKay's feet. He unfastened his jeans and shirt and scarf, his underwear. The yellow light of the lamp wavered against his body but he thought it was his mind vacillating. She held her arms out.

"Come here," she said. Then she undressed too and he lay down beside her.

"This feels strange," he said.

"Does it?" She put her hand on the small of his back.

"Call me something nice," he said.

"Sweet pea . . ."

"No . . ."

"Lamb chop . . ."

She raised up on her elbows and looked at him.

"Sweetheart," she said.

"Yes . . ."

She put her hand on the back of his neck and held his head to hers. "Closer . . ."

"I am," he said.

"Closer . . ."

He moved over her and she held him back.

"Wait."

"I can't," he said.

"Wait anyway—"

"For a long time?"

"No, not too long. I just want to see you."

When he lay back his gold hair rose on the pillow like broken waves.

"I can't stay like this too much longer," he said.

"I know. . . ." She pulled him over on her again.

"Hello," he said, touching her face.

She felt the warmth of the whiskey and his warmth in her body at the same time.

"Just stay like that," she pleaded. "Don't move yet—"

"I want to keep looking at you. . . ."

"I can't—"

"You can. . . ."

"Oh, McKay . . ."

"What?"

Her eyes opened wide.

"Are you all right?" he asked, but she did not answer.

McKay woke once in the night and stoked the fire, and when he slipped back into bed Madeleine was awake and turned to him, and they made love again.

In the morning they dressed quickly and rode to the ranch. The days were just beginning to get long, so they could do a day's worth of work before lunch and another day's worth by nightfall. The horses blew hard, sneezing and snorting. Their hooves pounded down like posts being driven into frozen ground. At the corrals they pulled their saddles and broke the ice on the water gap so the horses could drink. Madeleine watched a flock of pine siskins that had overwintered on the ranch swoop and spin and land on the haystack. McKay looked at her.

"I feel rotten," he said. "About Henry."

Madeleine looked at the birds again, then at him. "It was my idea. . . ."

McKay wiped the dust from his face with a blue bandanna.

"Well, this is a hell of a time to feel remorse . . . goddamn, McKay . . ."

McKay held the folded bandanna in his hand and turned it over once, then stuffed it into his back pocket. Something made the birds take off and they swooped overhead.

"It's not all right because of what we didn't do years ago . . . ," McKay said.

Madeleine gave a look of surprise. She had waited for McKay to come forward, to make some move, but at the last moment he always ducked out.

"I waited for you," she said flatly.

"I know." McKay took the bandanna from his back pocket again and wiped his face, giving the impression that it was hot, though it wasn't because the sun had just come up over the ridge and ice spanned the ditches. "I'm sorry," he said, though Madeleine didn't know whether he was saying it to her or to Henry or to himself. Then he picked up the two saddles, carried them into the saddle shed, and walked in silence to the house.

Bobby flipped pancakes, listening to the morning farm report, and the ones that weren't perfectly round he gave to the dogs. When McKay and Madeleine came in he turned, holding the spatula midair, and frowned at McKay, then went back to his work, whistling. On the table were platters of deer liver, fried eggs, pots of jam, and syrup. McKay and Madeleine took off their coats and chaps, then sat down to eat. When Bobby joined them, McKay caught the old man's eyes. The look on Bobby's face was pensive, then, as he looked at McKay and Madeleine eating together, he smiled.

"God, he always knows everything," McKay thought.

The phone rang. It was for Madeleine. She twisted herself in the phone cord and faced down the dark hall to the living room as she listened. Then she hung up and, wheeling, grabbed Bobby and hid her face.

"What? Tell Bobby. . . ."

When her head lifted, her eyes met McKay's.

"Oh God . . . oh God," she said in a hoarse whisper. "He's alive!"

McKay pushed his chair from the table.

"There's a letter at the post office. It's from a prison camp."

"Henry?" McKay said in disbelief.

"It's from a prison camp in Japan. . . ."

"Henry . . . ," McKay said again. He held her now. Then she wiggled from him.

After, Bobby filled McKay's plate again but he only stared at the food.

"You think Henry alive?" Bobby asked.

"Yes I do."

"Then you better leave Madeleine alone," he said curtly and took the plates away.

McKay put his foot in the stirrup and swung on the colt. From the road above the grainfield he could see the entire ranch—house, outbuildings, calving sheds, and Bobby bent over in the huge garden. People in town always talk about the bracing, stoical unity a war brings, how it makes a doer of everyone, how it makes for strange bedfellows . . . but hell, almighty, he had all that before the war. "That's city-talk," he thought. That's nothing a sheepherder doesn't know. And they say sheepherders are stupid. . . ."

He rode to the end of the road, then turned back. The spring sky changed every minute or so, but the feel of the horse under him always felt the same, the way home feels the same, even when someone changes the furniture.

The envelope was narrow and long and made of rice paper. Down one side was a string of Japanese characters. The part of the envelope where Henry's writing showed was wrinkled, though still legible. She opened the top flap carefully. Lidia, the postmaster, pressed herself so close, her breasts touched Madeleine's elbow, and the others who had come in for the mail slowly formed a circle around her. The lobby was small and after reading the letter through once to herself, she began to read aloud.

I am alive. I was taken prisoner of war in 1942. My health was good when we surrendered and it's good now. We've been growing a garden and we're getting more to eat now. I keep thinking how tough this has been on you and I'm sorry. I know you're taking good care of things. You always were a better hand than me. With luck I'll be home someday when all this is over and we'll see if I can still rope a steer or ride a bronc. Please say hello to everyone. I love you, Henry.

After, Madeleine held the letter for a long time and let her eyes run over the words. It was his writing, though a little shakier than usual.

"And all this time I thought he was dead," she thought, "because in that big ocean, how can someone missing in action ever be found?"

She looked up. The throng had thinned, but Lidia met her eyes.

"I wasn't prepared for good news," Madeleine explained. "I don't know what to do."

Lidia hugged her again, until finally Madeleine pulled away from her soft bulk. "You don't have to do anything," Lidia said. Madeleine looked at the date on the letter again: August 16, 1943. Her expression changed.

"This letter is eight months old. . . . Anything could have happened between then and now. . . ."

"Don't think like that," Lidia admonished.

Madeleine nodded wordlessly and walked out the door.

When Carol Lyman reached the post office, people were still talking about "the miracle."

"What miracle?" Carol demanded, and Lidia told her. Carol closed her eyes and pursed her lips as if she had just eaten a lemon. "How wonderful," she said at last in a choked voice. "That's what I've been waiting for."

"The new list is up," Lidia reminded her, but Carol did not look at it.

As Carol started her car she felt like exploding. "Willard, your uncle is alive," she said aloud though there was no one to hear. When she saw Madeleine on the street she wondered whether she should stop and say something. But Madeleine waved her down first.

"I heard the news," Carol yelled, rolling down the window. "It's glorious."

Madeleine leaned against the black coupe, clutching the letter to her chest. "I can't believe it," she gasped.

"This calls for a celebration, don't you think?" Carol said. "Hop in, you're in no condition to drive."

Madeleine shrugged. She didn't want to go home and face McKay. "Where are we going?" she asked, settling back in the seat. She touched Carol's sunglasses on the dashboard, then put them on. "How do I look?"

"Like a movie star," Carol quipped as she sped through town. "Is Snuff's okay? He'll be so pleased to hear. . . ."

Madeleine took a deep breath. "Sure."

Carol drove faster than usual. She wanted the exhilaration of speed. She looked over at Madeleine, whose eyes were closed.

"Is that the letter?" Carol asked.

"Yes," she said, and slid her finger over the ink on the envelope as if it were Henry's face. She thought about him—wiry, funny, impulsive. Nothing like the letter. Maybe the camp had broken him and he would come back with a blank look in his eyes, or maybe he was dying of malnutrition and all his hair had fallen out. Either that, or he was raising hell, charming the guards into doing things his way. Hard to know. Maybe he wasn't even alive anymore.

"Do you want me to read it to you?" Madeleine asked.

"Oh yes, that would be grand."

Madeleine read slowly: "I am alive," the letter began. Listening, Carol wished she could get her sunglasses back. She fought tears. "I musn't let anything show," she said to herself and tried to concentrate on driving.

Snuff's parking lot was empty.

"Did you hear?" Carol's voice rang out as they entered the bar.

Snuff looked up from washing glasses. "I hope it's good."

"It is," Madeleine said softly.

"Oh, I didn't see you."

"Henry's alive . . . ," Carol said. "He's a prisoner of war in Japan."

Snuff extended his hand over the bar to Madeleine.

"Great news. . . . It must make things a little easier, huh?"

Madeleine nodded.

"Drinks on the house."

"Have you ever had a Manhattan?" Carol asked. "Why don't you have one with me?"

Madeleine laughed. "Sure. Why not. What's in it anyway?"

"You'll see," Snuff said, shaking the container.

Snuff set their drinks down and the two women lifted their glasses in unison. After taking a sip, Madeleine whistled.

"Wow. That's one hell of a drink. It's not too bad," she said, making a face at Snuff.

"Here's to Henry. I wish there was more we could do for him," Snuff said, raising his glass.

"Henry," Carol said, relishing the sound of his name.

Madeleine and Carol shared another round.

"Now I won't have to go to the post office anymore," Carol mused. "I've been reading the casualty lists everyday, you know."

"I didn't realize you had relatives in . . .," Madeleine said.

"Oh goodness, I don't really. I'm quite alone," she said primly. "But you and I . . ." She paused and put her finger to her lips. "You and I are . . . related."

"What do you mean?"

"It's really Henry . . ."

"Henry?"

"And Willard. What I mean is that you are, in a way, Willard's aunt."

Madeleine put her glass down.

Clearing her throat, Carol touched her hand to the top wave of her hair. She caught Snuff's eyes, then looked away.

"Yes," she said, then took another drink. "I've kept it from you . . ."

"What are you saying?"

"Willard is illegitimate."

Madeleine felt her face redden. "I can't believe it."

"I couldn't tell anyone . . . but the war . . . and now with Henry taken prisoner and whatnot . . . I thought it best." Carol looked down at the front of her peach-colored sweater. She had spilled part of her drink on it and with her finger, tried to remove the stain. She knew she had misled Madeleine into thinking that Willard was Henry's child, not Carter's, but did nothing to correct that impression.

Madeleine set her drink down and walked out the door.

"What's wrong with her?" Snuff said, wiping the counter.

Carol looked up but her eyes followed Madeleine.

"Carol?"

When she stood, she staggered a little bit, then smoothed the front of her dress. "Oh dear. I think I've overdone it this time," she said.

22

Rain boiled over the mountains that night and did not let up for two days. Carol Lyman stood out on the front porch of her frame house and smelled the air. A flock of finches swarmed the tree. . . .

"Willard, come look. Those little birds are back," she called out.

Willard came to the porch carrying his willow. He ran his hand up and down the bark, feeling the scars and knots. It was the only skin he ever touched except his own.

"Can you hear those birds?" Carol asked.

Willard smiled and held his willow out from under the porch roof. Rivulets of rain ran down the tiny trunk, darkening it, wetting his hand and arm. Then one finch alighted on the top branch, then another and another, until the willow was full of birds. Willard gasped with delight.

"Look at them," Carol whispered, but the sound of her voice frightened them away.

Willard pulled the willow out of the rain. "Tree of life," Carol thought.

She had not seen the severed heads that time, but actual birds, and felt relieved. The front porch of the summer house where she had met Willard's father was similar, though much grander in scale, and at the time she had allowed herself to imagine watching the rain on that porch, with him, for many years. It was not happiness she had expected, but a purpose in life—a nest with many children and the hard work that goes with ranching. There was no work she felt was beneath her. She would have done anything.

Willard turned to her and held out the willow between them until the feathery branches touched her face. She grabbed his arm, wrenching the tree to one side so she could see his face.

"Willard . . . talk to me. Please, Willard, can't you talk?"

Willard looked frightened. He stepped back and one shoulder twitched. He lifted the willow again and held it out to her, this time as an offering.

"No, Willard, that's not what I want," she cried, grabbing his arm again.

Willard took her hand from his arm and, smiling, wrapped her fingers around the trunk. The branch made Carol's hand wet and she was afraid it would fill up with heads again, instead of birds.

When one of Mañuel's roosters crowed, Willard backed away, to the fence between the two yards, and peered into the cages. The brown cock with green and black neck feathers strutted, stretching his neck. He turned back to his mother, exuberant, and crowed.

On Sunday, Carol took off early, leaving Willard behind. It had been raining almost continuously. Where the railroad tracks crossed the river, wind lifted sprays of water and blew them against the green cliff. She liked driving in the rain because she thought no one could see her. Since she had revealed her secret to Madeleine—her secret and her lie—she felt horribly exposed, as if the sanctity of that night with Carter Heaney had been broken.

As she drove through town she saw Snuff's truck parked in front of the Catholic church. The thought of him there made her smile. She went in, and stood at the back by the font. Plain on the outside, the interior was fashioned after a mission-style church with white plaster walls, vigas, and a hand-tinted photograph of the Pope, much enlarged, attached to an oversized easel with two clothespins. Snuff stood at the

altar in purple robes. Under them, she could see his cowboy boots. After
the priest poured wine and water into the chalice, the two men turned
and the congregation came forward silently, kneeling at the altar rail.

"This is the bread of . . ."

Carol walked outside. She didn't believe in that god or any god, but
she had a certain feeling about things . . . like the willow branch and
the heads . . . that there were more than simple, literal truths. . . .

"What am I going to do?" she said aloud to herself. Her hands touched
the cold steering wheel.

She drove to Madeleine's ranch prepared to tell the truth this time—
the truth being that Carter Heaney, not Henry, was Willard's father—
but Madeleine wasn't there. She left a note: "There's been a misunder-
standing. Please call. Carol Lyman," then continued on, north across
Alkali Creek and Eagle Nest Creek toward the bar.

As she drove, the hood of her coupe shone like black patent leather.
She opened a box of fudge and bit into a dark square. Ten in the morning,
eating fudge. She preferred to eat alone like a wild animal. If only I could
live without the need for another human . . . without all these entan-
glements, she mused. She was a continual disappointment to herself.
Yet she had begged Willard to talk to her the night before. I've gotten
quite out of control, she said, cautioning herself. The fudge melted in
her mouth and she wondered if pleasure couldn't also be bitter, like the
news about Henry who was alive but not free, who lived close but was
almost a stranger. She opened the window and let rain hit her face.

The door to the bar was locked and she fumbled inside her purse
for the keys. Inside, gray light funneled through the porthole window
and the flannel curtains sagged heavily as if the rifles pictured on them
werc actually loaded. She put her purse on a bar stool whose leather seat
was torn. A single car passed and the whine of its tires on wet pavement
entered the room like screams. She knelt on the dance floor. Lifting her
hand, she crossed herself as she had seen Snuff do, though she didn't
know what it meant.

"Forgive me," she said. Then the telephone rang.

When Snuff came back from church, Carol did not mention that she
had seen him.

"Guess who I ran into," he said, carrying a load of groceries.

"Who?"

"The Wild Man. He's got problems."

"He's the strangest man I've ever heard of . . . driving around in that big yellow car with the top down . . . like royalty. . . ."

"He's got two girls in trouble," Snuff said.

"Two?" She switched on the radio.

"I sent him up to Venus, in Butte . . . she'll help him," he said, disappearing into the storeroom.

After talking to Madeleine, Carol had felt relieved. She had leaned the ladder against the side windows and took the curtains down. Up close, the duck hunters on flannel didn't look like men at all. She soaked them in a big tub in the middle of the floor—right where she had kneeled, under the bent chandelier that gave out no light.

Now she laid the curtains on the backs of three chairs to dry.

When the news came on, she heard about another local boy who was taken prisoner of war in the Philippines; how magpies were bringing a bounty of one cent apiece and that 1,650 of them had been killed by youngsters so far. There was a report on the nearby POW camp for Nazis—they had gone on strike—and that the basic diet of the American soldier in German camps was largely potatoes, cabbage, and fish. A local woman shot a black bear while panning for gold with her father, sugar for home canning was being made available without deduction of blue point stamps from War Ration Book Two, that the disallowance of weather broadcasts would continue indefinitely; a Presbyterian minister from the Heart Mountain Relocation Camp would speak in town Wednesday night; there were 17,083 American POWs residing in enemy countries. "And Henry is one of them," she thought.

After the news, "String of Pearls" and "At Last" played. She couldn't help thinking that the last item of the broadcast was just for her. "Henry . . . Madeleine's Henry," she thought a little enviously.

Snuff came in and stood beside Carol. "You washed the curtains."

"He's got *two* girls in trouble?" Carol asked again.

"Yes.

"Once he told me his name was Mutt," Carol said.

"No one's name is Mutt."

"No one's name is the Wild Man either."

"It's Lenny Weinstein."

"Who?"

"The Wild Man."

"Really?" Carol said.

"One's the banker's daughter, too," Snuff said.

"Oh my goodness."

Snuff continued: "Lenny's brother is some kind of physicist, a genius they say, doing something for the war effort. The Wild Man's completely opposed, of course."

"You mean he's for Hitler?" Carol said.

Snuff poked her chin. "No . . . he's not for Hitler, or Mussolini either," he said, laughing.

"I think whatever is going on he does the opposite; that's all," Carol said as she walked behind the bar and poured two cups of coffee.

Snuff sat on a stool. His bow tie hung straight down and his shirt-sleeves were rolled to the elbow.

"Remember when that dog of his died?"

"Whose, Lenny's?"

"Do we have to call him Lenny now?" Carol asked.

Snuff grinned. "No—"

She looked away. "I saw you in church today."

He gave her a surprised look. "I didn't see you."

"I only stood at the back."

"You could have come in. . . ."

"I know."

He looked at her. "What's wrong?"

"I did something terrible."

"Tell me."

"To Madeleine . . . I told her—"

"Shhh . . ." Snuff put his finger to his lips. "Listen."

They heard the whine of an air-raid siren.

"Oh no," she cried. "Not again."

Snuff caught her hand.

"Maybe it's for real this time," she said.

"Maybe so . . ."

When the whistle sounded an all-clear, Carol slumped back against the bar. She watched as Snuff went to the window and looked out. The rain had let up and in the west, a band of blue could be seen.

A roar woke McKay, and Bobby, and Pinkey as he lay in his bunk at cow camp, as well as Madeleine, who had dreamt that Henry was climbing down from a tall building on vines. The deep, persistent sound made her sit up in bed, and immediately upon waking she knew two things, or thought she knew: that Henry was alive and that the sound wasn't wind but water.

When she phoned McKay he was already dressed. They agreed to check three headgates, then meet halfway between the two ranches. It had been raining for four days. In Luster, a small tornado spirited a pig shed straight into the air like an upturned ship and three weiner pigs fell out of the sky. What Madeleine and McKay both heard was a wall of orange mud breaking loose from the top of Heart Mountain.

The ground was slick on the sidehills, but when the sun came out it dried quickly. Madeleine hadn't felt well the night before, and she still had cramps, but she rode at a good pace because there was a lot of country to cover.

She saw where the flood had taken out the first headgate. Orange mud covered the slope and buried the grass. Whole trees, carried down from the mountain, lay scattered above and below the ditch. She rode on.

When she arrived at the creek that divided McKay's ranch from the Camp, she saw that water had taken out part of the fence. The sun shone brightly now and already the streets between the Camp buildings had turned dusty. Up above, at the flank of the mountain, the irrigation boxes had been torn in half. She stepped off her horse to see whether they could be repaired, and when she tried to get back on, her legs went out from under her with pain. She lay in the grass holding her horse's rein. The cramps came in waves. She could see the tall smokestack of the Camp hospital, and near her head, sego lilies opened wide, exposing the magenta cross in the center. She unbuttoned her jeans. The sun felt warm against her abdomen. Once the cramps came so hard she yelled out, not from pain, but from a despair she could not name.

McKay rode quickly from headgate to headgate. They would all have to be rebuilt. It had been dry and he was glad it had rained anyway. He rode through the last gate and looked for Madeleine. It was three in the afternoon and he had had trouble catching his horse, which should have put him behind her. He waited and rode in her direction for a mile, then turned and rode home.

She had called. "Tell McKay I wasn't feeling so good and I turned back early," she reported to Bobby. When McKay came into the house the phone rang again.

"Madeleine?" he said.

There was a brief silence. "It's Mariko."

McKay dropped his hat on a chair as he listened.

"I'm in Cody. We're printing the paper tonight, and we have two hours before we can start folding. Can you come in? I'll be outside the May-flower Café. I want to see you," she said quickly.

He put the phone down, took his hat, and started out the door.

"Where you go now?" Bobby asked.

McKay turned. "Cody."

"What for? Too much work here."

"Can't."

"Where you go?" Bobby asked again, following McKay outside.

"To see someone."

"Her?" he asked again, following McKay outside.

McKay lay on his back under the truck and fastened the chains. Bobby went down too.

"Better stay home. Too muddy. You get stuck."

McKay came up with mud on his face. "I have to go."

"Madeleine called. She sick, I think."

"I'll call her in the morning. I got that headgate fixed anyway. . . ."

Bobby stood with his arms crossed defiantly. "Better you stay home."

"Bobby, for God's sake, I'm not a kid. . . ."

"No. You just crazy all the time now; that's all . . . ," Bobby yelled as McKay turned the key on and clattered out of the yard.

Mariko was waiting when he pulled up. He'd had to take the chains off at the highway and the chassis had shimmied because he had driven very fast. She was there, leaning back against the wall in wool trousers, boots, Will's black leather jacket, and her hair tied on top of her head.

McKay opened the door. The seat cover was torn where the working dogs had tried to scratch a warm nest and mud caked the steering wheel, floorboard, and gearshift knob.

She hid her head. "Let's get out of here."

Through the steamed windows of the café, McKay saw Kai watching. He made a gesture—thumbs up, palms up. McKay couldn't be sure, but Kai smiled when they pulled away.

"We're almost out of town," he said, stroking Mariko's hair.

She smiled. "I feel like Al Capone."

"You look beautiful."

They drove west, following the river toward the dam. In the long, narrow tunnel blasted out of rock, Mariko slipped her hand behind McKay's head and kissed him half on the mouth.

"Where are we going?" she asked.

"I don't know."

"It doesn't matter."

The rain made the rock black. A wind hit them on the other side of the tunnel and studded the lake with whitecaps. McKay pulled down where there were trees and a tiny beach. He turned in the driver's seat. She caught his hand in hers, then his eyes. The trance was like a river, holding them under its tight surface.

"Let's go for a walk. Do you want to?" he asked.

"Yes, but we don't have much time."

"I know," he said.

She slid out on his side of the truck. The wind came in fat gusts, shaking the trees. They could hear water hitting rock somewhere, and at their feet tiny waves collapsed. He held her and put his nose against the roll of black hair on top of her head, and her hands, strong as ever, pressed against him; he kept forgetting to breathe.

"I don't want to move," she said.

"I don't either."

There had been a half-moon, but the edge of the front moving in overtook it, though from time to time a portion of it shone through. McKay ran his fingers across her face. Her cheekbones seemed to absorb the moonlight and he wondered whether she were silver all the way down to the marrow.

When they walked, the wind pushed at them. Once, she turned her head and he saw her mouth a word but the wind took the sound away and he put his mouth over her soundless one and felt the smile. The strip of beach ended in rock. A branch snapped. When they looked up into the tree, rain hit them. Mariko rubbed the wetness over her face, then held her arms up to welcome more and it came.

They used a piece of canvas to shelter them and lay on blankets in the bed of the stock truck. The rain tapped all over the cloth.

"You don't hate me anymore, do you?" he asked.

"It's different here . . . away from all that."

"I know."

"Let's never go back. . . ."

"Let's not . . . ," he said.

"For a long time I didn't trust you."

"I know," he said, "but you can now. . . ."

She unbuttoned his long underwear and he found his way through her outer layer of clothes until their skin touched and he felt a burning sensation go through him and wondered if he went in deeply enough and reached her center, whether the errant bomb that had been following him since the beginning of the war would go away.

Finally she spoke.

"How did you learn to be so loving . . . way out here?"

McKay laughed shyly.

"I've never felt this way. . . ."

"Like what?" he asked.

"So loved."

"What did you expect?"

She touched his face. "You're not in love with anyone?"

"Yes."

"Who? Or should I ask?"

"You."

Mariko laughed.

"What's wrong?" he asked. "Why does that make you laugh?"

"I'm not used to it," she said. "But are there others?"

"No more than usual."

"What's usual for you?"

"The impossible ones . . . the ones who don't love me, or can't, or are dead."

She looked down. "I'm married."

"I know."

"But not really."

"How do you manage that?"

"It's just an arrangement."

"But wouldn't he still be jealous?"

"He doesn't think along those lines these days."

"What's wrong with him?"

"Nothing."

Then he held her tightly again until he found his way into her. Her hair looked like part of the sky but inside, he came to a brightness. "I can't help it," he kept saying, "I can't help it. . . ."

By the time the rain let up the blankets they were lying on were wet.

"How much time do we have?" she asked.

McKay took his watch from his pocket. "Forty minutes."

She pulled the canvas all the way back and touched his face.

"Let's sit in the truck," he said.

"There isn't enough time for anything," she said as she gathered up her clothes and climbed down to the wet ground.

The sky had cleared in the west. McKay helped her into the truck. For a while she lay with her head on his lap, then sat up and held both his hands.

"I can't stop thinking of the minutes ticking away," she said. "It's like being in a taxi when you can't pay."

"When are they going to issue passes again?" he asked.

"I don't know, but I think soon."

"Then you'll get one, and we'll have a day together."

"Yes."

McKay felt himself get hard again. She put her hand on him as if catching a bird. He bunched up his coat and put it behind her head for a pillow, and she lay back on it.

"Come here, my beauty," she said, laughing, because he had knocked his cowboy hat off on the ceiling of the truck, rearing up and coming down, and entering her.

When they woke the moon was straight up in the sky.

"Oh my God," Mariko yelped, buttoning her shirt.

McKay sat up with a start. He couldn't remember where he was, but being awakened suddenly made him think he must be in the calving barn. "What's wrong?"

"It's late," she said. "Hurry."

McKay started the truck and pulled onto the highway. They drove through the long tunnel in silence. On the other side, the town was quiet. Mariko saw the NO JAPS sign in the barbershop window, and the unilluminated theater marquis whose coming attractions were *Random Harvest* and *City Without Men*. The Mayflower Café was dark. McKay turned the corner, and saw the Camp car with a jack under it and Kai sitting on the spare tire.

Mariko jumped out of the truck. "Thank God, you had a flat. . . ."

"I didn't," Kai said, "but I sure as hell wanted it to look that way."

McKay helped Kai fasten the spare tire to the back of the car. The other staff workers were in the backseat, laughing.

Mariko turned to McKay. "I have to go."

"I can see that," McKay said, and Kai laughed.

"Come on, girl . . . we've got to make haste," Kai said.

"I'll . . ."

"When?" McKay interrupted.

"Soon . . ."

Mariko climbed into the car. As Kai started the engine, McKay stepped off the curb and grabbed his arm. "Kai, goddamn it, thanks . . . ," he said.

Kai laughed and the car pulled away.

Bobby couldn't sleep that night and he didn't know why. He closed down the cook stove in the kitchen and walked to his cabin on the hill. Below, the Camp lights blazed in the dark. He looked away because they reminded him of Henry. McKay had asked him what the Japanese would do to their prisoners of war, and Bobby had not been able to answer because he did not know, and even if he had he would have been too ashamed to say.

The rain had started again. This time it came softly, slowly. On the little bridge that crossed the ditch, he stood and listened. He could hear water running and was glad he had waited to put his garden in because one year the seeds had molded in the ground. At the house he had left needles and syringes to boil because he knew the long rains would bring on pneumonia in the calves.

Inside he took off his clothes and put his hands on his sagging buttocks. The heat from the fire warmed the small of his back and his short legs. He knew he wouldn't be able to sleep even before he tried, but sat on his bed anyway and slowly turned the potted flowers he always kept there— whose fragrance was supposed to help him sleep—around and around.

Long after McKay had delivered Mariko into Kai's hands and had driven home, the rain brought the pine scent onto the screened porch, and he did not know whether he liked the smell. The wind had turned bitter, like something bad you have to eat, a bitter root that's been in the ground too long. He wondered about wind. It unwound from the sky continuously, like cloth. Did the wind in Wyoming blow all the way around the world onto the beaches where Ted dragged wounded soldiers into hospital ships, or did their wind, stinking with decay and victory and defeat, blow this way?

The errant bomb had not gone away, but the carapace had broken. Now he felt as if he were carrying shrapnel. The sharp pieces had come down slowly into his body from the air. The edges were thick and sharp and rust-colored. He carried them the way a chunk of ice carries rock and sticks and bits of dirt. He did not feel anything when he walked around or when he held her but he knew the iron was in there, cutting its way through the center of his body, outward toward skin.

The moon rose over the ridge. One moon. Why not two? He took off his clothes and crawled under the heavy covers—seven wool blankets and a sleeping bag. Inside, the memory of Mariko's warmth enveloped him. He could feel the points on his body where it touched him—tiny fires. Did the moon spin or was he spinning? He wondered at the many disparate things strung on the same string. What had made him think life would be otherwise? The sand in Mariko's heat scratched him. Nothing was more redundant than desire, nothing more fragile than thought. For a moment he could smell her hair.

It had rained and continued to rain. He watched as the perimeter of the floor just inside the screens became wet. Then the rain turned white as if, coming down, it had aged.

23

The mud in April is the worst I've ever seen. I sink to my shins going from the latrine to the mess hall. The night I picked up Mariko—straight out of the arms of McKay—I realized I was tired of being the big brother, tired of being her chauffeur and covering up for her in front of Will. Spring is a cruel season. I try to understand what Abe-san has told me but some days it's one riddle on top of another and I find I don't much care. But I do, or at least I've begun to. Last night I dreamed of escape. Someone tapped me on the shoulder and said, "Come now," and I went with him. There was a plane waiting for me on the baseball diamond. The propellers were still turning. A rope ladder was let down but my feet were caked with mud and they kept getting tangled. Finally someone yanked me into the plane by my arm because we were taking off. I stood in the open doorway and watched the Camp recede.

Later, when I woke up, I remembered that when I first arrived here I *couldn't stop the sensation of movement after so many hours on the train, as if the physical fact of exile had made me sick. Waking up from the dream, I realized I'm still sick today.*

Even though it's only April we built a campfire out away from the barracks facing Heart Mountain. Drifts of snow were still hugging the north sides of buildings and the moon looked cold when it set. I can't remember who ran over to us with the news. Was it Ben or Shig? But when he told us about the old man at another Camp—Topaz—who had wandered over to the wire fence and was shot down dead by an MP, nobody could talk for what seemed like a long time. Then Will kicked dirt into the fire. I noticed the moon disappeared behind the tip of the mountain just at that moment, and if the floodlights had been turned out, it would have been a dark night.

We went back to Ben's place. There's always something to eat or drink there. But we didn't feel like drinking. Someone came in and said that the name of the old man killed was James Hatsuki Wakasa and that two thousand people went to his funeral. If we can't have a "happy camp," at least we could have a peaceful one. "But we're at war," Shig reminded us, meaning even though we're not at the front, war is everywhere.

Emi came by and I threw my arms around her. We sat curled up together on the floor against Ben's bed. I think we all felt a little lonely after the news. We tried to figure out when this new tide of hatred had turned against us and I said I thought it was when the announcement about the Doolittle Fliers was made: eight American fliers had been shot down over Japan, captured, held prisoner, then brought to trial, after which three of them were executed. That piece of information had been withheld for almost a year, and when it was announced, the outrage was redoubled, and somehow the press, who still refer to us as "enemy aliens," took out their anger on us. Illogical? But I think it's true. Ben agreed. If logic prevailed—or at least, the logic of the heart—there would be no wars.

The editor of the Sentinel *called us to a meeting early on May 5. The councils of two nearby towns have adopted a joint resolution demanding that "The visiting of the Japanese be held to an absolute minimum; that no visitor passes be issued except when absolutely necessary and that they be accompanied by proper or authorized escorts; that no permanent or so-called indefinite leaves be extended to the Japanese for visiting or working in the communities of Powell or Cody; that this request is in no way to interfere with or discourage Japanese on temporary leave who are engaged in gainful employment essential to the war effort and particularly labor on ranches and farms."*

After he read this statement to us, the editor let us have our say. As if we needed encouragement.

It didn't take us long to decide on a stand. Clearly they wanted to "keep us in our place" and at the same time use us for farm labor when it suited them. Very quickly we drew up a response which we would also hand over to the camp director. The editor wrote it out as we fed it to him. We decided to reciprocate by going a step further, that is, suspending all passes, thus immobilizing the work force which they wanted to keep open while denying us the few social privileges granted us. "It will be a labor strike, but we won't call it that," Ben said, and we all cheered in agreement. Tom read the first line of his editorial: "It's evident that not all of Wyoming's sheep are on the hillsides."

We set type all night and went to press the next day, only this time with an MP escort. I thought of how this "edict" would affect Mariko. We didn't go to the Mayflower Café this time.

Sitting in the press room, I listened to the machines. The sound they made was almost like breathing. I wondered where McKay had taken Mariko that rainy night and if a woman like that could ever love me.

I remember it was July seventh, because Mom made a big deal of the date. I had awakened early and saw her sitting at the rickety table Pop and I made, writing something on a strip of white paper. Pop was still asleep, lying on his back with his hands folded over his chest as if he were dead. "What are you doing, Mom?" I whispered. She looked flustered and covered up the piece of paper with her hand. "It's Tanabata, tonight." I asked what Tanabata was and she told me. "It's old feast celebrated on the seventh day of seventh month—some Issei say it's August, but here we celebrate in July. Tanabata comes from Chinese legend. It's about daughter of the master of heaven who lived east of Ama no kawa—that's the Milky Way. She was weaver—that's why we Japanese give her the name Shojuko. Her father chose husband for her, a herdsman who live on other side of Milky Way. They marry and love each other very much.

Go on very long honeymoon. That made father angry because no work get done. So, he condemn them to be separate—one on each side of the Milky Way—see each other only once a year, on night of seventh day of the seventh month, when a raven extend wing, make bridge for them to cross to each other.

"For many years, we celebrate this feast, especially young girls who want to have husbands, wait for them, no matter how long they are apart. We write our wish on piece of paper, like this," she said, holding up the strip of rice paper she had been hiding. "Then tonight, you will see two stars come together across the Milky Way . . . like two lovers. . . ."

"What's your wish?" I asked her. She looked away when I got out of bed even though I had underwear on. "Can't tell you," she said. "Wish won't come true."

"Can't I wish for something?" I asked, teasing her. She cut a strip of paper for me and laid it on the table with a pen. "Too bad you don't know calligraphy," she said as I began to write. I folded the paper and handed it to her. "Don't look," I told her, but I could tell she was dying to know. "Is it Emi?" she finally asked and I told her I couldn't say or the wish wouldn't come true. She fingered the paper, then Pop groaned and she put her finger to her lips—"Shhh . . ." Pop opened his eyes. I didn't feel like talking to him and watching him get dressed and watering his little plant—a cactus someone had dug up for him, now with a beautiful bloom. As I stood to leave I thought of Mariko. It was her name, of course, that I had written on the paper. I had a vision of her lying on her side on the bed, the top of her kimono loosened and one breast showing.

"What's wrong?" Mom asked. I shook my head. Then, as I left, I saw her open the screen door after me, attach the paper strips to a piece of bamboo and tie it under the barracks' eave.

"It's Mariko . . . not Emi," I yelled out to her, and she looked at me, dismayed.

Went for a walk with Will. The Heart Mountain Congress is all but dead and he knows he's going to be picked up soon and sent somewhere— probably Tule Lake, where all the dissidents go. "What about Mariko?" I asked, feeling guilty because I'd let my own fantasies about her go too far. "She'll be happier here," he said. "Without me." Will's own family—

the half that wasn't living in Japan—had been relocated from Seattle to the camp in Minidoka, Idaho, but he had not written to them. "In Paris, I helped a little in the Resistance, but someone gave the Germans my name. Otherwise, I would have stayed," he said, looking out across the desolate Camp, and swatting a mosquito.

24

McKay read the telegram he had received from his brother Champ.

I WAS GUTSHOT. LIKE A DRY DOE. OPERATED ON 3 WEEKS AGO. WILL BE
RELEASED TO REST CAMP, SAN DIEGO, CALIFORNIA. PLEASE COME. GIRLS
GALORE. HOT AND COLD RUNNING TEQUILA. CHEERS. CHAMP.

He could have read those words anywhere and known they were his
brother's. He and Champ were so markedly different. Their father once
accused their mother of having stepped out on him, and she had replied
curtly, "How could that be? Champ's just like you."

McKay slept on the train all through the night as they crossed the
desert, and when he woke he saw the turquoise and indigo sea, wrinkled
in the sun like skin. Far out toward the channel islands, the sea churned
into whitecaps, and the woman sitting behind him leaned forward to tell

him that the Indians used to paddle canoes back and forth between those islands and the mainland.

San Diego Bay was camouflaged. The roofs of all the buildings looked like a jungle canopy. On the water, destroyers, cruisers, aircraft carriers, and the big battleships were coming and going, gray against brackish water.

"Hey, cowboy!"

McKay looked up from the station platform and saw his brother dressed in a wildly colored, short-sleeved shirt.

"You look a little hot, kid," Champ said. He leaned on a cane.

McKay stood back, staring. "That's a hell of a getup you have on for a war hero." They embraced awkwardly.

Champ was so tanned the skin looked black where it wrinkled together on his neck and in the crook of his arm. His hair had turned gold in the tropics, and there were wet spots and blood spots on his trousers where the bandages needed to be changed. He had caught shrapnel in the leg and groin while climbing a tree. "I was trying to kill the bastards with coconuts," he claimed, though, in fact, he had been shot down running across a beach with his platoon on an island too small to have a name.

McKay thought his brother looked tired but steeled against fatigue, and the excessive tan looked like part of the armor. His eyes glittered. He showed McKay how one of his fingernails had grown long. "Christ almighty, everything grows in them damned tropics," he said. "It's like living in a big outhouse. You shit a seed one night and it's a tree the next."

They crossed the border at Tijuana and drove to their rented bungalow at Rosarito Beach. Out in front, McKay saw three vultures land on the beach and pick at a dead fish. Champ had turned sullen and silent during the rest of the drive. Sitting in the front room on a rattan chair, McKay found himself rubbing the scars on his knuckles where his hand had gone through the window of the car that day. It was a problem of beginnings. Where to start a conversation and how. After an awkward silence Champ leaned forward, uncorked the tequila bottle on the glass table between them, and said, "Let's drink ourselves into this. I never was any good at just sitting around making small talk."

McKay laughed. "Why did I think war would change you?"

Champ took a long swig and passed the bottle to his younger brother. The room was dark and because of the straw mats, it smelled of dry weeds. The front window overlooked the beach. Beyond, the sand was bright and the waves that rolled in toward the tiny house seemed to start somewhere far out in the ocean.

"How's that feel?" McKay asked, indicating his brother's wound.

"Like an old tom turkey with his stuffing sewed in," Champ said. "And I think they stapled my legs back together."

They talked about the ranch first: what the calves had brought in Omaha; how many replacement heifers McKay had kept; how things were going with Madeleine; the condition of the grazing land.

"We're getting rich," McKay said, shaking his head. "We're getting rich and everyone is dying. I suppose that's what wars are really for, but it doesn't go down very easy."

Champ stared at him with a blank, passive look. "No comment," he said.

McKay changed the subject. He dug into his suitcase and brought out the food Bobby had sent: all Champ's favorite foods—homemade peanut butter, rose hip jam, rum cakes, venison sausage, and oatmeal bread. So they ate in the bungalow that night, then went to bed.

In the morning they sat on the sand and drank beer laced with tequila. Children roamed up and down the beach selling chicklets gum, newspapers, and shoeshines. McKay inspected his brother's stitches.

"Not bad for a damned sawbones," McKay said.

"But you could have done better," Champ added, laughing at his brother's vanity.

McKay looked up. "Hell, yes. You should see that number 252 cow we cesareaned. She doesn't even have a scar."

When Champ grew restless, they decided to go to town. McKay watched him shuffle to the car.

"You look like you're in labor," he quipped.

Champ straightened up and pivoted on his cane. His eyes narrowed. "Hey, watch your mouth, gimp," he said and poked McKay in the ribs with his walking stick.

They followed the beach through Ensenada, past the harbor, up onto the bluff overlooking the Pacific Ocean, stopping once at a beer stand with a thatched roof to buy two bottles of beer. The old woman in the back, squatting on the ground and shaping tortillas with her hands, smiled at the two handsome, crippled men and McKay touched the brim of his cowboy hat to her.

"*Buenas—*" he said.

They drove on and parked the car on a cliff. From there they could go north into California or south over the top of Ensenada toward the ranch their father had once owned.

"Want to go look at it today?" McKay asked, looking down the coast.

"Naw . . . let's get ourselves a decent drink and some American girls in San Diego," Champ said and shook out two white pills into his hand.

"What are those?" McKay asked.

"These are my forget-me pills. You gotta take them to forget those army nurses," he said, swallowing them with his beer.

"That bad . . ."

"No, good."

McKay grinned.

"They make it worth a man's while to get wounded . . . but a foot-wound would have been handier. . . ."

"You'll heal."

"I need some of that pecker medicine Bobby brews up."

"He sent some. I threw it away about two thousand miles ago," McKay said, and Champ laughed.

At the border the customs agents looked in the front seat, under the hood, in the trunk, then waved them on.

"Hey, let's stop at this little joint," Champ said. It was a white adobe building with a red tile roof. "They know me in here," he said, climbing out of the car.

They sat at a bar and ordered whiskey. The bartender was voluptuous in a low-cut peasant blouse and wore a poinsettia behind one ear.

"Well, well, well," she said, looking at Champ. "Where'd he ride in from?"

"Wyoming, ma'am," McKay replied. Then he pushed his hat back on his head and downed the whiskey.

Two young women slid onto the stools next to the brothers. Champ threw his arm around the one nearer him. Her black hair hung to her waist. He bought them drinks, then lifted his shirt to show them the top of his war wound.

"How'd it happen?" the one with the long hair asked. She spoke with a lisp.

Champ told them how he was on an island in the South Seas and had climbed a coconut tree with his gun slung over his shoulder and had fired down on the enemy when they landed on the beach. But one got away and fired up at him. A bullet hit a coconut at the same time, and as he fell he remembered his face and chest were washed white with milk, and the next thing he knew he was being carried across water by one of his men.

The girls giggled. Champ shook out two more white pills into the palm of his hand, and the other girl brought him a glass of water. McKay ordered food: a platter of tacitos, shrimp cocktails with limes, and four beers. Then Champ directed McKay to another bar.

This one was filled with servicemen and had plush chairs and soft music. From his seat, McKay could see out over San Diego Bay and the gray masts of battleships, like crosses, rocking on the incoming tide.

"What's it like?" McKay asked finally, after they had sat in silence. Champ ordered a martini.

"You mean fighting or getting hit?"

"Whichever . . ."

Champ picked the olive out of his drink and rolled it from one side of his mouth to the other, then bit into it, chewed, and swallowed.

"First, you're not scared. Not at all . . . It's spooky, in fact. You just go along like something was pulling you up a terrible steep hill, like you're dreaming or something, and you can only think about crazy things like who in Luster has had sex with a sheep, or the way that horse of mine rolled in the waterhole with my saddle on, or opening up a girl's legs, or the smell of the grocery store. You think these things because you're not really thinking at all the whole time; you don't ever really think about what's happening, and then when it gets real bad it's like being on a big stout buckin' horse who kicks and squeals and turns midair, and you know you were scared a minute before, just as you pulled up the cinch and stepped on, but you've lost track of all that and then you're just flying. . . . It's dark, like some damned rockchuck hole—real dark—and you've forgotten that you're scared because you've forgotten to think, and everything gets darker. . . . Then you wake up and a lot of pale-faced strangers with delicate hands that haven't ever done no irrigating are leaning over you, and your mouth tastes awful and dry and they won't give you any whiskey for it, and then you know all that was fear."

McKay ordered another round. He rubbed his knuckles and looked at the swaying masts again. A destroyer glided up the channel between all the other ships and McKay thought how the wild ducks on the lake at the ranch did maneuvers every summer with their hatchlings, and wondered if militarism was perhaps a natural thing.

Champ took a deep breath. "How's that hand?"

McKay dropped his right fist into his lap and looked away.

"Well, Christ . . . I'm not still mad at you," Champ said.

McKay looked at his brother ruefully. "You were right. That's what I've been thinking all year. I don't have what it takes. I—"

"Bullshit. I've seen you ride colts a sane man would plumb run from."

"That's different—"

"It's still guts."

"But I'm not trying to kill the colt. I'm trying to be his friend."

Champ looked down at his damaged legs. ". . . Hell."

"I'm sorry for sounding like a goddamned Quaker. It's not quite that way either, it's—"

"Look. I fought without believing. What's there to believe? You go to the front with all that shit in your head and it doesn't mean a damned thing anyway. I just went and hoped to hell I was up to whatever came my way."

"And you were, weren't you?" McKay said.

Champ twirled his cane under his hand. "I don't know. How the hell would I know?" He lifted his martini. "Here's to—"

"Oblivion," McKay interrupted. "Oblivion is the cocktail of the people."

Champ grinned. "Gin with a dash of oblivion and a twist of oblivion, and two green olives."

"Rum and oblivion on the rocks."

"Whiskey and an oblivion back."

"Whiskey straight up with a side of oblivion."

"Whiskey and oblivion ditch."

They drained their glasses.

"God, I'm pie-eyed," McKay announced loudly. In the harbor, a second destroyer filed in and the wake from the ship made the gray masts swing harder. McKay stood and fell sideways. "The fuckin' tide's coming in," he said to a Navy man on the bar stool in front of him.

"You bet it is, pal," the man said, laughing.

Champ took a deep breath, eased himself to his feet, and, bent like an old man, limped out the door.

It was dark when they reached the bungalow. McKay thought he had never felt air so soft. It was still low tide and the wet sand shone. Two children approached, selling shells, just like the ones at their feet. Champ bought two sand dollars, then dropped them as soon as the children walked away.

Carrying their shoes, the brothers sat on the beach and let the water wash over their ankles.

"That island where I was shot," Champ began, "just before, I had seen a Jap on the beach. I was by myself and so was he. He looked to be kind of an older fellow. Had gray hair. Well, I'll be damned if he didn't take off his clothes and go swimming. Jesus, we were landing troops on the other side of the hill. I hid in these bushes and watched him. He walked into the water like there wasn't a war on and stood waist deep and splashed himself and wiped his face and hair. Then he swam out a little ways and floated on his back. Christ, one of our planes flew over him, but he didn't duck or hide. He just lay there, his arms stretched out. The ol' pilot dipped down and took a look, then flew on. That struck me funny, too. Why didn't he shoot? Then the guy swam back in and stood on the beach for a long time rubbing his head. Naked, out there while we were making a landing on the damned place. The thing is, I had my gun but I couldn't . . . I kept thinking . . . Ah shit—"

McKay looked at his brother. Champ stood and walked toward the water. He had taken his shoes off, but he had all his clothes on. A wave broke and the water rose up around his waist, then dropped.

"Come on, you landlocked sonofabitch, get your ass wet," he said and McKay followed.

They swam out. A wave came from a long distance away and they rose in its swell and watched it crash just beyond. Another wave came and another, followed by a lull, then a ripple of swells and they dove into the next wave's thick middle and emerged laughing. McKay circled Champ.

"God, this feels good," Champ said. "I don't limp when I'm swimming."

"Neither do I."

McKay saw that his brother's whole body was tanned bronze. Champ was shorter and thicker and the muscles in his arms were strung on bone like hardballs, and an arrow of dark gold hair ran from the top of his buttocks halfway up his spine.

"So who have you been screwing?" Champ asked, treading water.

McKay lay on his back, floating. "Someone you don't know," he said.

"Hell, I know 'em all."

"Not this one."

"Did you ask?" Champ said, smirking. "If she knew me—"

"Yea. That's always my first question."

"Who is it, then?" Champ asked, grabbing his brother's foot and pulling it down. McKay went under water for a second.

"Mariko Abe," he said, then dove.

"Who?" Champ yelled down into the water.

McKay emerged.

"What's that?" Champ said.

"Her name."

"I asked whose pants you've been in . . . God almighty, there must be a lot of choices with everyone gone. . . ."

"I told you," McKay said.

"What do you mean?" McKay started to say the name again. "Never mind."

"Mariko?" Champ said incredulously. "A Jap? You have the whole country to pick from and you're screwing a Jap?"

"Hey—" McKay started.

"You mean from that Jap Camp up there? Jesus, fucking Christ, McKay—" he yelled.

McKay swam away from his brother. He knew the look and the tone of voice. He knew what was coming and he didn't want that again.

"You lousy stinking traitor!" Champ yelled over a breaking wave, then swam hard after McKay.

The wave broke on Champ's back, pushing him down to sand, and when he surfaced again he let the next wave carry him to shore. Out of the water, he staggered to his feet. He picked up his clothes and cane

and walked toward the bungalow. "Come on, come out of there . . . ,"
he yelled.

A light in one of the houses down the beach went on and Champ saw
the door open, then close and the light go out again. Champ opened
the louvered side door of the bungalow. Inside, McKay stood naked.
Champ looked at him, and the smell of wet straw and salt and mold
filled the room.

"Did Bobby put you up to this?" Champ asked coolly.

McKay went at his brother, then stopped, holding his scarred fist with
his other hand. "Don't you ever say anything against Bobby, goddamn
you, don't you ever say his name again."

McKay towered over his brother, who held one hand to his groin and
the other out to fend McKay off.

"So you came all the way to San Diego to tell me about your Jap
girlfriend—" Champ began with a derisive smile.

"No," McKay said quietly.

Champ jackknifed with pain and stumbled to the wicker couch. McKay
looked at him, turned.

"I have to get my clothes," he said flatly.

"Don't run out on me, brother. . . ."

When the door closed, Champ lay in the dark. He grappled with the
cork in a bottle of tequila and took two more pills from an army envelope
on the glass table.

When McKay came in, he turned on the light. In another room he
put on a fresh shirt and jeans and brought the same out for his brother.

"Thanks," Champ said, taking the dry clothes, and after he had struggled with the wet pants, McKay had to help him.

"Where's the hooch?" Champ said.

McKay uncorked the bottle.

"You'd make a shitty nurse," he said, glowering and drinking. Then
he handed the bottle to his brother.

A few months before, McKay had dreamt there was a tidal wave and
he had saved Champ from drowning. He had awakened feeling an un-
accustomed tenderness toward him. That was gone now.

"I didn't think you'd care," McKay said, "who I slept with, as long as
it wasn't one of your—"

Champ broke out laughing. He had taken off his wet shirt. The long scar that began at the base of his groin was red and purple, and the skin on each side of the stitches looked sore.

"I don't," he said bitterly. "I really don't." Then he laughed again. "Here, Goldilocks, drink," he said, handing McKay the tequila.

McKay looked at Champ over the bottle and exploded with laughter, spraying booze all over the table. Champ bent forward, laughing. He held his incision, but when he looked up his face had gone pale.

McKay put the bottle down. "What?" he asked.

Champ's eyes moved down and McKay looked: the incision had split open.

"Put your hand on it," McKay ordered. Part of Champ's intestine showed. McKay went to the phone. "*Por favor, ambulancio* . . . hurry, please. *No! Pero* . . . *Sí, sí,* taxi . . . *Gracias.*"

McKay helped Champ lie back on the couch. He tore a clean sheet off one of the beds and held it firmly to the open wound. Champ's eyes were deep-set and he stared at the ceiling like an owl. A cockroach climbed the wall behind, then fell onto the couch. McKay flicked it away. Champ looked at him. His eyes were dry and vacant.

"Hell, I've done better sewing jobs on cows blind drunk," McKay said.

Champ smiled. "Feels like my guts are going to fly outta me."

"I won't let them," McKay said.

Champ grinned. "It feels funny, that's all. . . ." His voice trailed off.

"Hey, Champ . . . here, want a drink?"

Champ's eyes brightened, and McKay put the bottle in his hand.

Finally, there was a knock on the door. "*Venga,*" McKay yelled, and two men, one the proprietor, one the cabdriver, hurried in.

"Where you want to go?" the hotel owner asked.

"The hospital, San Diego. Now, please . . . it's serious. Five hundred pesos plus tip. Okay?"

The three men carried Champ to the backseat of the cab. It was an old Ford with rosaries and crosses and madonnas stuck to the dash.

"*Ciudado,* please. *Mi hermano.*"

The driver pulled out of the hotel blasting his horn all the way. Champ lay motionless, holding his wound. His head bobbed as the driver took the long hill up out of Ensenada.

"I saw that once," Champ mumbled.

"Saw what?" McKay asked. His voice was gentle now.

"Saw the guts come out of someone. See, the Japs shot my best friend. Shot him down right next to me, and the next thing I knew his guts were—"

"Here, have another swig," McKay said.

"You think of everything, don't you?"

"Yea, I'm sharp as hell," he said sarcastically.

"I like this driver we've got. Give him a hell of a tip," Champ said.

"What do you need?"

"More of that hooch à la Mexicana."

McKay held the bottle to Champ's mouth. "I should have brought one of those big black nipples Pinkey uses—"

Champ wiped his chin where the tequila spilled. "Christ, why do I put up with you?"

"Who said you did?"

After he paid the cabdriver, McKay waited in the hall while the doctor on call examined Champ's torn incision.

"How'd this happen?" the doctor asked.

"I was laughing at my kid brother," Champ said. "See, here I go off to this war and my brother gets himself an agricultural deferment to stay home and mind the ranch, and what does he do but start screwing a Japanese girl . . . can you believe—"

"How much have you had to drink?" the doctor interrupted.

"Not enough."

"We're going to have to give you a local then, while we sew this up."

"And with all those horny women around," Champ continued, "and he goes and screws a Jap. They ought to cut a man's dick off for that—"

"Mind your language," McKay heard the nurse say sharply. Then she closed the door.

25

Even at night the trip home across the desert was staggeringly hot and McKay felt drugged and heavy, but at the same time, as if he might break like eggshell. What had healed over or been put aside with his brother had come back, and it corrupted everything. McKay's idea of himself, his isolation, became fixed. As the train roared east on the same tracks that had brought Mariko to him and would take her away, his desire to see her redoubled. He thought of his brother's stitches bursting apart, everything inside unraveling.

Pinkey met him at the station. The cows were fine, Madeleine was sick with "some woman problem," Bobby's two hundred irises had bloomed, and a letter from Ted awaited him. Pinkey didn't have to ask how it went with Champ. He could tell by the look in McKay's eyes.

"I knew you two would quarrel. You're like a couple of sheepherders come to town."

The next day a cold front came through like a foreign visitor. McKay called the Camp and he was told no passes were being issued. The clouds took Heart Mountain from sight that same day, soft and thick and clinging, and did not relinquish their hold. When the rain changed to wet snow, a coat of frost bent green trees down. McKay felt the wrongness of everything. Day after day he looked for the mountain, even in his sleep, and when it showed, the midsection was gone, taken by fog.

When the mist lifted, a long, single cloud arced over the state like a bowed tendon. McKay looked through the mail that had stacked up. There was a card from Mariko.

McKay—
    Kai says that passes will be lifted soon. Come for me on July 24, 1:00 P.M.

                                               Mariko

"What day is it?" McKay asked.

Bobby looked at the calendar. A girl in a bathing suit sat in a brand new John Deere tractor. "July 7, 1943."

"I know what year it is, for God's sake—" McKay said.

McKay rode to Madeleine's that afternoon. When she opened the door he saw how pale she was.

"What's wrong?" he asked.

She barely let him in the door. It was a low-ceilinged house, cluttered with books, old bits and spurs and rawhide riatas, vet supplies, catalogues, and three-year-old magazines opened to unread stories.

"Nothing," she replied sullenly, sitting on the couch.

McKay stood in the middle of the room. When he went near her, she stiffened.

"Look, I don't really want to see you," she said.

"Madeleine—"

"Please, McKay," she said weakly, as if his presence had begun to overpower her.

"What's happened?" he said, though he had begun to understand.

She saw his face soften with dismay.

"I was pregnant," she said, "but not now."

"What do you mean?" he asked.

"I had a miscarriage."

"When?"

"That day, when the water came and I never showed up to meet you. Then you went off—"

"Why didn't you tell me?"

"Goddamnit, I didn't feel like it," she snapped.

McKay collapsed on the couch beside her but looked straight ahead. "I lay down in the grass. Then it was over."

"I should have ridden until I found you," he mumbled.

She closed her eyes.

"Are you okay now?"

She looked at him. "I feel very sad," she said slowly.

McKay searched his memory. Had he known all along? And if he had known, why didn't he go look for her that day?

"I had no idea," he said. "I should have kept riding. Then Bobby told me you were sick. . . ."

Madeleine sat with her chin tucked in, McKay at her feet.

"We could have had a child," he said, with a look of crushed astonishment.

"I'm not sure how we could have arranged that," Madeleine said bitterly.

"It wouldn't have mattered, would it?"

Madeleine shrugged.

"Come here." He put his finger under her chin. "I wouldn't have abandoned you."

"But you weren't there. . . . You were somewhere else. . . ."

He looked down.

"It's not your fault," she said softly.

"I should have called."

Madeleine drew her robe around her. "Why don't you go now, please."

McKay walked to the window but didn't see the storm had lifted. He went back to her. "God, I'm sorry, Madeleine. You've had to go through all this. . . ." He closed his eyes, then looked at her. "A child . . . It was conceived in love, wasn't it? They say those are the best children— the moment of conception . . ."

"I was thinking about Henry . . . ," she said, shaken.

McKay looked at her. "Don't make me go yet," he said.

She felt suddenly trapped, but when he put his head on her chest between her breasts, she touched his face. Her neck was all wet because he was crying. She hated his weight. His body rose under her hands like something yeasted and, touching it, she felt relieved and emptied; she felt desire. How perverse, she thought. His skin was smooth and hot. He was like a jewel—turned, cut, polished, inaccessible—and his wild, peevish frailty came from that near-perfection and from his ardent privacy.

"Even when I let you in, it didn't work," she whispered. "It's always wrong."

She wanted to push him off, to be done with him, but she couldn't. She held him and drove her hand into his gold hair.

On July 24, McKay drove to the Heart Mountain Relocation Camp as Mariko's letter directed. McKay proceeded through the sentry gate to the rec room of Block 4. It was the first day the ban on passes had been lifted and there were a number of visitors waiting in the hall. McKay took off his hat and leaned against the far wall, opposite the door. A gang of young children ran in and out, tied together at the waist with laundry line, screeching as one or the other fell and was dragged for a while. Three women from the Mormon church sat in chairs against the wall and a farmer and his wife from the valley told McKay they had come about rehiring a girl who had done kitchen work for them.

McKay saw Mariko coming. She wore boots and her long strides looked purposeful. She studied the ground as she walked, but when McKay stepped out of the shadow she broke into a smile. They faced each other on the steps.

"Hello," Mariko said, then dug into her pocket for a cigarette and a match.

"The paperwork's backed up on passes to get out of here. That's why . . ."

"How have you been?" McKay asked.

Her hand shook as she took the cigarette from her mouth. "Fine."

McKay held one of her arms in his big hand but she pulled away.

"Look, Will's lurking around here somewhere. He's gotten pretty embroiled. I think they're sending him off soon—"

"He hasn't hurt you again, has he?" McKay asked.

"No." She relit her cigarette and they sat down.

"I've missed you," she said under her breath.

"I've been out to California to see my brother," McKay said and played with his hat between his hands. He looked up. "I wish I could take you up there now," he said, pointing to the top of Heart Mountain. "There's a waterfall. . . . I've got this horse you'd like. Everytime I catch him I have it in my mind that I'm catching him for you. We call him Rudy after this old sheepherder who thought he was good-looking but he wasn't."

"How do you know I can ride?"

"You'd ride fine."

"How can you tell?"

"You really want to know?"

"Yes."

"By the way you make love."

Mariko laughed nervously. She saw Will in the distance, walking between barracks, but he did not see her.

"We'd go out at dawn and Bobby would make lunches for us and we could ride all day and make love whenever we wanted to," McKay continued.

"Pinkey told me about how Bobby came to your ranch when you were sick. He said Bobby saved your life."

"Probably," McKay said.

"And he raised you?"

"Since the folks died. Hell, he's still trying to raise me."

"What does he think of us?"

McKay scowled. "He's worried."

"That I'll hurt you?"

"Maybe, or that I'll hurt you, or Will, or the people in town."

"I don't care; do you?"

"No," McKay said. "Were you okay after I left you off that night?"

"Yes. I felt wonderful."

"So did I."

"Wouldn't it be grand to have a whole day?"

"A whole night."

"A whole week . . ."

"Or a very long time," McKay suggested.

"But it wouldn't be the same after a long time, would it?" Mariko said.

"Not the same but . . ."

"Maybe people are only happy for short periods. . . ."

"Is that what you think?"

"I've never been happy with a man . . . yet . . . where it was truly mutual . . . and even then, I don't know how long it would last."

"Maybe you can't think of that."

"Yes, perhaps not."

"But *were* you happy that night?"

"Yes. But let's not talk of it now—"

"Why?" McKay asked.

Mariko let out a shrill laugh as if she were being tickled. "Because . . ."

McKay looked at her. "Why?" he asked, teasingly.

Mariko leaned against him for a second. "God, I can't stand not touching you. . . ."

McKay let out a sound—a sexual laugh—and rubbed his forehead shyly. The sound erupted again despite himself, of pain mixed with desire. He stood abruptly. "Okay. We'll talk about cattle prices, hog fences, farm equipment, conception rates . . . no . . . that's too . . ."

Mariko shaded her eyes and looked up at him, laughing brightly. "Ummm . . . how about pickup trucks and squeeze chutes?"

"Tell me more about Bobby and your family. Tell me everything about yourself," she begged.

McKay leaned forward on his elbows so that his head almost touched her knees.

"Like what?" he asked.

"Pinkey told me your parents were killed. . . ."

"Yes . . ."

"And after, was Bobby like your father?"

"No one was like my father," McKay said brusquely. "They couldn't be, because no one knew him. He was always receding; he was always someone you saw on the horizon who never got any closer. The only thing he loved was his ranch in Mexico. For a while he used to bring up whole families from the village but when the snow flew, they did too. Sometimes he went with them. He took me once. I think I was about seven. We drove around in a jeep and the people in the villages came out and touched my hair. They'd never seen a blond. I don't know why he didn't just move us all down there. But there was a reason . . . he wouldn't tell me though. Maybe it was because he wanted it all for himself. He was ungenerous in that way. No . . . Bobby was more like a mother to me. Not quite that either . . . my mother and he and I did things together . . . collected flowers and worked in the garden, and talked about things. . . . She used to read translations of Japanese poems— from the Kokinshu—do you know it?"

"Yes, of course."

"She wanted Bobby to hear those things and some of the stories too. I was fifteen when they died. I was the youngest. . . ."

"That must have been hard—"

"Then Pinkey did some of the raising too . . . the hell-raising. . . ."

McKay sat down on the steps beside Mariko again. "But what about you? You have parents, don't you, or did you hatch?"

"They live in Japan," she said, looking out at the Camp. "Of course there's no way for me to know what's become of them until after the war. . . ."

"No . . ."

"And your brothers . . . are they in Europe or the Pacific?"

"The Pacific."

Mariko nodded her head. "My father's a potter . . . they live on a little island in the south of Japan . . . Tanegashima. . . . The Portuguese landed there in the 1600s and brought the first guns ever seen in Japan. My mother makes paper . . . dyes it. She makes an ink that floats on top of water and dips the paper in it. . . . But they've lived all over. They were bohemians . . . we lived in Paris and also New York—Greenwich Village—all kinds of places, sometimes with other artists because we couldn't afford our own rooms, but it was always lively and exciting for me. I met a lot of painters. But they always loved their little island and so they went back a few years ago."

McKay rubbed his calloused hands together. "I don't believe this war was inevitable, do you?"

"In Europe, it seemed so. Everything we believe in was threatened and everyone we knew. . . . What can you do but fight back?"

"But what made it begin . . . I don't mean what the damned papers said, I mean what made it something that could not be turned around?"

Mariko looked out over the Camp again. "I don't know."

They were silent for a while.

"Do you love me?" Mariko asked at last.

"Yes," he said. "Jesus . . . can't you get out of here today?"

"No . . . not yet . . . I don't know when."

They stood.

"How's Abe-san?"

"He wanted to see you, but he's working on a new mask."

McKay put on his hat and stood in front of the building's steps. The dust was like powder. "I've got to go and I don't want to," he said.

"Good-bye." She held out her hand, smiled, stepped forward, holding him for an instant, then turned on her heels and walked away.

When the leaves changed in late August, tufts of orange showed in the green, then the red rode up on the orange and the leaves on the south side of the tree fell first. It turned cold and a foot of snow dropped, breaking the tops of the cottonwoods, then the warm Indian summer days returned.

After, the warm days went on and on, rainless and windless until the end of October, when a bitter wind tore down out of the Arctic and the leaves that had fallen in the yard of the ranch house were carried away. McKay came to understand that when the war ended he might lose Mariko. But pain or pleasure, possession or loss—what did it matter?

He thought of his time with her as "passions," Stations of the Cross. Long ago, an old man his father had brought up from Mexico had read the poems of St. John of the Cross and St. Teresa—"Por qué, pues has llagado/ a aquaeste corazón, no le sanaste?" Why do you wound my heart and then refuse to make it heal?—and he had not known then what those words had meant.

Now he lay on his cot night after night. The swirling arms of war had embraced almost everyone, he thought. When the wind blew, his cot seemed to stand on end and when he slept, he dreamt that he told his brother, "There's no blood in my brain because they won't let me lie down anymore," and indeed, Champ had said that being at the front is like being picked up by a wind and thrown. "And I'll be damned if that's courage," he had said.

26

Dillon Meyer, the director of the War Relocation Authority, announced back in July that the so-called loyals would be segregated from the "disloyals" in order to "promote harmony in the relocation centers and facilitate the outside relocation for loyal American citizens and law-abiding aliens." In other words, he was ridding the Camps of the troublemakers. Will was on that list, of course, as well as Shig, Ben, Frank, and Masao. I remember when I saw them together after the list was posted, Will only smiled at me and said, "You should be coming with us," though not in the unkind way he had said it before. I guess it was too late for reprimands. I was sorry that I wasn't a "No-No boy," that I wasn't being segregated with them. By August 903 evacuees had been slated to leave for the Tule Lake Internment Camp. That included 242 children. The whole idea was absurd—just another disruption, as if we hadn't been torn apart enough— and I knew that many were going only to preserve the unity of the family, not because they had been activists. The only ones I wouldn't be sorry to *see go were the Kibei who had gone around denouncing America and singing the Japanese national anthem every time someone in uniform came to camp. They weren't doing our cause any good. . . .*

The day Will was to leave I saw Mariko bringing breakfast to their apartment so I went over. Will never ate breakfast—I knew that—and he said the Camp coffee was like weak horse piss but he drank it anyway out of a bowl he borrowed from Mom because, he said, that's how they drank their morning coffee in Paris. I pulled up a chair next to him. Mariko was wrapping a package full of food people in the Camp had collected for the men being segregated. For weeks and months Will had been venting his anger at all of us and at the U.S. government . . . now he was silent and those of us around him felt helpless. He sat on the edge of his cot wearing his white beret and black pants held up by suspenders— exactly what he wore the day we arrived.

I noticed Mariko moving around the room like a cat—a bit warily. And for good reason. He had hit her once—hard enough to give her a black eye—and I think he had struck out at her other times. Afterward, she had moved her cot to the other side of the room, against the wall that adjoined my apartment. That was the day I moved my bed to the same wall because I knew that when we slept, Mariko's face would be only a few inches from mine. How many times I awakened and thought I could feel her touching me. She'd pin my wrists above my head and put her hand against the small of my back, right where the spine ends. . . . Sometimes I really did hear her cough or moan and hoped it wasn't because of what Will was doing to her—good or bad—I wanted him to leave her alone.

I had told Mariko that when Will saw injustice he did not know how to fight, so he struck out—at everyone. He had uncovered a great moral void and discovered that racism is as American as democracy. He couldn't stand it. . . .

Sitting there, watching him sip coffee, I didn't know how to feel— relieved or sad. I would miss him. He's been my political conscience. Now it would be up to me to come to terms with the issues of loyalty to one's principles versus loyalty to a nation which has turned its back on us. I watched Mariko. She sat on Abe-san's low stool with one leg crossed.

"Do you have all your things?" she said to Will at the last. "I noticed you left some of your clothes."

"They're the ones you like to wear," he said.

"But you'll need them."

He gave her an absent look.

When the MPs came for him, they behaved as if he were a violent criminal. They handled him roughly and handcuffed him. I wanted to slug the self-righteous bastards. Will stopped at the door and told me to keep the spirit of resistance alive at the Camp. "Show them no concentration camp can be "a happy camp." I promised I would. The MPs jerked at him. The rougher they were, the more victorious he looked. At the last moment, he turned and said, "Tant pis," almost spitting the words. Then he smiled, but a smile that reeked of contempt.

I walked him to the waiting car. We didn't talk. The wind was like metal shavings hitting my head. I thought of the day we had arrived; walking to the edge of the Camp together. We were speechless then too, and that old wave of nausea—landsickness after so much travel—came back over me.

I touched his shoulder and when he looked at me, his face twitched. He's human, I thought, and I love him.

"Good-bye, Will," I said, but only after the car had taken him away.

When I went over to Abe-san's a few nights later, he was digging carrots out of his garden. He turned and said sharply, "What do you want?" Maybe he's just a flower grower after all—this other stuff has been a sadistic game.

Went to see Ben. Some of those tough Terminal Island guys were hanging around. They'd been drinking and when I walked in I heard one of them say, "Here comes four eyes." It made me laugh to think these guys are the sons of fishermen and they can't swim.

We all drank some home brew out of Ben's mother's flower vase. Went home after dark. I must have been looking at my feet, because I hadn't noticed the moon. Abe-san was out front with Mariko. They were sitting on a straw mat staring at that huge orb just rising. Abe-san held a mask in front of him. He'd stare at it for a while, then at the moon, then at Mariko's face, then at the mask again. I started to walk by. "Where you go now?" he asked. "Nowhere," I said. "How can you do that?" he asked, laughing.

I sat down with them. The moon, orange at first, had turned white.

Then I said the obvious: "It looks like a face." "Yes," Abe-san said, "but what kind of face?" He was sitting cross-legged with his hands on his thighs. He had thick, well-used hands—not like mine, which are small and soft. His face was lifted. Was it the moonlight that made his eyes look so tender? Mariko slid over by me. "We're writing a Noh play," she whispered, though I couldn't see they were doing anything.

Later, when we went inside for tea, we did not turn on the lights because the moon brightened the room. "They say it makes you go crazy," I said.

"What does?" Mariko asked.

"Moonlight."

Abe-san laughed hard. "Buddhists say, full moon means enlightenment." He laughed again. "But that's same thing, desu-ka?"

Mariko was sketching and I wondered how she put up with this mad old man and whether she missed Will. In front of her were drawings of a stage, and a backdrop, and masks that weren't human faces but animals, and a waterfall.

"Noh theater began in fourteenth century," Abe-san began. "Before Christopher Columbus," he added delightedly and looked at me. "What were you doing then?"

"Digging roots with a stick and making arrowheads."

Mariko lay on her stomach and continued drawing.

"Young boy, Fujiwaka, son of Noh master, made Noh live, even today. Changed name to Zeami. To understand Noh, have to begin training very young like he did. Seven years old. That's all you do for whole life. Study Way of Noh," Abe-san said, then put the mask he had been holding into its silk case.

"How old were you when you began carving?" I asked.

Abe-san looked dismayed. "Twelve. That's why I was no good. Look," he said, holding out his hands. "These grow flowers; that's all."

"Oh Grandfather . . . ," Mariko said, looking up at him.

Abe-san picked up a block of wood. "This wood give me much trouble. Always. Each time, just as hard. One mistake and . . . shtt . . . that's it. Throw away. Start from beginning. Each cut represent what I am, each stroke. If make bad one, then I'm bad. Have to know self first, then self of wood. Noh mask isn't for Halloween. They're alive! So, desu. See, I put it away," he said, indicating the mask in the silk bag, "but it's alive in there and when I put mask on, it takes me. There is no me then."

"How can there be no you?" I asked.

Mariko sat up and laid the sketches out on the floor. They were drawings of more masks—fantastic-looking things with antlers and fangs and long beards. . . . When I looked back, Abe-san had rolled backward on the floor and lay motionless. Mariko cupped her hand over her mouth, laughing. I didn't quite see how it was funny, but then his body began shaking and Mariko's laughter burst out and I found myself laughing too. But at what?

Abe-san sat up and gave me a fierce look. "What you call 'I' is swinging door. Wind go in and out. Birds too. When you breathe in like this"—he inhaled—"door moves. When you breathe out"—he exhaled—"door moves too. That's all."

I sat for a moment trying to understand what he had said. "How does one become a swinging door?"

Abe-san smiled. "I thought we were talking about Noh."

"Maybe we are."

"Yes!" he hissed.

Mariko poured tea, then lay down on her cot, the one that was so close to mine on the other side of the wall.

"Thank you," Abe-san said, tipping his cup. When he finished drinking he said: "Noh is same thing as Zazen. Zazen is same as life. Not your version of life, or my version of life, but life as it is. Not future or past—Noh is not made-up story. Each play, each mask, each movement of actor is epitome of all human emotion," he said, then shook his head in despair. "I talk too much."

Mariko turned over. She had been lying on her side with her back to us and as Abe-san talked I could not help but admire the line of her hip under the thin kimono.

"Who am I when I am not breathing out and not breathing in—that in-between moment?" I asked.

Abe-san either didn't hear or pretended not to. I asked the question again. Something about the room seemed strange then. Mariko's hip looked like a wave and when Abe-san turned his head, it was like a great ball rolling. He smiled.

"Now you are ready to learn," he said.

A hard driving storm came in from the north last night. Clouds all the way down to the ground, as if there were no mountains. That's when I *feel loneliest here. The mountains represent a freedom we all long for. A place to go, to get out of the noise and confusion of Camp, the noise and confusion of my own mind. Will would be pleased to know that Heart Mountain is not a "happy camp." Many agitators answered "Yes-Yes" on the loyalty questionnaire, tricking the administration in order to avoid deportation.*

Saturday. The "dissidents" formed the Fair Play Committee and Toki Ohara has come forward as a "Fair Play Committee of One." He gave a strong talk about the unconstitutionality of confinement and encourages us to protest it continually and vigorously and stand up for our rights as American citizens. After listening to him, I thought, here's a guy who speaks his own mind and seems to know more than any of us about the Constitution. He's in his early fifties, a Nisei from Hawaii, and a member of the ACLU. The talk was well attended and I wrote Will to tell him the resistance is in full swing.

Will's letter was returned by the censor. No explanation given. What a farce this democracy is.

Mom read a poem she had received from a friend at the Gila, Arizona, Camp:

> *My husband's interned*
> *And my son is a soldier.*
> *Oh, all so hard to bear:*
> *I lament*
> *Encaged behind wire.*

After, I asked whether she thought the guys who were soldiers would do what I've done—advocate draft resistance—if they were here, and she whispered, "Don't tell your father, but, yes, I think so."

Wrote a letter to Kenny, one to Li, and another one to Will. The ones to Li and Will were returned again.

December 5. Some young boys had been arrested for sledding outside the perimeter of the camp. The oldest boy was eleven. They were handcuffed by the MPs and taken into custody. The editor thought we should go over there and scoop the story. The kids looked awfully scared.

One was crying and I told him he hadn't done anything wrong and nothing bad would happen to him. When the parents arrived, one of the mothers became hysterical and grabbed her small child out of the MP's reach and the MP yanked him back. I grabbed him by the arm. "What do you think you're doing here?" I demanded. "These are just children."

That kind of shook him up. I guess he was used to bossing everyone around. Well, Nisei are pretty good bosses too. I told him he was going to be on the front page of the Sentinel. *"Maybe the wire service will pick it up too," I said, though Ben and I knew they wouldn't. When the director came, we left. Later the charges were dropped. In the morning we received even worse news. One of the Camp's great painters, Chiura Obata, stepped out of the shower and was beaten up by a pro-Japanese agitator—one of those wild Kibei. He had to spend three weeks in the hospital. Mariko knew of his work. "You see," she said, "that's what Will thought about me too. Just because I'm a painter he thought I had no political thoughts. That's not true. We're not pro-Camp, pro-administration, pro-anything. We want our freedom like anyone else. We paint about it, instead of talking, that's all."*

December 15. Lots of snow, Pop in and out of his slumps. In the summer he cheers up because things are growing, but as soon as winter comes, he suddenly realizes he's not the head of the family anymore. Mom is busy with all her classes and I with the paper and Abe-san and thoughts of girls. He has to make his way around camp on his own. I watched him walk to the mess hall. He has friends, but he clings to his Issei formality, then can't understand why he's lonely. The suitcoat he wears has gotten wrinkled and the lining is tearing out, something Mom would never have let happen before. He pays no attention. The only thing he cares for is his little cactus planted in a coffee can. First thing he does every morning when he gets up is turn it toward the sun. And every evening, turns it back.

I realized, watching him that day, something about giri—duty to one's parents. I have stayed here in this Camp because I thought the experience would give me insight into the workings of human society, and it has. But it's more than that. I relocated with my parents. Hate and resent them as I have, I'm bound to them now.

December 21. Winter solstice. The Issei walk around bowing and saying "Happy New Year" because they haven't been accustomed to celebrating

Christmas unless they've converted. Snow on the ground, Christmas decorations on all the barracks, even a tree in the mess hall. Mariko caught me in the office and held mistletoe over my head and kissed me. Yikes. I broke out in a sweat. It was all in fun to her, but for me . . .

December 24. Back in November, Mom and Pop had asked what I wanted for Christmas. Told them I wanted a swimming pool, a new bathing suit, and fins. This morning, opening my few packages, I had to laugh. Didn't get the swimming pool, but did get the trunks and flippers. I've hung them on the wall above my bed as a reminder of life elsewhere— California, here I come. . . .

After dinner, walked around the periphery of the Camp alone. All the lights on the barracks made it look like a ship at sea, but a ship on a voyage with no ports of call. We drift endlessly.

Christmas Day. McKay here with presents for Mariko and Abe-san and enough food for all us, baked by Bobby Korematsu. Mariko looked young in McKay's presence even though I think she's older than he is, and very beautiful.

Later. Went to look at Mariko's giant painting. It's a triptych and will hang from a big pine log McKay brought. The paper is thick—almost like cardboard. She smears the paint on with big cloths tied to brooms and brushes the size you'd paint a house with. After the first layer of watercolor has been applied, she wipes it off with a clean cloth, then paints over it again, then wipes that off, and so it goes, ten or fifteen times. The effect is stunning. The surface is absolutely even in hue and texture, almost polished, and with a depth you can't see but sense is there.

New Year's Eve Day. Mariko raised the sixty- by thirty-five-foot panels between the end barracks. Behind it, Heart Mountain looms, as if it were an extension of the painting, rising out of Heian clouds. The middle panel shows the tip of the camp, then a thick layer of clouds with a beautiful silver sheen covering the middle. The top panel is mountain, clouds, and waterfall. The painted mountain is so big, the peak is out of the frame. Above, the real Heart Mountain rises, snow-covered.

We hoisted it up at nightfall. No wind, thankfully, but a full moon. Went home to shower, then came back. The panels flap in the breeze like a big genoa jib sail. Many people came to see it, old and young. At the front of the crowd, Abe-san stood, legs apart, arms akimbo in kimono and new tennis shoes (a Christmas present from McKay), looking at the paint-

ing proudly. When I told him I was afraid it would get ruined hanging outside, that it belonged in a museum, he agreed, then laughed at me.

Went home. Mariko was asleep on top of the bed, her feet covered with paint.

Midnight. Now it's 1944. Another year in a concentration camp. We pause to celebrate the holidays, but the war goes on. Night battles off the Solomon Islands, heavy fighting in Italy, a sea battle in the Eastern Arctic, preceded by senseless deaths in the Aleutian Islands last spring.

How helpless I feel! We're not beaten or tortured or starved or raped here—but another sort of torture is inflicted. Our freedom to act has been taken from us. Last week, got so mad while getting our weekly pass to go to Cody to get the Sentinel *printed, I kicked a hole in the administration office door.*

Sat on my "thinking rocks." Drank a toast to Will and the others at Tule Lake, to Abe-san's wild spirit, to Mariko. Then I threw the glass against the rocks.

27

New Year's Eve. The last days of 1943 had been marred by a sudden spread of the flu, grown to epidemic proportions, and the graves reserved for soldiers coming home in boxes were beginning to be filled by both young children and old people who had succumbed to the virus. No bands were scheduled to play in Luster that night, and at dark, Velma Vermeer thought the streets looked nearly empty of cars. For two weeks she had manned the switchboard day and night, on call as the county's one doctor was, the only link between the doctor and his patients. The local hospital was filled to capacity, and once again Dr. Hoffman came out of retirement and put in his hours—inanely as ever—over the beds and bodies of the ill.

Though ravaged by wind, the Christmas decorations still hung over the main street of town. Velma thought the blinking lights on the scrawny pine trees wired to lampposts looked pathetic. Nevertheless, she took down one of the two New Year's hats she and Harry had kept from their first celebration together, unfolded it, and set it on the dining room table, along with one sherry glass and the cut glass decanter so rarely used the liquor it held had begun to look murky.

There had been one emergency call for the doctor since noon, but now the switchboard was quiet. It was not a night for social calls. She thought it must be grim business for him, bringing in the New Year at deathbeds.

Since Harry's suicide, Velma had become reclusive. She began to think of herself more as a voice than as a physical presence. It wasn't any particular incident that made her start to stay in, but a general feeling of insubstantiality. She envied the two gold stars that appeared in the windows of women who had lost sons or husbands in battle. But it wasn't that. "Anyway, Harry wouldn't have done well in battle," she thought as she dusted the black switchboard. But he could have entertained the troops. How many times they had pretended they were strolling down the Champs-Elysées when, in fact, they were only strolling down the main street of Luster to open the movie theater. She had sold the theater. Now she rarely appeared outside her house, away from the tangled lines and blinking lights of the switchboard, where the voices mixed inside her like colored waters. "I'm just a voice to all of them," she thought. "I no longer need a body."

The previous spring, she had planted a victory garden out of patriotism—but did the work at night so no one could see her. She had planted it during the week of a waning moon, with a silk scarf tied around her head, and, stooping over the ground, dropped seeds at random into the furrows. She let it be known that anyone in need was welcome to come harvest the garden. Peas came up with carrots, and broccoli and onions with beets and lettuce, and beans with peppers and corn and tomatoes and squash.

"You don't need much food if you are just a voice," she said to herself, while she watered the garden by moonlight, and, indeed, she had lost so much weight, her flowered dresses hung from her bones. She remembered the days when Harry had been alive—how busy they were, how much a part of the town. Harry had always said she had known things before they ever happened, implying not that she was prescient, but merely understood how a small town operates, and so could predict the goings-on. And because she could listen in on any conversation, she made it her business to know who was feuding with whom, who was in love with whom, when their babies were due, when the parties were held—as if keeping a record of such events in case someone wanted to know what life in Luster had been. She had had no time for Harry's dreams and light shows and operas, but put her calls through efficiently, her sharp, reprimanding voice reminding every caller that she could and would listen in, likening herself to a terrestrial St. Peter before whom every citizen would stand for judgment. Now, nearly bodiless, she imagined herself akin to an angel.

Sometime before midnight, Velma opened the venetian blinds wide enough to watch the street. It was grimly quiet. She held the paper hat in her hand. Once white with gold cardboard trim, the paper had yellowed unevenly. She saw Carol Lyman's black coupe race by. Was that Willard in the passenger seat or another man? The switchboard buzzed. Another call to tell the doctor a child was being taken to the hospital and would he please meet them there. As she put down the headphones, she thought of the years before there were cars when the doctor went from house to house with a horse and buggy, an oil lamp clamped between his knees to keep him warm.

At five minutes to midnight she stepped into the back room, poured herself a glass of sherry, positioned the faded hat on her white head, and lowered the heavy brown arm of the Victrola onto Harry's treasured record of Caruso singing an aria from *Aida*.

The tiny house filled with sound and for one glorious moment she thought she understood Harry, and what it must mean to be a great singer whose life begins at the lungs, surges up, vibrates the cranial cavity, and bursts forth from the front of the head. To be a voice and nothing else. To be song.

Willard couldn't sleep that night. Mañuel and Porfiria were laughing and talking loudly. Always, when Willard couldn't sleep or had been awakened by bad dreams, he went to his mother's room. She had lined the hall with nightlights—like a runway, she had said—so he could find his way. How many times he had followed the lighted path to her.

She had come home early from Snuff's. Willard went to her room an hour after she had gone to bed. He saw that she slept with a scowl on

her face and tried to smooth the skin of her forehead, then picked up
her hand by the wrist because he thought her long, painted fingernails
looked like the bloodied spurs of fighting birds. For years she had soothed
him by making designs in the dark with the glowing end of her cigarette.
He didn't want that now. He wanted to be driven, as she had driven
several times before, down the hill, across the river, to see, once again,
the furious glare of the Camp.

Not bothering to dress, she put on only a chenille bathrobe over her
nightdress. Soon the black coupe rolled across the bridge and up the hill.
When Willard saw the lights, he shook his hands in front of her face to
tell her he wanted to go slowly. She put the car in first gear and filed by
the endless fence, the nine manned guard towers, the bright sentry gate.
Maybe because it was New Year's, Carol thought it was like coming on
a carnival, whose rides were filled with prisoners of war. Willard rested
his chin on the dashboard and looked. He thought the awful, incom-
prehensible luminosity burning all through the night came from some
hot place underground.

That was the night the guards switched on the big spotlight. It swept
the ground on each side of the fence like a blade. No human entered its
beam. When the light came toward Carol's car, Willard ducked and held
his head in his arms. The next morning, January 1, 1944, he drew a
picture of a bodiless human head with spotlights for eyes, from which
rays broke loose and made small fires at the edges of the drawing paper—
in long, straight lines as if marking out a runway.

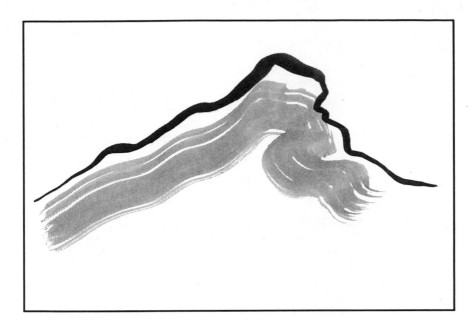

PART THREE
1944

Passion too deep seems like none.
—Tu Mu

28

The day Vincent, Pinkey's son, received his induction notice, he drove to Snuff's hoping to find his father. But the bar was empty at midday. Carol saw him lay the army envelope on the counter.

"The army?" she asked, wide-eyed.

"Um." Vincent nodded yes.

She busied herself making a sandwich for the boy.

"He's been called up," she shouted across the dance floor to Snuff, who was taking down the New Year's decorations. Festooned with red crepe paper, Snuff went behind the bar and poured Vincent a glass of beer.

"Have anything you want, Vince—it's on the house."

Carol opened the newspaper she had brought from the post office that morning. She scanned the headlines, then folded it again. When Vincent went to the men's room, she stood below Snuff's ladder, and read aloud: "JANUARY 28. ALLIED NATIONS STUNNED BY STORIES OF JAP ATROCITIES TO WAR PRISONERS," she began, then continued:

> On eighty-five miles of road from Bataan to San Fernando, the Philippines, Col. Dyess said U.S. and Filipino troops plodded for six days, thirsting under a piercing sun. The sick and delirious were dragged from straggling columns and cruelly put to death. In one instance, Americans were forced to bury alive three American and Filipino prisoners at bayonet point. . . .

She put down the paper when Vincent came back and gave him another beer.

Vincent nodded thanks and kept eating. He said nothing about his impending departure or what lay ahead because he couldn't imagine what that might be. He had never been beyond the reservation or the Basin and had only done the kind of work that can be accomplished on horseback.

"All the more reason to give him a good send-off," Carol said after he left the bar.

At ten the next morning, she went to the post office. She couldn't stop thinking about Bataan and what misery the prisoners of war—especially Henry—must be enduring. Her interest was selfish, of course: to lose Henry would be to lose the last link with what she knew of human passion, of opening out from the narrow way.

But for the moment she put those thoughts aside and concentrated on Vincent. She thumbtacked a poster to the post office wall: DANCE SATURDAY NIGHT. SNUFF'S BAR. FOR VINCENT COLEMAN, then drove back to start the preparations, even though it was a Thursday, her "free day," because the dance had been her idea. She hadn't hired on at Snuff's; instead, she had become indispensable and her awkward, brisk efficiency delighted him.

Days when she was most distant and restless, Snuff watched her from the corner of his eye, anticipating the worst—her flight from him, her inward rage exploding. He grew softer in her presence, and like rock giving way to a constant flow of water, she acquiesced. His tacit acceptance comforted her.

Yet if Snuff took her in his arms, she'd break away, straighten herself, reapply red lipstick, and get back to work. She washed glasses that had already been washed. At all costs, she thought, she must avoid losing herself—even to this kind man—avoid losing track of what was taking place.

It took twenty-four hours for the call to Janine Coleman Big Elk—Pinkey's ex-wife—to go through. There was only one phone in Crow Agency, and the man who answered it finally couldn't or wouldn't speak English. Exasperated, Velma Vermeer handed Pinkey the telephone, and with his pigeon-Crow-English, spoken with an accent, he was able to send out a runner to find Janine. When the operator rang the call through, Pinkey held the phone gingerly, then yelled into the receiver, knowing it was a long-distance call.

"Hello . . . !"

"Hello," Janine said in a soft voice.

There was a silence. Pinkey shifted his feet and scratched his head under the soiled brim of his hat.

"Well ain't you gonna talk?" he said.

"Didn't *you* call me?" she asked.

"Hell if I didn't," Pinkey said, grinning. "Well you can still talk, can't you?" He was stalling, because for a minute, he couldn't remember why he had called.

"Is everything all right down there?"

"What?" Pinkey yelled.

"What are you calling for?" she asked.

"Oh . . . Vincent's got himself called up by the damned army."

"Oh no," she gasped.

"We're giving him a send-off—you better come on down."

Another silence.

"Janine?" he yelled.

"When does he go?"

"Monday, I guess."

"What kind of send-off?"

"Just a dance over here at Snuff's. His gal's putting it on. . . ."

"A drunk you mean."

"Vincent hardly touches liquor. You know that."

Pinkey's hands were sweating. He waited for Janine to say something but she didn't.

"Janine?"

"What about you? You sober?"

"Hell yes. Don't I sound like it?" he asked, challenging her.

"Yes," she said meekly.

"You can get that afternoon train—"

"I don't want to come to no brawl—"

"Hell, Janine, we used to have good times—"

She snorted.

"Well damnit. Are you comin' or not?"

"Okay," she said flatly.

"Vincent asked for you—"

"I'm coming," she repeated.

"Janine?" Pinkey said in a softer voice. "It'll be fine. You'll see."

There was a faint good-bye, then Pinkey put the receiver down.

Pinkey met her at the station on Saturday. A Negro porter swung down from the day coach, followed by Janine and her father, a short, silver-haired man with a grotesque nose and twinkling blue eyes. His legs planted firmly on the station platform, he looked over the top of Pinkey's head, then down at him, and grunted. He wore wool trousers and a tweed jacket over two wool shirts and carried his dance moccasins, gaudily jeweled with silver and blue beads from heel to toe.

Pinkey watched Janine climb down. She had gotten wider, he noticed, and she wore her hair in braids. When she approached, Pinkey doffed his hat.

"Well ain't you a sight for sore eyes," he said.

She smiled shyly, and Pinkey thought he loved her just as much as he did the first day he saw her. She looked the platform over.

"Where's Vincent?"

Pinkey had forgotten to tell Vincent his mother was coming. He had no idea where he was.

"Packing," he lied.

Janine nodded solemnly and helped her father into the truck.

"Since when have you been driving again?"

"It's McKay's outfit—he was busy."

Janine stared straight ahead as they drove through town. Just after the state line the truck sputtered to a stop.

"Well I'll be go to hell . . . ," Pinkey said, got out, and lifted the hood. He climbed on the bumper and stuck his head down into the engine. Finally he climbed back in, blowing on his hands because of the cold. "Don't see a damned thing wrong with her."

Jimmy Big Elk leaned forward slightly. "No gas," he said.

Pinkey looked at the gauge. The needle was on empty.

They walked the last mile.

"Where you taking us?" Janine demanded.

"Snuff's."

"I'm not staying in no bar," she said.

"Oh hell, Janine, it's them cabins up back," he said, though he didn't tell her they were the rooms once inhabited by Venus and her ladies of the night and later, by bums passing through on freights.

Ahead they could see a cloud of white dust from the mill and as they moved closer, felt it on their skin. The road was snow-packed, and after a while they strung out single file, like cattle, Pinkey thought, as he fell back to the rear, hobbling, while Jimmy took the lead with decisive steps.

Carol Lyman clucked her tongue against the roof of her mouth when she saw the ungainly procession come in.

"That goddamned McKay . . . ," Pinkey muttered, heading for the bar. "I need a drink. That's the one thing a man shouldn't ought to do, is walk."

"Help yourself then," Carol snapped.

"Well, how am I supposed to know when there ain't no gas in the outfit?" he said in his defense.

"Try looking at the gas gauge," she said, leading Janine down the dark hall.

"Hell . . . my pony don't have no gas gauge and we get along just fine."

"You mean that ugly mare of yours?" Snuff interjected as he came in from the back room.

Pinkey turned. "Jimmy . . . whiskey?" he asked, lifting his glass to show the old man.

Jimmy sat at the booth against the wall and nodded yes. He saw no sense in talking with white people.

Carol Lyman led Janine out the back door to the Wild Man's cabin. Unused since he had taken to living in his car, it had been cleaned by Carol for the occasion. The trunk with the candelabrum was gone, but the bookshelves still stood, and she had brought fresh sheets and blankets from her own house, plus a down comforter because of the extreme cold.

Janine sat on the edge of the bed and took a book from the shelf. She turned it in her hand like some foreign object.

"Good?" she asked Carol.

Carol glanced at the thick volume. "Oh goodness, I've never read it."

Carol opened the door to Venus's room for Jimmy Big Elk. She leaned over the bed where God knows how many men let their seed go into that one woman and smoothed the green wool blanket as if passing her hand over the backside of a man. Six wooden straight-backed chairs were stacked in one corner, and over the bed the red flocked wallpaper had pulled loose. Two pictures hung on the wall, cut from magazines. One was of a square-rigged schooner on the high seas and the other was Titian's painting of an odalisque.

"Your room's right here. First door down the hall," Carol told Jimmy.

He stared at her, expressionless, then growled. His joke—to see whether he could make the woman frightened of him. Carol laughed, unfazed. Jimmy pulled a thick wad of money from his pocket. The bills looked old and worn and the corners were bent back. He slipped the single rubber band that held them and peeled two bills off. Carol approached him, shaking her head.

"It's on the house. This party is for Vincent and his family," she said, then saw they were not ones, but hundred-dollar bills.

"You be careful with all that," she admonished.

Jimmy turned the money over in the palm of his hand and when he laughed, she saw he was toothless.

That afternoon they decorated the bar with red, white, and blue crepe paper, twisted and taped to the walls, and tied back the flannel curtains with balloons. At six, the barroom began to fill quickly. Pinkey and Vincent arrived on horseback, not from the direction of either of the two ranches where they lived and worked, but from north of the calcium mill, though no one knew why. Vincent's long hair had been combed and rebraided and he wore a ribbon shirt. When he felt everyone in the room looking at him, he hung his head. One whole wall was lined with women waiting to dance with him, or anyone else they could find, and when they ran out of men, they danced with each other, taking turns leading and following. The men who came were either too young to be called men and too young to drink, although they ended up with drinks anyway, or else were too old to go to war, except McKay. The women who didn't dance handled the food. They had brought frozen salads, hams, homemade bread, pies, cakes, and whatever they still had on their shelves in the way of canned beans and pickles. Jesse and Pinkey asked every woman in the building to dance, then retired to the bar.

Velma Vermeer arrived late in a fussy pink voile dress, her arms and legs so thin and white they looked like clothesline. When Orval and Clementine stood in the door, they swung their matching but worn cowboy hats down. "Powder River, let 'er rip," they yelled in unison, then leapt to the middle of the dance floor and two-stepped straight into a wall.

"Down in that hole-in-the-wall country we had one of these brawls, and damned if ol' Clementine didn't pick up a big rock and drop it on this ol' kid who was trying to kill me. But it killed him instead, so we drug him all the way to the outhouse and dropped him—" Pinkey heard Orval telling one of the wallflowers as he walked by to find Janine. The music had stopped momentarily and someone else who had brought his fiddle stood on the little stage and sawed a tune. Out back, one of the sheepherders from a Bridger, Montana, outfit had ridden in. He sat on his horse, holding the harmonium he had brought all the way from Spain, through Ellis Island, and his dog lay under the horse's tail.

"Better get on in there and get yourself something warm to eat and drink. A man could freeze plumb to death out here," Pinkey said jovially as he hobbled by.

The sheepherder stuttered something, but by the time he got the words out, Pinkey was gone.

Janine was sitting on the edge of the bed in the Wild Man's cabin with the book she had picked out of the shelves opened on her lap, though she wasn't reading. Pinkey knocked, then opened the door.

"Vincent wants to dance with you," he said.

"Tell him to ask me himself."

"I ain't drunk and I'm asking you to come in to his party," Pinkey said,

Janine glared at him.

"Why the hell did you come all this way if you wasn't planning on being here?" he asked, then walked away.

When Vincent came to the door, she made a place for him beside her on the bed. "Don't let whatever happens to you take your heart away," she said.

Vincent nodded, his eyes on the floor. "Will you dance with me?" he asked finally.

There was a hurt look on his mother's face. "It's no good in there," she said.

He kissed her good-night.

Jimmy Big Elk sat in the middle of the back booth as if it were a throne. People came and went, paying their respects, though he seemed not to look at any of them, but instead, gazed beyond the crowd, out the window to the two-lane highway pocked with potholes and beyond, past the mill, to McKay's hundred square miles of grazing land where it was so cold the moisture in the air glittered. Between songs, Pinkey could hear Jimmy's thumping foot and the low, cracked voice droning a chant that had no end.

The temperature dropped. By eight in the evening it was twenty below zero and by ten it was thirty below. The windows frosted into opaque screens framing a black sky too cold to snow. Pinkey stood on the edge of the dance floor greeting couples as they passed, not out of courtesy, but because he found his legs wouldn't take him where he wanted to go and it was easier to stay in one place. Carol and Snuff made the drinks behind the bar and Velma Vermeer took shots of Cobb's Creek to Pinkey.

Once, over all the heads, Pinkey caught another glimpse of Jimmy Big Elk. He was surrounded by three women and looked content. He and Pinkey had never known each other well, not because of the language barrier, but because he and Janine had worked on a ranch out of Missoula in western Montana until a drunken night when he swore the pine forests were moving in on him—literally mowing him down—and they hopped a freight with their baby, Vincent, bundled up in a new Pendleton blanket, and landed in Luster, where Pinkey claimed the tallest thing growing was a jackrabbit standing on his hind legs or a rattlesnake coiled and striking.

When McKay and Madeleine came in a waltz played, and before he had even been to the bar, McKay pulled Madeleine out on the floor and spun around so gracefully, no one could tell which of his legs was the shorter. After, they paid their respects to Vincent, who was, by then, sitting next to his grandfather at the back booth, then went up to the bar.

"Could you make us a couple of whiskey ditches, please?" McKay asked.

When Carol pulled her hands from the dishwater, she discovered she had cut her wrist on a broken glass.

"Are you trying to kill yourself?" Snuff asked and tied a bar towel above the cut.

"Silly me," Carol said to Madeleine, who insisted on looking at the cut.

"It just missed that artery," she said.

"Oh." Carol laughed gaily, then primped her hair as Snuff applied a bandage.

After, she went out for fresh air. The line of cabins—all vacant except one—wound up the hill as if connected like lives but were not. Beyond were the Pryor Mountains, over which she had ridden to that party long ago and had sat on the edge of a bed with a man so sick his whole body felt almost too hot to touch, and to whom she had lost herself. "How quickly you've gotten to the inside of all my thinking," she had told him, and by the time she had ridden back over the mountains and packed her steamer trunk with a summer's worth of ranch clothes and boarded a train for Denver, he was dead.

In Snuff's parking lot in the backseat of a car, she saw a woman's head bob up, then duck down, then a man's. She clucked her teeth and returned to the bar.

When McKay looked around, Pinkey was gone. Then he saw him with a reluctant Janine on his arm, coming down the hall. They danced a polka. The tempo increased until Janine's feet left the floor. The other dancers made room for them. Janine pounded Pinkey's back with her fist to make him stop, but he would not. He fell ignominiously to the floor.

Vincent went to him.

"Dance with your mother," he pleaded, laughing. "She's too much for me."

Vincent helped his mother up. She brushed a loose strand of hair back from her face and when the bombast of the polka stopped and something slower played, Vincent took her in his arms and moved off in an awkward two-step.

Four men Snuff didn't know appeared at the front door. Carol Lyman saw them scanning the room. "They've come to make trouble," she thought.

"Who's that?" Madeleine asked.

"I don't know," Carol said.

Vincent followed McKay to the back door.

"Where are you going?" McKay asked.

Vincent motioned toward the parked car. "Some guys said there was a present for me in that car."

McKay raised his eyebrows and smiled. "I bet there is."

The waning moon's half-light seemed to drill the cold even deeper into the ground. A kid who'd lost an arm in an auger pulled an unlabeled quart of booze from under his coat and handed it to Vincent.

"Drink this first and you'll see more than stars," he promised. "Then you can look in the back of the car."

Vincent took a swig, then handed the bottle back to his friend.

"No, take another one. Live it up, Vincent; this is your last night of freedom."

Vincent drank. McKay buttoned his jeans and sidled over to the parked car. A young woman, bundled in blankets but apparently naked, because he saw her white slip and bra on the floor, lay across the backseat.

"I'll be right back," the one-armed boy said as he opened the door for Vincent, then handed the bottle in. "Have some fun," he said. McKay filled his lower lip with snoose and went back into the dance.

The four strange men stood in a knot in the middle of the dance floor. Jimmy Big Elk also saw they were looking for trouble but when he tried to get out from his booth, his legs would not hold him, so he stayed.

"Hey, Harry—" McKay yelled over the crowd from the end of the hall. He recognized his friend, the guard from the Camp, among the strangers.

"Come have a drink," he yelled again.

The knot of men moved toward him. He thought the malevolent look on their faces was a joke, or else, they were bringing bad news.

"You fucking Jap lover," Harry screamed, then fell on McKay, kneeing him and slugging him in the face. McKay tried to shield himself from the blows of the others but could not. The fists were coming from all directions. He tasted blood and felt his breath sucked from him before the men were pulled away.

Snuff pushed toward McKay and jerked Harry backward by his collar.

"You get the hell out of my bar and don't ever come back," he said. Orval, Jesse, Pinkey, and Clementine pulled the others off, and before anyone else could get there, Madeleine was on the floor beside McKay, holding his head on her knees. Carol handed her the bar towel Snuff had used on her wrist and Madeleine dabbed at the two cuts on McKay's face.

"What was that all about?" she asked.

McKay looked up at her. "You don't want to know."

After midnight some of the well-wishers left because they couldn't find Vincent to say good-bye. McKay's left eye had swollen shut but he kept dancing and Pinkey lay head down at the booth next to Jimmy, who kept droning his one song. When the fiddler played "September Song," Pinkey jerked awake and called out for Janine, who had gone to bed a few hours before. When no one paid any attention to him, he stumbled out on the dance floor and teetered in circles as if dancing with a woman, though he was by himself.

"Hell, by morning he'll be telling me he danced that one with her," McKay quipped as Madeleine fished another ice cube out of her drink to put to his eye.

When the song stopped, Snuff turned on the lights, and everyone laughed as Pinkey wobbled all alone in the middle of the room. Jimmy Big Elk was snoozing, ensconced in his red booth.

"Where's Vincent?" Pinkey barked.

The party-goers didn't know.

"Well goddamn—" he said, then began looking under all the tables and behind the bar. He opened the door along the hall—Venus's rooms and the broom closet, where he found only brooms. When he opened the back door a blast of cold air blew in.

"Hell, it ain't that cold out," he mumbled and stepped down into the snow. The parking lot in back, paved with bottlecaps, many of them his, was empty. He walked to the Wild Man's cabin. The moon had set and very quickly his feet and hands felt numb though he didn't care. Janine was sleeping.

"If you're drunk get out of here," she said, lifting her head.

"I can't find Vincent," Pinkey said.

She sat up, her long braid hanging down the front of her nightdress. "I haven't seen him. Maybe he just went home."

Pinkey could feel himself weaving a little bit in the dark.

"Can I sit down for a minute?" he asked.

She glared at him and before she could protest he dropped heavily onto the edge of the bed. He felt the weight of an inconceivable anguish. He wanted to lie down and sleep next to his wife and feel her ampleness press against him; she had always been so warm on those cold nights, at least the ones she would sleep with him, which in the last years of their marriage weren't many because he was always on a tear or sobering up from one enough to start another.

"Help me look for him. I ain't too steady on my feet anymore."

Without a word, Janine climbed out of the narrow bed and put on her clothes.

The clouds had dissipated and now the stars wheeled around Pinkey's head.

"Look, the Big Dipper's all screwed up," he said.

She looked.

"The sonofabitch is upside down, see . . . the dipper's stickin' straight up—it's all goin' to spill out. . . ."

She gave him a disgusted look. They walked through the cobbled parking lot, then around to the front of the bar where the flashing sign drove its red and pink stains into the snow. He took Janine's hand.

"Here, let me help you cross this busy street," he said mockingly. He looked up and down the narrow highway. No cars in either direction, not even the distant roar of a truck. "Silent fucking night, silent fucking night . . . ," he began singing. Snow squealed under their feet.

The calcium mill was a hollow wooden shed all dusted white, which seemed to rise out of the snow the way an adobe building rises out of dirt. At one end a mound of powdery mineral bulged from two open doors. An empty railway car was parked at the back. Pinkey steered Janine over to it. He stood on his toes and peered in. No bums, he thought. Where in the hell are all the bums? "Where is everybody?" he cried.

"I used to could jump into one of these things when she was a-movin'," Pinkey bragged.

"You could not. We were both too short," Janine reminded him.

Pinkey appeared not to hear.

"I'm going back. It's too cold out here," Janine said and began walking.

Pinkey followed behind her obediently. The wind was in his face and he tucked his head down under his coat collar. Now the bar seemed to be a long way away. The snow from the ground whirled up, mixed with the calcium dust, and he couldn't see.

"Hey . . . where are you? Where is everyone?" he yelled again.

He heard a scream and pulled his head out of his collar, opening his eyes against the stinging snow. He saw something dark huddled down near the great white mound.

The scream didn't stop, but was amplified. It had come from the top of Janine's lungs and now a new sound surged, a low, trembling wail. Pinkey bent down to whatever horror she had stumbled upon. When he crouched next to her, he saw Vincent.

Finally, he stood. He felt as if his clothes had emptied out. No flesh filled them, no human commotion. Nothing came from his lungs, though he wanted it to—the nothing he had been singing about earlier, the nothing night, and now the nothing son. When his body contorted into motion, he found himself running toward the bar and an image of Vincent fixed itself before his eyes: the blue face whitened by a skiff of snow, the black cowboy hat tipped off the back of his head, and the beautiful braids flung out, then bent under like broken legs.

McKay ran back across the frozen highway with Pinkey. He ripped open Vincent's shirt and lay his head on the strong, hairless chest and put two fingers against his neck where the jugular should have been pumping blood, but was not, then, slowly, sat back on his heels.

McKay hung Pinkey's black gabardine suit on the iron triangle Bobby rang to call them in for dinner because the fabric smelled like mothballs. Bobby lent him one of his clean dress shirts because they were similar in size, and McKay polished his boots. Just before it was time to leave,

Pinkey slumped on the stool and asked for something to wet his whistle.

"What you need?" Bobby asked, standing in the middle of the kitchen floor.

"I don't know," Pinkey said. His voice sounded hoarse but inside he felt lighter than he had ever felt, not the lightness that comes from relief, but the featherweight emptiness that comes when death is so near.

Bobby took a bottle of the ranch's best whiskey from the shelf and filled a small glass.

"Please—" he said to Pinkey and placed the glass in the old cowboy's hand.

Pinkey drank.

"More?" Bobby asked.

Pinkey shook his head numbly. "You know . . . when I took Vincent into that funeral parlor I had to wait in line. Someone else had gotten in there before us." He set his glass down hard. "It was the middle of the goddamned night," he yelled.

Bobby nodded, listening, then set a glass of ice water by the whiskey.

"I guess a man has to wait in line even if he's dead . . . ," Pinkey continued. "It was that Markham kid from the Three Six's Ranch, come in from the front in Italy. . . ."

Bobby refilled his glass.

Vincent's body was laid next to a big hole in the ground. Janine and Pinkey and Jimmy filed by the casket, then stood by as the others in the funeral party did the same. Janine was wearing an unfitted flowered dress with a silk jacket her daughter had won running barrels at Crow Fair. She had wanted Vincent to be buried on the reservation, but Pinkey wanted him "planted on the outfit," as he put it, because that's where Vincent had spent most of his childhood, and this one time she conceded because she had her way about not having an autopsy. "I don't want no white man's hands inside my boy's body," she said, not so much because of the bitterness she felt about Pinkey, but because she did not want the process of dying, of being dead, to be tampered with. "It's none of our business," she said. "He's gone. We have to help him now."

When everyone had viewed the body, the pallbearers—McKay, Snuff, and two Indian boys who had come on the train that morning—closed the casket and lowered it down into the hole with ropes. The ground was frozen but because of the war, the gravediggers had dug extra graves and covered them in order to accommodate the soldiers coming home in boxes.

Pinkey looked at his wife from under the brim of his Stetson, which he had brushed clean and sprinkled with talcum powder to cover the stains. Suddenly he wanted to go home with her, to her Indian house, filled with the smell of fry bread and stew. They would play cards and learn how to hurry up and die since now there was no child to live for, and in the meantime, they would move cattle together the way they used to—across the rolling hills of the Wolf Mountains, whose dense thickets of wild plums lining every draw reminded him of the way a woman looked with her legs spread.

The Lutheran minister started a prayer. Lutheran, not because Vincent had gone to that church, but because the owners of the ranch where he worked were German pioneers—and Pinkey took off his hat and bowed his head but could not pray. "There ain't no God and there never has been anything like one in the whole world," he thought. His shoulders felt tight. He wanted to yell at the top of his lungs. When he looked up, he caught Janine's stare. It was a sharp, sad look, and her dark eyes . . .

"Amen."

The pallbearers began covering the coffin with shovelfuls of dirt. Pinkey knelt by the grave and stared in. A chinook wind had come up and it blew warm air around his ears. He wanted to lie in the dank hole with his son.

Then Pinkey heard the voice, the low, crackling growl of the old man, the grandfather. Jimmy Big Elk tapped his cane on the hard ground and the volume of his voice doubled. Janine joined in along with the high, falsetto voices of the boys from the reservation. The minister's prayer was drowned out and the mourners could not hear anything else but song. The chanting continued. The wind picked up and the sudden warmth melted the top of the snow and Pinkey thought he could smell something from the mountains, maybe pine. He was glad when the minister left, sneaking off like a hyena, and after, he stood by Janine and let the vibration of her voice enter him. Then as suddenly, the song stopped. Very quietly Janine said there would be a feast at McKay's. She clasped Pinkey's hand as she talked because she was shy and Pinkey looked down and saw her big brown hand over his white one and in the first truly sober moment he'd had for years, felt ashamed of the pain he had brought her.

The mourners came by to pay their respects. Then the need for a drink seized him. It was winter and already the sky was getting dim. He wished it would get dark and stay that way. He wanted that. He took more steps, then climbed over the picket fence around the graveyard, out into the white sea of a plowed-up, snow-covered grainfield. Once he stopped and looked back. Janine was watching his disgraceful retreat. He tried to make himself return to her, but couldn't. "I'm just a running fool," he said to himself. All during the funeral he had wanted to rip open the casket and prove it wasn't true that Vincent was dead. "Let them have their marriages and funerals," he thought, "none of it is true." When he reached the highway he thought he saw Vincent's pickup coming toward him, beginning to slow, slowing to give him a ride to the first bar in town.

29

Secretary of War Henry Stimson announced that the Selective Service was "throwing open its arms to Japanese-Americans" and we Nisei would now be eligible for the draft. Many had been in the army before Pearl Harbor but after, were immediately reclassified 4-C—ineligible because of ancestry. In that way they invalidated our efforts to prove our loyalty long before the camps came into being. I don't think there is one of us who wouldn't have gladly enlisted if we had not been put into Camps. Why must our "struggle back to America," as someone called it, have to be paid for with one big leap from imprisonment to giving away our lives?

The draft aside, Mom and Pop and I have given some thought to relocating to a midwestern city; 1,566 evacuees have relocated out of this Camp to places like Des Moines, Chicago, Milwaukee, Cleveland. After dinner one night, I told them that I had turned down an opportunity to go back to graduate school.

Mom looked surprised. "But why?" she asked. "We wouldn't have minded, would we?" she said to Pop, who nodded in silent agreement. I hadn't expected that; I was glad I had decided to stay. It's not just out of giri—duty—but out of curiosity, as well. There's every kind of person here, from every kind of background, all ages and states of health, all kinds of minds . . . and there's Abe-san too. Mom realized this when she said, "It's good for you to stay. You will learn about life here, and about where you came from."

Later that week—the last week of January 1944—I made my first step toward fulfilling my vow to Will and took part in getting the Fair Play Committee into full swing as a response to the draft notice. We elected a president and a vice president and announced that membership was open only to American citizens whose loyalty to the United States is indisputable. We declared a two-dollar membership fee, and in short order, tallied up 275 members, bought a mimeograph machine with the dues, and began distributing daily bulletins to keep people informed. That same week, a new ally appeared: James Omura, editor of the Rocky Mountain Shimpo in Denver, gave us a column in his paper. Our articles will appear regularly there.

We will resist this draft!

While I was writing this, Mom was scrubbing the apartment from top to bottom for the second time. Pop and I had to take the furniture out, wash the curtains, straighten up the rocks around the flower garden, and rake the dirt in front of the barrack. Why? Because Kenny telegrammed and said he was coming for a visit. The thought of meeting my brother for the first time has been almost more than I could ingest. I struggled with the thought—going over and over in my mind what he would think of me, a nearsighted Ph.D. candidate going soft in the head and soft in the body from years behind barbed wire. What if, after all this, we found we couldn't get along? But I don't think either of us would let this happen. Too much time had already been wasted and who was to know whether Kenny would survive his next missions? Nothing could have deterred me from liking him. No, the word like isn't strong enough—I need him probably far more than he needs me.

Later. Ben came around just as I was going to dinner. He looked stony-faced, then he blurted it out.

"The guys think we ought to boycott Kenny's talks. He's talked to the *papers and publicly denounced the Fair Play Committee. If we boycotted, could we count on you too?*

I looked at him incredulously. At that moment I didn't give a damn about politics. "How can I boycott my own brother?" I said.

"In the Civil War, there were cases of brothers fighting against brothers . . . ," Ben said.

"I've never even met him . . . ," I said.

"That might make it easier."

Then I exploded. "You can say that, Ben," I began. "You have a big family. You have a wonderful father, and brothers and sisters . . . what's another brother to you? How could you understand what it's like to be alone all your life . . . you can't know . . . try to think what it's like. It's damned lonely. I'm not going to go against Kenny and I'm not going to change my mind about Fair Play either. . . ."

I stormed off and ate alone. The next thing I heard was that the committee decided not to stir up any dust, and I was glad. "Maybe we'll learn something from each other," I told Ben later that night, and he apologized.

The Camp Director has quite a celebration planned for Kenny's visit. I wonder if I'll have any time with him at all. There's a welcoming reception and banquet, various meetings, a dance, and on Thursday, he'll give his talk in the high school auditorium.

Monday. When Kenny came to the door of the apartment, Mom just put her hand over her mouth and stood there, struck dumb. He was smaller than I thought he'd be—small and lean—but he carried himself like a soldier. Mom went to him and felt the medals on his chest like a blind woman, while Pop bowed. Kenny had to wait until Pop's head bobbed up so he could shake his hand. Then Kenny turned to me.

"Hello, Kai," he said and I laughed with embarrassment.

"You know who I am?" I asked, after the fact.

"I know—"

Then I tripped on something and fell against him. He clapped me on the back as if I had choked and we laughed. He's small and tensed like a bobcat ready to spring. When I looked up, I saw Pop wiping away tears.

Before I knew what had happened all of us had our arms around each other, our heads together in a circle—crying like babies and passing Mom's

Kleenex box around. A family. For the first time. I hadn't known it would feel that good.

Mom made Kenny sit down in an overstuffed chair she had borrowed from a friend in another block. Pop and some other men had carried it on their shoulders to the apartment. Then Mom had stayed up all night reupholstering it, but as soon as Ken sat down, I heard something rip. It didn't matter—all those preparations seemed silly compared to just having him there.

Friends from all over the Camp had brought food to have around while Kenny visited. Other soldiers had visited the Camp and each time, it was an occasion for people to show their appreciation of what any soldier had to endure. But Kenny was even more special—the first Nisei to break the color line and join the rank of fliers. He had been all over the United States giving speeches and his picture had been in magazines.

Mom laid out food on a white tablecloth on two tables pushed together. We wouldn't have to go to the mess hall for a week! And neighbors— mostly Issei—filed by, bowing at the door, and moving quickly on.

I couldn't stop staring at him. He was in army uniform. His boots were shiny enough to see your face. His cap, pulled down on his forehead, pushed the skin against the bridge of his nose and his eyes moved quickly from Mom and Pop to me. "I can't believe it," I said. And he said, "Believe what?" "That you exist—that you're alive." Then Mom told me to stop talking that way; it was bad luck she said, though I couldn't figure out why.

When Kenny stood, I could tell he was a soldier just by the way he held himself; I kept thinking he was going to salute.

He's about five foot nine and couldn't weigh over a hundred and fifty. He wears a silver ring he bought in Egypt—it cost all of forty cents, he told me—and on it are engraved three pyramids. "It's my good luck charm," he said when he saw me examining it. He's already won two Distinguished Flying Crosses. Mom and Pop wait on him as if he were royalty. He suffered frostbite on his face during one of his missions and only one side of his face moves when he smiles. Finally he took off his cap and rubbed his face. "I'm so tired," he confessed. "Could I sleep for a little while?"

Mom's face went blank. This wasn't what she had expected.

"How many missions have you flown now?" I asked and he shrugged

at first, then he said, "Around thirty-seven." I wanted to pull my chair up close and start asking questions, but I could see he needed sleep.

He lay down and Mom covered him with two extra blankets. We watched him sleep. I didn't want to let him out of my sight—ever. In a way it was like watching a stranger, but I like to think I saw myself in him too—whatever traits we shared. We stayed like that—around his bed— all afternoon.

Later, I lay on my cot. I must have fallen asleep because a terrible scream woke me. I didn't know where it was coming from, but I yelled out, "What's wrong?" Then I saw Kenny lying face down on his bed, shaking. His hands were over his face and his body twisted horribly. When he screamed again, I grabbed his arms. "Kenny, it's all right; you're here with me." This time he didn't know who I was. Mom came over with a lantern and said his name and his face relaxed. "Oh no . . . I'm sorry—" he said. I held him and kept saying his name. Finally he looked at me. "Hello, Brother. I guess I was having one of those nightmares. . . ." Then he lay back again and I gave him one of my cigarettes and we smoked for a while without speaking, and when he turned to put his out, he said, "I'm glad you're here with me."

The next morning Kenny washed his face with a hot towel Mom had brought. She pushed his ear forward and looked: "Soooo . . . desu . . . still there." "What's still there?" I asked and felt behind my own ear for something. "No . . . no. You don't have them," she said. "Have what?" Pop glared at me. He thought I talked too much. Exasperated, he said, "Lucky holes behind ear, that's what." Kenny wiped his face. "Can I have a look?" He stood patiently, like a horse being inspected. There was a tiny pinprick of a hole behind each ear. "What's that supposed to mean?" I asked my parents. They looked at each other and smiled. "Good luck," my mother said. "He has it." Kenny shrugged, embarrassed.

After breakfast Mom and Pop picked up the mail and went to the Camp store run by a man who had lived not far from them in Richmond. When they had gone, Kenny lay down again, propping his head on his hand. I pulled up a chair but was speechless.

Sensing my difficulty, Kenny asked what was on my mind.

"How long have you known about me?" I asked finally.

Kenny lay on his back, turning a Zippo lighter over and over in his hand. "Since I was about fourteen," he said.

"But I only just found out. . . ."

Kenny looked over at me. "I know. I made Mom and Pop tell you . . . in case something happened to me on a mission. See, I made out this will so that all my stuff will be sent to you."

I wanted to stand up and move around the room but I sat, frozen. "Who raised you?" I asked.

"A foster family—like you. Mom was afraid Pop might hurt us—not hit us or anything, but by acting, you know, crazy—so I went inland, and it was different for me when the war came. I wasn't evacuated. Anyway, they had a real nice little ranch in the foothills. Gold country like where Bret Harte used to write about. I was in the 4-H, I did all that ranch-kid stuff—showed pigs and steers and got laid the first time in a great big haystack." Kenny paused to look over at me. "What about you?"

"I ended up in an orphanage," I said. "It was really okay. I learned to fight—like a little Filipino." Kenny laughed because Japanese and Filipinos never got along.

Then he sat up and put his feet on the floor. "Do you think Pop is any better?"

"No."

"Poor Mom."

"She's got a hell of a lot of patience."

"I didn't get any of that."

"Neither did I."

"I noticed."

The door swung open. "Very special surprise for you boys," Mom said, putting a package down on the unsteady table in the middle of the room. She opened it. Ice cream.

"Read it," she said to us.

"Rainbow sherbet," we sang out in unison as if we had always done these things together.

"Mom, can you say that yet?" Kenny asked, smiling.

Mom took a deep breath as if to speak, then collapsed in giggles, shaking her head.

"We eat, not talk. Okay?" she said.

Kenny and I shared a spoon.

Later, I told him about Li and he told me about his girlfriend Betty, who stopped writing him when she found out he had signed up for more missions, and about his friends in the Air Corps, and all the trouble he'd had getting in. "Even after they let me into the army, I was questioned all the time in the barracks about what nationality I was, or if I was Chinese, or if I knew how to write English . . . and always, we were called Japs. Then I was on KP duty for twenty-one days and no one in the barracks talked to me until finally this big guy from Chicago just came up to me and said, 'Hey, want to go to the movies with me tonight?' and I almost cried with relief." Once the ice was broken, things changed for him, he said, and he was assigned to a squadron and a crew and after that he never had to worry about not being accepted again.

Talking . . . talking . . . with my own brother. I still can't believe it. Even Mom and Pop became quite animated during Kenny's visit and the four of us were able to have some experience of what a family is like.

In the meantime, he had obligations to fulfill. He talked to the kids at the grammar school and high school, as well as the Boy Scouts, the USO club, and a parent's group. I had work to do. We were putting out an especially big issue at the Sentinel to cover his visit, and he told one of the groups that he had never seen as many Japanese-Americans in one place, and was disappointed in the attitude of some of the Nisei toward the draft.

What he doesn't know won't hurt him.

Thursday, Kenny put on a clean uniform, which Mom had brushed off and hung up, and he combed something through his hair to make it stay in place. An MP came for him in a jeep and asked whether we wanted to ride with him, but Mom and Pop wouldn't get in. So Kenny got out and we all walked to the other end of the Camp and people came out of their barracks all the way along and brought him little gifts or flowers and crowded around to ask for his autograph. Near the last row of barracks someone threw a tomato at me. It hit the back of my leg. Kenny stopped. "Was that for me or you?" he asked. "Look, Kenny . . . there's a lot of things going on here you don't know about yet. I'll explain later," I said. He gave me a funny look. "Should you tell me now?" he asked. "No," I said, "not now," and walked on.

It must have looked odd—a war hero and a troublemaker walking side by side. In my mind, however, there was no contradiction. I wasn't a conscientious objector; I was fighting on principle for our rights and hoped that if Kenny had been in my shoes or I in his, we would have done the same things.

The front row of the hall had been roped off—like at a theater—for Mom and Pop and me. Almost two thousand people turned up for the talk. I was glad they hadn't boycotted him and even felt proud. Kenny told what it was like to be a turret gunner—about the fear and the loneliness and the cold, and how great the Air Corps is; then he reminded the audience that he was the first and only Nisei allowed in that branch of the armed services and how this must change. Typically, the audience took these messages in silence. No hoots and hurrays—that's why the younger generation, the Nisei, have to be the troublemakers. . . . When he got off the train in Denver and tried to hail a cab, he told how another man came from behind and hopped in. The driver leaned out and asked where he was going and when Kenny told him, he said it was close to where the other guy was going and to hop in. But the passenger slammed the door closed and said, "I don't want to ride with any lousy Jap" and the cab drove off, leaving him on the curb. Then he recalled the day he had to give a talk in San Francisco at the Commonwealth Club to some wealthy Caucasian businessmen. The headline in the Chronicle read: JAP TO ADDRESS SF CLUB. He began his speech: "I learned more about democracy than you'll ever find in all the books. Because I saw it in action. When you live with men under combat conditions for fifteen months, you begin to understand what brotherhood, equality, tolerance, and unselfishness really mean. They're no longer just words. . . ." That's how he began, and afterward those men came up to him and shook his hand and called him "Sir."

Like those businessmen, I used to read war stories in the papers—Ernie Pyle's reports and the hard news. But I had never heard them firsthand, especially from a brother.

Turret gunners could go home after twenty-five missions—if they survived—but Kenny signed up for more. He described the raid over the Polesti oil fields, watching the planes next to him burn, then waiting all night for the others to come back. Fifty-four Liberator bombers were lost on that raid.

But there was more to his message than bombing missions. He said: "I *find prejudice directed against me and neither my uniform nor my medals have been able to stop it. I don't know for sure if it's safe for me to walk the streets in some parts of my own country. This war will not be over until my fight against intolerance is won."*

Afterward, a huge mob formed around him. One girl had him sign his name on her arm and swore she wouldn't wash until she got out of Heart Mountain. He was kind to everybody, but I could see he was still very tired so I helped him get away and we took a devious route back to the barrack. I was shaken—not by the mobs but by his stories. What kind of lard-assed coward was I, pontificating from this Camp while Kenny flew through sheets of gunfire and watched his friends drop out of the sky?

"Are you going to tell me about that tomato?" he asked when we were back in the room.

"I'm a draft resister," I said, very coolly, and he asked me to explain. I told him about Will and the Heart Mountain Congress, and how, after they segregated the loyals from the disloyals, the Fair Play Committee was formed. I talked as eloquently as I could about constitutional rights, how refusing to go for our physicals was a way of fighting for democracy, against American fascism.

"I believe in fighting to prove our loyalty," he said. "It becomes un-questionable then. That's why I keep signing up for more missions. I'm going to ram it down their throats," he said, slamming his fist into his other hand.

"That's what we're doing too—that's why we're resisting—"

"I can't go along with that. The only way to prove our loyalty is to put our lives on the line."

"What are you?" I yelled. "A JACLer?" I hadn't realized how angry I'd become.

He scowled at me. "I'm a fighter. I'm a soldier. I'm an American citizen. I don't need anyone else to tell me how I feel. I've lived it. I've sweated it out in the tail of a plane."

I looked at him. "Are you really my brother?" I asked.

He said yes.

"Then don't go against me."

"I'm doing what I know is right."

"So am I," I said. "We stand for the same thing; don't you see that?"

"No. You're disloyal."

"I'm not!"

"That's what it looks like to me."

"But you said yourself that this is a war against intolerance, against racism. . . ."

"Yes. But that's the only thing we agree on."

"You're not making sense."

"Look, I'm very tired."

"Wait."

Kenny started to walk off and I grabbed him. He spun and his hand came toward me. When I ducked, he laughed. His face looked ravaged for a second, then he regained his calm.

"I'm not going to change my mind," he said calmly.

"Will you go against us if this comes to court?"

He looked at me. "I can't say."

We walked. I felt a terrible repulsion toward him, as if I didn't want any part of our bodies to touch.

"You're not my brother, are you?" I asked.

He smiled faintly. "I think we are."

I ran ahead of him past the end of the barrack into the dark.

That night I couldn't sleep. I had pulled Kenny's bed near mine, and later I wished I hadn't. Pressing my ear against the wall, I listened for the sound of Mariko's breathing. Abe-san coughed in his sleep. Light from outside shone on Kenny's head. I couldn't believe what had happened. . . . If I said I felt torn before, I didn't understand what those words meant. It was more like being clawed to death than being torn neatly like paper. Looking over at him, I thought of the night before when a nightmare had awakened him and I held him and he was sweating even though it was cold . . . and how only one night later, I felt deeply betrayed. I lay down and stared at the ceiling. "Don't let him intimidate you," Ben had said. This was much worse than fighting with a friend because, if it were true that we were brothers, somewhere the root had divided and bent in opposite directions. Who or what was to blame? Yet, the fact that he's my brother . . .

I turned over. Just before daylight, sleep came.

Saturday. I had to swallow my pride when the Sentinel came out. The headlines read: "NAKAMURA 'TAKES' HEART MOUNTAIN. COMMUNITY

CELEBRATION FEATURES VISIT OF HERO. *Sgt. Kenny Nakamura, who blazed his name in the eternal halls of fame from the turret position of a Liberator bomber over Europe, Africa, and the Middle East, this week literally captured the Heart Mountain residents. Speaking informally before many groups, Sergeant Nakamura impressed his listeners with his modesty and sincerity . . . ," etc.*

Monday. Kenny's gone. Maybe it's too hard to compare waging a war against intolerance from a tar paper barrack to waging one from the tail of a plane. Mom and Pop have been hurt badly by what happened between Kenny and me. Pop has gone comatose again. Abe-san came over and massaged his feet and talked to him but it did no good this time. He has shut us out. Later, went to Abe-san's to talk. I tried to take the larger view of things, to understand what wars are about, then go backward and understand what divided Kenny and me so deeply. I kept thinking of the things Abe-san has taught me: how to follow my breathing, how to empty my mind.

Mom came over, removed her shoes at the door, and sat down with us. She had never behaved so informally before. Abe-san poured her some tea. He was so gentle with her. . . .

They call the two fronts "theaters." What an appropriate usage. I couldn't help compare the theater of war with the theater of . . . what should I call it . . . the spirit? That which Abe-san has been teaching me. People are always talking about ART versus LIFE. That was Will's big stumbling block. I see them as the same. What passes for "life" these days—i.e., the frontline, is perhaps more "theater" than Abe-san's Noh. I doubt that the army teaches much about the ideals of the warrior. They teach you to kill and brainwash you into hating the enemy (even though, in the next war, that "enemy" will probably be the ally), and the good things that come out of that situation—what Kenny talked about: democracy in action, selflessness, color-blindness, democracy without discrimination—seem to arise despite the drill sergeant's teachings, and from this we know the goodness of human beings. But I can't help thinking of that "theater" as compared to the theater of yugen—grace, natural elegance, tenderness, loneliness, radiance; of hana, that which is rare, haunting, flowering; or ran-i: effortless effort, emancipation, harmony.

Does the soldier on the battlefield learn these things? Does the student of Noh learn selflessness, tolerance, unconditional bravery?

Why must we take lives to become human? We sat for a long time in silence. My thoughts were tangled. If I hadn't liked what I was before, how did I know what to become, and by which vehicle? How does one learn how to live?

30

Long after the funeral the sky turned black with rain, then the heat came. Bobby found a rattlesnake curled up in the sun at the kitchen door. He didn't try to kill it. Instead he picked up a broom and hit it and told it to go away, and it did.

McKay rode more than he needed to that spring.

When he went to mend fence, he led two packhorses loaded with wire, posts, fence stretchers, a hammer, pliers, and a shovel. It took a week to ride to every fence. He crisscrossed the ranch. In one place, Alkali Creek went underground as if it had been shot in the hip and drowned in its own waters. The sinking feeling he had been experiencing for two years happened when he was with Mariko, as well as when he was alone. Her waters were a kind of liqueur that weighted him, submerged him in a sweet, asphyxiating trance.

He heard the sandhill cranes before he saw them. At first he scanned the horizon down by the lake. The sound they made was like a consonant rolling back and forth in water, a wavering "rrruuu, rrruuu," a cry of longing. He looked straight up. Two eagles rolled in opposite directions across high thermals, and a pair of cranes, mated for life, flew one above the other, their long stretched bodies gold and white. McKay knew there was no hope of their nesting on the ranch. Not enough water. "Not here," McKay thought. "Death, that's all we've got going on down here."

He and Bobby arose as usual at 4:30 A.M. Bobby made breakfast— oatmeal, bacon, and coffee. When he took the deck of cards down for their usual winter morning game of gin, McKay said, "Not now. I'm going to the Camp to ask Mariko to live with us."

Bobby looked at McKay.

"What are you doing?" he said. "You fill every room up with women? Madeleine coming soon to live here during calving. . . . Did you forget that? Did you forget her so fast?" he asked, dashing his hands together. "What Mariko do on this ranch? You make her into cowboy? You marry her? Abe-san must come too, then. Can't leave him all alone. . . ."

McKay sat back against the breakfast table as if he'd been pushed.

"Damnit, Bobby."

"Sooo . . . damn Bobby . . . you blame me, but you don't think. You only think with this!" he said, clasping his hands to his groin.

McKay looked away, pained.

"She very beautiful, very great painter . . . I know that. But what she do here? This—" he said, indicating the ranch, "worse than Camp. Worse prison for her. She would be like caged bird here," Bobby said, then retied the sash of his kimono. He stared at McKay until McKay turned to him.

"Sooo . . . you love her, *desu-ka?*" he asked gently.

Madeleine burst through the door.

"Did you hear those cranes? They just flew over. Here's the mail," she said brightly, tossing it on the table. "Are you going to check those heifers or am I?" she asked McKay.

McKay pulled on his boots. "I've got to go to town. Could you do it this morning, Mad?"

"Yep, but you owe me . . . ," she said, smiling.

"That's just what Bobby's been saying."

*   *   *

The guard at the sentry gate—not Harry, he had been fired—let McKay through after he signed the visitor book. He walked to Mariko's block. It was breakfast time and he could hear the clamor of the mess halls as he passed them, one by one. The roads in the Camp were deeply rutted from spring rains. Soon they would be dust, a kind of veil that isolated the prisoners from the green irrigated farms on the outside.

He saw Mariko walking down the lane, arm in arm with Kai. They stopped once and pointed at some children who were playing naked in the mud while their parents ate breakfast, and she and Kai were laughing. McKay did not know what she did at Camp when he was not with her or whom she saw. He had never asked. She looked so domestic at that moment and happy in an ordinary way. The sight shocked him. They didn't cook or eat together, or pull calves, or go to the grocery store, or pay bills, or clean house, or go to the movies; he hadn't thought there was anything casual about her. Yet her laugh was different from any he had heard before.

He walked to the far end of the barrack. He could hear them talking and laughing as they approached their rooms. He stopped and filled his lower lip with snoose. The wind kicked up black from the coal dump at the end of the building and he wiped the tobacco and dust from his chapped lips.

He knocked on Abe-san's door. No answer. Then he heard the old man's bright peel of laughter outside. McKay went around back and there was Abe-san, straddling a blue bicycle with wide handlebars and a wicker basket. He stepped on one pedal, standing for a moment above the hard seat, then sat and pedaled strenuously out away from the building onto the rutted lane.

"Haaaa . . . ," Abe-san cried out. His brown kimono dangled above the bicycle chain.

At the end of the lane, he put one foot down, paused, then mounted the bike again and rode toward McKay. The handlebars shook from side to side as the front wheel hit ruts. He stopped and let the bike fall to one side.

"Here, you ride now," he said to McKay.

"Hell no, I'd get flat bucked off. . . ."

"Ahhhh . . . ," Abe-san growled and tapped McKay briskly on the chest. "Be cheerful!"

McKay picked up the bike. He rolled it out onto the dirt track, then hopped on, the way he hopped onto a calf-roping horse, and let it roll.

"Faster . . . ," Abe-san yelled delightedly.

McKay pedaled hard and the front of the bike lifted a little. He rode to an intersection, turned, and pumped until he was in front of Abe-san again.

"Whoa, Blue." He skidded to a stop.

"That's good," Abe-san purred.

"Where do you want this bronc?" McKay asked.

" 'Bronc.' What's that?"

"A horse that's hard to ride."

Abe-san laughed.

"Where do you want it?" McKay asked.

"Inside, here—" he said, pointing to the wall inside the screen door, then stood and admired his "steed."

McKay heard Mariko's voice in the next room—Kai's room.

Abe-san watched him.

"I came to see Mariko," McKay said.

"I know," Abe-san said. "She is right there." He pointed to the wall.

McKay listened, nodded, then walked through the door all the way to the sentry gate and went home.

31

Madeleine would remember 1944 as the year when more people died than animals. The flu had taken nineteen lives so far, Vincent had died, twelve "boys" had arrived home in coffins from Italy, and she'd had a miscarriage. She had more time to contemplate these events than she wanted. She and Pinkey were feeding that week, and Pinkey, still stunned by grief, hardly talked. It amazed Madeleine that so much could change on a ranch, where sameness would seem to prevail—the same seasonal routines year after year for a hundred years. But what happened between and to people changed everything.

Madeleine climbed on the wagon and Pinkey slapped the lines across the horses' backs. Where the thaw had come out of the ground, the wagon wheels made sharp ruts that froze into a mass of crystals until the sun hit them and the ridges softened into mud. The oldest calves were six weeks, which is old in a calf's life. They jumped and bucked together, then ran to their mothers' sides as the wagon approached.

Madeleine drove while Pinkey pitched loose hay to the cattle. The line of green behind the wagon was like the wake of a boat. Madeleine drove the length of the field, then turned the team and came back the other way until the wagon was empty. After, they drank coffee from a thermos and watched the calves play. Madeleine took off her jacket and gloves and let the sun pound down on her shoulders. Pinkey asked whether she had heard from Henry, and she said yes, but his letters were always months late. "I'm so afraid he'll be dead while I'm reading his latest letter, thinking he's . . ." She stopped and looked at Pinkey. "I'm sorry," she said. Pinkey grinned. "Yep. It's tough, ain't it."

"What I was waiting for in 1942 is different from what I'm waiting for now. How stupid to have thought otherwise. But how was I to know?" she said.

"Yep," Pinkey mumbled again, though he didn't know what she was talking about and didn't care.

When she finished her coffee she jumped down and walked through the calves to check for scours. One calf butted his head against her leg, and when she reached down to touch his ears he twisted away and jumped backward. Descriptions of the Death March turned through her mind. She had collected all the clippings and articles she could find from the *Billings Gazette*, the *Casper Star Tribune*, the *Kansas City Star*, and *Life* magazine. Thirst, delirium, dysentery, malaria, and hunger; bayonets, live burials, executions—she had found Henry's last letter unbearable because he had mentioned none of these things, yet he had been on the March, and his cheerfulness and concern struck her as patronizing.

At the end of the long line of mother cows, she found a calf who had not suckled all day. He was too weak to stand, and his mother's teats were hard with milk. She held the calf in a standing position between her legs, pried his mouth open with her thumb, and pushed a bolus to the back of his throat, massaging his neck as it went down. Then she held him at his mother's side as he sucked.

Her boredom—the boredom of waiting for Henry—embarrassed her now. Had her night with McKay happened because of the cheerlessness of her life? Yet, his weight on her had seemed to push her through the floor, to some unspoken tenderness that both frightened and pleased her.

Now, waiting was like straining against gravity. "How high can I jump to reach him?" she wondered. She envied the women who passed the time doing their nails, planting their victory gardens, and playing cards. Surely, she thought, they must wake in the night fearful and crying as I do. In '42, even '43, she marked her calendar. Absence could be counted in days then. Now she didn't bother.

After the calf had his fill, she walked back to the wagon. Pinkey watched her as he sipped whiskey from a flask. He could no longer be counted on for cheerful words, or even for help on the ranch. When she climbed on the wagon, he stood and spit over the side. The younger of the two horses backed nervously, then lunged forward as Pinkey picked up the lines.

"Blackie, Bud, come up."

McKay had been waiting for Mariko since morning because that is when the note, scribbled on a piece of cardboard, said she would come—April 1, 1944. She had lied to the Camp Director, saying she was interviewing for a job.

Twice McKay went outside. Had she walked? Would she drive? He heard Pinkey and Madeleine unharness the team and turn the horses out. The ducks that had returned to the ranch the day before wheeled over the house.

He went inside and sat down to pay bills. Long before, Bobby had stopped going to the general store or the grocery store, but called in his orders, which were charged to the ranch, and McKay picked them up when they were ready. He used the same big checkbook his mother had used, four checks to a page, and wrote out the amounts hastily and signed his name. April first. Maybe she's playing a joke on me, he thought. He looked up from the table. No one. Then he felt the errant bomb move into the room, felt its weight against the back of his neck, and when the wind outside shifted against the kitchen, a metallic smell filled the house. He put down his pen. He thought he heard a sound—the noise of an engine. But still she didn't come and he went to the window over the sink, and no one was outside.

The bomb mocked him with her absence. It had come to stand not for loneliness in general, but for the specific hardship of separation, from which almost everyone in the world was suffering now, he thought. He

closed the checkbook and walked to the corrals. Then the bomb shrank
to the size of a football and jostled the air by the side of his head and he
wanted to swing around and smash it with his fist.

He turned the colt into the round corral. It was the blue roan gelding
he was breaking for Champ. He was easy to catch and saddle, though
sometimes he still struck out with his front foot when McKay was getting
on. Pinkey told him to hobble the horse with a gunny sack, and get on
and off for a few hours, but McKay preferred to let the colt figure it out
on his own, come to trust his passenger in his own way.

"It'll take longer," Pinkey had warned. What else did they have in
1944, but time?

McKay stepped on smoothly. In the saddle he wasn't lame and the
colt moved out gracefully from the round corral into the roping arena.
As he trotted toward the chutes at the other end, McKay looked down
the lane to see whether Mariko was coming and still there was no car;
he could see Pinkey walking to the house with Madeleine and Heart
Mountain going purple and gray with a spoke of sunlight piercing the
clouds.

McKay touched the colt's ribs with his left heel and the colt turned.
What time was it now, he wondered? Nine? Ten? Halfway down the rail
he touched the colt's ribs with his other heel and the colt turned into
the middle of the arena and McKay let him stop. The colt was a natural
athlete but it had been difficult to teach him to stand still while he got
on. This he had to learn because Champ would need extra time to get
his bad leg over the saddle.

McKay nudged the colt with his right heel again and pulled back on
the bridle rein until the colt backed, then he touched his right spur to
the colt's ribs and the horse spun. He did the same going to the left. He
asked the colt to back ten steps, then McKay kicked the horse into a lope.
He felt the muscles in the colt's hindquarters bunch up and when the
horse bucked, McKay jerked the colt's head around sharply, let it go,
and the colt bolted in another direction.

"What the hell's got into you, anyway?" McKay yelled at the horse,
pulling him around quickly the other way. The colt fell on his side.
McKay fell too, but pulled his foot out from under the horse before the
full weight landed on him, then stood, and with the long mecate, pulled

the frightened horse to him. McKay rubbed the horse's head. "April Fool's, huh?" he said, then got on again.

When McKay was a little boy Pinkey had told him how smart a horse is. "Hell, he knows you're coming out to catch him before you get out of bed in the morning," he always said. "So you better have your head on straight by the time you've finished breakfast."

Pinkey had learned the hard way. Horses had broken almost every bone in his body by the time he was thirty-five. The year he rode the rough string on a big outfit in Montana and came on a colt nobody could get near, much less ride, he devoted the entire winter to understanding that horse's mind. "He's an unridable horse, not even fit for glue," the foreman had warned him, but Pinkey said, "I know we can get along," even after the colt struck out at him and shattered his thigh.

"I never did conquer that horse," he'd told McKay, "but I got him to trust me . . . ," he said, grinning.

"How?" McKay had asked.

"I went out there one morning and front-footed that waspy little shit and down he went. He was sure surprised . . . but not half as surprised as he was later. . . . I got a real soft rope and while he was down I tied him up . . . wound it around his legs and back and under his tail and around his chest. . . . He looked like he'd got caught in a big cobweb. Then I lay on him and petted him all over, and talked to him kind of softly. I did that all day long. It was worse than shacking up with a dame . . . I mean more tiring."

When McKay asked what happened next, Pinkey told him.

"I did the same thing the next day and the next. That went on for just about a week. Then one morning I went out and that ol' colt looked at me and I looked at him and we both knew the game was over. I could see it in his eyes and the way he acted. So I got my saddle out and I put it on him real quietly . . . I didn't tie him up or anything. He knew he could get away if he wanted to . . . but he just stood. Then I stepped on. I tell you what . . . I took a deep seat at first, but he didn't do much—just moved around enough so I knew I had a horse under me. From that day on he wasn't scared of me and I wasn't scared of him and he only gave me enough trouble to keep me awake . . . to kind of check up on me so I didn't get lazy. . . ."

Remembering this story, McKay smiled as he loped the colt in figure eights, stopping each time they came to the middle; backed the colt; turned him one way and the other; then loped out in the opposite direction, giving him so much to do and think about he wouldn't have time to buck. McKay worked him until the horse was covered with lather, but not so much that it would sour him. "See, I wasn't mad at you, ya dummy," McKay chirped affectionately. He could feel the colt relax as soon as he relaxed, and then he didn't have to think about what the horse was doing because the movement took on its own internal rhythm, and the horse's legs and McKay's legs were the same legs, and his hands holding the bridle reins telegraphed the horse's mind.

The colt worked smoothly and well and sometimes McKay felt as if he were moving toward Mariko, then spinning away from her, only to turn quite suddenly into her arms . . . and still she did not come.

A shiver went through McKay's body when he saw dust from a car rise stiffly. He watched. It was the car Kai drove when they took the paper to press. The colt worked his mouth on the bit and when the car came to a stop between the house and the corrals, McKay opened the gate from horseback and rode through.

A mountain thunderstorm had passed earlier that morning and the ground was still beaded with hailstones—"just like a broken strand of pearls," McKay's mother always said. Now McKay wanted badly to string his broken feelings for Mariko on a single strand. He remembered something Bobby had told him—something like "relax with things as they are"—and he wondered what it took to be smooth and natural and happy.

Mariko got out of the car. She stood for a moment and watched McKay dismount. She brought a handful of flowers from behind her back.

"Look," she said, smiling. "They're from Mr. Nakamura's greenhouse. Freesias." Her voice vibrated. She held the delicate blossoms under his nose and he inhaled deeply. Laughing, her eyes danced wildly.

"Why didn't you wait for me when you came to the Camp?"

McKay shook his head. Some of the petals broke loose and fell back on her arms and McKay leaned forward to kiss the places where they touched.

"I don't know if I can stand this anymore," he finally said.

"Stand what?"

"Not being with you all the time."

Mariko looked at the ground. *"Shigata ga nai."*

"What's that?"

"It means, 'There's nothing to be done.' "

"Isn't there?"

She stared at him.

"Maybe we should stop," he said.

"Stop?"

"It's tearing us both up."

"So will stopping."

McKay looked away. The horse sneezed and rubbed his head against McKay's shoulder.

"Let me see," Mariko said, stepping closer to touch the scars on his face. "Have they gotten to you? Is that why you say these things?"

"Who? Gotten to me how?"

"That guard who beat you up."

"How could you say that?"

He turned away, then looked. But what good did it do to read her face, to know every inch of her when it only led to more passion, another impasse? He led the colt back to the corral and pulled the saddle. Mariko followed him, carrying the flowers. He threw the saddle blankets over the horn and slung the bridle in the crook of his elbow.

"I feel like I'm dying all the time," he said hoarsely.

"From it? From us?"

"Yes."

The colt went down on his knees, then rolled in the dirt, first one side, then the other, stretching his neck out to rub the sweat spots behind his ears.

"Would you come here and live with me? You could get a permanent leave. . . ."

Mariko watched the horse rise to his feet and shake. "I can't."

Stunned, McKay felt like an elk that's been shot in the leg and keeps running. He wanted to start the day over again and not have to wait so long for her and, when she came, not have to hear what he just heard. He sat down in the loose dirt. So that will not be my life, he thought, a life with Mariko in it: it will be something else. But all he could think of was the life he had now, doing the work of three men and loving the only two women he had ever loved, and waiting for his brothers and friends to come home, if they survived.

"McKay?"

He shielded his eyes from the sun. A truck drove by the house and he saw Madeleine look in his direction.

"Come sit by me," he said.

Mariko sat with her legs stretched out. "I did apply for a long-term pass," she said in a soft, clear voice. "It was denied."

"When?"

"A month ago. Because I'm married to Will and he's what they call a 'disloyal'—that makes me one too, in their eyes."

McKay rubbed his forehead. "What do we do now?" he asked wearily.

"What we have been doing . . ."

"I don't know if I can."

"What do you mean?" she asked and her voice broke.

"What's the point?" he said.

32

It was summer, and Carol Lyman's house was hot by seven in the morning so she went for an early drive, heading north for Warren through the rocky foothills of the Pryor Mountains where the wild horse herds were. She and Willard had washed the black coupe in the yard after Willard finished with the roosters, but already it was covered with a film of dust. She looked at herself in the oval rearview mirror as the car bumped along. The Wild Man once said her hair was the color of burnt umber, a color darker than rust. What had carved such deep lines in her face? she wondered. She rolled down the window and let the wind hit her, but it made no difference—nothing softened the brittleness. Stretching her neck, she held her hair back with one hand: she hated the way her ears stuck out. Then she wrapped her fingers around the steering wheel until the long, painted nails stuck into the palms and made them go white.

The road climbed through blasted rock. Up above the world she could see the white mounds of mine tailings; the empty, waiting boxcars; the winding layout of Snuff's. She continued on what had been the freight road between Montana and Wyoming for fifty years, passing the cave where the Outlaw Gang had spent a night on their way to the Hole-in-the-Wall country. The road switchbacked up and up. She came to a fork and recognized the road to the right which had led to the secluded Heaney Ranch.

She decided to walk. It was a narrow valley with a long meadow bounded by pine forests. How far was the house? She couldn't remember. Once, she bent down and drank from the creek with her hands. It was a hot day, but the breeze on her wet face cooled her.

She tried to remember Willard's father: one front tooth was crooked and his fingernails had grown long from not working and his dark hair was gray in the front and his voice was soft and gravelly. . . .

She remembered the Chinese lanterns swinging from the veranda and the green lawn bordered by sagebrush, and the man's black-haired Irish mother who greeted the guests bedecked with Indian jewelry and gaudy Crow moccasins, and she remembered a young boy, Henry, with deep-set green eyes, exploding with laughter everywhere he went, and the cool hallway, the sound of fiddle music, the dark room where he lay.

The gate was open. She stood on the grass and called out. No one answered. The trees were bigger than she remembered, but why shouldn't they be? She walked to one end, then the other. She felt so brittle as she moved, she thought she could hear her bones breaking.

She leaned against the edge of the veranda. "Ossification of the bone results in extreme . . ." She stopped and drummed her fingernails on the weathered wood floor. "Narrow . . . so narrow . . .," another thought began. She pushed her hip against the planks.

She thought of his seed climbing the ladder of her body and the one egg, imploded by sperm. . . . At that moment she held the hard edge of the porch with her bony hands, then threw herself against it again and again. I must break myself, she kept thinking, break myself open. The wood gouged her abdomen. I must break into where I held him, held his beauty. . . . The wide planks squeaked as she threw herself, and she heard the hard sound her body made every time it struck.

"Ma'am?"

She jerked awake. A young cowboy with a mustache wearing a hat that had been through too many rainstorms stood before her.

"Ma'am, are you all right?" he asked.

She was lying on the lawn in front of the veranda because she was afraid to go back, afraid that Snuff would, at the last minute, find her unsuitable, unbendable, impervious.

"I'm so sorry . . . I walked a long way, then I must have fallen asleep." She primped her hair and ran her finger over her uncolored lips.

"Yes, ma'am, I saw your car."

"Goodness," she said, getting to her feet. One deep wrinkle ran diagonally down her dress. "I must be . . ." The shadows of pines swept across the grass. She looked back at the young man. "Are you a Heaney?"

"No, ma'am, I just ride for the association. . . ."

She looked at the house again. "I went to a party here once," she said weakly.

"Yes, ma'am, I heard they used to have some good ones here before the Depression."

"Everyone came. . . ."

"Yes, ma'am . . ."

Carol straightened the front of her dress and buttoned her sweater. "Well, I best be going."

"On foot?"

"Oh yes . . . it's not really far, is it? Then the drive back to Warren. Do you know what time it is?"

"No, ma'am. My sundial's plumb broke."

She smiled. "You must like it up here. . . ."

"Yes, ma'am, it's good country."

"Yes . . . ," she said and began the long walk back to her car.

Carol drove down the mountain too fast because she didn't want to use up her brakes. Some mornings Willard's father did not seem dead, merely away, as many of the men were in those days, and she reported to him under her breath about the condition of his ranch house, about the snowpack, and war casualties. Always, at the end, she added something about Willard—what he had done that week, what a good job he was doing with Mañuel's roosters.

Sometimes she felt irritated that his death had impeded the future, but lately she saw how pure and unblemished by life he had become, and when she talked to him, his presence surrounded her like a pure gas.

*   *   *

Willard rode a horse older than he was, a black mare with feet round as pancakes and heavy fetlocks, and thick ears that bounced forward and back like a mule's when she walked, which was as fast as she moved in twenty years. It wasn't just that she was approaching thirty, but she had brains. She knew more about Willard than Willard knew, understood that he had a different scent, not a man smell, a mix of sweat and sperm and beard, and not a sweet-salty woman scent, either. His was the slightly stale smell of innocence, guilelessness bottled up for so long it had become an unwitting beatitude.

The mare knew all this when the pear-shaped boy rambled across the pasture in her direction, coming not to catch her, kidnap her, put her into service, but rather to pull carelessly toward her warmth and bulk. Everyone had seen the boy and the mare walk side by side in the borrow pit, the one not leading the other, but strolling together, stopping to swat flies. Sometimes Willard rode her bareback with a piece of twine looped loosely around her neck, giving it a shake each time he wanted to talk to her, but couldn't.

Mañuel had given Willard the first week of July off, though he continued to water and feed the roosters every morning, and only after did he ride. It was a hot day and he smelled the irises a homesteader had planted on the hillside, which had been left untended for fifty years. He slid off his horse and hid behind the screen of a low juniper and saw them, saw the backs of the two riders and the huge haunches of the horses churning muscle, and her black hair so long it touched the horse's back as if it were trying to become another tail. He saw them climb through the breaks and go up into the shaded grove of juniper trees where the water came out of the ground, from between two rocks. He saw the glistening rumps of the horses where they were tied in the trees.

Now he watched how the woman with the hair like a tail knelt by the spring and, cupping water in both hands, brought it between the man's legs, and later, how he held her breasts with his wet hands and sucked her like a calf. Then they lay on their sides with the yellow slicker thrown over them on the juniper needles, her back fitted against his front as if there were not two of them, but one. He knew what they were doing because he had seen bulls with cows and rams with ewes, and the way roosters hopped on each other's tail feathers and tried to hold the captive's neck down, but it troubled him to see the woman lying on her back facing the man. Later, she turned and he saw the man climb on her from behind, and he felt better because that's how it was supposed to be done.

He forgot they could see him and he stood. McKay rose up from under the slicker. "Willard . . . what are you doing up here?"

Willard held onto the black mare's mane with one hand and closed the other over his eyes, as if to make himself invisible.

"Willard?" McKay said again.

Willard felt the aqueous part of his mind jostling, and he reached for the sounds that make words but only faint squeals came out, and when they were gone, the words McKay had spoken settled on that interior lake the way mallards land on water.

Now the woman was sitting with her knees pulled up to her chest, and she was laughing. Willard came out from behind the juniper and walked toward the grove. McKay stood at the edge of the shade. Mayflies and mosquitoes swarmed him and he hit himself with little slaps and Willard stopped where he was, thinking the slaps were intended for him. The woman was still smiling: a shaft of hot sun pushed down on her shoulder and Willard felt drawn to her heat and repelled by McKay's shade, so he didn't know which way to go. One strap of his overalls was unhooked and his big forehead shone with sweat, and he made a noise that was almost a word but sounded like a door creaking.

"Hello, Willard," McKay said.

Then Willard smiled broadly and the woman who had stopped laughing smiled too, shading her eyes from the sun with her hand and holding the slicker across her nudity. McKay took the metal cup off the nail in the tree and held it where the water came out of the ground and, when it was full, handed it to Willard and he drank. McKay filled the cup again and offered it to the woman, then filled it again and drank himself.

"Willard, this is my friend Mariko," he said, and the woman held her long arm out toward him, and Willard could only stare at her beautiful hand. He sat down in front of her and crossed his legs like a schoolboy.

When Mariko laughed this time, he saw her eyebrows lift high on her forehead. He peered over the edge of the slicker and watched her breasts shake.

"We were just going to the falls, Willard," McKay said.

Finally Mariko stood. Her nakedness rose over Willard and shafts of sun moved across one breast, then the other, as McKay's hands had.

"We're going now," McKay said again, and Willard stood, his eyes still fastened to the woman. When she turned he saw her straight back, how it narrowed suddenly at the waist, how her buttocks stirred the way a horse's haunch does. McKay put on his shirt and draped the slicker over Mariko's shoulders, then picked up their clothes. Willard was standing at the edge of the shade, his face in shadow, his back doused by sun, and McKay and Mariko walked up the hill away from him. He watched them go arm in arm, and saw how once McKay's penis stuck straight out from his body, fell, and rose again, as if lifting some invisible cargo. He saw how the ends of her black hair bounced and swung across McKay's groin.

They picked their way through the sagebrush up the hill. When Willard couldn't see them anymore, he took the cookies from the pocket of his overalls and ate some and gave the others to the mare. Then it was no longer a matter of hide-and-seek, but of being drawn by them as if being led.

He could see the falls from the spring, but as he moved closer, the long threads of white water disappeared behind bushes and trees, and he walked not to any specific place, but toward the wild noise hidden within the thicket of willow and rose hip and gooseberry and pine, until he was closed in too, and wondered whether he had ever been made invisible by sound.

The mare had stopped at the edge of the thicket, but Willard pushed through until the water bubbled at his feet, and he entered the feminine cleft of the waterfall. He climbed the slick rock, falling once into twin streams of water, though now he didn't think of it as water, but as noise. He walked to where the ground was level. A shallow pool surrounded by rocks was dappled by light. He took off his wet boots and rolled up his pantlegs, and put his feet into the bitter cold and pulled them out again. The driving water sound was constant and even when a squeak pushed up from the top of his throat, he could not hear it and he wondered whether sound swallows sound as well as all that is visible.

He climbed higher. No difficulty could assuage him now. Once he saw them naked under the falls. Long threads of white water twined themselves in her black hair, hitting her shoulder and spraying sideways, then falling again on rock older than Willard knew how to count, if he knew at all. Their skin shone like fish scales. They turned to each other once, and where Mariko's head had been, he could only see McKay's, and this scared him because now there was one head and two very different bodies. Later, he saw them step out of the water, in toward rock, and the water cascading by them looked solid, like one silver flash, and he could see them no longer.

He climbed. He found footholds in giant, granite boulders and belly flopped over the top, then scrambled to the next one. He stopped to get his breath. When he looked again, he saw them lying, joined and motionless on a rock far above. The roar of the water gathered in a higher pitch as he gained altitude and the air sizzled with droplets that found their way to his overheated face. He pulled himself up to a level place. A huge snout-shaped rock towered overhead, and before him was a room scoured out by water.

He had not known until then that rocks were also houses. He entered the grotto. Streams of water blackened the wall and the hollow echoing sound it made when it hit the floor was almost as loud as the rushing water sound outside. He wondered about McKay and Mariko. Had he come up underneath them? Had he climbed that far? Were they lying on the domed rock over his head? Something stirred in him he had not felt before, as if helium and hot sand had been sent shooting through his body, and he looked at the ceiling covered with lichen and moss and then pressed his hands up and up and up into that dark wetness and green sponge.

Three of the roosters crowed an hour before first light, and soon the whole chorus chimed in. Willard knew which bird crowed first, because he knew their voices. Sometimes in the predawn dark, he ran outside in his pajamas and put his flashlight on the one crowing and watched how the bird's neck arched and lengthened and after, how the neck feathers ruffled and smoothed, as if making that sound were like sucking a lemon. His own rooster, the one Mañuel had let him raise and train, was never the first one to crow. He kept off by himself, sometimes jumping the fence when Willard let him loose, only to eat with the goats and rabbits in the next pens. He was a friend of the goats, the way goats are natural companions to horses, and they tolerated the brown bird as he scratched the dirt between and around their legs, but when Willard went into the yard, the bird everyone referred to as "Drumstick" flew to Willard's side.

Willard had seen him hatch out, the point of his beak fracturing the shell and the chick feathers drying off into something that looked to Willard like milkweed spore. Later, when the adult plumage had turned brown, Willard saw how an iridescence began to spread down the neck, across the wings, over the top of the head, and when he touched it the first time, he thought it would feel wet, but it didn't. Later in the month, he saw the rooster stretch his yellow legs and run faster than he, Willard, could.

When the rooster was eight months old, Mañuel started training him to fight. Once a week for eight weeks he wrapped the bird's beak and leg spurs with white tape, weighed him, and put him in the portable ring with one of Tony's birds and let them spar for fifteen minutes, after which Willard was allowed to feed and water them.

The ninth Saturday, Mañuel emerged from the house with his best white shirt and a red cotton scarf tied tightly around his neck. He didn't tape the rooster's beak or spurs, but instead covered him with a gunny sack and told Willard to hurry with the evening feeding. Then he lifted the portable ring into the back of his pickup, and they drove to the place under the railroad bridge by the river where the cliff looked green.

The other men were already there—Tony, Mañuel's oldest son, and Chico, Pedro, Pete, Miguel, and the ones Willard didn't know, cousins and nephews of the others. The ground had already been swept clean of rock and the lanterns lit, throwing the shadows of the men and the fighting cocks across the water, and Willard wondered how they had grown so big, and why they were not carried away by the current.

Tony's rooster was gray-white with black streaks in its wings, and long plumage at the crown. Its red comb had been trimmed and the shorter feathers down its legs and under its wings had been plucked, and Willard could see the bird's bare skin and the way it shook from the cold. The bird's head moved in short jerks and his lidless yellow eye fastened on one thing, then another.

Mañuel and his son held their two birds up off the ground, facing each other, and when Chico saw the second hand of his stopwatch point straight up, he said, "Go," and the men dropped the birds into the little ring.

Then Willard thought something had happened to time, because he couldn't feel its passing. All the minutes—fifteen of them—that it took for the birds to go at each other, squawking and jumping and pecking, shrank as if the beginning and the end of the match had become the same thing.

Amid human shouting, the birds lifted and fell, springing straight up and coming down at each other, sharpened spurs first. The gray and white cock pecked viciously at Drumstick's shoulder, then he struck back with his claw and came down on his opponent beak-first. Once, Mañuel lifted both hands to the sky and made a sound, a howling prayer. The cocks lunged again, and Willard thought that each surge of human sound brought another bead of blood onto the neck feathers of the rooster. The two birds jumped away from each other, wings half-lifted, until the brown rooster's spur came down and stuck deep in the other's neck and blood spilled from the jugular onto the ground.

Willard saw that the little piece of tape Mañuel always had stuck to the side of his nose had come loose. It flapped up and down as he fell to his hands and knees at the edge of the ring, eye level with the two birds. Sound rolled out of his throat like something passing over ball bearings, and the white rooster fall sideways. Chico stood over the bird. Its gnarled yellow feet jerked and shook. Willard saw Mañuel step into the ring and snatch up the brown rooster and hold him over his head in victory.

As usual, the tequila bottle was passed, but passed to Willard first, because it was Willard's cock and Willard's victory. He thought how sometimes the fighting roosters had looked like McKay and the woman that day by the falls.

As soon as Mañuel put the bird into Willard's arms, time began again. The rooster's warmth penetrated his thin windbreaker, as did the blood from the cut by the bird's eye. Willard made cooing sounds only the bird could hear.

When he felt the ground shake he looked up and saw the light from a train's engine telescope forward and bury itself in the green cliff above the river. A spray of sparks streamed down from the wheels as the train flew over their heads, and the rooster's wings lifted against his arms in fright.

McKay helped Chico lift the portable ring into the back of Mañuel's truck while the other men settled their bets. All the money that had been bet on Tony's cock was handed to Mañuel, who told them to give it to Willard, and after, Willard felt them shove the green paper into his overall pockets and then pass the tequila around again. Then the men started up the gravel sidehill to their trucks, and Willard saw Tony carry his dead rooster upside down by the feet. Its neck felt like rubber when Willard touched it.

Mañuel and Porfiria's kitchen smelled of food cooking. Mañuel took the brown rooster from Willard's arms and set him on the Formica table. He told Porfiria to bring him the sewing kit, which meant the needles and catgut thread, and he and Chico held the bird down while Mañuel made two stitches above the eye. After he let the rooster down on the floor, Porfiria covered the table with pots of food—*chile verde*, sopapillas, tortillas, frijoles, tamales, and enough plates and silverware for everyone who had been at the fight.

She asked Willard to sit at the head of the long table, the place of honor where Mañuel usually sat, then everyone ate, laughing and re-telling each detail of the fight. Willard tore a tortilla into small pieces and fed it to Drumstick on the floor.

"That bird, he likes *la cena Mexicana*," Pedro said in a voice that sounded like singing. When the dog came in, he sniffed the rooster and the bird pecked his nose.

After dinner Willard took Drumstick to the yard where the cages were. The bird tilted his head so his lidless eye met Willard's hooded one, then craned his neck and crowed.

Willard filled the containers made of cut-off soup cans with water and feed. The rooster drank thirstily. Then Willard pulled the loose money he had won from his overall pockets, all the time making a rolling "Rooo, rooo" sound. He shredded the green bills into narrow strips and laid them on the bottom of the cage; they looked like green feathers. The rooster eyed him, cocking his head, then settled down on the new bed. Willard smiled. It was a warm night, and in every direction he could hear water moving and in the distance another train shook the green cliff by the river.

33

During the last week of February 1944, Ben and I began staying up all night once a week to put out our bulletin:

FAIR PLAY COMMITTEE—ONE FOR ALL—ALL FOR ONE

It began: "The Fair Play Committee was organized for the purpose of opposing all unfair practices that violate the constitutional rights of the people. . . ."

As I cranked the handle of the mimeograph machine, paid for with dues collected from FPC members, I thought of what Kenny would do if he walked in the door right now. I'm still in a state of shock. First I had no brother, then I had one and loved him, then he turned on me. Losing Li, giving up my studies were nothing compared to this. Losing what you've had only momentarily is a more bitter pill.

When my arm wore out, Ben took over and I went outside and smoked. Abe-san said of Kenny's and my quarrel: "If you run after freedom you won't find it." Then he made me clean out my room, from top to bottom.

Mom came home from her class in ikebana and found my bed and clothes and radio outside on the ground. "Are you going away now?" she had asked stoically, and I laughed. "No, just cleaning." She thought I had gone mad. When I restored order to my room, Abe-san slipped in and whispered: "You have to start at emptiness and go in the direction of emptiness."

I went back inside to spell Ben. As I cranked and cranked I tried to stop the continuous drumming sound of the machine and start again with no sounds or thoughts, but I failed. Ben and I had worked hard on the bulletin and when we had a pile of four hundred copies in front of us, we sat down and read it over again:

Bulletin 4. We, the Nisei, have been complacent and too inarticulate about the unconstitutional acts that we are now subjected to. If ever there was a time or cause for decisive action, IT IS NOW! We, the members of the Fair Play Committee, are not afraid to go to war—we are not afraid to risk our lives for our country. We would gladly sacrifice our lives to protect and uphold the principles and ideals of our country as set forth in the Constitution and Bill of Rights for on their inviolability depends the freedom, liberty, justice, and protection of all people, including Japanese-Americans and all other minority groups. But were we given such freedom? No. Without any hearings, without due process of law as guaranteed by the Constitution, without any charges filed against us, without any evidence of wrongdoing on our part, 110,000 innocent people were kicked out of their homes, literally uprooted from where they have lived for the greater part of their lives, and herded like dangerous criminals into concentration camps with barbed wire fences and military police guarding them. AND THEN WITHOUT REC-TIFICATION FOR THE INJUSTICES COMMITTED AGAINST US AND WITHOUT RESTORATION OF OUR RIGHTS WE ARE ORDERED TO JOIN THE ARMY THROUGH DISCRIMINA-TORY PROCEDURES INTO A SEGREGATED COMBAT UNIT. Is that the American way? No!

WE MEMBERS OF THE FAIR PLAY COMMITTEE HEREBY REFUSE TO GO TO THE PHYSICAL EXAMINATION OR TO THE INDUCTION IF OR WHEN WE ARE CALLED IN ORDER TO CONTEST THIS ISSUE. We are not being disloyal. We are not *evading the draft. We are all loyal Americans fighting for justice and democracy right here at home.*

Despite our efforts, on February 28, seventeen men showed up for their preinduction physical. That surprised me. I thought we had allayed any fears of reprisal—the one the administration announced: arrest for sedition. Our legal stand is this: If the existence of the Camps is unconstitutional, then drafting Nisei out of the Camps is illegal as well.

Now it's March. Yet I have no feeling of spring or of time passing. My old happy-go-lucky Camp life is a thing of the past. No more sake, no more girls, no more sulking late in the morning abed. Ben returned his mother's washtub—the one he had been using to make sake. "We might as well be monks," he said, but I could see he loved the work and loved using his legal mind again.

I try to apply what Abe-san tells me to these daily activities, to work with great energy, to avoid narrow-mindedness. Sometimes I feel a sudden lightness, a sense of well-being that is different from gloating—then it goes and I'm my old self again. "No you aren't," Abe-san insists. Then he thumps me on the chest and says, "It's okay."

Mariko is bemused by my unexpected industry. She's always working too and we rarely see each other, except in passing.

March 5. I quit the Sentinel *this morning. Nothing the editor said could have kept me there.*

To be associated with the paper is to be connected with the JACLers, the Yes-Yes boys who believe that the only way to prove our loyalty is to let ourselves be drafted straight out of the Camps.

Got a job at the tofu factory. What a change for me. Have to get up at 4:00 A.M. There are two huge round stones, one on top and one on the bottom, and a big crank which we turn to grind the soybeans into a mash. After it sets up, we put it into sacks and deliver it to the mess halls for the noon meal. Then we're off for the day.

When Abe-san found out, he laughed at me. "Got off your high horse, huh?" he said. Mom and Pop are proud. But of what? Getting up early.

March 23. The Powell Draft Board reported that 53 out of 315 evacuees have refused to report for the preinduction physical examination so far.

Attorney Carl Sackett in Cheyenne has issued warrants against them. MPs broke into the FPC president's room, arrested him, and sent him to Tule Lake.

Ben and I decided to make a test case out of the constitutionality of being detained in these Camps. Things are coming to a head now and we'll need evidence if and when this goes to court. On the morning of March 23, Ben "went for a stroll." He walked through the sentry gate, right past the guards without a pass. I watched from a distance. The dumb guards didn't even see him, which doesn't help prove our point, but so it goes. Ben said that if he got through he'd spend the night in Cody and come back the next day, voluntarily returning to Camp.

That night I lay on my bed and wondered what he was doing. Probably getting drunk, but maybe not. Feeling lonely, I went next door to find Mariko but she was gone, and Abe-san was snoring.

Ben returned in the morning. He said he stayed at the Irma Hotel and ate at the Mayflower and didn't get drunk or laid. He went to the movies but the projector broke during the newsreel and they couldn't get it going again. He brought me a present—a new notebook for my journal keeping. When he announced to the MPs that he had left the Camp without authorization, they didn't believe him at first. After checking with the office, they found his statement was true, detained him for a few hours, then let him go, subject to further interrogation. But in the meantime, the guards caught hell.

Just to drive our point home, I attempted a similar stunt today. But the guards stopped me. "Where is your pass?" they demanded. "I don't have one," I said. "You're supposed to have them to get out," the MP said. "But we're American citizens," I protested. "I can't let you out," he said and took me into the guardhouse.

They kept me for two days. It was kind of cramped but I enjoyed the change of scenery. The guards turned out to be good guys. They shared cigarettes, cookies, and candy, and we played some good games of poker. One of them took a note in person to Mom and Pop, assuring them that I was okay, and when Mariko came back from wherever she had been— probably McKay's—they let me talk to her.

I also had a chance to try out Ben's and my ideas regarding the Constitution on the average Caucasian-American. It took a while, but they gradually came to see the logic of it, even though they refused to turn me loose. "But if you really understood, you'd act on it," I insisted, though I knew I wasn't in the company of idealists. "We need our jobs," they said and that was all.

On April 4, Ben and I were escorted to the Camp director's office. He's still as ruddy-faced as ever, almost jovial, but he didn't look amused that day. What came next was a kangaroo court, a mock trial, and it made the whole question of who had power over whom and the ways power might be abused very clear.

ROBERTS: Which of you is . . . Kai Nakamura?

ME: I am.

ROBERTS: Will you read the charge, Mr. Horn!

HORN: It is alleged in this complaint that on the twenty-ninth day of March 1944, you attempted to leave this center, to pass through the gate, without a pass or permit.

ME: If this is going to be a trial, I would rather have an outside attorney represent me. Just when he will come down I don't know.

ROBERTS: You know we have to try these cases within forty-eight hours. You understand, Kai, I am only trying you on a project charge. You have violated a project regulation; you know that. There isn't anything complicated about what I am going to do. If you can prove you had some . . .

ME: Here is the reason I did that, Mr. Roberts. As far as guilty or not guilty goes, I personally believe I am not guilty because I am an American citizen and I wanted to find out how far my rights went. I wanted to find out how long I could be detained here against my will.

ROBERTS: I understand that. You are supposed to obtain a pass before you can go through the gate. Lieutenant Kellogg is supposed to apprehend anyone who goes through without a pass. As to your rights in the matter, that will be taken care of later. If I can prove that you violated a project regulation, it is up to me to assess a penalty regardless of your rights in the matter.

ME: In other words, Mr. Roberts, you imply that you have more power than is set forth in the constitutional Bill of Rights?

ROBERTS: No, Kai, I have the power to do what I am doing.

ME: *Then I contend what you are doing is against the rights I have as an American citizen.*

HORN: *You have known as a matter of fact that you cannot leave this Camp without a permit or pass though?*

ME: *No, I don't.*

HORN: *How long have you been in the center?*

ME: *About two years.*

HORN: *How old are you?*

ME: *Twenty-eight.*

HORN: *You have a high school education?*

ME: *Yes.*

HORN: *College education?*

ME: *I'm a Ph.D. candidate.*

HORN: *I would like to ask you one other question. You attempted to leave the area without a project pass the twenty-ninth. Where were you going?*

ME: *I had no particular place in mind.*

ROBERTS: *If you are thoroughly convinced in your mind that it is an order that you can't go in and out without a pass are you willing to obey that order!*

ME: *If that order is declared legal by the Supreme Court and if it is constitutional, I will obey. I will abide by anything the Supreme Court says because that is the law of the land.*

ROBERTS: *I don't want to deprive you of your constitutional rights to test the law. You have a perfect right to do that, but as long as that regulation is in force it is my duty to enforce it. That is my job. They would fire me tomorrow if I didn't do it.*

ME: *Another thing that may have motivated me to stroll out there is the fact that as American citizens we are being pulled into the army just as any other American citizen would be so I didn't think there was any restriction.*

HORN: *Have you had a leave clearance hearing?*

ME: *Yes. I don't know just how it stands now.*

ROBERTS: *For your information, Kai, you haven't been cleared by the Joint Board in Washington yet.*

ME: *Will you give me that pass?*

ROBERTS: *Not until you get leave clearance. I can't give you a pass without leave clearance.*

ME: *Why have I been denied that leave clearance?*

ROBERTS: *You haven't been denied that. The Joint Board just hasn't decided your case yet.*

ME: *Under whose authority is the leave clearance board?*

ROBERTS: *The WRA.*

ME: *In other words, if the legality of the leave clearance . . .*

ROBERTS: *Just for your information you can test the legality from the project just as easily as you can from the jail. I believe you are on the Stop List.*

ME: *I am curious why I was put on the Stop List.*

ROBERTS: *I don't know that myself. In almost every case the Stop List is compiled by someone in Washington. The Stop List means that you are not eligible for leave clearance and eventually will be transferred to Tule Lake. They expect to finish this group of leave clearances by June.*

ME: *I would like to understand. . . . Am I guilty in this case as far as you are concerned?*

ROBERTS: *I think you are guilty.*

ME: *I want you to remember, Mr. Roberts, that I haven't pleaded guilty. Any action that I have taken, it is not with the intent of disloyalty; it is purely from the standpoint that I consider myself a loyal American citizen.*

After the "interview," they let me go. It seems I'm not considered radical enough, dangerous enough to be removed to Tule Lake, though someone suggested they've left me here to separate me from Ben. The Fair Play Committee is no more.

Later. After I got off work at the tofu factory, Hideo pulled me aside and said they'd heard that Tule Lake had gotten bad. The MPs have set up a stockade for dissidents and resisters. It's called the bullpen and the prisoners are housed in wall tents with no heat and only two blankets. The bunks are on the ground. Many have been beaten but given no medical care. I turned away when he was still talking—I didn't want to hear any more.

*   *   *

May. The Federal Grand Jury in Cheyenne has indicted sixty-three Heart Mountain draft resisters and charged them with "willful and felonious failure to report for preinduction physicals." They've all pleaded not guilty. Their lawyer from the ACLU says they have a strong moral case, but not a strong legal one. They'll probably lose.

June 13. My brother, Kenny, is back in the country. He didn't write to me; I heard it from Ben. Despite censorship, Ben's letter reached me because one of the MPs, who has been kind to us, delivered it by hand. Ben said their trip to Cheyenne was marred by the presence of a Caucasian prisoner who had escaped. He was in chains and every time they went into a restaurant, everyone stared at them. The trip wasn't unpleasant, but took several days. They stayed in county jails along the way.

The FBI interviewed them, though Ben felt he answered without giving any information. Anyway, there was nothing to hide. All was public information to begin with. Right before the trial was to begin, Ben said a JACL team came to interview them. My brother was one of the interviewers. They tried to get Ben and the others to drop our case. "I feel badly having to tell you this, but you would have found out anyway," Ben said.

July. The Heart Mountain 63 lost. The judge said: "Two wrongs don't make a right. One may not refuse to heed a lawful call of his government merely because in another way it may have injured him."

Hardly any of the papers covered the trial. But a Basin, Wyoming, paper published this: "If these Japs are good American citizens as some people insist they are, why didn't they enlist to show their love and respect for our country? The phrase 'good American citizens' sure has a hollow ring when applied to most Japs. Ask the mothers and fathers of the thousands of real American boys who bled and died from gunfire of the Japs. Let them be the jurors when the next group of Japs are granted a hearing for draft violations."

Thursday. The Heart Mountain 63 were sentenced to three years in the federal penitentiary. They asked for bail pending their appeal but didn't get it. In another note from Ben he said the worst thing that happened was the introduction of a false witness—an informant among us, an old man who befriended us but was really spying for the administration. Ben said when he saw him in the court, he couldn't understand why he was there. Then he took the stand and realized we had all been betrayed.

34

Without Will, without Ben, I've sought out Abe-san's company again.

"I've been waiting for you," he said.

I didn't feel like talking so I watched him work. He held a half-carved block of wood.

"In old days," he began, "we used better wood—palowanea . . . sometimes camphor tree. . . ."

He set the mask down on a block of pine and, hitting the chisel with a wooden mallet, made a long, deep cut between the cheek and the nose, then held the mask up close, for inspection. With a smaller chisel, he made several tiny gouges under the eye.

"The ideal is to copy an old mask exactly. But always, personality of the carver shows through. . . ."

He put the mask away. "If I cut away too much, all I have is this," he said, laughing, and took a handful of wood shavings. We walked back

to the barrack. On the hillside above Camp we saw three deer. Abe-san
stopped.

"See those. I need them. Nikawa. Mix paint with glue made from bone
of deer. . . ."

We walked on.

"Carving take two weeks; painting take one week or more."

The moon rose in the east, over the shadowed canyons of the Big Horn
Mountains. "It looks like that," Abe-san said, pointing to the moon.
"White like that. Paint five or six times, then sand it, then paint over
again. That's how I make it look like flesh—I paint and sand and paint.
Later, use very fine brush to paint hair, eyes, lips, teeth. Last thing . . .
make holes for ribbons that hold mask to head."

He stopped at the door to his room but didn't invite me in. "You'll
see," he said.

Another day, I walked in the direction of the waterhole. Some of the kids
had made a small raft lashed together with bailing wire and a paddle out
of scrapwood. When I topped the hill I saw Abe-san out on the water. He
was singing Shigun—Japanese ballads—and the sun, having just risen,
made the sky go red. Steam rose from the water and Tanabata poems
rang in my head:

. . . frantically I
wandered the shallow shoals of
the great river of
heaven still lost amidst the
white waves when dawn lit the sky. . . .

A raven swooped, cawing, then looped around, cawing again. I thought
of the fabled raven who extended his wings across the Milky Way as a
path on which lovers could meet. But it won't be me who meets her, I
thought, and shivered—Mariko. . . . I turned and walked back to the
barracks before Abe-san saw me watching him.

I had already gone to bed when I heard his singing again. I got dressed
and went outside. Weeks before, Abe-san had set up a small portable
stage floor in back of the barrack. A bright moon shone on Heart Moun-

tain. For a long time he sat on his knees with his legs under him, facing the mountain. Once, he leaned down and brought a bottle up from the grass. He took several swallows, then, pressing his thumb over the opening, held the bottle up as an eyepiece through which to view the moon. He sat back again. He picked up a silk sack from the floor, letting it rest in the palms of both hands, and held it skyward, then drew the mask from under the cloth. "When I put mask on, I am not me," he had told me once. "And when there isn't any self, there isn't any time. In Noh, I step out of time."

He tied the mask behind his head and sat motionless. I waited for him to get up and move, but he lifted his hands suddenly and took the mask off. He stood. A low, howling note of music came from him. "Noh plays, very short on paper, very long to perform. One sliding step—a hundred years," he had told me.

He drank again. I felt thirsty too and wanted to show my face so I could share the bottle with him, but decided not to. This time, when he put on the mask, it stayed on, and he rose slowly to his feet and walked to the back of the stage. He had told me many times about the swishing sound the brocade kimono made when a Noh actor made his entrance down the bridge—hashi-gakari—but this soft cotton kimono made no sound at all as he took his first sliding step. "Outer form in Noh—mask, movement, robes—all indicate inner soul, inner mind. When you see mask on outside, you understand mind on inside," Abe-san had explained.

He wore white tabi socks and slid to the center of the stage, then turned slowly. The mask he was wearing was "a madwoman" mask. The eyes were slits and the eyebrows painted at the top of the forehead, and the mouth opened in anguish. "This Degian mask is face of woman devoted to lover. But also, could be enlightened woman or bodhisattva. That's why whites of eyes are mud mixed with gold powder," he had said.

The effect was chilling. Abe-san, portraying a woman, moved with a lightness and delicacy. He was not impersonating a woman, but had captured the feminine spirit. Masked, buoyant, moon-drenched, he moved swiftly to the edge of the stage. Then, almost imperceptibly, he raised his fan, unfolding it, as if unfolding the sun. His arm rose until the fan covered his face—anguish overtaken by anguish. His feet slid and he began a slow dance. The fan came away and his mask tipped moonward. A sound came

from deep in his chest, a deep roar, a wolf's falsetto: yooooooooo. Then he
stamped his foot and spoke:

> *My heart finds no solace*
> *at Heart Mountain—*
> *not even wind obstructs my love,*
> *not even snow.*
> *I wish I had sown*
> *seeds of forgetfulness*
> *when we first met if*
> *I had only known how hard*
> *it would be to see you. . . .*

Mariko's words.

Abe-san glided to the center of the stage, lowering his head slowly. The
moon cast shadows across the mask. The delicate hair painted down the
sides looked like lines of aging.

Watching him I thought about the news I had heard the day before,
something new and terrible, called kamikaze. Pop said the word means
"divine wind" and refers to the typhoon which broke apart Kublai Khan's
invading ships in the thirteenth century. It no longer refers to an act of
nature, but a human act: using the body as a weapon. I looked at Abe-
san gliding with such stillness over the tiny stage, frail and delicate.
. . . They said that at the Battle of Leyte Gulf, Japanese pilots—kami-
kazes—crashed their small planes onto the decks of American battleships,
right into the holds where the torpedoes were kept, starting devastating
fires. A human bomb falling . . . Watching Abe-san move effortlessly: he
could have carried a tea tray on his head because there was no up-and-
down movement—only sliding—yet it always looked as if he were being
lifted or, like yeast, rising. . . .

He turned, his fan unfolded and held stiffly, then stopped suddenly
when he saw me.

"What are you doing here?" he asked.

"Watching you," I said. "It's beautiful."

Abe-san turned away and methodically went through the ritual of
untying the mask. When it had been removed, his face was another mask.

For a moment, I couldn't think which was flesh, which, carved wood. Sweat streamed down the sides of his cheeks. Reverently he held the mask in the palms of his hands and the soft ribbons hung and swayed. Then the mask that was really his face broke. He looked at me.

"Can I see it?" I asked.

He handed it to me carefully. Away from the actor's body it looked no more, no less than a mask. Quite lifeless. Light from the setting moon lodged itself against the gold and mud eyes. I handed it back. "It's so light," I said.

I could smell the liquor on his breath. He let the sweat drip. His white hair, in a severe bun, pulled the skin on his face back. Even though he was in his eighties, he had no wrinkles and he stood straight.

He contemplated the mask. "I try to carve each one exactly like the very old ones, the ones Zeami's carvers made. But always, the personality of the carver shows," he said. He held the mask up once again. "My face can't express what mask expresses. All my face does is show confusion— self, whirling. . . ." I had never seen him as calm and melancholy. The sky darkened. "Look," he said, then I saw the moon go into eclipse, or was it only a cloud?

35

Pinkey's free-fall had started when he backed away from the graveside service for Vincent and it had not stopped. He did not wait for a storm to start drinking. The night the eclipse occurred, he knew it was Vincent's shadow he had entered, knew by the smooth, silent, agile way it pulled over him. He had ridden from town to cow camp to Snuff's to town again and thought the passage from one point to the next must be like the lines drawn between stars to make a constellation.

When Vincent was young, Pinkey pointed out the stars because of the times cowboys have to ride home in the dark—the Big Dipper, Orion's Belt, Sirius, the North Star, the Pleiades—Vincent had wanted to know why he needed stars when his horse knew the way home, and Pinkey told him about the time his horse drank from a creek in the winter and the cold water gave him a heart attack and he fell down dead, and he had to cut the cinch and carry his saddle over his shoulder. "A man wants to know where he is every once in a while . . . ," he had said, laughing, "at least once a week or so. . . ."

When he looked up, a corner of the full moon was already black. He crossed Sand Coulee and Little Sand, then loped down into a draw where one tree grew by a spring. He looked at the darkening sky and thought the shadow must be permanent. He stepped off his horse. He did not need to look at the moon anymore; he had seen enough. A fragile scent of mountain mahogany drifted through the air. He had to keep reminding himself that it was spring, or was it winter? He couldn't remember.

Out on the flats again, he tipped his mare into a lope. The pressure of the stirrup made his badly mended leg hurt. It had been weeks since he had thought about the war. Vincent used to read parts of the newspaper to him when they met at the bar. Everything he read was spoken in the same monotone voice and Pinkey liked that. It made the bad news sound solemn without the rash headliner emotionalism and the frivolous news sound more substantial, less at odds with what was going on in the rest of the world. Pinkey's mother had read to him on their Alabama farm. Like his father, he hadn't bothered with school, content to raise mules and dogs and chickens. After that, it was Janine who became his "eyes," then Vincent. Now he had no reader, but it didn't matter because he didn't care about the news anymore. "I'd rather read the clouds," he liked to say. The rocking gait of his horse lulled him. He could tell the difference between a coyote and a dog track, a grizzly and a black bear track, a weasel and a mink track, a skunk and a bobcat, and he knew the stars and could read the weather in the clouds and the cloud shapes as omens, and he could read the look on a man's face. But to read the papers only made things worse, blew things up bigger than they were, and they were big enough. "I'm just getting to where I know as much as this ol' mare," he thought. "And that's enough for me."

When he looked up again, the black shade had drawn itself over a third of the moon's surface, over the rough craters and shadows the craters made—shadows over shadows. The eclipse drew over the moon's slate seas and Pinkey wondered whether there was anyone like him up there on the moon, anyone as lost as he was. . . .

He crossed Pole Cat Creek, and when he rode up through the breaks, the pines that grew in the sand didn't shine, and the skyscraper-size rock tablets were blanks. He pushed his mare harder. He had to get to the cabin before the moon had been taken from the sky, light a lamp, uncork the bottle, and lift it to his lips, the way he might have lifted some part of a woman to his hunger long ago. He thought of kissing someone— how else can a man know what a woman is thinking—and puckered his lips in the dark. He thought of Janine . . . no, Loretta. . . . But nothing came back, no lips, no warmth, and his kiss skirred into the same void from which Vincent's shadow had come.

The cabin loomed ahead. The moon was all black now, like a face destroyed, but the stars shone. To drink, not to read, not even to kiss, was all he wanted—to drink his way out from under a shadow that blackened what he knew, moved the coming of the year 1945 from him.

PART FOUR
1945

And say to thy life: Am I thine? Art thou mine?
Am I the blue curve of day around thine uncurved night?
—D. H. Lawrence

36

"Is it January yet?" McKay looked at his watch. He and Bobby had not bothered to ring in the New Year. It was four in the morning, the first day of January. "Nineteen forty-five," he said out loud and wondered whether this was the middle of the war or only the beginning or almost the end. He was hungry and he dressed and went to the kitchen. It would not be light for three hours. He did not want to sit by himself and think about the year that was just over and the year that was to come. "Life is all denials," he thought. His brother had been wounded and his best friend was rotting away in a prison camp; he had conceived a child with Madeleine and she had lost it, and he loved Mariko in a way that made him blind to everything else and yet he could not have her. The more despair he felt the greater his thirst for life.

He went outside and stood in the snow wearing his bedroom slippers. A warm wind had come up in the night and it rolled soft and warm

against his body and even before first light, he heard the delicate drumming sound of water dripping from eaves.

Snuff opened the windows on the south side of the bar. The flannel
curtains lifted, and he straightened his bow tie in the mirror. "It's a
chinook," he called out.

Carol Lyman appeared at the end of the long hall. She had never spent
the whole night at Snuff's and felt awkward now. She had to wear what
she had worn the night before—her New Year's dress and high heels.
She was glad no one was there besides Snuff to see her. Taking a deep
breath, she walked to the window.

"You're right. It does feel warmer," she said. "Maybe we're in for a
January thaw."

"That's what made me think of it . . . ," Snuff said. He stood behind
her.

"Think of what?"

"Here." He led her away from the window onto the middle of the
scarred linoleum dance floor. "Come here."

She was almost as tall as he was and did not have to bend her head
back to look into his eyes. Yet she had always avoided them. Then she
remembered her New Year's vow. "I must break myself open," she
thought.

"Are you cold?" Snuff asked, because she was shivering.

"No." Was she afraid of him or afraid of herself, she wondered.

When he took her in his arms, she gasped, then burst out laughing.

"Oh, Snuffy, what are you doing? It's eight o'clock in the
morning. . . ."

He released her, knowing how fearful she was, even though, the night
before, she had had more than usual to drink and had screamed out with
pleasure.

He pulled two chairs to the middle of the floor and they sat facing
each other, under the bent chandelier. He cleared his throat. "This year
has gone awfully fast," he began badly. He felt like a boy at confession.
"It's because you've been here all along. Now I can't remember . . ."

"What?" Carol asked.

"How I got along without you."

She turned her head from him. He thought she looked like a statue. Her long, birdlike neck stretched as if she were about to crow.

"Let's get married; what do you say?"

Carol's head swiveled. "Oh, goodness," she began. "I've embarrassed you into . . . ," she began, swallowing hard. "I shouldn't have spent the night."

"I'm glad you did."

She looked down at his hands holding hers. "What do you want with someone like me? I'm just a spinster," she said, shrinking from him.

Snuff leaned toward her, smiling. "I like spinsters," he said.

Carol had trouble catching her breath. She put one hand to her chest but couldn't speak.

"You're not unworthy," Snuff said. Her eyes met his. "I've watched you . . . since the first day you wandered in here. For God's sake, no one ever said you have to believe what you think about yourself."

A smile came slowly over Carol's drawn face. Snuff continued. "You've had some bad luck, is all. You've been nursing your grief like a damned sheepherder, rolling it over and over in that head of yours. And I'm not saying it's self-pity either. You've been hit hard a couple of times and you raised that boy alone and you didn't hide him away. But that night with Carter Heaney—that was twenty-three years ago, Carol. . . ."

Her eyes moved quickly around the room, then Snuff brought her hands to his lips as she watched. It was excruciating for her. Those hands, she thought, aren't mine. He's not kissing me.

"It's over now," he said softly.

Carol took a deep breath. She felt the hair on the back of her neck rise as it did before a close lightning strike. They stood. She let her eyes go into his and the sensation was not terrifying as she had expected— some kind of tumbling plunge—but, rather, one of rest and ease.

They held each other as if to dance.

"I think we're like two storks together," Carol said. "The way we're both built . . ."

Snuff smiled, but they didn't move.

That night Carol went home and the next day returned to Snuff's to work. She didn't know what came next—what she should feel or say or do. When she opened the door a woman sitting on the end bar stool swung around.

"Hello, honey," she said. "I suppose Snuff hasn't told you about me. . . ."

Carol's eyes darted between the woman and Snuff.

"I'm Venus," she said, standing with her arms outspread.

"Oh, goodness . . . yes. Well, you threw me for a loop there." She gave Snuff a look of astonished relief.

"Prince Charming here hardly recognized me. See, I've gotten fat," she said and pulled the flesh at her waist, laughing heartily.

"Don't be silly . . . he told me about you the first thing . . . we were sitting on the floor under that table . . . ," Carol said, pointing to the oval oak table Snuff had taken from the lawyer's office in town.

Venus leaned forward. Carol could smell the liquor on her breath, and the low-cut angora sweater revealed a voluptuous chest. "You're not really going to marry this gambling fool, are you?" Venus whispered, then erupted with laughter again.

"I thought you would be older," Carol said. "He said you raised him."

"Hell, I did, but we were both just kids. I knew more, that's all."

Venus set her empty glass out in front of Snuff for a refill.

"Venus, you lie like a . . ."

Venus drank, then set the half-empty glass down. "I raised him good, too. Made him into a good Catholic, made him good with women."

"Ohhhh . . ." Snuff turned his back to the women and shook his head with embarrassment.

Venus finished off the Manhattan, then stood under the chandelier and looked up at the bare bulb hanging down through the middle. "Fancy," she said, then crossed the scarred dance floor and sat at the blackjack table. She reached up and switched on the green lamp.

"Snuffy . . . you come over here and deal me and Carol a game."

Snuff reached in a drawer for a fresh pack of cards, pulled on his visor, and escorted Carol to the table.

"I'm going to powder my nose," Carol said.

Venus watched her go. "God, Snuffy, you've got her skinny as an old rooster. Don't you take care of her?"

"She has her own place . . . and a son."

"I mean in bed."

Snuff looked at Venus's bare shoulders. The rhinestones on the angora sweater caught light and sparkled like stars. He saw her breasts swell, almost lifting above the neckline, and shuffled the cards.

"I think I'll go powder my nose too," she said winsomely.

When Venus opened the bathroom door she saw Carol's face in the mirror, and the hand that resembled a claw, and the red tube of lipstick moving across her mouth.

"Oh . . . ," Carol murmured when she heard Venus coming in. Venus hiked up her skirt and sat on the john.

"I've always thought this was the best place to talk. Those other rooms are too big . . . everything gets lost in them. . . ."

Carol tried to smile with the lipstick still applied to her upper lip. "Uh huh . . . ," she agreed.

"My room used to be down the hall two doors. I worked here for a couple of years."

"I know," Carol said, licking her lips together, then blotting them with a rumpled handkerchief. "I've been in that room. Aired it out one day when we had people staying over. An old Indian. I don't think he ever went to bed. Just sat in that booth out there while this young kid went and fetched him drinks all night. Just sat there kind of chanting . . . had to carry him to the funeral."

"Who kicked the bucket?"

"Pinkey's son . . . Vincent."

"Oh my God . . . no one told me."

Carol turned to her. "I'm sorry. . . ."

Venus wiped herself and pulled the chain on the toilet. The tiny room filled with noise. Carol stepped back from the mirror as Venus moved closer, stood in profile, and examined herself out of the corner of her eye.

"Look at all that fat," she exclaimed, then clamped her hands on her voluptuous breasts and laughed. Carol stared frozenly.

"He'll be loyal to you," Venus said. "He almost became a priest . . . did he tell you that?"

"Yes." Carol leaned against the wall.

"I guess he should have, really . . . but it's a long way from Venus Alley to the Vatican. I didn't push too hard. Then he got wound up with Daley and that gang, and got to running race ponies, but he wasn't like all the rest. You see these other fellows were always acting out of desperation; that's why they came to me. They were on the downside of life. I mean, they were falling . . . they didn't really believe in life, and that's what you've got to believe in. They think they do something and then life is over; for men like that it's over as soon as they come, which is always too fast. But Snuffy, he was different. Even as a kid he could see things. It was kind of spooky, like he was an old man inside a little boy."

Venus stood back from the waist-high mirror, then made a face.

"I let them use me . . . but I did it with revenge . . . ," she said, smiling. She flipped up the back of her hair and let it drop two or three times. "I could have done other things. Lordy, when I think of it . . . I was good in school, but where's a girl going to get a job that pays anything decent? I had mouths to feed and I wanted to work for myself. I could have raised myself up . . . oh hell, that's water over the dam, isn't it? And there were always these," she said, putting her hands on her enormous breasts again and laughing hoarsely. "Oh, they were in demand. First they all wanted to get a peek at them, then they wanted to touch them, then . . . but I tricked them . . . you know what a trick is, don't you? What that really means is that I turned their attention back on them . . . I turned it into a kind of power over them. They were always at my mercy," she said, dropping her hands and smoothing the angora sweater at her waist. She gave Carol an assessing look. "You must think I'm some kind of freak."

"No," Carol said solemnly. "Quite the opposite. I'm the freak. Truly."

Venus looked Carol up and down. "Well, he's got you too skinny, that's one thing."

"What else?"

Venus put her hand on Carol's hair. "You need some curl in here or something, something soft around your face. . . ."

"I know. I'm just not very good at these things. . . ."

"Oh, honey, it doesn't matter anyway . . . sometimes it just helps your outlook on life. You'll need that after you've been married for a while. I don't know why you girls do it—"

"Do what?".

Venus shook her head.

*   *   *

The day Venus left, Carol unlocked the door to the room that had been Venus's for those two years. She knelt by the bed. When she was seven, she had said her prayers that way, but by the time she was ten, she had given up any notions of safekeeping or delivery through divine intervention. Now she knelt at the bed of a whore and asked for something quite different. "How can I be a person someone could love?" she entreated, not God, but herself, because she did not feel sufficiently significant to presume any God could be bothered with her.

She smoothed the green wool blanket with her hand as if to feel the backsides of all the men who had lain over that one woman, then leaned back. The blanket was cold against her skin. She lifted her hips a little to hike up her skirt, closed her eyes, and tried to conjure up the feeling of a small room with a man in it, a strange man whose mouth she had never tasted, whose thoughts she knew nothing of. What would he do? What would he say? Where would he put his hands first? Where would she put hers?

She lay for a long time in the half-dark, with her long legs sticking straight out from her skirt. She could not even allow herself to bend her knees, and her hair spread across the pillow like needles. She thought of the difference between the birds who sought out the upper currents of air and glided gracefully and the earthbound ones—like grouse—whose short flights looked fettered. . . .

"Carol?" She heard Snuff calling and lay rigid. He walked past the room to the back door and yelled her name, then came back. He paused in front of the door, walked away, then opened it slowly. The light in the hallway made a fan shape on the far wall.

Carol swung her legs over the side of the bed.

"Carol?" Snuff said softly.

When he saw her, he came to the bed. Carol's eyes widened.

"Carol?" he said again. He sat beside her. "What's wrong?"

Carol looked at him. "I know you love me," she said, "but I don't know how you could."

In March the wind came like a claw that loosened every stick and string of human civilization. Carol and Snuff had made a date for the wedding— April 21—and she had already begun looking through magazines for a wedding dress. It was a Thursday and she and Willard would drive somewhere, she decided. Anywhere. Just drive until she felt like coming home again.

"Hurry up," she snapped at Willard. "We've got places to go."

He looked at her quizzically and did as she said.

They drove southeast out of Luster. The narrow road finally crossed the river at Meeteetse. The black coupe continued south, down to the town with the hot springs, across a wide plain where antelope ran parallel to her car but faster, over the Medicine Bow Mountains, past the hotel where Owen Wister wrote part of *The Virginian*, south, but upward in altitude, onto the Laramie Plains. Here, she was stopped by a roadblock. She had run out of "A" ration cards for gas.

"We can't allow you to go any farther unless it's an emergency," the uniformed man said.

"But it is—" Carol pleaded. "My sister is sick in California."

The man scowled at her.

"My son and I are going to take the train from Laramie," she continued, and the man let them through.

"But I'm warning you, there's another roadblock on the other end of town," he yelled after them.

Carol drove obediently to the train station. An east-bound train had just arrived and the platform was filled with returning soldiers. She told Willard to stay in the car. Inside the station she looked at the big board by the ticket office. There was a west-bound train in two hours.

"How long will it take to get to Los Angeles?" she asked.

"Twenty-six hours, ma'am."

"I'll need two tickets then," she said. "On that train today."

After, she sat in the car with Willard.

"We're going on a trip," she explained to him. "I have a sister, Aunt Emily. She lives in the desert. She says there's sand and cactus and date palms and a place where we can ride camels. She has a swimming pool. We'll teach you how to swim. . . ."

Willard grinned. He made motions to get out of the car and go to the train.

"It won't be here for a while, Will . . . ," she said patiently.

She leaned her head back against the seat and closed her eyes. Why am I running away? she wondered. She thought of the moment she had allowed herself to look into Snuff's eyes. The thought made her smile.

She was not frightened by him. Yet, she wanted to be alone. "My my, perhaps loneliness has become a habit with me."

She roused herself and went back into the station. This time, Willard tagged along. She asked to use the phone and placed a call through an operator who sounded nothing like Velma Vermeer, but rather, young, and sweet, and helpful.

"Snuff? It's Carol. I'm in Laramie. How? I drove. Willard and I are going to California. My sister is sick . . . I don't know . . . I know you do . . . I'm fine, Snuff. No, I don't need anything. Yes, I will. Good-bye."

She sat with Willard on a hard, polished bench until the train came.

The wind stopped and it began raining. A yellow Dodge convertible pulled up to Snuff's. The Wild Man stood at the bar.

"Aren't you going to say hello?" he asked.

Snuff turned and smiled. "Where have you been?" he asked. "Here. Have one on the house. You drinking these days?"

"Champagne," the Wild Man said heedlessly.

Snuff set two glasses on the bar top and filled them with whiskey. "It's good to see you," Snuff said.

"I need something," the Wild Man confided.

Snuff nodded his head. Under his blue eyes, the skin was dark. He had lost weight and his face looked wrinkled. The Wild Man stared.

"You don't look too good yourself. . . ."

"Naw . . . here's to . . ." Snuff raised his glass.

"My brother," the Wild Man interjected. "He's making bombs," he said bitterly. "Here's to all the killers."

"No. Lenny, come on. . . ."

"Who's Lenny?"

"You are."

"No, I'm not," he yelled and took a swipe at all the glasses on the counter. An ashtray broke.

"Hey, now . . . what's got into . . ."

The Wild Man stretched his arms in front of his head and squeezed the palms together hard. "She's going to have my baby," he yelled shrilly. "And my brother's making bombs. . . ."

Snuff looked at the Wild Man, whose beautiful face had become transfixed with a bitter grimace. "Take it easy . . . okay?"

The Wild Man opened his eyes and let his arms drop. When Snuff held out the bottle in a friendly gesture, the Wild Man looked as if he were being accosted and backed up across the dance floor.

"Ow . . . ," Pinkey said. He had just ridden in.

The Wild Man had stepped on him.

"You stuck in reverse or something?"

The Wild Man stepped forward without an apology.

"I'm going now . . . ," he said blithely and made his way to the door.

Snuff followed him outside. He could see the empty bottles and some dirty clothes strewn in the backseat of the convertible. The canvas top was torn and the floorboards were thick with mud. The Wild Man started the car and backed in a half-circle around Snuff. He rested his elbow on the rim of the door.

"Los Alamos," he yelled, then spun his wheels on the cobbled parking lot and drove north toward the dark rain clouds that reached all the way back to Billings.

When the rain came, Snuff ran for cover and shook himself inside the door.

"I knew it was going to storm," Pinkey said. "My bones told me so I thought I'd get a little head start on it," he announced. He pulled up a stool as Snuff went behind the bar. "What's got into him?" Pinkey asked, looking in the direction of the highway.

Snuff looked up wearily. "The same as the rest of us. He's lost his marbles. . . ."

Pinkey howled with laughter, even though it wasn't intended as a joke.

A bottle of Cobb's Creek sat on the counter in front of the old cowboy.

"Might as well bar-up until this sonofabitch is over," Pinkey said, then looked at Snuff. "What's eatin' on you?"

"You're looking kinda rummy . . . ," Pinkey continued, pouring himself one shot, then another. The wind shifted and rain slapped at the windows. "I better get to drinking before this baby gets over with," he said and tipped his glass.

Two more men came into the bar. They worked at the ranch where Vincent had worked, and Pinkey bought their drinks.

"Thank you," the tall one said, lifting his glass. "I owe you one."

"You greenin' up over there?" Pinkey said.

"Oh, it's starting," Stubby said. "We'll be branding next week."

"Not us," Pinkey laughed. "We're doing double work . . . got all them cows of Henry's . . . and we're running late as usual."

The others laughed appreciatively.

"Had a set of twins the other night, and I'll be damned if that ol' cow ain't supportin' the both of them. Two little heifer calves. God, if she ain't a dairy lookin' ol' rip. . . ."

Pinkey passed the bottle of whiskey down the bar and the other two men refilled their glasses.

"Where is this Cobb's Creek, anyway?"

"Tennessee," Pinkey said.

"I bet there ain't no brookies or cutthroats on that whole damned creek," Stubby said.

"I bet not either."

"You been there?" he asked Pinkey.

"No."

"I heard from some hunter was through here that a man can't even pull his fly rod out without it getting snagged on a tree. I guess that's all they have is trees in that country."

"That's about how Alabama was," Pinkey said.

"Damn . . . how could a man live ass-up to a bunch of trees? I'd go plumb crazy not being able to see."

"Wouldn't want to run no cattle in there," Stubby said.

"Hell no, it'd be like ridin' blind."

Even though it was raining hard, Snuff went outside without a coat or hat on and stood in the parking lot looking down the road.

The phone rang. The three cowboys glanced at each other, then the tall one stepped off his stool, reached over the bar and answered it.

"Snuff's," he growled into the receiver.

"Who? Can you talk louder?"

"You bet . . . no . . . he's right here," he said, holding the phone out to Pinkey.

"It's for you," the cowboy said.

"Who?" Pinkey asked.

The man shoved the receiver into Pinkey's chubby hand.

"My, my, my," Pinkey chortled, then held the phone to his ear.

"Hello? Who? Loretta? That you? Well, where are you? You are? When? I'll be there. You bet. Who? Dutch? Hell, you don't want to see him— he's off somewheres. . . . You do? Hell, kid, I knew you loved me. You too. I will." When Pinkey held the receiver out, Stubby took it and put it back on the cradle.

"Oooowwweee," Pinkey yelled. "I'm in love!"

Snuff came back in. His hair was plastered down and his clothes soaked through. Pinkey lifted his glass in a wordless toast and gulped the whiskey effortlessly, then spun on his stool to greet Snuff. Snuff gazed expressionlessly at the three men.

"Close up for me when you're done, will you, Pinkey?" Snuff said and walked down the hall.

"What's eatin' on him?" the tall one asked.

Pinkey shrugged.

"Boys, I'm in love," Pinkey announced again.

"In love or in lust?" Stubby asked.

Pinkey threw up his hands in the air. "Let's not sweat the little stuff," he exclaimed. "She's been working in one of them airplane factories."

"You gonna tie the knot?" the tall one asked.

Pinkey scratched his head. "Hadn't thought that far along . . ."

"Come on, Pinkey . . . why not ask her?" Stubby urged.

Pinkey rubbed his forehead, then looked up. "What if she said no?"

"In my opinion, you'd be coming out of this thing a lucky man," the tall one said.

Stubby laughed, then went behind the bar and brought out another bottle of whiskey. "Don't forget to put this on your bill," he said to Pinkey and winked. "I'll bet you another bottle she'll say yes if you ask."

The tall one reached into his pocket and pulled out a bill. "Me, too," he said. "Who the hell are we marrying, anyway?"

"Loretta Wilkins . . . ," Pinkey said proudly.

Stubby choked on his whiskey.

"Hell, she ain't that bad," Pinkey said.

They all laughed.

"Hand it to me again," Pinkey demanded.

The tall one reached across the bar and gave Pinkey the phone. He dialed zero. "Velma? I want to send a telegram. This is Pinkey. Oh hell, charge it to the ranch."

When Velma was ready, he dictated the wire: "Loretta. Wanna get hitched? Please reply care of Snuff's. Pinkey."

When Pinkey put the phone down, he ordered another round of drinks. "How long do you think it'll take to get an answer?"

"Hell, Pink, I don't know, but I aim to stay right here until that phone rings."

"You're on," Pinkey said, drinking. He looked out the window. The rain came down straight and heavy now, and it was getting dark. "I don't even have to go home until it stops raining. Ranch rules," Pinkey exclaimed cheerfully.

"That McKay's a real understanding man," Stubby said, laughing.

"Yea, here's to the kid," Pinkey said, raising his glass.

"Here's to the beautiful Loretta," the tall one said, and all three drank.

Snuff got up from Venus's bed, where he had been lying. He smoothed the green wool blanket, then walked out the back door. Up from the row of cabins, he heard pond ice crack and saw a pair of mallards moving effortlessly on the water. He walked up the winding road. He couldn't understand what had happened—why Carol had run out on him before the wedding. Halfway up the hill he turned and looked down on the ramshackle buildings and the way the white dust from the mill had coated a hundred acres of greasewood. Under his ribs a knifelike pain turned in his gut. He doubled over, reeling. "Goddamn you!" he groaned, looking skyward. "Who are you anyway?" he yelled in a fury, straightening up. He stood with his hands held, not clenched, but straight like knives at his side. "Was I really asking too much?" His own answer was no. Another pain hardened below his heart and he fell to his hands and knees in the mud.

37

January. Heavy damage from kamikaze attacks. Mochi making for New Year's. I think of the green dragon weaving through Chinatown. The longer the dragon, the longer one is expected to live. If I did not like myself a year ago, or even yesterday, what am I to think today? A warm chinook blew through and I heard birds. They say that by the time the snow melts off, green grass will have begun to grow. So it is with me. My cynical troubled, doubting mind churns and yet . . .

Abe-san says I must "cultivate my spirit," that everything I am, everything I need, is inside me, and it is no longer necessary to destroy what I do not like elsewhere. What I want is to see clearly what's been done and to whom and why.

I realized at some point that my single-mindedness and bitterness had become obsessive. But after last March, when the Fair Play Committee broke up and I returned to my "studies" with Abe-san, the narrowness melted away. Even this place looked changed—wider somehow, flatter, *but more vivid. Abe-san says that is because I have started to live with emptiness. Yet I have to keep asking him what that means.*

The night I watched him perform his Noh and asked what Noh was all about, he said, "When you do something, you should burn yourself completely, like a good bonfire, leaving no trace of yourself."

Heard last week that the West Coast Exclusion Act has been lifted. This was announced in Public Proclamation 21. "The people of the states within the Western Defense Command are assured that the records of all persons of Japanese ancestry have been carefully examined and only those persons who have been cleared by military authority have been permitted to return. They should be accorded the same treatment and allowed to enjoy the same privileges accorded other law-abiding citizens or residents."

This means that if we can get a leave clearance pass, we will be allowed to return to California, Oregon, and Washington—these being the coastal regions from which we were evacuated three years ago.

February. Mom and Pop heard from Kenny. He doesn't write to me. He is now flying missions in the Pacific and is the only Nisei to be allowed to do so. "I wanted to make a point about loyalty," he wrote. No comment from me. Even Mom and Pop looked a little stunned by the news.

March. Had another "interview" with the Camp director, who said I still didn't have my leave clearance pass, but thought I would soon. Then Mom, Pop, and I would be free to leave Camp and go home. But home to what? We have nothing there and will have to start all over again. Mariko can't get her pass either because of her association with Will. So it looks like we're all stuck here for a while. Pop tapped me on the shoulder as I was writing in my journal and said, "Don't want to go back. No store, no house, no car. What old man like me do? Want to die here."

April. Emi and her family are to leave tomorrow. There was a going-away party for her and we danced like two bears, hugging affectionately. But the news from Los Angeles is not good. They owned some property and left it in the hands of a "friend," who apparently sold it, for a fraction of its value—sold it to himself—and the money they received for it is already gone.

Another day. Pop said he'd been thinking of flowers. In the old country, they'd go on all-day outings to every city park and view the cherry blossoms: at their peak; when the wind blew through them; and when they had scattered on the ground. "Beautiful every way," he volunteered. The Danish sea captain who is caring for his bonsai wrote him a note in a rough hand and said "The little tree, she is healthier every day." We sat outside on the doorstep and I shared a candy bar with him. He said he worried about the cherry trees in Japan during a war with no one to view them. "Maybe they're happy just being trees," I said. I'll always remember the first spring we were here. One morning he jumped out of bed excitedly and motioned us to the window. But what he thought were cherry blossoms in the distance was only snow.

38

In April the winds abated, and for a week the temperatures reached eighty degrees. The war in Europe was rapidly coming to an end, and the war in the Pacific had intensified with Operation Iceberg, the invasion of Okinawa. Four hundred and fifty thousand army and marine troops were landed there, among them Champ, recently sent back into action. On April 1, Roosevelt died and Truman became president. The first German death camps were liberated by American forces—Bergen-Belsen and Buchenwald. Snuff's wedding day, April 21, came and went. Snuff was admitted to the hospital again with another ulcer attack and told to keep off the bottle. A few days after, Mussolini and his mistress, Clara, were shot and hanged by their heels in the main square in Milan. The next day, April 29, Hitler married Eva Braun, only to commit joint suicide on the thirtieth.

"At least he got the old gal to marry him," Pinkey said, putting the newspaper down. The steam from his coffee cup wetted a corner of the front page. He was disconsolate because Loretta had not answered his telegram nor shown herself in town since the phone call, nor had Snuff heard from Carol.

"We're a hell of a pair," Snuff said, sipping tea. "Look at me, drinking tea like an old maid."

"We're eclipsed," Pinkey said, because he still believed the eclipse of the moon he had ridden under was a permanant shadow, one that had no end or edge.

That night Snuff offered to take Pinkey to the movies to see *For Whom the Bell Tolls*. Halfway through, Snuff regretted his choice. He could not reconcile himself to the loss of Carol, who had come into his life— like a stray, he liked to say—though Ava Gardner she was not. . . .

"Ah hell," Pinkey exclaimed when the lights went up, because he was caught dabbing at his eyes. "You better take me on into the ranch," he said. "I've had enough excitement for one day." The two men drove home silently.

Carol Lyman lay out in the sun by her sister's pool. Emily's husband had been killed in the early part of the war and it was 1945 now, and she already had several boyfriends under tow. Her victory garden consisted of cactus, hot peppers, tomatoes, muskmelons, and watermelon, which she watered in the middle of the night when the air was still hot but the blistering sun was gone. For days the two women waded back and forth across the pool suspending Willard with their hands under him. Will he ever float, Carol wondered. Whenever they touched his back he laughed, then began thrashing, sinking head first like a punctured blimp. After the lessons, they stretched out in the sun until their skin was very dark and the white stripes under their bathing suits looked like scars. The dry air had a mineral and flower fragrance. Carol wore hibiscus in her hair. Each time she thought about Snuff she made herself put an X on a pad of paper until the pad was filled and Willard drew a picture of a rooster and their house in Luster. He wanted to go home.

Carol packed their belongings and took the train north and east again. It was May 6th, and the heat was so severe she found it hard to breathe. Before leaving they bought a basketful of dates, oranges, and nuts, which they ate while watching the scenery go by. The land changed from sand to red cliffs, to mountains, to high sagebrush plains, and within thirty hours they were in Wyoming again.

She had not stopped thinking of Snuff. All the way to Laramie, she blamed herself for her failure with him, blamed it on her rigidity, her lack of spontaneity, her bad genes. When she contemplated starting a new life elsewhere, her ties to Luster pulled her. What, in all that desolation, could it possibly be? Her sister, who went nowhere, had given Carol her gas coupons, which she used in Laramie. She had the coupe filled. They started north slowly. At the Big Horn River, she and Willard roasted hot dogs and marshmallows over a twig fire, and at dusk she saw a tree with five herons perched in its branches. They were hulklike, almost grotesque, too big for the narrow trunk. The bright sky silhouetted them. She pointed out the tree to Willard, and he raised his willow so that it looked like part of the tree, as if the birds had come to rest on its pale branches.

"It's our tree of life," she whispered.

Willard grinned.

Then they heard the wing bones creak as the herons flew over.

May eighth, VJ Day in Europe. The Germans surrendered and came to Eisenhower's advance headquarters in Reims to sign the truce. They sat around a plain wood table in a school building and the mood was tense. Carol Lyman heard on the radio how Trafalgar Square and Times Square went wild at the news but in the tiny Wyoming towns she drove through that day, the celebrations were grimly quiet. In one, with a population of twenty, the two stores were closed, a church bell rang, and the spacious community hall, built of logs before the turn of the century, was decorated with black crepe paper because five of the seven men who went to war from that town had been killed.

Carol and Willard drove home that night. From the hill she could see the lights of the mill and the string of green roofs. Willard wiggled in his seat when they passed Snuff's, then he squealed and hit his head on the dashboard until she stopped.

"Willard, what's gotten into you?" she asked.

He turned around in his seat and motioned toward the bar.

"Oh, for goodness sake, we have to go home."

He threw himself against the dash again.

"Stop it," she screamed, then turned the coupe around.

Just inside the front door she paused. Her hair was shorter now because she'd had it cut in Palm Springs for the "softer look" Venus had suggested, and in the dark entry, she smiled at her small victory over self-hate.

"Hello . . . ?" she called out tentatively.

A pot of coffee simmered on the stove and the back door banged shut. Willard seated himself at the bar and stuck his big hand into the pickled egg jar. Carol called out again, but no one answered. Down the hall, she peered into Snuff's room. The bed was made and both windows were wide open. She sat on the bed, their bed. Had she come home? she wondered. She pushed her hand into the V neck of her dress; her skin did not feel like her own.

"Is that all you wanted, a pickled egg?" she asked Willard. He peeled a second egg slowly, then deposited it, unbroken, into his mouth.

"Well, no one's home, I guess," she said, and hung her heels over the rung of a stool. She poured herself a cup of coffee. The wind had come up and after the back door slammed shut for good, she could still hear some part of the roof banging. A car drove up but she could not see who it was because the flannel curtains had been closed against the sun. She took a sip of coffee and waited. A car door opened, and another one, then two doors closed and one car pulled away. She put her cup down and went to the window to look. Just mounting the hill some distance away, she could see the tail lights of an automobile going north.

Carol went outside. A drift of white dust hit her and she could feel the grit in her teeth. Next to her coupe she saw footprints and tire tracks. Shading her eyes, she peered inside. A bundle lay on the seat. She opened the door cautiously. It was an old blanket, faded by sun, and the satin trim had torn half off. When she reached her hand toward it, the bundle moved.

"Oh . . . ," she gasped and jumped back.

The baby howled and she saw a tiny hand make a fist.

"Oh my God," she said, clapping her hand over her mouth, then reached in again and slid the baby across the seat, toward her.

The baby yowled. Her hair was one black tuft that stood up from the top of her head, and her dark eyes searched Carol's face. She carried the baby inside.

"Carol?" Snuff stood in the middle of the room with a grocery bag under his arm. He set the bag down slowly as she approached.

"What's—"

"I found her on the front seat, someone just left her there." She pulled the blanket back from the baby's face. "Look at this hair," she said, touching the fuzz. "You can still see the tracks. They go north. . . . "

Snuff nodded and looked at the baby. She opened her eyes for a moment, then shook her fists again and cried.

"She's hungry," Carol said.

"It's a girl?"

"Yes, I looked."

"I don't have anything here to . . . I mean we can't feed her whiskey."

"Call Ora Smith . . . tell her I need some formula and bottles and diapers," Carol said over the child's screams.

Snuff went to the phone. Looking out the porthole window he could see the tracks of the car that had come and left, and as he watched Carol walk the baby around and around the dance floor, the shock of seeing her again and the added surprise of the foundling made his heart race. He had never succeeded at putting things together for himself and often wondered if it might not have been better to have become a priest, where one's weaknesses and dependencies are subsumed by the larger order of the church. Yet he found that if he stayed in one place long enough, things came to him: a man fallen from a train, a lonely woman, a child at the door. The bounty, not taken but received, no longer surprised him.

"She's coming right up," Snuff said, then emerged from behind the bar.

Carol sat under the bent chandelier and rocked the child. Snuff pulled up a chair, but this time he looked at her instead of the baby.

"You came back," he said.

"Yes."

Willard stumbled in from the back door, dragging his willow. When he saw the baby, his face brightened.

"Look, Willard, it's a baby girl."

Willard smiled, then leaned down to kiss the child on the cheek, and after, touched his fingers to his lips and laughed.

Snuff brought another chair for Willard. "Do you know whose car came and went?"

Carol looked at him. "I think so, don't you?"

"Is it who I'm thinking it is?" Snuff asked.

"Yes. He came back by, too, while I was holding the baby."

"So he saw you with her?"

"And kept driving," she said. "Snuff . . . what are we going to do?"

Snuff gazed at her. "You had your hair cut, didn't you?"

Carol smiled shyly. She touched the baby's forehead. "What's wrong with that man?" she asked.

"I don't know. I don't think he believes in anything anymore. He can only see what's wrong and terrible in the world."

"He couldn't see this?" Carol asked, looking at the baby.

"No, I don't think so."

"But he came back by—"

Snuff nodded. "He's not heartless. . . ."

"Are you going to try to find him?"

"I don't know how."

The door opened slowly. Ora held a stack of diapers in one arm and a basket of formula and bottles in the other. She was a big woman, not fat, but tall and strong and rangy. She had raised eight children alone and had done ranch work with a team of white mules because her husband had died shortly after arriving in Wyoming by wagon from Utah.

She gawked at the room, her eyes roving from the shelves lined with bottles, to the poker table in back, to the scarred dance floor, to the chandelier.

"Come on in," Snuff chirped. "Before the bishop sees you . . . ," he said, laughing.

"I've never been in a bar in my whole life," Ora exclaimed, dumbfounded.

"Well, you're in a real den of iniquity now, Ora," Snuff joked as he took the basket from her arm.

Her eyes caught Snuff's. "It's really not as bad as I thought it would be," she said.

They spread a blanket on the oak table and changed the baby's diapers. Willard looked on with the same hooded stare he gave to his roosters and horse. Ora glanced at Carol.

"That was a quick nine months," she quipped.

"We adopted her. She just came earlier than we expected."

Snuff smiled at Carol as Ora pinned on the clean diaper. A child wasn't news to her, nor did she care how or why a baby came into the world. "A blessing is a blessing," she said. "God doesn't go by the calendar."

"How hot is this stuff supposed to get?" Snuff asked from behind the bar. He was boiling two bottles of formula and carried one to her. Ora touched the nipple to her wrist.

"Just right, Snuff." Then she handed the bottle to Carol. "It's best if you feed her."

Carol took the baby in her arms, and when she put the bottle to the child's mouth, Willard clapped his hands and squealed.

"Ora, can I make you something?" Snuff called from behind the bar. "I mean, since you're here, maybe you want to have the complete experience. I won't tell the good bishop."

"I think I've had enough excitement for one day," she said. "Well, I've got to get back. We're having Relief Society tonight. You're welcome any time," she said breezily and walked out the door.

When Ora was gone, Snuff quickly poured two small glasses of brandy and took them to the table. He looked at Carol pensively. "Did you come to stay?"

His eyes caught hers. The baby grabbed his finger. "What shall we call her?"

"Snuff . . . you don't have to get involved in this if you don't want to. I'll take care of her."

He shot a look at Carol and his gray eyes narrowed. "I'm glad you came back."

Carol's face softened. A car went by and they both looked, then Snuff touched the baby's hair.

"How about *Venus* for a name?" Carol asked.

"Oh no . . . that wouldn't be fair to the poor kid. Venus is a great old gal, but let's not put that on someone just starting out."

"Then we'll call her *Lenny*, no, *L-E-N-I*," she said, spelling out the name.

Snuff looked astonished. "I thought you hated that name."

"Just on him," she said, looking from the baby to Snuff. "I can't think of a name right now that would ever fit him."

"Leni?" Snuff said, looking into the baby's dark eyes. "Hello."

The baby smiled, then shook her hands in the air.

When the child had her fill of milk, Carol held her over one shoulder and walked the length of the bar. She heard Snuff talking on the phone. When she sat down again, he came back in and pulled up a chair close to hers. He looked excited and serious and a little scared.

"You won't ruin me, will you? At the last minute?" he asked.

"Snuffy," Carol said, moving her head close. "What are you talking about?"

Snuff sat up straight and smiled. "Good," he said, satisfied. "We're going to town now."

Carol looked at him, baffled. Snuff stood before the back mirror and tied his bow tie and smoothed his hair. Then he turned and spoke again. "You know, most women wouldn't do what you've done."

"You mean take in a baby?"

"No, I mean come back."

The baby squirmed, and Carol shifted her to the other shoulder. Then her eyes met Snuff's. "That's false pride," she said briskly. "We don't have enough time left for that."

Snuff put on his suit coat.

"Where are we going?" Carol asked.

"We have an appointment . . . with the JP. I just called him. He's even sober. I'll hold Leni while you get ready."

Carol stood, stunned. "You're not kidding, are you?" she said. "Are you sure? I mean, now, right now? Like this?"

"Hell, Carol, we can't have a baby if we're not married," he said, smiling, and took the baby from her arms.

They found Willard curled up in the backseat of the black coupe when they were ready to go. Snuff let him hold the baby part of the way while Carol drove. Everyone knew that Snuff fell asleep at the wheel, so it wasn't unusual to see him being chauffered, even to his own wedding, by his bride-to-be.

Willard was the best man and the witness. He locked his soft arm in Carol's until the justice of the peace told him he could let go. Then Willard saw Snuff kiss his mother, and he laughed. The jailer, a gruff, stocky retired rancher they called "Hard Winter" because, the legend went, he was born in a snowbank during the hardest Wyoming winter on record, held the baby all during the ceremony. After, Willard signed his X on the marriage certificate, and Snuff slipped Frank a twenty-dollar bill and invited him up to the bar.

Within an hour, news of the wedding spread through Luster and by the end of the day the speculation that there was a baby was confirmed, but they wondered why Carol had bothered to go away to have it.

Cars poured into Snuff's parking lot, and the sheepherder, who spoke no language, neither English nor Spanish, but some amalgam of the two with animal sounds punctuating each vowel, played the Jew's harp and fiddle. Bottles of milk simmered on the stove, while Pinkey and McKay poured drinks. The miraculous presence of the child, who was passed from Carol to Snuff, to McKay, to Velma Vermeer, to Pinkey, to Madeleine, to Willard, and back to Carol again, mitigated the usual rowdiness, and the festivities were graced by a dignified glee.

39

McKay had two horses saddled and tied under a tree. It was June 1945 and already there had been a heat wave with temperatures well into the eighties. Mariko's day-long pass had finally been approved and McKay was at the Camp's sentry gate before breakfast. Since his mix-up with Harry, he no longer talked to the guards, but instead stood by his truck with one leg tucked up, leaning against the front fender. He heard the short blast of the siren for roll call, then the breakfast bell. The noise and smell of the Camp repelled him. He knew he should have gone in to visit Abe-san but he was impatient. It had been four months since he had seen Mariko.

She strode down the dusty avenue. At the gate, she pulled out a cigarette and asked the guards for a light, taunting them. She showed her pass, then stepped through to temporary freedom.

When McKay walked toward her she noticed his limp. It was always bad just before a rain. She searched the sky; to look directly at him now would be overwhelming, she thought. Her shoulders rose stiffly as he drew near, and she closed her eyes. When he took the cigarette from between her fingers she felt as if he were undressing her.

"It's going to rain, isn't it, on our one day together?" she asked, peering up at his face. The skin under his left eye twitched and in the gold at his temples, she saw glistening strands of gray.

"Let's get out of here," he said.

Nothing seemed natural. The movement of the truck matched her roaring thoughts, if they could be called thoughts at all. The horizon slid—like lumber at a sawmill—and endless sagebrush bumped past, grazing her eyes. She felt carsick.

She laid her head on McKay's lap and he ran his hand through her long hair, twisting it into a loose knot around his knuckles, reentwining himself, gently invading her.

As soon as they turned off the pavement he stopped the truck. Mariko sat up. The earth was still. It was the brutality of their separations and reunions that frightened her now.

"Where are you?" she asked and pressed toward him.

His chest seemed huge and she clung to him. He touched her nose to make her look up.

"I'm here . . . ," he said, almost tentatively, and she marveled at how they seesawed between sureness, power, the unmistakable physical weld— and uncertainty. Uncertainty because there was no surfeit, no frame, no end point.

"I don't doubt *you*," she said. "I doubt love."

She felt her heart cramp, then jerk into motion. There would be no end to wanting or loving him, yet she knew that nothing could ever meet the expectations of desire.

They stood in the V where two creeks met. A kingfisher, perched on a branch, dove into the water and came out again as if untouched, unscathed. She looked at McKay. In his eyes, slabs of gray were cut into the blue. It's the kind of imperfection Japanese love, a sign of beauty, she thought, smiling, and grabbed him around the waist.

"Your bones are so light. I always forget that," he said, touching her wrist. "Like a bird's."

They heard flapping and laughed. Upstream and around a bend, a blue heron lifted into sight and flew behind a screen of willows.

"We better go. I've got two horses waiting." Mariko let herself be led back to the truck.

As McKay drove, she kissed his hand on the steering wheel, then the cuff of his shirt and the sleeve and the seam at the shoulder and his neck. She thought of all the ways she would open herself to him, the way layers of self would drop away and burn like paper scraps. The thought did not frighten her, but the unquenchable longing did. Maybe there's no stopping it, she thought, shuddering because it made a joke of love. She promised herself that at the moment of orgasm she would try to grasp some meaning—she would fashion it into a hook on which their two lives would swing. But to grasp at anything . . . how that would make Abe-san laugh. And to feel sadness in the attempt to join with anyone . . . that was laughable too because it was only something becoming empty, and the emptiness taking on form, and so on. . . .

"I hate it," she cried silently and pushed her hand under McKay's shirt, sliding her fingers over his heart.

They untied the horses and rode and when it started raining, they stopped in the breaks above the ranch and found shelter under a tree. The soft needles brushed her face, wetting it, and she inhaled the rain smell. He held her and his tenderness seemed to irrigate her bones. The scent of mountain mahogany sweetened the air. But it was too wet and cold to take off their clothes. McKay sat against the thin trunk of the white pine and held her with his legs. As he rolled his heels back and forth on the rowels of his spurs, she thought how desire, gone beyond knowing, ends up as nothingness. Perhaps it was tenderness that made up for loss. She liked being rocked between his knees.

"If we were in Paris," she began, and he listened, smiling. She told him about the café where she met with her friends in the afternoons, and a place called the Mermaid Tavern where musicians from the major orchestras—violinists and oboists and cellists—came to play chamber music on their free nights; she told him about Pablo Casals, and Pablo Picasso and another Pablo, who made love only to women's feet; and about going to see racehorses warm up in the Bois de Boulogne on Sundays and about the trains you could catch in the middle of the night and find yourself in another country by morning.

"But it's like that here too—for me," McKay said. "It's just like that."

"Yes," she said.

When it stopped raining a mist rose from the ground. They stood up and looked out across the basin and everywhere the earth shimmered in steam. They left the horses tied and he took her hand.

"I'll show you," he said, leading her downhill.

His long strides broke into a run.

Three sage hens lifted out of the sagebrush and he turned, thinking Mariko was behind him. Wind ruffled his blond hair. When Mariko caught up, he walked straight toward the ridge, and when he stopped once to inspect a tiny flower, his hand looked impossibly big. But how tenderly he touched things, she thought.

From the top they could see down into a small canyon. "I want to show it to you," he said, barely stopping long enough to catch his breath.

The canyon was human-size, scaled to fit an animal. Runoff water had scoured sandstone into basins like baths. Rock walls the size of houses were nicked with shelves and nests, and here and there a thick juniper root split the rock like a hairy arm, twisting back in on itself.

How different we are, Mariko thought. I look at all this but he is made of it. He is not separate from it as I am.

After, they climbed up and out and across a sandy hill and down another canyon which they followed north. A wall of red rock rose out of the ground, its smooth side facing east.

"Look," McKay said, and pointed.

Mariko squinted into the sun and stepped closer. Carved into the rock were images of elk at a run. She traced the lines with her fingers.

"How old are these?" she asked.

"I don't know. Maybe ten thousand years, maybe five hundred years."

They walked on. Up a ridge, down a steep slope, up through another set of breaks where blocks of sandstone had tumbled like boxcars. A trail wound through them. She had to catch her breath once, supporting herself on a jack pine. On top, she saw a low fence. She looked at McKay as they approached.

"You mean you have your own graveyard?" she asked.

"Yes. This is where my parents are buried."

She touched one headstone, then the other.

"I planted blazing stars on my father's grave—see?" he said and held the tightly closed blossom in his hand. "They only open up at night. My father was like that. He traveled like a ghost and whenever he went away from the ranch, he always left at night."

By his mother's grave he had planted wild iris, small and brilliantly blue. He said, "They're like her eyes; that's why I put them here."

"What else?" Mariko asked, meaning about his mother.

McKay knelt down at the head of the grave. "When Bobby came to the ranch she embarked on what she called her 'Japanese studies.' She was like that. She wanted to know who Bobby was because she had never known any Asians before. She used to read to me from Genji. . . ."

Mariko smiled delightedly. "My prince . . . ," she said tenderly but with a wry smile.

They walked back to the ridge above the house. The sky hazed over, yet there were no clouds, no front moving in.

"I smell something," Mariko said.

"So do I," McKay said, scanning the horizon.

Mariko stood next to him. "Oh, McKay, look," she said, pointing.

A flame shot up from behind a ridge.

They rode to the ranch.

The fire was up behind cow camp, Bobby said, and helped McKay catch four more horses.

"You coming or not?" McKay asked Mariko brusquely. "Because it's going to be hell up there."

He fitted two horses with pack saddles and filled the panniers with water canteens, towels, gloves, a first-aid kit, and the sack lunches Bobby brought out. Then he top-packed them with shovels and axes.

"I'll come," Mariko announced.

McKay looked at her. "You'll have to keep up."

He saddled two more horses, and while Bobby opened the gates, he grabbed the pack string and led off at a trot with Mariko following.

It was not a big fire yet. Riding out through the sagebrush, he gauged the wind and tried to think about how the fire would burn if it took off.

At the river he saw tracks: elk, deer, cattle. He let the horses drink, then turned north, up the trail to cow camp. He wondered if Pinkey was up there, turning the cattle for home. When they emerged from a patch of timber, he saw elk. They weren't grazing. They were on the move. The air was thick with smoke, and as he pulled off the trail so they could pass, he saw there were cattle with them.

Mariko watched McKay from behind. She thought she could see his thinking by the way he moved with his horse. His mind ran fast and fluid. . . . When they reached the camp, Pinkey's mare was gone. McKay turned to Mariko.

"Pinkey must be turning down those cattle . . . the ones we passed." He made a twisting motion with his wrist and thumb. Then his face lit up and he smiled at her. "You're beautiful," he said and rode on up the hill.

He could see where the fire had burned across the top of the mesa a few miles away. Now it was in the trees and the tops of tall lodgepole pines burned like torches, single flames going up into the air.

"I think we better dig a trench here," he said, pulling the shovels from under the lash ropes. He tied the horses. The wind blew in sharp gusts, and each time the fire brightened. McKay loosened the hard ground and Mariko dug after him. The ditch was a foot wide. When they hit boulders, they dug around them. Sometimes they stopped and drank water from the canteen, then continued their work. When he saw that she was tiring, he told her to check the horses, and she did, and by nightfall the trench was dug.

The air didn't cool down with darkness. Now, when the wind fanned the smoke into flames, they could see sprays of sparks cascading and the burning grass crept toward them. They stopped once, sat by the tiny creek.

McKay handed Mariko a sandwich. "We better eat while we can," he said.

Her hand was black with dirt. They ate without talking. When she finished the first sandwich, McKay handed her another one, and after they drank from the stream. The smoke was thick and it made McKay cough.

"When you were sick, you coughed like that. . . ."

"Did you really come to see me?"

"Yes. Pinkey came to the Camp. He said you were about dead—"

"I don't remember—" he said.

The air grew hotter. McKay led the horses out from the trees and they rode higher. In a coulee, he found four head of cattle and pushed them on down toward Pinkey's cabin. He wondered where Pinkey was and how soon they would run into Madeleine.

The wind shifted in their favor—that is, away from the cabin—then it came around and blew from the northwest again. They rode up and down the fire line, putting out small blazes. McKay thought he saw someone at the top of the ridge and called out, but there was no reply. It must have been a falling branch, he told Mariko.

They worked through the night. Mariko's eyes took on a wide dry look he had not seen before and her delicate, pale skin blackened with soot. Wind shook flames into the trees and balls of fire jumped from treetop to treetop. Then they heard thunder. McKay looked up from his shovel work at Mariko. She held out her hand, and a raindrop flattened itself on her palm. The tree flames caved in first, burst sideways, then dissolved into smoke, and the trenches filled with water. McKay caught Mariko by the shoulder and turned her to face him.

"We've got her licked," he yelled, then picked her up and let her down against him.

They rode to the wide bowl rimmed by the lacelike remnants of a cornice. Ahead, in a clump of aspen, McKay thought he saw something again. The rain didn't let up. It came in undulating waves. As they approached, he saw a horse lying on its side.

"Pinkey!" McKay ran to the old cowboy. Pinkey's mare, Eleanor, was down.

"She broke down on me . . . ," Pinkey mumbled, "my mare broke down . . . ," he said, leaning against her and looking up with glazed eyes.

"Are you okay?" McKay asked.

Pinkey looked at him uncomprehendingly.

"Is the mare's leg broke?" McKay asked, running his hand down her back leg.

"I don't know," Pinkey said. "I can't find my gun."

"Can you stand up, Pinkey?"

Pinkey got to his feet slowly, obediently.

McKay looked the mare over. She lifted her head once and eyed him imploringly. Pinkey slumped beside her again.

"I don't feel a break, Pinkey . . . did she fall?"

Pinkey laid his head on the mare's neck.

"Pinkey?"

"You old broke-down mare . . . ," Pinkey said, stroking her neck.

"Why don't we ride to the cabin, then I'll come back and see what needs to be done," McKay said.

Pinkey didn't move.

"For God's sake, Pinkey . . . come on."

Mariko helped McKay lift Pinkey onto a horse. The rain came in soft gusts that made the fire twitch and there were no flames.

As they rode to the cabin another figure came out of the dark.

"McKay?" the voice said. The rain had misted into a steady drizzle when Madeleine met Mariko on the trail. The two women stared at each other without moving. Mariko's hair was wet and it hung in strings down her soot-blackened face.

"Hello," Madeleine said. "Where's McKay?"

"He's coming. He's got Pinkey with him. Pinkey's horse is hurt."

McKay and Pinkey, riding double, came around the bend. The mist, mixed with smoke, made it hard to see.

"Is that ridge out now?" Madeleine called ahead.

"Yep," McKay answered. He looked at the two women. "Madeleine, this is Mariko," he said.

Madeleine smiled. "That horse treating you okay?" she asked Mariko.

"Fine, thanks."

"I'll bring the rest of the cattle on down and pick up anything I see on the way," Madeleine began.

"Eleanor's broke down," Pinkey said in a weak voice.

"How bad, Pinkey?"

"She's just broke down. . . ."

Madeleine gave McKay a knowing look.

"A horse as ugly as that is hard to hurt," Madeleine said.

"Just went down on her knees, sudden-like. She's never done that before . . . ," Pinkey droned.

Madeleine picked up the bridle reins and backed her horse so the others could pass. "Nice to meet you," she said to Mariko.

When McKay passed, she grabbed his hand as if to signal both understanding and dismay. Then she continued on down the trail.

The cabin was dark when the trio rode in. Pinkey slid off the back of McKay's horse and stumbled lifelessly to the door. When McKay and Mariko walked in, they found him sitting in the dark. McKay lit a lamp and when the room lightened he saw Pinkey's desperate eyes.

"You've just been waiting to shoot my mare," Pinkey yelled, standing. He grabbed the salt shaker and threw it against the wall.

"Oh, quit it, Pinkey," McKay growled.

Pinkey sat down, quieted. He looked frail suddenly.

"We'll grain these horses and let them rest a little bit, then I'll go back and see what I can do for her," McKay said, putting coffee on. "Okay?" he asked the old cowboy.

After taking care of their saddle horses, McKay and Mariko walked toward the creek. It had stopped raining and the sky cleared to its former haze.

"Let's clean up a little," McKay said and nudged Mariko toward the water.

She sat at the edge of the creek, then slipped in, trying to wash the soot from her face. McKay crouched, facing her. He cupped his hands and brought water to his mouth, then took off his hat and doused his hair. She laughed when she saw him drip.

He thought about the two women meeting on the dark trail. They were like negatives of each other: blond and black, physical and cerebral, companionable and passionate. But there was no question of choosing.

He rose up suddenly like a bear: "For God's sake, Mariko, don't leave me," he cried.

When McKay went to shoot Pinkey's mare he found the horse at the bottom of the hill, alive and unharmed, and grazing, and up above, the ridge of charred lodgepole pines smoldered.

40

High water came and stayed through the first week of July that year and even in August, during cloudbursts, the creeks rose suddenly and overflowed. McKay rode the colt on a ten-mile circle every day and never went the same way twice, so the colt could see as much of the world as possible. He rode to the waterholes where the ducklings hatched; rode through the bonsai field; rode the ridges above the Camp and the ranch where the clouds blew through and around him; rode through plowed fields, circled the Camp in the evening when the lights went on; rode the highway to Snuff's, rode the pastures where the elk were; kicked him up through bogs and over ice, through deep mud, along steep sidehills; and showed him all kinds of weather except heat, which was still to come.

The day McKay rode the colt to the river was the day—August 6, 1945—a solar eclipse occurred.

Pinkey had ridden from cow camp before dawn. He rode north against the flank of Heart Mountain, saw that the bulls were in with the cows, checked for pinkeye and hoof rot, then traversed a long point of land to its end, from which he could see the two-thousand-acre pastures below. The sun had just risen when the eclipse began. Pinkey thought it was his eyes. His friend Dutch, who had had a cerebral hemorrhage once, described the way black blotches came over your eyes and the world dimmed. Pinkey tried to look directly at the sun but couldn't, yet he knew the darkness—Vincent's shadow—was coming again. The sun looked big on the horizon but by the time it lifted completely above the ridge, Pinkey couldn't tell if the sun was blowing up, or becoming lost. Then the whole center went black, and the last Pinkey saw, a bright halo flared out from behind it. "I'll never get out from under you . . . ," he mumbled, meaning Vincent's shadow. The eclipse was like a foot on his heart. Below, in the valley, he could hear roosters crowing because they thought it was night again, and east of the ridge, a band of sheep bedded down halfway up a hill. How long did the darkness last? Pinkey couldn't tell. He leaned forward in the saddle: "The days get shorter and shorter," he said to his mare. "Are we dead now?"

After, moist Pacific air brought snow squalls, as if someone were puffing smoke, and McKay rode the blue colt to the river. The wind came in three directions at once: on the north side of the ranch it snowed, on the south end the sun shone, then for a moment it rained. The river was high. It had brought down whole trees, which caught in jams along the banks, and the water whirled under them. The gravel bar had been reduced to the size of a coffin. Only the high part, where the tall bunchgrass grew, was visible.

In his pocket he carried the letter he had received from Champ. "I didn't even know he could write," he had told Bobby jokingly. The letter had said:

McKay—

Our brother has been busted up pretty bad—I guess his ship got the hell torpedoed out of it. He lost blood and a little of his skull. He said they gave him forty units of plasma. They found him topside—he struggled because he thought the ship was sinking, just like the time he fell out of bed during a nightmare and we had to pounce on him. Squirrelly older brother, huh. Some dumb newspaper man who was on the ship stumbled on this scene and wrote: JUNIOR MEDICAL OFFICER

FIGHTING TO SAVE LIVES OF MEN. Ted said it made the front page of *The New York Times*. So don't believe a damn thing you read about this war. If any of us do anything heroic, it's only because we've gotten the shit scared out of us and we've lost control. Anyway, Ted's being transferred from a hospital ship by DC-3 to good old dry ground. Expect a call. I'm off to do battle. We're being moved to a forward area tonight. Squeeze a girl for me.

Champ

When McKay looked down at the river again, the rocky banks were submerged and the turquoise pools with the cool gravel bottoms were muddied.

He hadn't been thinking about Mariko—yet no thought arose in his mind that didn't have something of her in it. It didn't matter that he had tried to stop seeing her. His edict rid him of nothing, but only acted as a further link, a kind of negative bond. Nor did it matter that he would lose her. He knew she would not, could not stay on the ranch and marry him. He'd had no experience with a woman whose life could not be grafted onto his, and the impossibility of their love strengthened his feelings for her. Yet he had not expected her to take such a hold.

He moved the colt up to the edge of the river. The river was fast, and a twig, floating by on the surface, made the colt balk. McKay let him turn, then took him back the other way to the water. The horse put his head down, touching his muzzle to the current, and blew air, then tucked his rump to run. McKay pulled the colt's head around sharply and let him trot up river, then turned him, up and down. His father always told him to make a good situation out of a bad one: if a colt balks, use it as an opportunity to teach him to turn.

The colt stopped suddenly and pawed the water. McKay talked softly, then made a forward movement with his hips in the saddle to urge the colt on. The horse pawed and snorted and pawed. McKay felt the muscles in his rump tuck and picked up on the bridle reins, but not soon enough. The colt bolted into the water, bucked, and fell.

When McKay went out of his body, he was lifted by the thermal of Mariko. Lifted and dropped and lifted again. It was neither hot nor cold and he couldn't tell if he was moving. For a moment, the water cleared and he could see: the thick carpet of sedge leading up to the rock and the rock itself looked like mere casings—for something else.

Water rushed against him, into him, tinged white and blue. The rapture worked its way down from McKay's head into his body. One hand rose limply and one foot pushed out in spasm against a tree trunk, then a rock. He remembered wiping sweat from his face. Was it sweat? Then he saw Mariko, saw the heat rise in her cheeks. He was damp under the arms and the water worked in his lungs like fear.

McKay's head broke through the windshield of water and a piece of grass unwound itself from his neck and let go. His mother's dead face came down on him . . . he gasped for air. Something caught in his side when he breathed. He looked up: Heart Mountain's tusk loomed and he felt as if he had been gored. He gasped again. The colt had fallen backward and was righting himself. One rein undulated toward him, just below the surface like a watersnake, then sank.

"Mariko . . . ," McKay cried out. He touched the side of his head and his hand came back with blood on it, staining the water pink.

At that moment she went from him. The rapture worked its sweetness all the way through his body. Breathing was hard. He had broken ribs. Then he felt light-headed and the double, embattled constraints of desire and solitude floated. . . .

He laid his face on the water, on her, on the place where the pink stain had been, and cried out for her again. "Foolish me," he thought. For a moment Heart Mountain shimmied at his waist, then the horse, clambering onto the bank, shattered the reflection.

Out of the water, McKay lay on gravel. The big colt grunted as he shook. McKay rolled on his back and opened his eyes. There was no place the sky stopped when he looked and the water roared and there was no other sound.

41

July 1945. The "Powell War Dads"—a group of men from the nearby town—have signed a petition asking that when the war ends we promise to leave the state of Wyoming. In addition, they requested that in the meantime, our passes be suspended. The Camp director retorted that 748 boys from the Heart Mountain Camp are also fighting and are as dear to their "war dads" as the boys from Powell.

We were pushed into the interior deserts by racism in 1942; now we're being pushed back out.

Later. No farming this year. Seems strange. We're simply waiting for the end, but when will that come? In the meantime there's talk of home —California—for the first time: Guadalupe, Santa Maria, Terminal Island, Lompoc, Hollister, Salinas, Oxnard, San Jose, Gardena. . . .

Will the Buddhist temple near my father's hardware store still be there? Will they be able to lease their lettuce farm again? Will the art goods store in Little Tokyo be reopened? Will they have time to plant winter crops if the war ends, say in October? Will they be able to find a place to live?

Will the old neighborhoods have changed? Will we be shot down on the streets? Will we be able to get bank loans, buy a car, go to public schools? Will our belongings in storage be made available to us? "After Camp," that's what everyone's talking about these days. . . .

Saturday. A letter from Emi arrived. They went back to Los Angeles and found strangers living in their house and the strangers have refused to leave. Her father has had to take a job washing dishes in a skid row restaurant . . . he used to be a prosperous strawberry farmer. Her mother works as a cook at a farm labor camp, so Emi went to live with her. She says, "If you come back, expect nothing. Love Emi."

July 7. Tanabata again. Mom wrote out another wish on a streamer of white paper and gave one to Mariko, too. I remember how upset she was when she learned it was Mariko I had my eyes on, not Emi. Now, since Pop has become so difficult, almost impossible to live with, she has taken a kindly attitude toward Abe-san. "He's a hotoko no yo na hito," she said, "a man just like a Buddha."

Later, I went with Mariko to the big bonfire where some old Issei men were reciting Tanabata poems. We lay in the grass. The day before there had been a dust storm—just like the one that had hit the afternoon we first arrived here and the grass was gritty with dirt. Mariko lay on her back and looked at the stars as the poems began: "Hisakata no / ama no kawara no / watashimori / kimi watarinaba / kaji kakushite yo." "If my love should come / to me from across the broad / waters of heaven's / river oh ferryman please / hide your oars."

We had finally convinced the administration to turn out the guard tower lights for Tanabata. It was wonderful to be able to view that thick bright ceiling. The Milky Way twisted over us. . . .

"ama no kawa / asase shiranami / tadoritsutsu / watari-hateneba / ake zo shinikeru. . . ."

I held Mariko's hand and she turned to me.

"*I've grown so used to you. What will I do without you?*" she said, then rose up on her elbow to listen to the old men:

"*ima wa to te / wakaruru toki wa / ama no kawa / wataranu saki ni / sode zo hichinuru. . . .*" "*The time to depart / has come I have yet to cross / the great river of / heaven but already my / sleeves are drenched with tears. . . .*"

42

The morning after his fall McKay awakened Bobby and said he'd have to help him get to the hospital because he couldn't move very well or breathe because of the broken ribs. Bobby sat up straight in bed, and even after McKay left, he couldn't shake the dream he'd been having. He dressed quickly. He hadn't been to town for three years and now Pinkey and Madeleine were nowhere to be found and he'd have to take McKay in himself.

"Keep it pretty slow on these bumps," McKay said, holding himself in pain as Bobby drove the truck toward the highway.

It was also the morning Velma Vermeer opened her blinds and saw the young boy running down the main street of Luster carrying a radio almost as big as he was. It was early—only the café was open—and she couldn't imagine where the boy was going. She watched him cross the street. The top of the radio was rounded and the woven cloth over the speaker made the dark wood of the radio look like an arch. "L'Arc de Triomphe," Velma thought. "He's carrying victory." The black striped cord and heavy plug bumped and dragged on the ground behind him as he disappeared into Rose's boardinghouse.

Coming into town, someone stopped and waved a little frantically as they passed. Bobby craned his head. It was Velma Vermeer. "Oh, she's gotten so thin and old," he said. The front windows of the grocery store sported sale signs hand-painted in blue and he slowed the truck to read them.

"Come on, Bobby, you can look at those later," McKay said. It was hot and he wiped the sweat from his forehead.

Bobby turned up the hill to the hospital. The dream still hounded him. As they came to the top Bobby rolled the window all the way down and looked out. The sky was clear, an impossible dark blue, almost indigo, and in the west thunderclouds rose to dizzying heights, sudden uncontainable growths. . . . At the front door of the hospital—also the emergency entrance—Bobby helped McKay out. Bobby had seen him with broken ribs before. After the nurse signed him in, Bobby went back outside. The band of clouds had become one immense cloud moving toward Luster. In the dream, the sky had been like that: cobalt blue, but with threatening clouds. Then, when it rained, the rain was black and came down in thick streaks like iron splinters and everything it touched turned black, and even after the rain stopped the tarnish would not go away.

A train's whistle blew as it crossed the iron bridge over the Shoshone River. Bobby went back in. McKay was sitting, bare to the waist, as Doc Hoffman wound a thick piece of white tape around and around McKay's ribs. McKay read aloud from the *Billings Gazette:*

TERRIBLE FORCE OF ATOMIC BOMB UNLEASHED ON JAPAN

August 7. The most terrible destructive force ever harnessed by man— atomic energy—is now being turned on the islands of Japan by the United States bombers. The Japanese face a threat of utter desolation

and their capitulation may be greatly speeded up. Existence of the great
new weapon was announced personally by President Truman in a state-
ment issued through the White House at 11:00 A.M., Eastern War
Time. He said the first atomic bomb, invented and perfected in the
United States, had been dropped on Hiroshima 16 hours before. The
power of the bomb, Secretary of War Stimson reported, "is such as to
'stagger the imagination.' "

McKay looked up and saw Bobby standing at the door silently.

"How many ribs broken this time?" he asked.

"Not more than three or four," the doctor said casually. "He'll live."

"Good," Bobby said, then turned quickly from the room.

Outside, the big cloud had dissipated as if someone had poured water
on it from above. It spread horizontally and clouds behind it were racing
to catch up. The week before he had heard on the radio about the fire
bombings of Tokyo, Osaka, Kobe, Yokohama . . . and had already
assumed that the pickle factory where he had worked as a child had been
bombed, like a single target, as if it were a munitions factory or a harbor
or a bridge, but he had not yet thought of whole cities and everyone and
everything in them—Buddhist temples, noodle shops, geisha houses, sake
bars, Shinto shrines, houses with polished floors, and the families within
them—all flattened.

The sky was completely dark. Another car pulled up to the front of
the hospital. Bobby felt afraid. He had not seen a strange face since the
war began, except for the two army men who had come to the ranch
and now he wished he had not come to town at all.

He sat in the truck. Watching people come and go from the hospital,
he felt sure he could tell what their ailments were—he had been treating
people for such a long time with his potions: powdered bark and flower
teas. Then he remembered the rattlesnake skins he had left on the clothesline. If it rained before they got home, they would be ruined.

He dozed for a short time and woke with the same sense of dread,
only now the dream was replaced by a picture of the city where he had
grown up: its two rivers running through the middle and the arched, iron
bridges . . . and dense smoke touching the ruins softly.

"Bobby." McKay opened the door on the passenger side and Bobby
slid over behind the steering wheel.

The truck coasted down the hill, then Bobby turned left on Main Street, slowing.

"Bobby . . . do you think we could make the grocery store another day . . . I'm hurtin' pretty bad. . . ."

Bobby nodded his head, perused each sale sign, then drove out of town.

McKay spent the next days reading the papers, since he could do no physical work. The news from Japan worsened, though it seemed sure now that a surrender would come. On Wednesday morning, August 8, 1945, the *Billings Gazette* ran an update on the bomb, saying it "devastated 60 percent of the city or 4.1 square miles of civilization," though the American army had long since ceased to think of anything Japanese as "civilized." On the same page, a story from San Francisco said the Japanese had labeled the bomb "barbaric."

The next morning, Thursday, August 9, Velma Vermeer called the ranch—one of twenty or so calls she made that day—to notify McKay that a second atomic bomb had been dropped on the Japanese city of Nagasaki. It was a port city, she said, and that's why they picked it. Also, President Truman was calling the atomic bomb "the most powerful weapon for war and peace" and hoped surrender was near.

McKay thanked her and hung up the phone. Bobby looked at him inquiringly.

"It was Velma," he said. "They dropped another bomb . . . on 'Nag . . .' "

"Nagasaki?"

"Yep . . . that's it."

"Ahhhh . . . ," Bobby said and sat down. "Very beautiful city . . . look like San Francisco . . . very many boats and ships. Houses all up on hill, looking down at them. . . ."

McKay nodded solemnly. He looked Bobby in the eyes. "This is terrible, isn't it?" he said.

"But maybe peace now," Bobby said bravely.

"Maybe so . . ."

A loud clatter on the roof made them look up. Then they saw the hail, big as golf balls, smashing onto the ground.

*   *   *

Earlier that morning when the sun was hot, Willard had walked to the horse pasture where he kept his mare, taken off his overalls, and sunk down in the mossy bathtub where the horses drank. The sudden darkness of the sky made him remember the eclipse and also wonder if maybe it wasn't suppertime.

When the hail started Willard thought someone was throwing eggs. He saw the stones bounce on the ground and squealed delightedly. A moment before, the horses had run, tails in air, to the other end of the pasture, water streaming from their mouths. The hail came harder. Willard climbed out of the tub and dressed quickly. He tried to look up once, but a hailstone banged him on the forehead. Then the ground was white.

He ran. The stones battered his head, belly, shoulders, and his feet rolled over the tops of the ones that had not melted. He ran past the schoolteacher's house and the horse trader's, across an empty pasture, through a downed fence, across the road, past his own house, and into Mañuel's yard.

Carol Lyman was pulling the blinds shut when she heard the scream. It sounded like a pig being butchered. Then the scream stopped and she heard the word *help* being yelled. It wasn't quite "help"—more like "hup." She ran from the house. Willard stood on the other side of the fence with a dead rooster in his hands.

When Porfiria saw what had happened she raised the skirt of her apron to her face and mumbled something in Spanish as she walked into the yard. Everywhere, at her feet, hailstones big as golf balls were piled like ammunition. She bent over and picked one up. She was amply built, with big breasts and delicate ankles, and her flowered dress fluttered as she leaned down. She walked lightly through the rows of empty cages. The hailstones had lined up neatly where Willard had raked. Then she went to Willard and put her hand on Drumstick's brown feathers. A hailstone had broken his neck. Another was still alive but his legs looked broken and he lay on his side and made a hissing sound. The night air was warm because it was summer and where the hailstones had melted, pools of water had formed.

Carol held Willard's big head on her shoulder. Another neighbor, the horse trader, climbed in and quickly surveyed the scene. "By the gods," he mumbled excitedly, "it tore the whole country to hell. Said the alfalfa's nothing but damned sticks, by God, and them cornfields is all flattened to hell."

Willard put his head down against the rooster who had won the fight for him. The bird's lidless eye was open but unmoving and he stared past Willard at the sky.

43

Velma Vermeer dropped the shades against the setting sun shortly after five. As she pulled the cord, she noticed the same little boy carrying the big radio down the street. He walked out of the funeral parlor and headed south on Main Street, then she saw him go into the side door of the big Mormon church. After, she went into her living room and turned on the radio.

At five o'clock Mountain War Time, President Truman announced the Japanese acceptance of the surrender terms. They will be accepted by General Douglas MacArthur when arrangements can be completed.
"I have received this afternoon a message from the Japanese government in reply to the message sent to that government by the secretary of state on August eleventh. I deem this a full acceptance of the Potsdam Declaration, which specifies the unconditional surrender of Japan. Arrangements are now being made for the formal signing of surrender

terms at the earliest possible moment. Great Britain, Russia, and China will be represented by high-ranking officials. Meantime, the Allied Armed Forces have been ordered to suspend offensive action."

Velma returned to the switchboard. She thought of this as her most important duty: to inform the citizens of Luster that the war had ended. She told each person she contacted to spread the news, and very quickly the sidewalks outside her office began to fill with people. They were quiet and inquisitive at first, then, when she heard yelling and shouting, she opened her blinds and saw two grown men dancing in a circle in the middle of the street. The upstairs windows of Rose's boardinghouse opened and she saw Dutch's head pop out. He swung a flask back and forth like a flare and people yelled cheers up to him. Larry and Rose stood quietly in front of their grocery store and Willard, dragging his willow branch, walked through the streets gaping at the citizens gone wild. A man walked out of the florist shop and asked Rose if someone was getting married, and when the 5:20 train pulled in, two soldiers inside threw the windows up and asked if the news was true. Then one of them, elated, jumped out the window onto the platform and danced wildly, throwing his cap into the air.

As Velma pulled the shades all the way up, light from the setting sun stretched across the floor and touched the ancient switchboard. After the last call—to McKay—she pulled the earphones from her head and stood, clasping her hands, in front of her chest. "It's over, Harry," she said, as if that would make him come back. If you lose your husband during a war, but not in combat, does that make him a hero, she wondered. He was too delicate, she thought . . . for this life. . . . The switchboard lit up and she answered the call.

"Yes, that's the news as of 5:00 P.M. Japan surrendered. The war is over."

McKay saddled his roan colt and rode toward Pinkey's cabin. "I ought to let the old fart know," McKay told Bobby, "even though he probably doesn't give a damn. . . ." Up above the breaks, there had been an early snow and the aspen leaves had curled and blackened. He passed the still where Snake River Pete made whiskey during Prohibition and let his horse drink from the spring. The still was there but Pinkey and the kids from town had long since drained it dry. McKay thought about the news of the surrender as he rode up and over a ridge into the next drainage. He didn't feel like dancing in the streets—he knew that—and the relief of peace was overtaken by something else, a disorientation, as if the war had occurred in his inner ear and the inner ear had been damaged.

At the end of a war, when those who survived come home, things don't go back to normal, he thought, because war is not something that happens far away. It happens everywhere, to everyone, and new things occur in the absence of others and there's no way of making things the same again.

Pinkey opened the screen door and looked at the dark sky. It had been a week or two since he had broken all his stashes of whiskey, vowing never to touch booze again. Later, when the shakes came on, he had resorted to an old sheepherder trick—drinking vanilla, which didn't work—and he writhed for a day in pain. Sitting in the dirt in front of his cabin, he had licked the broken pieces of whiskey bottles. For a while he couldn't stand the smell of food. Then when the shakes died down he became ravenously hungry and made a pot of chili. He ate his fill— four bowls. Then he went outside. Everything looked bright. A full moon appeared on the horizon—a pumpkin moon—and the great orange globe made him smile.

Stepping away from the cabin, he listened. He thought he had heard something. . . . A fragile scent of dying leaves drifted through the air. He had to keep reminding himself that it was autumn and, looking, pulled his hat down low. There's no time of year darker than this: an autumn night before it snows. Then he unbuttoned his pants and peed into the void.

"Pinkey?"

Pinkey jumped. "What the hell?"

"Evening," McKay said, smiling.

Pinkey squinted at him. "You runnin' away from home?"

"I just came up to tell you . . ."

"You ought to put a phone in up here . . . like them first-class outfits. . . ."

"The war's over, Pinkey. Japan surrendered this afternoon."

"Well I'll be-go-to-hell. . . . Put that bronc up and come on in. I've got some chili on . . . and deer steaks. . . ."

"Poached?"

"Hell no. Fried."

When news of the surrender reached Kai's barrack, Kai ran out the door. He wanted to see for himself how people at the Camp would react. Nothing happened at first. He could hear radios carrying the news report, and after, an eerie silence. He went back inside. Mr. and Mrs. Nakamura sat on their bed, holding hands.

"Mom . . . it's over. The war is over. . . ."

She looked at him blankly. "It's just that we can't believe . . ."

"What?" Kai asked impatiently.

"The emperor . . . he had to tell the people himself."

"It's not a disgrace," Kai said. "It's best that it ended."

Kai sat on a chair facing them just as he had the day they told him he had a brother. "We can go home now," he said slowly, hoping his father would hear. "We can get something planted. . . ."

Mrs. Nakamura rocked the old man's head against her chest and gazed out the window at the dust blowing by.

The next morning an urgent knock woke Kai.

"Special delivery," a young voice yelled.

Kai staggered out of bed, fumbling for his glasses, and signed for the two letters—addressed to him, not his parents, from Kenny:

Onamachi, Japan

Dear Kai,

I thought I better write and tell you what it's like here; it's bigger than any of our differences.

It took almost as much prodding and finagling to get assigned to this Division as it did to get into the Air Corps. Always the same thing is implicit: Why does a Jap want to go around liberating American prisoners of war in his own homeland?

I'm in a town about a hundred miles south of Hiroshima. No bombs were dropped here because the location of the prison camp nearby on the island of Ikuno was known. Spent the day supposedly liberating American war prisoners, but they had already liberated themselves. Tried to bring order to the process, but some guys have gone wild as March hares: wild for food, clean clothes, and women.

On arrival I was met with bafflement. What nationality was I? Chinese? If I was Japanese-American, why was I with the U.S. military and why didn't I speak Japanese? No amount of explaining could make them understand. Instead, we were shown to a hotel where a lineup of beautiful girls was paraded into the lobby for our "enjoyment." The colonel dismissed them; that didn't make the men very happy.

Met a merchant and his family who have a big three-story house at the edge of town. Just before the war ended they housed a regiment of Japanese soldiers; now they have opened their doors to us. He's a kindly man. He showed me a picture before the war—he was standing in a room full of expensive kimonos and had a big paunch. Now his clothes hang on him. I don't think there's a person in the whole of Japan who isn't suffering from malnutrition. We pay for everything we buy in food.

Mr. Shibota's five children are quiet and polite except for one. He's only fourteen, but he speaks some English. Here's what he told me, paraphrased:

"The day the bomb was dropped my sister and I were on our way to school. The sun was rising. Then we looked around and saw another sun. That's what the bomb was like for us—two suns. It wasn't until the next day, the seventh, that we heard what happened, but still we don't know what it was. My uncle lives in Hiroshima. The glass in his house blew all the way to the other side. He had been playing Gō with a friend. The whole house came down on him, so he was saved from the flash rays. The first thing he remembered was that he had no pants on, so he crawled around and found some diapers and put them on. Then he looked for his friend under the house and pulled him out. They walked around the city. They couldn't recognize anything. They saw people walk into the river because of their burns and drink the water and die, and he saw many people with their skin hanging off. They walked away from Hiroshima that day and a farmer took them in. Another uncle had half his face exposed so the skin on one side was gone and the other side looked normal. He was walking over a bridge when he saw his brother. When he called out his brother didn't recognize him. That's all I know about the bomb. I have other relatives there and I think they're all dead.

"Near the end of the war we had thirty-five soldiers living in our house. My mother and one of the soldiers cooked for all of them plus seven of us. That's how we got food—the soldiers had rice and some fish. But before that we had nothing to eat. A cup of rice for all of us lasted four days. One guy in town went to the beach and gathered seaweed, dried and curled it, and sold it as noodles. We tried it but it was full of sand. Then we had an uncle who owned a silkworm farm and he brought some of those worms over here and we ate them. They were awful.

"One day an American plane was shot down right on the beach. This was last year, 1944, and there wasn't anything to sell in the stores then so the owners of the big store here went down and took souvenirs— the prop, the window, the pilot's dark glasses—and they made a window display out of these things. I liked the big prop best.

"In July about a hundred B-29's flew over us so low we could see the bomb bay doors. I did drawings of them. They flew right over and about five minutes later it was like an earthquake. They had dropped the bombs on a town about a hundred miles away. We had an anti-aircraft gun. We followed the soldier who rolled the gun up the hill to the temple and set it up. Then he said, don't worry; we won't get hurt because we don't have any bullets. By this time we had nothing. No food, no ammunition. Their bayonets had blades made of bamboo.

"After the bomb was dropped the planes dropped leaflets that looked like ten-yen notes but on the other side they said *Surrender* (in Japanese). When the American prisoners got out they looked like dead fish. Eyes staring out of heads. They were hungry and so were we. Then the planes came back and dropped food for them and the next time I saw them they looked alive. They made shirts out of the parachutes. Our soldiers ran and hid in the mountains, but American-ji brought all kinds of things for us—food and cigarettes and gum and candy. They wanted something for it. They showed me with their finger. They wanted women so we told them where to go and they gave us food. Everything's happier now. They even have a band. I followed it down the street and they let me play their drum."

August 16
Dear Kai,

I asked to be driven to Hiroshima today. By now, maybe you've seen the pictures. Where there was once a huge city, there is now only wreckage and carnage, a terrible smell, dead horses in the river, and bodies everywhere. People are building little shanties with the debris because the rains are coming soon. For once I'm glad I have a Japanese face, because I could walk around without people staring at me. Talked to one woman. She must have been very beautiful, but half her face was burned and she was wearing rags and holding her child. When I asked her how she felt about the bomb, she gave me a blank stare.

Later. Just before leaving, walked by the place where there was supposed to be an American prisoner of war camp. We looked through the wreckage for any trace of who had been there and how many, but there was nothing to see, and so we walked on.

August 20, 1945
Dear Kai,

The last day I saw the Shibota boy, he showed me his drawings of the town and people during the war: the department store with the propeller in the display window; the temple on the hill above his house with a gun in the garden, the bomb bay doors of a B-29; his uncle with only half a face.

He asked me why I looked Japanese but wasn't. I told him about all the Issei immigrants who had come to America on ships. "Maybe I come to America someday too and paint," he said beaming, as if there had been no war at all.

On August 14 Emperor Hirohito told the Japanese people to "bear the unbearable." They had been defeated in war. The next day was VJ Day where you are; here it was solemn and quiet. I saw old men crying in the streets, heard of suicides.

My orders were to gather and deliver these American soldiers to Tokyo Bay by September 1. It took some doing to track some of them down. The ones that are here are shaping up their marching band and fresh uniforms are being airlifted to them for the signing of the surrender on September 2.

It's taken me a while, but I'm getting my "ground legs" back. Fighting

an enemy is easy; victory is bittersweet. I'm shipping out to San Francisco on nothing less than the *Luraline* September 3.

Your brother,
Kenny

The morning after the surrender was announced, McKay took Bobby
to the grocery store as promised.

"Wish I was in here yesterday," Bobby said, soaking up the passing
scenery.

"Why?" McKay asked.

"Velma—she tell me over phone about it."

"You still listen to that old gossip?" McKay said, teasing.

Bobby shot him a defiant glance. "Big doings, that's what," Bobby
said, pushing his chin out a little. Then he wiped his forehead because
the sun beating through the pickup window was hot. "Fire chief turn on
siren—let blast for long time," Bobby continued. "Then close street. No
car. Big dance everywhere."

"Well, hell . . . ," McKay said. "That would have been fun."

Bobby got out at the grocery store and stood under the blue hand-
painted signs, reading each one carefully. Then he went in. Larry walked
out from behind the butcher case. His hands were red from the blood
of a beef he had just gotten in but he shook Bobby's hand enthusiastically.
"It's good to see you in here," he said. Willard had taken back his old
job of sweeping and spreading sawdust after his rooster had died, and he
stood, resting his big head on the end of a broom, and stared. Bobby
lingered in front of the meat counter. They didn't buy meat because he
and McKay butchered their own, but he liked to look anyway.

"Go look around, Bobby, and take your time."

Bobby walked the aisles slowly, up one, down another. They seemed
wider to him, but weren't. He lingered over decisions, carrying his willow
basket over his arm—the one he and McKay had made when McKay
was ten. Rationing had stopped and the shelves were beginning to fill
again. Even coffee and sugar could be bought and the news around town
was that the café where Carol Lyman had worked would reopen when
the ranchers began shipping calves in September.

Bobby strolled to the front of the store to say hello to Rose. He noticed
her hair was a different color. She had been a blonde—or was it a

brunette? He couldn't remember. "Hair very pretty now," he said to her.

"The old hotel's got a new color to it, too," she said, pointing to the clapboard building across the street.

"Ahhh," Bobby crooned appreciatively. The horse trader walked in to buy snoose as Bobby placed his groceries by the cash register. He looked at the old man. "I thought you'd up and died, it's been so long since I've seen you," he said to Bobby.

"Willard . . . ," Rose called.

Bobby watched the string unwind from three spindles over Rose's head as she and Willard filled two cardboard cartons, tying the flaps to make them stand up.

"Thank you, Rose," Bobby said as he signed the receipt.

"Are you going to be coming in regular, now?" she asked.

"Yes," Bobby replied cheerfully.

Willard carried the boxes to the truck.

"I guess your boys will be coming back soon, huh?" Larry said, moving to the front of the store.

"Ted and Champ coming soon."

"You must be proud of them," she said gaily.

"Very good, they come home. All over now . . . sooo . . ." His eyes were watery.

"Yes, it is, isn't it?"

At the truck, Bobby slipped Willard a dime.

Carol Lyman stood behind the bar all afternoon without a single customer. She had given her nails a second coat of red polish and the baby slept peacefully, lying in a basket the Mormon Relief Society women had brought along with all the diapers and clothes a baby would need. Carol looked out the porthole window. The geranium had bloomed. When she touched the flower, hanging heavily from a thin stem, she noticed it was the same color as her nails. A feeling of contentment had come with the baby. Maybe that was the point of the gift, she thought. "The Wild Man knows what it's like not to be able to keep still." She had expected him to come back on a day like this, a quiet day. He would appear unannounced . . . sneak in through the back door and lift the baby out of the basket and carry it around. But he didn't, and no one coming or going from Billings, Big Timber, Bozeman, Livingston, or

Butte had seen him. Carol thought about the scientist who had helped make the bomb, who, after the bomb dropped, had said, "I am the maker of death . . ." and wondered if that was the Wild Man's brother.

Snuff had fixed up the back rooms. The two rooms—Venus's and his—were now one with a double bed, a crib, and two purple overstuffed chairs. A coffee table stood where Venus's bed used to be.

Now Carol smoothed her dress the way she had smoothed the green wool blanket on Venus's bed a year before as Snuff had watched her.

"Come over here," he said and they lay down with the baby between them. The next day she told him she thought she was getting milk in her breasts. "That happens sometimes when you adopt a child," she explained. He unbuttoned her blouse and held her breasts gently as if weighing them . . . so gently, her knees buckled and she felt herself go unconscious for a moment, and when she woke up, she was lying in Snuff's arms and her crumpled blouse was wet.

44

September. It's been two months since we were told we could get passes to go on hikes and picnics nearby. For the first time, many of the Issei have been able to enjoy the wildflowers and cottonwoods and aspen when their leaves have turned. Abe-san takes walks too. I'd go to his room and find him gone and Mariko would ask me to look for him because she was worried. We celebrated his eighty-fourth birthday in April and now he seems more frail than ever. I could have picked him up with one hand.

The next thing I knew, he wanted to climb Heart Mountain. We've spent three and a half years looking at its twisted form, seen how storms swallowed the top and gave it back, mist-shrouded and white, but we had only that one view from the east, which makes it look like the tipped smokestack of an ocean liner.

We arranged for a ride to the base. On the way, we passed a ranch set back against the hills with a creek winding through and huge mountains behind. Abe-san poked his head out the window and swallowed up the *sights. We were all hungry to be out, away from the barbed wire. I had learned that the legend of Heart Mountain came from the Crow Indians because it stuck up sharply like an animal or human heart. They called it* awaxaum dasa, *meaning "mountain heart." A Crow medicine man once fasted there and received revelations from the Great Spirit, who said that if any part of the mountain broke off and fell, he would die. Soon after, a rent in the top of the mountain appeared and slid down and the old medicine man passed away.*

After climbing a ridge and topping out on a steep hill, we stopped the car. Nearby were the remnants of a hermit's shack. It was said he'd run a still up there during Prohibition and after, stayed on until he died. Abe-san pivoted on his heels, surveying the mountains hemming us, then dropped and drank from the creek with his hands.

We crossed the creek on stepping-stones. Walking ahead of me, Abe-san began singing. He wasn't wearing a kimono, but a Japanese workman's short jacket, pantaloons, and the tennis shoes McKay had given him, a gift he treasured. It was a steep climb to treeline. I had to stop every few minutes to breathe. How soft I've become, still in my twenties, and that old man outwalked me. We ascended the north slope. A huge rock face, shaped like a heart, towered over us. "Mountain heart," I said aloud, but Abe-san was so far ahead, he didn't hear me.

At treeline, we could see down the other side. Far below, the Camp was laid out in all its bleak monotony. Only the smokestack stuck out— the barracks and mess halls sprawled. Abe-san sat cross-legged under a bent seedling pine. The wind that had beleaguered us all these years wrapped itself softly around us now. I heard birds and looked. They flew from tree to tree, and I felt as if they were the one link pulling me away from barbed wire, toward life.

Abe-san laughed when a big gray bird landed in the palm of his hand and ate the scrap of bread offered. Then he proceeded on. The trail was easy to find and followed the ridge up toward the tusk, the nipple. I cut a walking stick for Abe-san and one for me. Wind touched the tops of the pines, setting off a hushed music. The trail rose steeply and often we had to clamber over dead trees. Abe-san walked ahead effortlessly, as if climbing stairs. Once, when I stopped to catch my breath, I heard a crashing sound, then saw cattle below the face, running through trees. When I looked back, Abe-san was out of sight. I kept climbing. It wasn't hot, but my face was wet with sweat and my glasses clouded up. A wide root growing across the trail provided a bench on which to sit. Just ahead, a skiff of snow covered the ground and I could see where Abe-san's foot had slipped. His was the only human track—there were others, but I'm no mountain man. What animals inhabited this mountain, I didn't know. I stood and climbed, falling several times. What an ass I am out of water! Abe-san's tracks were smaller than mine and with each footstep, I annihilated his delicate ones.

Around a bend I entered a stand of dead trees. The needles were brown and every trunk was bent toward the Camp below. Above, the rock face of the mountain was streaked red. It was like looking at a movie screen from the side of a stage, across which a raven and two eagles flew. I heard a few notes of a song—it was Abe-san—then the wind came again. After a steep pitch, the trail leveled off where the rock merged with the trees. Perhaps there had been a landslide. . . . A sound startled me and I jumped. I heard laughter, then saw Abe-san, crouched in a tiny hole in the rock wall—probably an eagle's nest.

"How did you get up there?" I asked, shading my eyes, for there was no obvious route.

"I flew," he said. "What's wrong; did something scare you back there?" I made a face.

"Look."

I turned. A huge valley opened out below, bordered by high mountains that seemed so close I thought I could leap to them. Between were swaths of brown grass. It looked so smooth . . . brown valleys folding into ones that the distance had turned blue. . . .

"I sure hope there isn't a landslide today," Abe-san called out, laughing.

I sidled along the rock face, touching it with my hands. It was smooth and cold. I came on a place where snow had lodged itself in a crevice and a tiny pine grew there. Halfway across I figured I was next to the center of the mountain and put my ear to the rock. Abe-san's laughter spilled out of the cave above. I continued on. Then I did hear something. Looking down, I saw water oozing out of broken rock.

"What do you see?" a voice said in back of my head. Abe-san had climbed down and was behind me.

"Look." I pointed to the water. "I wonder where it comes from."

Abe-san laughed. I couldn't tell if he was laughing at my naiveté or laughing with delight. I counted the lines that radiated from his eyes—crow's feet—there were four on each side.

"Everything comes from emptiness," he said.

I groaned. "Then why doesn't this mountain fall over if it's empty inside?"

"Oh . . . it will . . . ," he said, smiling.

45

The Chevy convertible Mariko bought in Luster was gunmetal gray. *"Très beau,"* she had said to the salesman. "It looks just like a destroyer." Even before she reached the Camp the back wheel fell off and the horse trader, who happened to be passing by, stopped to help her.

Abe-san liked to sit in the backseat with the top down and be driven. Mariko gave him a tour of the whole Camp that way. So many evacuees had left, whole sections of barracks were closed down. By the time the windows and doors were boarded up, the little gardens were already covered with weeds.

McKay had invited Mariko and Abe-san to visit the ranch. Abe-san settled himself in the back of the car, his white hair tucked into his dark kimono, while Mariko drove. As a going-away present, Kai had made a walking stick for him. It was a long twisted limb from a cedar tree, more like a staff than a stick. When Kai presented it to him, Abe-san smiled. "My friend," he said, "I have started to cast a very thin shadow."

It was early autumn and up on the flank of Heart Mountain Abe-san saw hot spots of aspen, their leaves reddened in among the pines. His hair floated behind him in long wisps.

"I want to see everything," he told Mariko, though what he meant was that he wanted to see anything.

When she drove through the sentry gate Abe-san threw his arms in the air as if batting at insects. He howled with laughter. She took the long way to the ranch, going south toward Cody, then west and north again on the back side of Heart Mountain. When they crossed the river he could smell sulfur from the hot springs and peered over the car door at the baths far below. Then she turned off on a narrow dirt road and drove to the "bonsai field." There, in the wind, he saw how the trees were stunted and why. After, Mariko followed a track north.

"That's where the falls are," she said, stopping the car and pointing to a cleft in the rock. How many times she had painted those falls in the style of Hiroshige: filling the entire page with emptiness, a white band of water. Abe-san half rose in his seat and looked. He nodded his head when he saw how the tumbled rock lifted straight up. The falling water made a steady sound, like someone silencing a room: shhhhhhh. When he sat back, Mariko drove on.

They took the highway to the ranch turnoff. Abe-san liked the tan screens of corn shaking stiffly in the wind. After the corn, there were miles of grazing land, then the emerald of irrigated pastures.

She stopped once to check the back wheel. Abe-san followed her with his head, then leaned out and said, "Used to wander when I was boy, only walking. So many treasures everywhere—didn't matter which direction. Never knew if I was at home or on the way."

Small clouds broke open over the ranch and the moisture that was let down from them evaporated before it hit the earth.

When Mariko and her grandfather drove into the yard, they found McKay and Bobby digging potatoes. The ground was wet and when McKay wiped his face with the back of his hand, he left a smear of mud.

"This is some outfit," McKay said as he opened Mariko's door.

"Godawful, isn't it?" Mariko said.

For a moment, Abe-san let the sun beat down on his head and closed his eyes.

"*Konichi wa*," Bobby said.

Abe-san smiled, holding out his hand to Bobby. "My friend . . . very happy to see you."

"*Samisen* . . . come in for tea. We have red tea and Mormon tea, no tea ceremony tea, I am sorry . . .," Bobby said.

Abe-san smiled. "Please, I would like to sit here for a while. We've been inside for so long. . . ."

Bobby looked from the old man to McKay and back to the old man. "Then we have tea out here."

When he returned with a tray, McKay and Mariko were nowhere to be found. Balancing plates of fruit and cookies on the dusty fender, he served tea.

"Bitter melon," Abe-san said, holding the handleless porcelain cup up to admire the color.

"May I?" Bobby asked, indicating the seat next to Abe-san.

"*Hai, dozo.*"

Bobby looked at the old man. "You go home soon?"

"Sooo . . .," he said in a faint voice.

He tipped the cup delicately to his mouth. The afternoon sun blazed down on the two old men and on Heart Mountain, and the yellow went up in the cottonwoods like candle flames. Fruit had been difficult to get during the war and when Bobby held the one orange in the palm of his hand, Abe-san accepted the gift, turning it slowly as if the orange were a globe.

McKay led Mariko through the house and outside to his porch. She touched one of the screens.

"Is this where you sleep?"

McKay laughed. "Yes."

"Even when it snows?"

He nodded and tried to rub the mud from his face. She held his arm, turning it palm outward, then knelt and kissed him where the mud came down to his wrist; she kissed the front of his jeans. McKay lifted her. She took her sweater off. She wore no bra.

"You look like ivory . . .," he said, running his finger along her collarbone.

She unfastened his pants. As he watched, he tried to rehearse in his mind the days after she left. He would get up early and do chores. He would ride the pasture below cow camp and come home . . . he would not drink . . . no, he would drink excessively. . . .

She looked up. "What's wrong?"

McKay took her hand. "This can't be."

"What?" she said softly.

"That you are leaving tomorrow."

She bit her lower lip. "Come here," she said, lying on the cot.

The sound of her voice made him shiver. He pulled the rest of his clothes off hurriedly and lay down on her. He knew she could feel the wetness under his arms—his excitement and sorrow and joy and fear. He bit her arm gently and thought how the bullet that had gone through her grandfather's arm years ago had also entered her, and in that way they had become inextricably linked.

When he touched her a flush came to her face. He was trembling and could not make his arms and legs stay still, yet the bullet that had preceded his own entry into her always made the passage seem shockingly familiar.

"Mariko," he cried out.

"There's nothing but this, is there?" she said.

"Shhhh . . ." He kissed her mouth.

After, she watched him as he slept. She buried her head by his ear and whispered: "I'm not going to forget you." Then, starting at the top of his head, traced his body with her eyes. But it was his mouth she loved most, the way the upper lip barely touched the lower one—such natural elegance, she thought. The straight nose and the princely mouth and the powerful legs . . . I'll remember these. . . .

"Are you still here?" he asked sleepily.

Then he lifted up and embraced her and as the smell and taste of him filled her again, the idea of leaving dropped away.

She put her hand on his chest and watched it move up and down. "I'll always love you," she said.

He looked at her, anguished. "I don't want to be consoled."

The wind made a door inside the house slam closed. Then Bobby came running. When they saw the expression on his face, they simply rose naked in his presence, dressed, and followed him—through the living room, down the dark hall, through the kitchen, into the yard. There, on the gray fender of the car, the tea tray teetered and Abe-san sat motionless in the backseat.

"He was peeling orange. So happy, eat orange. We share, then he go back like that," Bobby said breathlessly as Mariko and McKay climbed over Abe-san. McKay took the old man's pulse and Mariko opened his kimono and laid her head against his chest. He was thin and the skin was stretched taut over the sternum and the sun was like a light on his domed forehead.

Mariko looked at McKay. He shook his head. She leaned toward her grandfather again, touching his chest with her long hand.

"Look, he's still holding the orange," she whispered at last.

Bobby collapsed on his knees in the dust. "So sorry," he whispered, then McKay helped him to his feet.

The wind came in gusts and McKay felt it push at the back of his head and saw the row of willows by the ditch wave tendrilously, though it was the car that seemed to be moving, not the trees. Mariko lay against her grandfather. Her hair had come loose and it mixed with Abe-san's white strands. Finally she closed his kimono and stepped out of the car. His head had rolled to one side, facing west, and held the sun.

For a long time, Mariko, McKay, and Bobby watched the dead man as if to see the moment when the soul went from him.

When the coroner came he was wearing a double-breasted suit and dark glasses.

There was to be no embalming, only cremation, McKay explained. The undertaker had come to the house after McKay's parents were extricated from the canal. Now he waited with McKay in the kitchen while Mariko dressed her grandfather in a white ceremonial kimono, and after the body had been taken away, Mariko drove back to the Camp alone to tell Kai.

The Camp was nearly deserted now. The guards waved her through the gate without checking her pass. She parked the car in front of the barrack. No one cared now. The life she had had with her grandfather was over . . . and the life she'd had before evacuation . . . what would be left of that? Will was in prison; her parents were somewhere in Japan, perhaps dead, perhaps alive . . . and Kai was nowhere to be found.

The moon, having reached the other side of the sky, lit the room.

She lay down on the floor. It was nearly empty now—just the stove and the beds. Four years in here, she thought. Now he's gone. Slivers of cold came up from between the cracks in the floor. . . . He was going to Paris with me and we were going to paint together and carve masks and write plays. . . . She could not look at his empty bed. Instead, she turned on her side and pulled her long hair back with one hand. For the last five months Abe-san had looked like a ghost, his white hair spectral, and she wondered if he would return now like one of the old men in the Noh plays who had been dead for years. . . .

She pulled herself up until she was on her hands and knees and slowly raised her head: no one. Exhausted, she slumped down. She closed her eyes. How long did she sleep or did she? Wind rattled the door and *shakahachi* music came from another barrack. She woke to it and to the sound of the screen door slamming back, then opening.

"*Grandpère?*" Mariko shouted.

"Mariko?" a voice said.

She opened her eyes. At first she didn't know where she was. A hand pressed down on her and she turned.

"Mariko?"

"Kai?" She looked into his eyes. "Kai . . . where have you been? I've been looking for you."

"You have?" he said.

She took his hand. "Come here. . . . Oh Kai, I have to . . ."

Kai lay down on the floor beside her but she buried her face. He wondered what she wanted of him. . . . "Mariko, don't hide. . . ."

She rolled so her back was against him. He ran his hand across her arm and breast and clasped her hand.

"No . . . no . . . ," pushing him away, and began sobbing.

"I'm sorry," he whispered and withdrew his hand. It's not going to happen, is it? he said to himself and pounded the floor with his fist in anger.

When Mariko woke she was alone and cold. She sat straight up and listened. The wind had stopped. She heard Kai say something to his mother in the next room and the lid of a trunk slam closed. She got to her knees and slid to the edge of Abe-san's bed.

"Grandfather . . . are you a ghost yet? Why have you not come to me?"

Kai carried two of the family suitcases to the mess hall, where they would be picked up and delivered to the waiting train. An old man approached, a crony of Abe-san's who was also an aficionado of Noh theater. He motioned Kai aside.

"You hear?" the man asked.

Kai shook his head. Then the old man held up a white but soiled handkerchief, as if that gesture would tell the story.

"What is it?" Kai asked.

"*Sensei . . .*"

"Who? What teacher?" he said.

"Abe-san . . . dead."

Kai backed away. Very slowly, he took the wire-frame glasses from the bridge of his nose because they had clouded up. He knew then what had been wrong with Mariko—she had tried to tell him and couldn't.

"My God, I'm so stupid," he yelled out.

The old man looked at him quizzically. "Not your fault. Abe-san old man. Know he die."

Kai collected himself. "When did it happen?" he asked.

"Yesterday. He go in big car. Die then."

Kai put his glasses back on.

"He tell me you best student," the old man continued. "You mask-carver too?"

Kai gave a faint smile. "No."

"So sorry," the man said and bowed.

Kai ran all the way back to the barrack and threw open Abe-san's door, calling for Mariko even though he could see the room was empty.

Abe-san's ashes were returned in a coffee can. Mariko and McKay drove toward the falls with the can between them on the seat of her car. It was dark by the time they reached the base of the mountain. The limestone tusk towered above them but they could not see it. McKay lit a lantern and they climbed up through gooseberry bushes and willows, past Willard's cave, onto a promontory of rock. From there they could see the lights of the Camp—no longer a furious glare, but only a bright cluster;

and to their left, against the mountain, the three lights of McKay's ranch, because Bobby had gone to town and settled the five-year feud with the REA, and had the electricity turned on.

McKay and Mariko huddled under a blanket on the flat rock and she held the can with Abe-san's ashes in the crook of her arm against her chest.

"I don't know if I can do this now," she yelled over the roar of the water.

"You don't have to . . . ," McKay said.

The moon rose over the Big Horn Mountains. It was a hunter's moon, a huge orb that looked deformed. Mariko stood and stepped cautiously to the edge. Sprays of water flew back on her. She opened the jar and poured its contents—small and large grains and bits of bone—onto her hand and let the wind and spray take Abe-san's ash away.

There was no conversation between them in the car. When they reached the ranch, the light in the kitchen was on. Bobby had left food: his sacrament, his continual offering. They ate the sandwiches and cake and drank cognac out of one teacup.

"Do you feel like talking?" McKay asked finally.

"No," she said. "I can't."

He touched her cheek.

"I don't want to cry," she said and wiped her eyes.

"Have some more," McKay said, holding out the teacup to her.

"Thanks." She took a sip, then cleared her throat. "That's better."

McKay led her up the creaky staircase to bed. She sat in a chair. They were in Ted's room, not Champ's, and it looked out on the mountains. McKay thought about Ted's lying wounded in a hospital. So many sorrows at once—he found he was unable to give himself to all of them.

"Here," he said. Undressing, he turned down the blankets.

Mariko sat rigidly. "I'm going to be sick," she said and ran to the bathroom.

McKay went in and held her, though she tried to push him away.

"Don't. I'm all right. . . ."

"I don't mind," he said. After, he wiped her face with a damp cloth. She was shaking and he helped her back to the bedroom and undressed her.

"I'm sorry," she said.

They fell asleep holding hands. No mention of the fact that they had never spent a whole night together in a real bed was made. Her grief about the loss of her grandfather had not shown through completely yet, but it would come, and he was ready for it. He lay awake for a long time. It wasn't the reasons that she was leaving that would hurt, but her absence. You only have love when you have it, he thought, and the rest of the time you have nothing. Much later, he woke and felt the bed shake with her sobs.

Mariko left in the morning while McKay slept. Bobby saw her go but did not try to bring her back. A mist hung on Heart Mountain when McKay woke. He felt sluggish, as if he had been drugged, and when he discovered she had driven only as far as the highway he realized she must have walked without a coat or hat in the rain.

46

"Madeleine? It's Velma Vermeer. You have another letter."

Madeleine was just going out the door when the call came. She had brought five calves sick with pneumonia down from the mountain, and had bedded them with fresh straw in a sun shed, and they needed to be watered and fed.

Now that the war was over she felt more apprehensive, not less, because soon she would know Henry's fate. Was he dead or alive? Was he coming home? At weaning, she and McKay would divide their cattle into separate herds again after four years of running together. But she had felt her intimacy with McKay coming to an end for a long time. The war had brought to him sorrows of a different nature and he was preoccupied with them now. To have suffered an absence or to have experienced a great love—finally they came to the same thing, Madeleine thought.

Hurriedly, she finished her chores. She wondered how recent or old this letter from Henry was, because sometimes they arrived out of order.

A letter written in 1942 had come in 1944, though others had been written only a month before. The drizzling rain that had begun after sunup had turned the road to mud. She put on her slicker and overboots and hoisted the heavy chains over the back wheels of her truck, lay on her back and hooked them, then tightened them across the hubcaps and drove to town.

This time it was a thick envelope with something soft inside. She opened it under the inquisitive gaze of the postmaster. There was a long scroll of toilet paper folded neatly and the lettering was very small.

She pushed the wad back into the rice paper envelope and drove north. Halfway there, she pulled off the road and read what Henry had written. It was not a letter, but part of a journal he had been keeping during the years since the Bataan Death March. A note was attached:

Madeleine,

I don't know what will become of us when and if liberation comes so I'm sending this now, care of a Nisei soldier who has a brother at that camp near us. He said he'd send it by air to you. Looks like the end is here.

Love as always,
Henry

1

1942. Bataan, the Philippines. The War Plan Orange III called for us to hold up in Bataan and wait for the great American fleet to sail in from England. It never did. MacArthur had been recalled to active duty and was responsible to the Filipino president. There was a certain urgency in the air when we arrived, but we were pitiful. Like Boy Scouts. We'd never seen combat and we had very little ammunition around— three-inch guns, that's all. From time to time we had drills. The rest was like a weekend house party. We wore white uniforms and had formal dinners in the mansion that served as the major's quarters. If we could find a car, we drove to Manila. There was an Army-Navy Club there and the Polo Club. The guys tried to get dates with army nurses when they could.

The training center for Filipino soldiers was something—they wore coconut pith helmets, bluejean fatigues. Some were barefoot and the guns they carried had been outdated during WWI. The communications system consisted of a phone with miles of wire which had to be connected to battalion headquarters. None of us was prepared in any way for war.

It was Sunday and I was reading the paper when a big V formation of fifty planes flew right over us. Of course, I thought they were ours; then someone started yelling, "It's the Japs," and just then the bombs came down. I rushed out and had a man set up a Browning machine gun. He was digging when a row of bullets went right between us. I picked up his BAR and shot. Got a Zero in the wing. The strafing went on for an hour and when it stopped the commander came around and told me to go eat lunch while I could. I went back to the officer's quarters. Brado, the Filipino houseboy, was hiding under the bed. After I got him out, we had a lunch of cold fried eggs and papaya together. After, I got orders to move to a canefield with our artillery. We found the crashed Zero there. I put some guards on it and carried out my orders to strip it of armament and bury the dead pilot. When it came to getting the pilot out, I was elected. I stuck my arm in and he came apart in my hands, he had been burned so badly. I threw up all over the plane. That was the beginning of the war for me.

2

January 8. The Japanese hit us and hit us hard. We formed a line with combat teams called the Aliikai Line, which stretched across the Bataan Peninsula, but when we were hit, the 51st—a battalion made up of Filipinos—broke and ran. It went back and forth like that for two months. Then the fighting got heavier. MacArthur finally came and pulled us out of heavy fighting after the Battle of the Points, which I fought with a Springfield rifle. That might give you some idea of how ill-equipped we were. The 57th was sent in, but on Good Friday the Japanese made a push and things fell apart. We folded up pretty bad. I had been made forward observer but I lost track of my unit. Couldn't find any of the men, except the radio man, who had been killed. In the middle of the night I heard a jeep. There was a white flag on it. A one-star general stepped out and said, "I'm going forward to surrender Bataan." I headed out to find my unit. It took me until evening. I ate a can of abalone, because I hadn't eaten for a day or so. I wanted to clean up before we surrendered so I bathed in a creek and put on a clean uniform. When we surrendered, the Japanese troops held guns on us and tied our hands behind our backs. They had us kneel down and started shouting. They played with us—like a cat with a mouse—all night. They got drunk. They made one soldier kneel while they swung a sword at him. Others held pistols behind our ears. In the morning we were formed in a column and marched to a big field. We stayed there all day. I don't know why but one guard saw that I was hungry and brought me a can of milk. That night they separated us from the Filipinos and we started the march up a road. We'd had no food for 48 hours and no water. When we marched by a creek, some men broke for water. There was a dead horse upstream and the water was all bloody, but they drank it anyway. That was the beginning of the dysentery problems. They marched us to Pampanga and put us in a compound still with nothing to eat. Later, groups of us were marched to railroad cars. I had been put in a liaison group with some Filipinos and they got their hands on some rice and meat, so I was in better shape than some of the others. When we got to Capas, they let us out. Three American soldiers in our car were dead.

3

After the march we were put into our first camp. The barracks were made of split bamboo walls and thatched roofs. There were no screens so most of us got malaria. There was very little food—a rice gruel, that's all—and no medicines except for the little the medics had brought. Fifty or sixty men began dying every day. The bodies were carried out slung in blankets on a bamboo pole. We heard that Corregidor surrendered. I was put in charge of medicines with the chief medical officer and assigned to the hospital unit but there was very little we could do. The men were dying of malnutrition, malaria, dysentery, pellagra, and scurvy. We had a typhoon in camp. The guards made us lie on the roof, thinking we could hold it down, but the roofs sailed out across the fields. No one got hurt. We thought it was great fun. After, we were moved by train to another camp. It was here that we put our "Yankee ingenuity" to work. Between the chemists and doctors in the group we concocted an extract from one of the grasses that grow in the Philippines. It was full of vitamins and with it, we got rid of some of the scurvy.

November 1942. Boarded the Magato Maru—*a Japanese ship, which* we dubbed the "Maggot Maru"—and were moved to a camp in Japan. We prisoners were put in the hold of the ship and stacked up like cordwood. They pissed on us from above. It was very hot. My best friend died in there. At one of the stops, they cremated him and put the ashes in a box tied with a furoshi and gave him back to me. I tied the box to a beam. One of the men who had gone crazy thought I was hoarding food and during the night he stole the box. I never saw it again.

4

When we arrived in Shinoseki on Thanksgiving it was snowing. We sat down in the railroad yards. Six men died right there. Then we were put on a warm train and given a box with rice and a piece of fish. Never tasted anything better. Arrived Tanagawa that evening. Issued flannel blankets and pillows stuffed with rice hulls and put in new barracks with stucco and flat wood shingles. We were issued little oval tags with the name Tanagawa and a number. Mine was 57. Then they gave us tattered Japanese army uniforms to wear and a kind of tennis shoe with tabi socks. We welcomed all this, but some started dying anyway. They'd picked up diphtheria along the way. The next day we formed into work groups. The officers were assigned special tasks. We put the dead bodies on little carts with slab wood on top and hauled them to the crematorium. Buddhist ceremonies were performed. The priests scattered rice, which the prisoners caught and ate. The next day wooden boxes with the ashes were returned to us. This was regular procedure all winter, every day. One of the guards, Moto, from Nara, was quite friendly to us. He got his girlfriend pregnant and needed money for an abortion, so we lent him money in exchange for garden seeds. With those seeds we put in a huge vegetable garden. A hundred prisoners were brought in from the Dutch East Indies. As soon as they arrived we gave each one a soupbowl full of fresh tomatoes. From then on, we started saving lives.

5

During the long year of 1943, I read Spengler's Decline of the West. It made a great impression on me at the time. Some of us also read about Japanese culture and learned some Kanji so we were able to follow the progress of the war on the commander's maps. The second camp commander was a fine fellow, a very compassionate man. He had been a teacher at a school in Kobe and when he realized how starved we were, not just for food, but also food for thought, he went back to that school and returned with a whole library. After the death rate declined the worst thing about our days was boredom. We got up at five, ate a small bowl of rice and drank tea, then went to work in the garden. Cleaned the latrines and used the night soil for fertilizer. The foot soldiers were made to work helping build a dock. Soon they were allowed to operate the big steam shovel. They were very ingenious at sabotage, and before long they made the shovel inoperable. We officers weren't allowed to do that work, so we served the workers a hot lunch every day. We'd put twenty kilos of rice and vegetable soup in buckets and balanced one at each end of what we called "yoho poles," and took them to the work detail. The rest of the day we read or whittled out chess sets. Once in a while we were allowed to mail a letter. I wrote you during the fighting on Bataan and the letter went out with MacArthur's escape, floating in a mail sack in the Pacific. I wonder if that sack was ever picked up.

6

Christmas 1944. Saw our first American B-29 fly over. Within two months navy aircraft carriers came in and the fliers bombed the dock the men had been building. So we were moved to a factory between Kobe and Osaka and given the assignment of moving big sacks of charcoal. We were moved in the afternoon. That night attack bombers came in and blew our last camp to smithereens. We had mixed emotions. "Hit everything but me," we yelled. Then the heavy bombing began— Nagasaki, Kobe, and Osaka burned. There was so much smoke, day and night looked the same and the fires were as bright as the sun. I don't think the Americans had any idea where we were, but the Japanese kept moving us. The next camp was the mining village of Ikuno. There were wooden barracks with tile roofs and bedbugs that rained down on us. We'd been prisoners for three years now and the big preoccupation was with food. Once in a while a Red Cross relief package got through. Men would stay up all night writing and rewriting recipe books and one MIT engineer with a slide rule spent hours computing how to cut up a can of corned beef among us all.

7

July 1945. American planes overhead day and night in August. Went out on a work detail and a guard came out and hustled us back into the barracks. Then an interpreter came to me with a tube sock filled with rice and said, "If you hear commotion, take this and run. Don't look back." The morale of the Japanese was deteriorating. Their leggings were not wrapped very tightly, so to speak. One day we officers were invited to a meeting with some Japanese officers. We cleaned up and went in. There was tea and rice cakes. These young naval officers were part of the kamikaze. They said they were going to die by "jumping down the smokestack of an American battleship." They wanted to meet some American officers first because when they died they would be surrounded by Americans and they wanted to know something about us. These were men of great character. They knew they had lost the war. This was their way of atoning to the emperor.

8

August 6, 1945. All we could see was smoke and fires. The smoke of one bomb could not be distinguished from the smoke made by another. Things are in a terrible mess. We heard that a camp near Hiroshima burned to the ground. Later in the day the guards came in and painted POW on the roof of the barracks. After lunch we heard planes. One plane flew so low we all rushed out. It went by. A little later it came back over. We rushed out again and climbed onto the roof and waved vigorously and the plane wagged its wings at us. At that moment the camp came unglued. I saw a man who had been wounded in the leg and couldn't walk get up and walk. I've never seen men behave that way in my life.

The plane went south and came back. This time it dropped leaflets about a half-mile from camp. Five of us walked right through the guards and went out across a wooden bridge and up a hill into a grove of trees to get the leaflets. Just as I picked up the first one I heard another plane and that terrible sound of bomb bay doors opening, then the whistle of bombs. We hit the dirt. I heard trees crack but no explosion. I reached up and felt something wet on my shoulder. It was shaving cream. I looked up. One of the other officers was stabbing a can of peaches with a knife and eating them. The American fliers had put food and clothes *and all kinds of supplies into fifty-five-gallon drums and let them out of the bombay doors. There were parachutes on them, but they never opened. The transfer of power took place at that moment.*

9

Most of the camp guards disappeared. We had to lock up the rations and give them out a little at a time so the men wouldn't get sick. Someone found a radio and we heard the battleship Missouri *was anchored nearby. Someone else made his way to a bombed-out naval base, found a radio plus a lot of band instruments, and brought them back. He radioed the* Missouri, *told them where we were and requested a food drop—with parachutes—which came almost immediately. We saved the chutes and made flags of all nations and put them up flagpoles. Maintaining discipline was very hard. One prisoner stole a Japanese truck full of rice, checked into a hotel, and paid his bill with rice. The next morning a plane flew over and the flier dropped a note. It read: "Clear the cookhouse." Then he dropped a ham through the roof.*

The Americans sent in rescue teams accompanied by reporters. They didn't know how to get things done in Japan, and we did. They got drunk on whiskey and we made arrangements to take a train to Yokohama, where we'd be picked up. When we got off that train, we were met by a general with the First Cavalry band. It made a hell of a racket. I lined up the guys. We were very thin, but we had fresh uniforms on and when we stood there and saluted, the general collapsed in tears.

I have no doubt that I'll be home soon.

Madeleine put the letter down. She realized she had been sitting in the cab of the truck staring without seeing. Someone stopped and asked if she was broke down and she said no, thank you, then instead of going home, she drove on past her lane to McKay's. When she reached the ranch McKay had already gone. She threw her slicker on the floor and called out for Bobby. No one answered.

"Well, sonofabitch," she sputtered and heated the coffee on the wood stove. Now she knew that what Henry had been through was much worse than she had imagined, worse than he knew how to describe, and she was angry at herself for not being as tough as he was.

When the coffee was hot, she wandered around McKay's house with the steaming cup in her hand. In the living room she looked at the photograph of McKay's parents and at the incense burner Bobby always kept there. She walked to McKay's screened porch. She had never walked all the way in. A pair of jeans lay crumpled in the corner and on the night table by the cot was a pistol, a can of snoose, and a book about the "Fighting Cheyenne Indians." She sat on the cot. The wind was cold and hit her feet like a tide coming in and she wondered how he stayed warm at night. Despite the note and journals, Henry still felt distant to her and as she lay back she knew she would always be in a condition of wanting McKay—it was one of the givens in life, like the color of someone's eyes. Perhaps he *was* the first person I saw when I was born, she thought.

The phone rang in the kitchen. She hated being roused from her daydream and wondered if she should bother answering it. It rang five times, then stopped. She lay back, relaxed, then it began ringing again. She ran down the long hall in her bare feet and picked up the receiver.

"Hello?"

A loud noise like a hiss came through the line, then she heard an operator's voice, not Velma's, but a long-distance operator.

"Hello?" Madeleine yelled into the phone.

"Hello. . . . Is this McKay's?"

"Yes . . . I can barely hear you. . . . He's not here. . . ."

"Who's this talking?"

"Hello . . . I'm losing you. . . ."

"Don't do that, gal, I've been lost. . . ."

"Is this Champ?"

"Hell, no."

Madeleine waited. "Are you still on the line?"

She held the receiver away from her ear. The line went dead. She hung up. In a few moments, it rang again.

"I have your party on the line, sir," the operator said.

"Madeleine?" the voice said.

"Yes."

"It's me."

"Who? I can't hear. . . ."

There was a pause.

"It's *Henry*."

Madeleine held her hand to her mouth. "Oh my God, my God . . ."

"Madeleine?"

"Is it really you?" she asked softly.

"What? Speak up. Are you okay?"

"Henry . . . where are you?"

"San Fran . . . Army Hospital . . . they're gonna keep us here for a few weeks. . . ."

"I can't believe it. I just got your letter today."

"You've been getting them?"

"Yes."

"Good . . ."

"Henry? Are you really alive?"

"Well this ain't no ghost you're talking to."

"What's wrong . . . why are you in the hospital?"

"I've got worms, like a damned dog. They're delousing us. Sheep-dip . . ."

"You sound good."

"I'm a little shaky on my feet but I'm okay. Had my first steak yesterday. Made me sicker than a dog. Just not used to it. . . ."

"When can I see you?"

"I'll be home in about three weeks."

"It'll be wonderful . . . everything's good here. McKay and I ran our cattle together and it's worked out. . . ."

"Look, I've got to go . . . there's a line of guys wanting to call home."

"Okay," she said in a small voice. "Henry?"

"Yes?"

"Nothing. I'll see you soon, I hope."

She ran outside and stood in the middle of the road between the house and the corrals.

"McKay . . . where are you?" she called out. "*Where is everyone?*" Only McKay's dog came out and lay between her feet.

47

Kai's alarm clock went off at 4:00 A.M. He woke with a feeling of great dread, then he remembered. Abe-san was dead, and also, the Camp was closing and it was the day to leave. He thought of the morning in his parents' bare house in Richmond, the final sweeping of already polished wood floors, the giving away of bonsai, the train ride with the blinds closed, the terrible desert, the armed guards. He had felt the same dread that morning, four years before.

The day the announcement that the camps would be closing and they were free to go home whenever they chose—in other words, the day their democratic rights had been restored—he had been called up for his preinduction physical, and the next week the notice came that he had been inducted into the army.

He no longer felt sure he was a person who could make life change. History was not an interpretive act, but the theater in which he had been made an indentured servant. Life happened to him, to everyone—during these years, at least. He rolled with the punches.

When he threw the blanket back there was light in the sky. He saw that it had rained during the night. He remembered being awakened by something, a loud rumble like an earthquake, but the ground had been still. The blanket, hung on nails that had partitioned his side of the room from his parents', moved, then fell. He watched his mother fold it neatly. Behind her, his father sat on the edge of his bed. His glasses were crooked. Kai said good-morning but his father didn't answer. He even ventured to say it in Japanese—still no response. Mrs. Nakamura bustled around the room packing the belongings they had acquired—the English language textbooks, the ikebana tools, drawings and prizes they had received at various functions. One of their friends came by to say good-bye and Kai watched as Mrs. Nakamura and the visitor bowed to one another over and over, lower and lower, until the visitor broke away.

Kai helped pack dishes, winter clothes, and a painting from Mariko. When Mrs. Nakamura stripped her husband's bed she had to pull the sheets and blankets from under him because he would not move. After she dressed him, she picked up his felt hat, brushed the dust from the soft brim, and plunked it down on his head. "How gray he has become," Kai thought. "He's like a frozen fish."

When it was time to leave they had to carry him. Mr. Nakamura held his body rigid, legs bent at the knees as if sitting, elbows stiffened truculently. Some of the young men carried him on a little sawed-off pallet, like a palanquin, only this was not royalty they were carrying, Kai thought, but a silly old man who would not face reality. Kai fought back the great irritation he felt. He doesn't even know about Abe-san, Kai thought bitterly. He noticed how his father's thick lenses looked opaque as if frosted over and even when he could see into his father's dark eyes, there was no sign of life in them.

Mrs. Nakamura trotted by her husband's side. Once the pallet tipped precariously and she held her hand to her mouth and screamed. He made no attempt to save himself but at the last moment, the carriers righted the "chair" and proceeded toward the waiting train.

Kai thought of Kenny. Home from more than fifty missions, he had survived, then volunteered to go to Japan and help liberate American prisoners.

Kai was glad Kenny couldn't see this farce with his father. Perhaps he already knows and that's why he makes himself scarce, unafraid to die, he thought. Now he, Kai, would take the same steps. To be inducted into the army after the fighting was finished was not the same. He felt foolish for a moment, then relieved to have a reason to leave his parents, even though it would not be to resume his old life of study and lovemaking on Grant Avenue. The old life was gone. Like Li's failure to respond to his letters, the past no longer called for his return.

Kai pulled his father up the stairs of the railroad car under the arms, then carried him to an empty seat. He bent down to ask his father if he was all right. Though it was only nine in the morning, the sun was very hot and beads of sweat dropped from his forehead onto the scuffed floor of the train. Mr. Nakamura sat rigid. His glasses were half off and Kai straightened them, then dusted off his father's jacket. Someone bumped Kai from behind, going by with luggage, and he fell over his father's knees. Righting himself, he felt exasperated.

"Stop being a child. Stop acting this way, you stupid old man," Kai burst out at his father, then turned away, thinking only of Abe-san.

Someone tapped Kai on the shoulder and he jumped.

"Mariko, what are you doing here? I thought you had gone . . . ," he said.

"He's dead," Mariko said, then collapsed in Kai's arms.

"I know," he said. "You should have told me that night. . . ."

Mariko looked up and gave him a crushed, astonished look.

Kai held her tightly. People pushed by and Kai pulled her into the seat across from his father. Two teenage girls took the seat behind them and began whispering and laughing loudly. A baby screamed and hit its mother's chest with its fists, and two Issei couples fanned themselves, staring at the woman draped across Kai. When Mrs. Nakamura returned from checking on the baggage, she sat down next to her comatose husband and glanced furtively at Kai and Mariko, then turned her head away from what she could not understand. Mariko's hair had fallen from the knot at the top of her head and Kai brushed it gently from her face.

"Oh my darling," he said. "My darling . . . ," and held her again.

The train lurched once, then a great burst of steam came from the engine. Outside he could hear someone yelling to wait.

At first he thought it was McKay's voice, then he saw it was one of the *hakujin* who had worked at the Camp, holding up a teddy bear left behind by a child. Kai felt relieved before he knew why. He looked at Mariko.

"Are you coming . . . with me?" he asked.

"Yes."

"What about your things? Where's your luggage and car?"

"I don't care," she said.

"I know, but—"

They looked at each other. Under the porcelain lids and eyes, the extravagant cheekbones, her full lips were chapped and half-opened. It wasn't a smile nor was it pouting and self-pity, but a wild vulnerability showing, as if daring life to give her whatever it had in store and more. The train lurched again, then started to move.

"But this train is going to San Francisco," Kai said.

"I know. Do you mind?" she asked.

"No."

"Abe-san gone. I can't believe it," Kai said to himself. He thought of the first time he had seen the old man. It was in a train and he was sitting a few seats ahead. His gray hair was tied back neatly and tucked into his kimono and the great expanse of his forehead shone and wrinkled when he smiled, like an ocean.

The train stopped and bursts of steam rolled across the train window.

"Are you all right?" Kai asked Mariko.

She nodded yes, but fidgeted in the seat. Kai closed his eyes too. His forehead felt hot and his glasses clouded up as if he were about to cry.

He mumbled something.

"What?" Mariko said sleepily.

"Nothing—"

Kai covered his eyes with one hand. Was the train moving or was the Camp moving like history itself, on a great scroll, turning in and out of time? Kai looked out the window and saw the sentry gate go by and the rows of barracks, the tall smokestack of the hospital, the mess halls, the latrines, the store and office buildings, the baseball diamond, the hill where the boys were arrested for sledding, the rock gardens, and more than that, he thought he could see the days go by, about a thousand of them, a thousand days filled with whatever one fills waiting with, days like hollow trees and the edges of days breaking off into the next morning and the odor boredom brings of something burning, something dead.

Now this, he thought. Has history brought me this woman? She leaned against him. He did not know why she was there or how long she would stay. He had seen the narrative scrolls of the Heian period, the *emaki*—multiple lives painted in what she called "flat depth," nothing like Western perspective. How moving that flatness was, because it portrayed no past or future and therefore no history, only what was in the present, what was multiple, what was possible to bring before his eyes. Now she was here, with him, she who had eluded everyone, astonished everyone with the power and seamless beauty of her work. . . .

"Mariko . . .," he whispered. She lit a cigarette and pulled her hair to the top of her head, then let it drop loosely. He wondered if he had lost all the strength in his arms: four years away from swimming. At times all he could think of was water breaking over his shoulders and hands like knives cutting a way through oncoming waves. Abe-san dead. He took a deep breath and looked at Mariko. Her eyelashes were wet but there were no tears. The feel of her body had surprised him. How many times had he made love to her in his mind over the years; and then, the other night, he almost . . . She smiled at him, but there was a distant look in her eyes. Kai leaned back and propped his feet up. The train stopped, then lurched backward. Mariko pulled her wild, roped hair back into a knot again, but already a few strands had come loose.

"What about McKay?" Kai asked at last.

Mariko looked surprised. "We had to stop," she said solemnly.

"Just like that?"

"No. We love each other as much as two people can love each other and we gave each other up."

Kai stared out the window. He could not help wonder if there was anything for him in this. He felt his shoulder touch Mariko's again. It sent electric shocks through his body. Perhaps the army wouldn't be so bad, he rationalized. He'd get an intelligence job, maybe learn Japanese. The irony alone delighted him. He looked at Mariko. Her eyes were closed but she was not sleeping. He wondered where she would be while he was in the service and if she would wait for him. The whistle sounded and the train lurched forward again. He had forgotten they weren't moving. That's the effect Camp has had on us—you don't know whether you're going backward or forward and you don't give a damn, he thought.

As the train picked up speed, Kai felt his heart race. The twin reali-zations of Abe-san's death and Mariko's intimate presence hit him like shock waves. He kept looking at her.

"Mariko . . . ," he said breathlessly. He took a strand of her black hair between his fingers and delivered it to the top of her head. "I couldn't tell you before . . . I was inducted into the army."

She pulled away and looked at him gravely. "No . . . ," she began. "No you weren't, were you?" she asked incredulously.

Kai nodded. He felt like a child.

"Oh, you poor boy . . . you poor, stupid boy."

He looked out the train window and watched the last of the Camp slide by. It seemed as though they had been on the train for many hours, yet they had moved only half a mile.

"I'm sorry," he said.

In the distance a single cloud wrapped itself around Heart Mountain like a tourniquet. When it unwrapped itself, he saw the place where a piece of the mountain had slid. He couldn't believe his eyes. "Look," he said to Mariko. He had never felt her against him before this day and now he wanted to stand up in the middle of the aisle of the moving train and hold her tightly until her eyes glittered the way they did the night she stepped down from McKay's truck around the corner from the May-flower Café in the rain.

"It's like in the legend—when the medicine man died. . . ."

She didn't know what he was talking about.

The train rocked slowly on the tracks and the Camp was gone. Now, the landscape was only sagebrush. When the whistle blew, Kai's mother stood suddenly and lifted the window. She leaned into the dry rushing air and looked back toward the place that had been her home for four years. Then, half in and half out of the train, she bowed deeply to what had already passed by.

McKay had spent the day in a tree. It was an Englemann spruce, an easy tree to climb. Twenty feet off the ground he sat on a limb and rested his back against the trunk. He could see where some of the branches had been torn off in the blizzard, torn and thrown down on the ground. He wondered if a tree has the same sense of inviolability as a human has—

and despite that, loses its limbs anyway. He thought of soldiers coming home.

The branches above him rattled. A locust held itself vertically to the trunk. McKay climbed higher. The view is always changing, he thought. Sap from the tree made two of his fingers stick together. He hated it when people came to the mountain "to see the view" because, as Mariko always said, "Everything is a view of something." The limbs on the tree spiraled up and down the trunk as if the trunk had been spinning when they grew there.

He stretched out. "Out on a limb," he thought smiling, the way Mariko stretched out in his mind, bright and soft and sharp as the needles that brushed his face and powdered him with yellow pollen.

When the wind came again he thought the tree was a finger that stirred life and death and especially death into the world. The wind tore at the branches and the finger stirred harder, digging into the ground, burying the war dead or else sculling them on homeward currents of air. There was movement every place he could imagine: prisoners in Germany going home to Poland, America, France, Holland; prisoners in America going home to Germany; prisoners in the Philippines, Manchuria, and Japan going home to England, Australia, and America. . . .

One twitch of the finger causes such a stir. . . . He didn't want to move. Then he did. He climbed higher and farther out on a limb. "Out here," he thought, "beyond victory and conquest, beyond despair, beyond possessiveness. . . ."

The branch sank and lifted. He thought of the day he had been bucked off in the water, how the rapture worked through his body.

When he looked down from the tree, what was left of the green pastures leeched into a white sky. "Out there is something beyond happiness," he said aloud, though he could not think of what that might be.

Two miles down the line the train stopped to pick up freight and while Kai was getting beer, Mariko opened the door of the passenger car and jumped to the ground. She walked north toward Luster. Some people stared at her; some did not. What difference did it make? At the reservoir, ten Canadian geese rose up, honking and circling, then landed again. It felt good to walk. A thin mist obscured the top of Heart Mountain so that it appeared to rise and then disintegrate. "*Grandpère,* I can't leave you yet . . . ," she said under her breath, though she did not know why she was going back, if it was to get away from Kai, or . . .

She saw a man on the street corner holding a willow. When she passed, he waved the branch at her and she waved back and he smiled. A huge sign across the grocery store window proclaimed: PEACE * VICTORY. She passed the hardware store and lumberyard and funeral parlor where the walls were pink, and across the street, the Cactus Bar and Rose's yellow boardinghouse, whose windowpanes merely reflected the sky.

A truck stopped in the middle of the street. When she turned, she saw McKay. He opened the passenger door. For a moment she did not move. Is this why I came back? she wondered. He leaned toward her and extended his hand. Finally, she let herself be lifted into the cab.

The truck moved down the street. She looked out the window at the sidewalk, then at McKay.

"I didn't come back to stay," she said at last.

"I know," he lied.

She leaned her head back against the seat and let her legs splay out in front of her.

"I was on the train. I was going to San Francisco with Kai . . . ," she said, as he braced his hands against the steering wheel.

"He was going to show me the sights. . . ."

McKay nodded silently.

The truck rolled past a cornfield, then he turned up a hill and drove into a stack yard. The hay had already cured in the sun and the stack, neatly and tightly arranged, looked like a Mayan temple. McKay pulled to a stop. The wall of hay was golden with sun. He turned to her slowly.

"My brothers are coming home," McKay said.

"When?"

"Champ's coming in two weeks."

"That'll be wonderful. . . ."

"No it won't. Has the train left yet?"

"Yes. I jumped off down the tracks a few miles."

McKay leaned back against his door. "Look . . . you can stay at the ranch until you're ready to go. . . ."

Part of her long hair fell across her face. She lifted it. "Then it would start all over again."

"It hasn't ended. . . ."

"But it's just easier if we don't see each other. . . ."

"Easier?" McKay said bitterly.

She put her hand on his thigh but didn't look at him.

McKay leaned his blond head against her shoulder. "Do you want to go somewhere?" he asked. "We could use Pinkey's room. I have the key."

She closed her eyes, then shook her head.

McKay started the engine and backed away from the towering haystack.

"Where are you going?" she asked.

"Wherever you want—"

At the highway he stopped, resting both arms on the steering wheel.

"I guess I'll get my car now," she said at last.

McKay turned north onto the pavement.

Ahead, Heart Mountain had reappeared. The pine trees growing up its east slope looked like shorn hair and the huge outcrop of limestone facing north was stained with red threads.

"Is it over, then, or should I visit you when you get settled?" McKay asked.

She turned to him. "I want you to visit."

"What about Will?"

"We're getting our marriage annulled."

The truck slowed at the turnoff to the ranch. Mariko's car, mud-splattered, was parked on the gravel road.

"The battleship," she said, looking at it.

"You can't drive to Paris, can you?"

She laughed. "Maybe I'll drive it off a cliff. . . ."

They got out and McKay opened the door of her car. The inside smelled musty. Mariko poked her head halfway in and drew back.

"Now I don't want to go . . . ," she said.

"You don't have to. . . ."

He kissed her. Then they walked up a hill behind the car, away from the highway, and down the other side. There were no trees, no privacy, so they lay down by a low juniper. The ground was littered with blue berries and soft twigs—unlit kindling, McKay thought.

Passion is not always a fire. He unbuttoned her sweater and she shivered. It was September 1945 and the earth had already grown cold. He told her he loved her and that he understood he must let her go and that lying with her now was not part of trying to make her stay. She nodded, then pulled his shirt apart and kissed his chest. He looked at the sky and remembered Bobby's dream the night before the bomb was dropped on Hiroshima—how the rain was black and streaked the sky with needles; how it fell into a terrible fire. Now, the sun set below the horizon and the sky looked like a blue flame. There is an end to war, he thought, but there is no end to time.

48

"Where is she?"

Those were the first words Champ uttered when he stepped in the kitchen. Bobby clucked his teeth once, then pulled a sheet cake down from the cupboard, ice cream from the freezer, plates and forks and laid them out on the kitchen table, newly endowed with an extra leaf so that it almost stretched to the hall door.

At the sink, McKay cupped his hands under the cold water and washed his face. Then he turned to his brother.

"She's gone," McKay said flatly.

Champ pulled out a chair. His cane dropped noisily to the floor.

"Thought about getting the damned thing cut off and wearing a peg leg, but those sorry butchers they call doctors wouldn't do it," he said, slicing the cake.

"When you're finished, I have something to show you," McKay said.

Champ squinted at his brother. "Looks like it's been a pretty good year," he said with a full mouth. "Grass looks good."

"Yep." McKay sat at the table but didn't eat.

"Good cake, Bobby . . . better than ever before," Champ said.

McKay picked the cane up from the floor and handed it to Champ.

"Okay . . . I'm coming . . . ," Champ said, grinning.

The blue roan colt was saddled and Champ's bridle with its silver Garcia bit and reins with rawhide knots hung from the saddle horn. When McKay stepped to the middle of the corral, he snapped his fingers once and the colt laid his ears back and walked to him. McKay bridled the horse, then handed Champ the reins.

"He's yours, Champ. Welcome home."

Champ's cane sank in the soft dirt. He limped toward the colt, looked at his head and ears, the deep chest and long neck, then back at McKay.

"Where'd you get him?"

"He's out of Lena. . . . I raised him, started him when he was two. God, he was a scrappy little bugger at first."

Champ appraised the horse once again. "Who'd you breed Lena to?"

"That Driftwood stud of Jesse's."

Champ nodded, never taking his eyes off the horse. "How's he feel about 'crips'?"

"He's broke to canes and crutches and he'll stand all afternoon while you get on. The rest is up to you, I guess," McKay said.

"How hard does he buck?"

McKay grinned. "Oh, not too bad . . ." He kicked the dirt with his boot. "Try him."

Champ smiled and pulled down his hat. "You dirty bastard," he growled at McKay and stroked the colt's neck.

"I'll leave you two alone. Bon voyage," McKay said, then walked back to the house.

Champ picked up the bridle reins and the horse stepped toward him. He rubbed the horse on the front on the face, then let his hand slide down the soft muzzle.

"Hello, you good-looking sonofabitch," he crooned. "Jesus . . . where d'ya come from anyway? You weren't here when I left . . . ," he said, and struggled with his balance as he lifted his foot into the stirrup.

McKay woke and heard laughter. It was four in the morning and he couldn't understand where the noise was coming from. Then he remembered he wasn't on the screened porch. He got out of bed and walked to the landing of the stairs. Below, in the living room, alive with kerosene lamps and candles lining the mantle over the fireplace, Champ and Pinkey sat on Mexican stools with a bottle between them. McKay watched as Pinkey tried to pour. When he brought the bottle to the rim of the shot glass, both hands were shaking so hard, the whiskey splashed over the top.

"Here, let me try," Champ said, amused, then pressed his hand to the damp spot on the rug and wiped his face with it.

Pinkey handed him the bottle and shot glass. Champ's hands shimmied.

"Hell, I can't do it either," he said, laughing, then tipped the bottle to his lips.

McKay moved toward the stairs.

"Hey there," Pinkey yelled up to him. "He's got the shakes worse than I do. Did you see that?" Pinkey's chin was wet and he needed a shave.

"Can't sleep either, huh?" Champ said cheerfully.

"Too goddamned much noise. It used to be quiet around here," McKay said, smiling.

"Yeah, I bet, with you and that girlfriend tiptoeing around. . . ."

McKay glared at his brother.

"Here, tits up," Pinkey muttered.

"It's supposed to be bottoms up," McKay said.

"I don't care. I don't like that other stuff. . . ."

"What other stuff, Pinkey?" Champ asked, teasing.

"Hey, are you going to pour me a drink or not?" McKay interrupted.

Pinkey handed McKay the bottle. McKay filled the shot glass twice, then wiped his lips and passed the bottle around. Champ and Pinkey talked about women and horseflesh and army nurses.

"Yep, not a damned thing's happened since you've been gone except that I got laid in '43. . . ." He turned to McKay. "Was it '43 or '44?

Hell, all them years are the same to me, but anyway, that's not a bad average for an old man like me."

McKay looked at Pinkey. "God, if your eyes ain't red . . ."

"A man's got to live up to his name," Pinkey retorted. "Besides, it's from the hay," he said, holding his arms out. "Lookee there," he said and showed the scratches on his arms to McKay. "You'd think I'd been in a catfight."

"And you lost," Champ added.

When Pinkey went outside to relieve himself McKay and Champ sat in silence. McKay could hear Champ's body shaking the whole chair. "Flak happy," "shellshock," "battle fatigue"—those were the words Champ had used earlier. He had been in the hospital again, this time for paralysis and a loss of speech. "They put me in the nuthouse . . . can you believe that? Then they'd wake me up real early in the morning and take me down to this room for an 'Amytal chat'—some drug that put me to sleep. It was sleep, but I talked during it. Then they taught me how to walk again and I was reassigned . . . see, everyone in my unit had been killed but me."

McKay turned the shot glass in his hand. There was nothing to say now. Champ was home; Mariko was gone. Ted and Henry would be home soon.

He thought about how Champ had limped into the corral using his cane, how when he caved in with pain once and fell to his knees, how the horse had gone to him and put his nose on Champ's shoulder as if that moment had been rehearsed. That's why he and Champ didn't have to make peace. They both hated that sort of thing.

"I'm hungry," McKay said. "Have I ever made you my special eggs?"

Champ groaned. "You mean the ones that smell like formaldehyde?"

"Can't we have something normal?" Pinkey said, stumbling down the dark hall.

McKay held the swinging door to the kitchen open. "What would you know about normal?" he asked as the old cowboy pushed in.

The sounds in the house, the human sounds of laughter and cooking and talking, continued to trouble McKay. Bobby began a siege of cooking and weekly trips to the grocery store in town. Their meals were boisterous. Bobby made special tonics for Champ and settled their quarrels by cluck-

ing his false teeth, then whittling them at the table until the anger had
passed.

McKay had taken down his screened porch, folded his cot, rolled up
the screens like maps and tied them with canvas straps. It had been hot
and once the screens were gone his "cell in wide-open space" filled with
darting mudswallows. Now it was no more. Even if the cell was gone
and the Camp emptied out, the mountains hemmed him and solitude
smeared the walls and floors of the house with its shine.

Later, sitting on the cement slab of his screenless porch, he had felt
a sudden, foolish sense of well-being. How could that be? Where did
unfounded pleasure come from?

McKay lay on top of the bed. He couldn't sleep and it was hot but
the air had something of autumn in it—it smelled of dry ice. He dressed
quickly and left the house by the back stairs. He didn't know which horses
were in the corral and he couldn't see—one looked like another—so he
caught the first horse who let himself be caught, saddled him, and rode
to the river. It was late in the year and what water there was ran shallow.
The sandbar had widened and what started as river rock was fine sand
in the middle of the island. The driftwood had dried and bleached all
summer in hot sun and the grasses were grazed to nothing.

McKay took off his boots and spurs and curled his bare feet over rock.
Above, the Milky Way had slipped from the middle to the west side of
the sky. Once, McKay had seen the river shift. High water—water that
seemed to move over the top of water that was already there—took the
gravel bar as its center. The next year it shifted back. But the "Great
River," as Mariko called it—the Milky Way—was always on a slide. It
was the great heart of the sky.

McKay walked the length of the tiny island. He could see where the
elk had been. Tracks covered one end. He thought about what Pinkey
always said: how reading tracks came more naturally than reading words.

He caught his horse and crossed the river. On the other side the tracks
were visible, then disappeared in grass. But the grass showed where they
had gone: it folded out from an invisible trail and here and there, seedless
heads were bent down and had not straightened. Ahead, a patch of timber
was collared by snow.

He led his horse into the trees. Darkness was another hue there—it had no sheen; it was all purples and blacks drenched by black. The errant bomb had gone, the hard carapace, the shrapnel—all behind him. What lay ahead?

He came on a deadfall, a ruin of pines and spruce lying across each other, midsections broken, torn roots lifted into air, and the slender, lighter limbs crosshatched in a rotting canopy over his head. He and the horse threaded a way through, picked up the tracks, and followed them to a clearing.

Where the elk had grazed the grass was nipped down to roots. McKay stepped on his horse again. The tracks widened into a game trail: down a hill, across two dry creeks, then out onto land that had shelved to a high plain. Now the black was broken; a long tail of stars hung down vertically like a ladder. He wondered how far the Milky Way had slid, if it was under him now like a belly band, if it slid at all. Once, when he got off his horse to look at how the elk's hooves had stamped the dirt, he thought he could smell the musk of their passing.

The trail dove down into the breaks. Ahead was a fence. He saw where they had jumped it. One calf hadn't cleared the top wire and died hanging there. He pulled the calf to the ground and rode down the fence line. He knew where the gate was because it was his gate, the gate to his lower pasture. The tracks led through the grainfield to the lake. There was just enough starlight to see the animals and he could hear their clattering on rock. As he rode closer he could see some of the calves still had spots on their flanks. His horse was thirsty and McKay let him drink. The elk calves made soft barking sounds and played half in, half out of the water, and the water looked like the shadow timber makes—a hard shade.

Then there was only Venus, the morning star, and the sky, having lost its darkness, went blank, unable to pick up another hue. McKay thought about the errant bomb, how its metallic glare must have fallen onto the lake because when dawn came, the water hardened into sheets of silver.

Turning his horse for home, he glanced back. Wind blasted the lake into tiny crenulations that peaked and flattened, took the light as it came, and carried it forward to water's edge where the calves gamboled until the errant bomb's lid of solitude had been trampled into day.